SMOG
THE ARDELEAN BLOODLINE
BOOK FIVE

SARAH JAEGER

BEARLY CONTAINED ROMANCE

© Bearly Contained Romance

E-Book ISBN: 979-8-9900360-2-4

Male Model Paperback ISBN: 979-8-9900360-3-1

Wolf Paperback ISBN: 979-8-9900360-4-8

Editing - Indie Edits with Jeanine

Proofreading - Nay's Notions

Book Cover - Sandra of Mando Designs

Pack Publicist - Kelsey Schneider

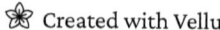 Created with Vellum

Smog

Mountain Laurel

Kalmia latifolia

To anyone who has been the one holding it together for everyone else
while silently losing yourself to the chaos within.

I'm glad you're still here.

Chinese Lantern
Physalis alkekengi

"Just stay."

— BENJAMAN HARRE

"Maybe the journey isn't so much about becoming anything. Maybe it's about unbecoming everything that isn't really you."

— PAULO COELHO

A QUICK NOTE ON CONTENT

This book is a traditional shifter romance book. As such, it contains events such as physical on-page violence, graphic discussions of death, and character deaths. These events may be handled or discussed in ways that may not be acceptable by all readers.

Smog is a book based in a world very much like our own and deals with a wide variety of heavy topics. These topics may cause individuals to have negative feelings or reactions.

The list of topics includes, but is not limited to, mental health, revelations of biological parentage, drug and alcohol use, addiction, sexual intercourse, gambling, misogyny, conversations relating to firearms, use of firearms on individuals, infertility, medical trauma, health struggles, suicidal ideation, and suicide.

Deacon and Henri must embrace their own diversity and confront their trauma within this book. Some of these topics include, but are not limited to, stalking, childhood neglect and abandonment, sexual assault, domestic violence, death of a parent, food insecurity, adoption, and estranged parental figures. Also included are scenes of consensual use of an edged blade during intercourse, near-deadly assault on a female, miscarriage, graphic revenge killing, and interactions with police following a car accident.

These topics are not always handled in the most politically correct way. As often seen in real life, my characters can sometimes be insensitive to those around them and their struggles.

None of these words written were chosen without thought. All choices were debated at length. Ultimately, it is my intent to highlight the struggles of humanity as we work toward acceptance of all the differences among us. Even if that means allowing my characters to be imperfect as part of their growth, as part of our growth.

And while it is never my intention to cause any reader any distress: reader discretion is advised.

If based on this warning, related to the potential triggers listed above, you have any additional concerns or questions that you'd like addressed, you may reach out to me, the author, via email: sarah@authorsarahjaeger.com or on Instagram: @author.sarahjaeger

A QUICK NOTE ON CONTENT

If you are in a dangerous situation and need help or support, please call the National Domestic Abuse Hotline at:
1-800-799-7233
https://www.thehotline.org/

988 Suicide & Crisis Lifeline 988 Suicide & Crisis Lifeline provides 24/7, free and confidential support via phone or chat for people in distress, resources for you or your loved ones, and best practices for professionals. Includes information on finding your local crisis center.
Phone: 988
Website: http://suicidepreventionlifeline.org

ALDEN'S PACK HOUSE
GROUND FLOOR

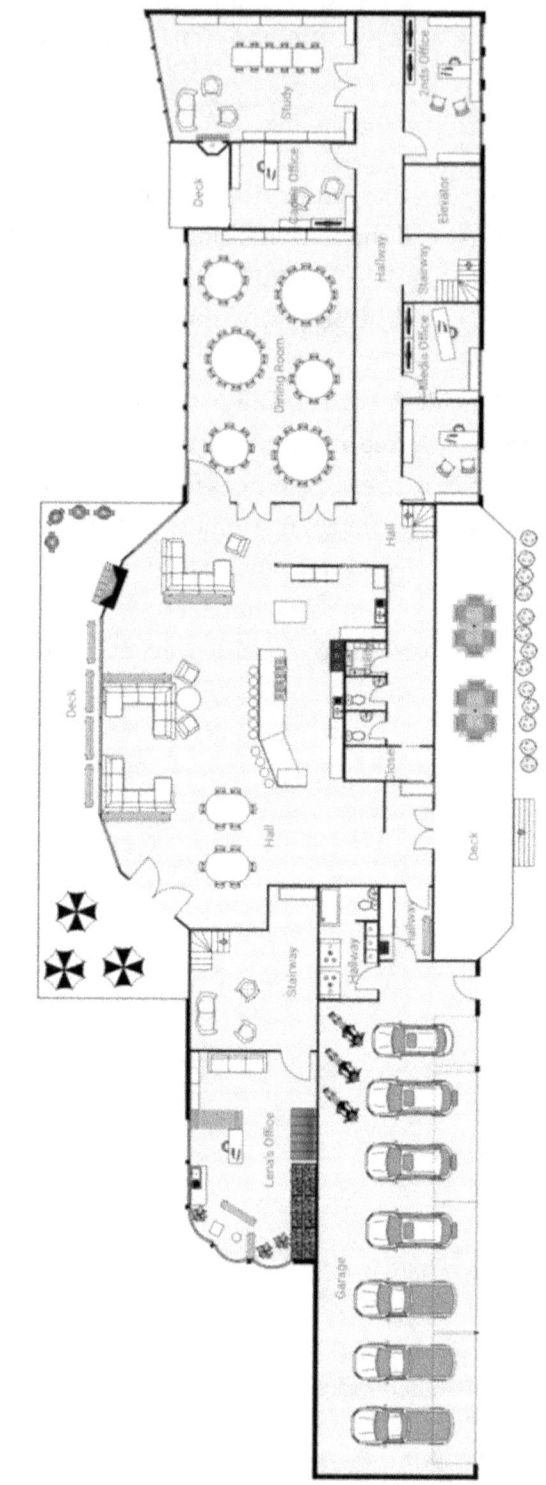

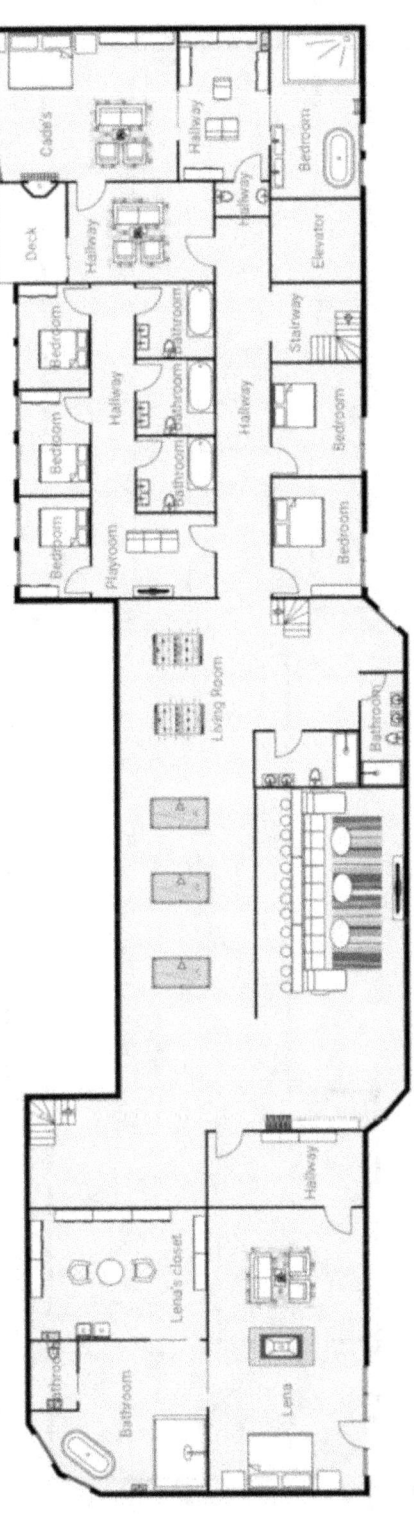

SECOND FLOOR

ALDEN'S PACK HOUSE
THIRD FLOOR

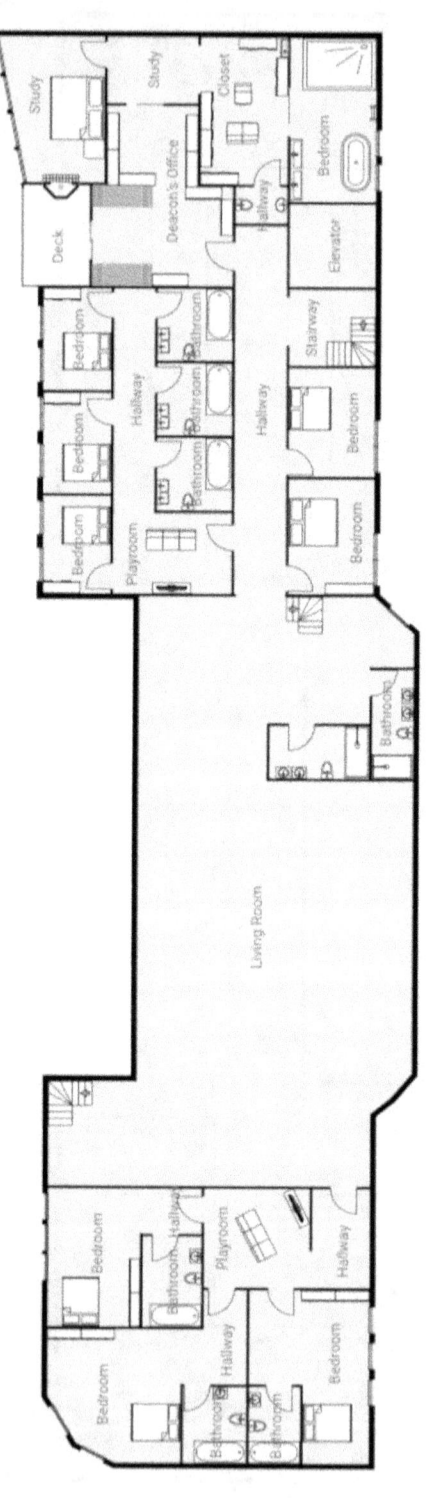

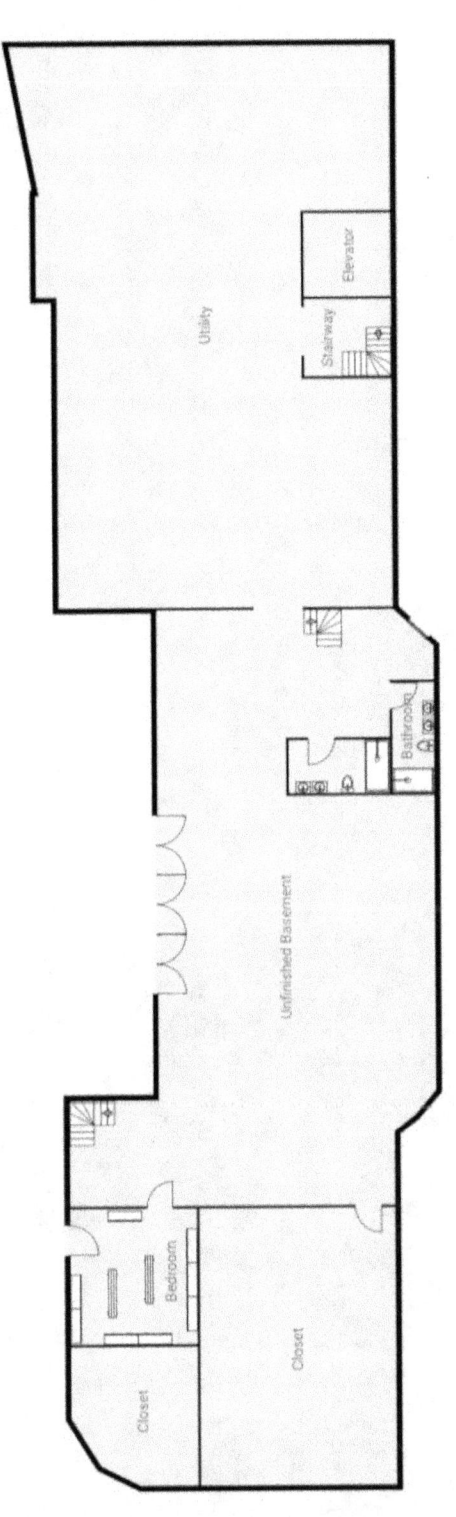

BASEMENT

THE WISCONSIN HOUSE

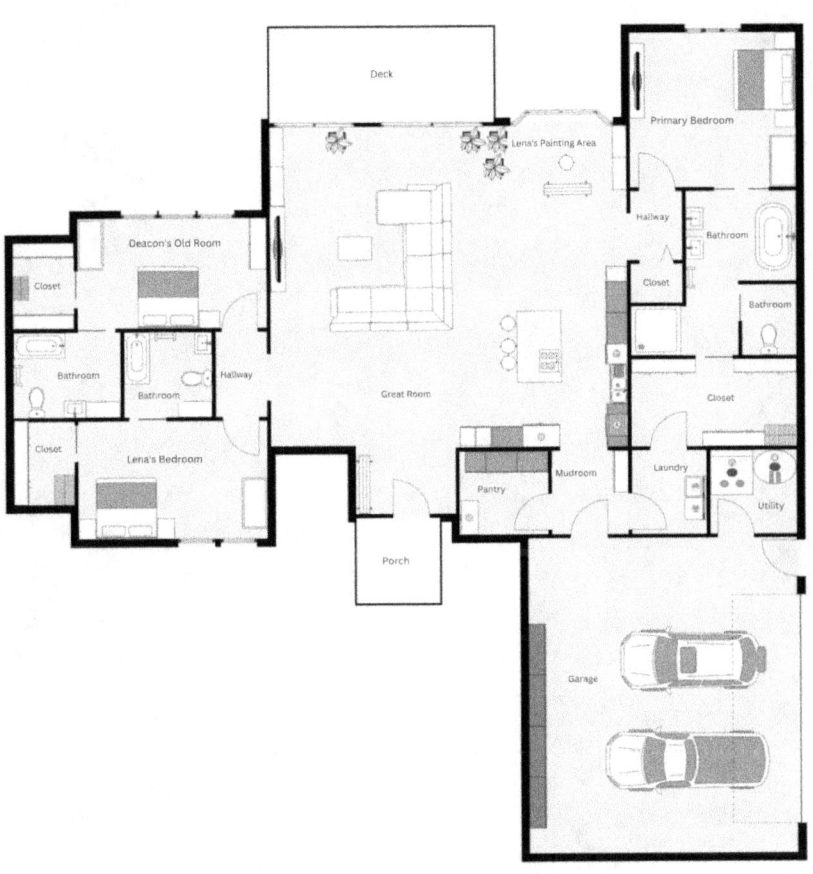

Pinkshell Azalea
Rhododendron vasey

APRIL

DEACON

THE ENGINE on my bike purrs beneath me. It's an impractical vehicle a lot of the time, but riding is the closest thing I have to feelings. I round the corner on the last straight stretch toward home and open the throttle.

My life is fundamentally changing. The quiet comfort of my home in the middle of the Northwoods is about to relocate to the prison where the darkness started. My bike and the high of riding at nearly top speeds, despite the imminent danger, are the only things that distract me from the pain of returning to the pack.

I'll go back to my childhood bedroom and memories of the nights at the kitchen counter in a standoff with the man who raised us. For Cade, his new, soon-to-be mate, Thalia, and Lena, I'll do it. And if the mask holds, I'll pretend to be, at the bare minimum, content with it.

A half mile down, someone's parked on the side of the road. Squinting, I slow way down. A woman stands in the middle of the road, waving her phone around in the air. The most ridiculous little silver car on the shoulder next to her. My bike is more practical than that death trap.

I inch closer, making out more beyond the feminine shape. Long blonde hair, impractical heels, pencil skirt, floofy blouse poking out underneath black business blazer — she's completely out of her element.

As I approach on my bike, she glances toward me but doesn't even try to move off the road to behind her car. She's glued right back to her cell phone.

The left lane, marked with the double line for no passing, is awfully tempting. I might blow past her in it. *Not my circus, not my monkeys.*

My cock twitches as I give her one last look over. Small thing like that, I could fuck her over the top of my bike. *No one will be coming down this road for hours. I only need one to fuck her, feast on her, and send her on her way.*

I come to a stop, idling fifty feet behind her, and cut the engine. And with the silence of the cut engine, she turns her attention to me, her piercing blue eyes catching mine. The delicate features I've stared at in her personnel photo no less than four dozen times dash my hope of an impromptu sexual encounter. *Off limits.*

Henri Greene, Alden pack publicist, shouts, "Hey, do you know where the Aldens live?"

"Unless they moved recently, probably," I answer.

Henri's a wolf, so she has every right to approach someone without fear, and she does.

"Oh, it's you." Henri's cerulean gaze locks on mine.

Nodding, I look at the aluminum can that doubles as a car. "Yup. And you're Henri Greene. Is it dead, out of gas, or are you just lost?"

Henri looks away. The wind picks up, blowing her golden locks across her face.

"I thought I had enough gas. It's so embarrassing. Now I'm late, and I can't get ahold of Mr. Alden, and my GPS won't reconnect and —" She pauses and draws a big breath of air before putting her polished self back together. "I would love directions or to borrow your phone to call the roadside emergency company."

"I'll take care of it. Hop on."

The devil on my shoulder is suddenly very glad we took the performance bike today. The smaller seat will push her closer to me. *I might not be fucking her, but having her close will still be awesome.*

She shakes her head. "No, directions will be fine."

"It's five miles." I point to her shoes and furrow my brow. "I mean, if you want to shift and run it, I guess?"

Henri points to her skirt. "I hardly think this will work on that."

"Gird your loins and come on." I slide the backpack off my shoulders.

Henri wiggles her nose, and it looks like the wheels turning in her brain are working overtime.

"Listen, I know you're probably worried about how this all looks." I try cracking a joke. "But if you're worried about how this looks, I'd say it looks better if people think you're being eaten out by me rather than by a black bear."

Henri straightens up, looking suspiciously at the woods. "Okay."

It's not a lie, there are bears, but little black bears wouldn't fuck with a wolf, even one as petite as I assume Henri's is.

I offer my hand to Henri, and she pulls her pencil skirt up a little bit. "Excuse me, eyes on the road."

I look away, feeling her maneuver herself onto the back of my bike.

"Fucking death trap," Henri mutters under her breath.

3

She slides forward, but from riding with Lena on the back, I know she's sitting with her ass at the tail end of the seat.

"You're not even on the bike." I look over my shoulder at her.

"I am too," she argues.

Sassy. I love sassy so much.

I laugh and rest my bag on the fuel tank. After hooking my hands under her knees, I pull her forward. She yips from being startled but doesn't try to slide away.

"Do I have to explain hanging on?" I look over my shoulder at her again.

With a sigh, she wraps her arms around me. I pull my backpack off the fuel tank and turn the engine over.

"Two hands!" Henri scolds as we inch forward.

I don't bother answering. With a flick of my wrist, I toss my backpack onto the roof of her tin can death trap on our way past before obediently putting my other hand on the handlebar. I want it wrapped around her thigh. But I'm pretending to be a good boy right now.

When I pick up the speed, she holds tighter to me, her cheek pressed against the back of my shirt.

The faster we move, the tighter she pulls up to me. The drive back to the house is supposed to take six minutes from where we started, assuming one's going the speed limit. I normally do it in three. With Henri though? She's precious cargo, and I wouldn't forgive myself for denting something so pretty.

The drive takes seven minutes.

I ease the bike into the garage and back it into its space before offering my hand to Henri to help her off.

"Thank you." Henri straightens her skirt.

"You're welcome," I answer with a nod. I get off the bike

and stand in front of her. With heels on, she's about as tall as Lena in flats. "I'll go get your car fuel and bring it around."

"Uhm." Henri swallows hard, looking up at me. I'm short, but even with her heels on, there's almost six inches between us. "Uhm," she repeats before continuing. "There's like ten dollars in the glove box. I think that'll be enough to get it back to the land of cell service. My boyfriend promised to —" Henri cuts herself off. "This is so unprofessional. I am sorry. I don't know why I'm telling you this."

"Everyone tells me things. Just one of those faces, I guess. Why is your boyfriend transferring you money?" It's insensitive, but I get away with asking inappropriate questions regularly.

My fingers itch wanting to touch her. The wind whipped her hair around a little bit, and while it suits her, Henri doesn't come across as someone who likes to be less than polished. It'd be easy enough to smooth it back into place for her.

"Uhm. Well, he's covering my expenses." Henri lies. Badly. But not as badly as Thalia. She reaches up and tucks the flyaway strands I had been eyeing behind her ear.

"He controls the finances, and you're left with an allowance," I deduce. If I had feelings, they'd hurt right now.

She doesn't answer my question but reiterates, "The ten is fine. It'll be okay."

Ten won't be fine. That vehicle is getting a full tank and a full look over.

Piece of fucking shit boyfriends. What wolf in their right goddamn mind doesn't take care of their mate? *Boyfriend. She said boyfriend, likely meaning he's human.* I mean, I guess we've all slummed it with someone before. Well, usually I'm the one people are slumming it with but whatever.

Dismissing herself, Henri is halfway across the garage

5

before she speaks again. "Any advice to get on Cade's good side for being late?" She pauses and looks back at me.

"Yeah. Tell him you ran into me. He'll calm right down."

"Thanks." Henri gives me a small wave before heading toward the house.

I pull my phone out of my pocket.

ME:

Be nice to Henri.

CADE:

I would be if she'd get here.

She's here. Be nice to Henri.

Cade doesn't answer.

After grabbing the full gas can I keep in the garage, I take the game trail through the woods back toward Henri's car.

Water Hemlock
Cicuta maculata

NOVEMBER

CHAPTER 1
DEACON

"Why does it feel like I've been summoned to the principal's office?" I ask Cade, my older brother and the Sovereign Alpha of all wolves, while strolling leisurely into his office.

Henri Greene, our pack publicist and, until very recently, Cade's jack-of-all-trades, sits in one of the chairs across from him, leaving the other open for me. It's been a week since I've laid eyes on her directly, but I know she got here at eight thirty this morning and has been in this meeting with Cade for almost an hour.

It's not stalking, it's just being aware of your surroundings.

I climb over the chair and sit on the back with my stocking feet on the seat.

"Really?" Cade glares at me, eyes flicking back and forth from my chest to my feet on the seat.

Giving Henri a big sigh and eye roll, I drop down into the seat. "Better?"

"Much." Cade huffs and then does that thing he does right before he's about to irritate the fuck out of me: scrub his hand down his face and purse his lips. He starts slowly. "I've a proposal."

The thick pause in the air gives me the space to speak. "This'll be good."

Cade ignores me, looking at Henri and addressing her. "Now that we've semi-settled the news outlets in relationship to Finn and Lena, I hear you and your request that we get ourselves out among the humans. The proactive method to minimize media swarms that you recommended by seeming accessible and part of the people makes sense."

This is so not good. Catching onto the trajectory of this conversation, knowing the outcome of the media storm with Lena and Finn, I can see the impending impact, and I don't like where this is going to ultimately explode. My sister and her new mate had it rough. Fucked over the coals, so to speak, and now he's trying to make it my turn.

"Between you and Thalia and Fi —" Henri must be picking up what Cade is putting down.

"Deacon." Cade cuts in, shaking his head.

I follow suit, shaking my head. *No. No. No. He can't be serious.*

I look over, and the furrow in her brow and the pen poised on the electronic tablet sitting in her lap indicate that she thinks this is going to be a short, easy discussion.

Henri chews on her bottom lip. I'm hoping she comes to my rescue on this.

Come on, Henri. Any of our conversations over the past six months would tell you I can't do this.

Instead, with no way to hear my internal pleading, she gives a solemn nod. "The public loves Deacon."

"Yes." I cut in.

If Henri won't save me, I'll save myself.

I put my feet up on his desk, and Cade cuts me a sharp look, but I don't move them.

I keep talking before he can interrupt me. "What's not to love? The billionaire playboy with attachment issues." I sum up what social media has concluded about me with an easy shrug, and then I glare at Cade. "I, on the other hand, do not love the public. I don't like most of the pack, if we're being frank. This is part of why I willingly let my ass get kicked by Finn in front of the pack and submitted."

I swallow hard, forcing down the words 'because you made him promise not to kill me.'

"I know." Cade hangs his head in an apologetic glance downward before he slides his hand back through his hair. "Believe me, I know you're going to hate this, but . . ."

"Thalia is pregnant." Henri nods, cutting off our sibling discussion.

It's still surreal in a good way that Cade's mate, my best friend, is pregnant.

She continues. "Finn and Lena are both trying to get the new lab up and running. Lena needs some time to adjust to her life and what that's going to look like interpersonally first before adjusting to the media."

Cade takes my silence as acceptance of the situation and turns back to Henri, who looks like she's as many parts terrified as I am pissed off about the arrangement. "So, I want to hire you three to five more people. My executive assistant, Meaghan, is almost up to speed, so we'll lean on you less. That gives you more open reign . . ."

I tune Cade out, knowing he's about to tell Henri everything he thinks needs to be done with the situation. I'm simply here because Cade is trying to 'include me' in the decisions about my life.

Out the window I'm watching for snow. It's been an

incredibly dry season, and I don't mind. There aren't a lot of years I can still take the motorcycle out this late. Motorcycles don't really care for snow, after all.

"Deacon," Cade snaps, teeth clicking, pulling my attention back to their conversation. "I would appreciate if you would work with Henri and do more of the public meet and greets. Maybe show people not all wolves are as scary as Senator Clark keeps trying to tell people we are." Cade is picking his words very carefully.

He knows I'll push back if he keeps being too forward, and if he doesn't give me reason and incentive, I won't agree to it.

But I push back anyway. This can't happen. "How much time are we talking? Because let's be honest with each other, what are you really expecting of me? How many of the Pack Second's, Pack Alpha's, The Sovereign's responsibilities am I supposed to just shoulder without argument?"

Henri goes completely still, and it's only in the silence of the room that I realize I raised my voice.

"Ideally." Cade pauses, and there's a soft rumble in his voice as The Leviathan rises in his eyes. "At least half, or so, of all the appearances on the books already, and anything additional that Henri can make do without needing me or Lena specifically. I'd prefer three-quarters as I go head-to-head with Senator Clark and Congress in the new year."

I stand up out of the chair. *Fuck this.*

"Deacon. Sit down." Cade hits me with an Alpha command straight from The Leviathan, so I have no choice.

"Fuck you," I snarl.

"I know it's a lot." Cade sighs but doesn't apologize, dismissing me as a threat. He's back to scratching that spot in his beard, clearly grasping at straws. "I know that means you're going to have to travel together across the country from time to time. I'm hoping you two can get more things booked here where you're both more comfortable, at least to start."

Henri is scary quiet. I can barely hear her breathing. I don't blame her, but she hasn't seen the two of us really get into it. She hasn't seen it because it's been years since I've really stood my ground with him. The fact is his unilateral decision-making is just who he is as a person.

I don't know how long we sit in silence, but Henri's voice, soft and full of fear, breaks it. "Deacon needs to be more sober for a lot of this."

Cade looks at me like he's waiting for an answer, but there wasn't a question in Henri's statement. Her voice didn't pitch up like she wanted an opinion, so I remain silent.

My family knows how uncontrollable my gift can be if I'm sober. The micro-dosing self-medicating I do to keep my wolf under the surface isn't for fun. It is bred from the necessity of passing as 'normal' enough for people not to ask questions. 'Normal' people don't talk to ancestors no one else can see. 'Normal' people don't have to see the dead.

"And what's in it for me?" I leverage because it wouldn't be a conversation with Cade if I didn't give him a little shit.

"You help make it so people don't try and kill us all? Think of it as a good deed for our people." Cade doesn't sweeten the pot at all.

"Did you ask the Alloways? Like, Judah would be *really* good at this." I push back again.

I look to my older brother and try to get him to hear me. I know his mind's made up, but fuck, am I above begging? *Come on, Cade. Don't make me do this.*

Cade looks over at Henri and then back at me. I can see he's not even considering it. Probably because Judah's already drowning under his own responsibilities.

You've got Thalia. Lena has Finn. I was planning on saying goodbye to Ansel at Equinox and being done with it. I draw a deep breath and let it out. *I should probably wait until Thalia gives birth anyway. All the stress of planning a funeral can't be good for a pregnancy.*

The silence speaks volumes.

There are no negotiations here.

Accepting defeat, I turn toward Henri. "So, which minion of yours do I get to terrorize first? Can it be Kyle? I really think Kyle likes me." I smile at her.

That guy fucking hates me, and Henri isn't his biggest fan. I bet I could do her a favor and get him to quit. I'm nothing if not exemplary at getting under people's skin.

"You'll work directly with Henri." Cade spells it out.

Henri tenses in her chair, and it's what I would have expected.

She and I have been dancing around each other since we met. The way we stalk each other, always aware of where the other one is. On days when we're not in the same building, it feels strange to me. Granted, it's unavoidable when I have to go on longer hauls to pick up the drugs I need to survive. But when I'm not around, I miss her not-so-veiled attempts at hiding her stalking of me.

We can spend time with Henri? My wolf perks up at Cade's offering. *You'll convince her to come off the suppressants. You hold yourself together for a few days. We can see if she is our mate.*

My wolf circles back to every single spare thought we've had about her in the last seven months. Many times even pushing me to stalk her right back.

And I'm better at it, he reminds me.

Numbness sinks into me because it doesn't matter if Henri comes off her heat suppressants and I get sober. I don't want nor can I have a mate. Fate wouldn't be so cruel as to give me one. I laugh and shake my head at my thoughts because, let's be real, fate, hope, a higher power, they all abandoned me a long time ago.

This time, when I stand up, I'm not ordered back to sit down. "Sure thing. See you tomorrow, Henri."

"Wai —" she starts.

I don't look nor turn back. It's one thing to have obsessed about her and stalk her while she stalks me. It's another thing to have her interjected into my life. I've purposefully forced myself away from her for so many reasons. Those reasons — abusive boyfriend, obsessive fantasies of her in my bed, and my self-medicating — aren't less valid now.

Tonight, I'll try and figure out how I'm going to live through this or figure out how to say goodbye faster.

You can't end this without knowing, my wolf demands.

By the time I've reached the third story, the quietest part of the house, I'm no longer sure what my plan of action is going to be beyond the next five minutes.

CHAPTER 2
HENRI

Yesterday's meeting was . . . intense. Cade was positive he wanted Deacon to take over doing a large share of the public outreach events going forward. Unfortunately for me, Deacon seemed to have the exact same level of excitement about the new arrangement as I did.

My wolf wags her tail, knowing we're about to go upstairs and see him.

It'll be easy. I lie to myself. *All I have to do is get the world to see Deacon the same way I do. Quirky, fun, and witty. He's good with children and smart.* It's not hard to list Deacon's good qualities because, since the first stupid moment I saw him, I've been enthralled.

Despite the fact that I have a boyfriend.

As much as I've learned Cade's schedule, likes, dislikes, and tolerance, I've learned Deacon's. Granted he wasn't supposed to be my job at all, but I already know enough about him from my notes and worry — I mean concern — for his well-being.

Being Tuesday, he most likely stayed up most of the night reading. But the question is, which substance was he on last

19

night? That depends apparently on the weather? I still haven't figured out his drug use.

Because I shouldn't be doing that, I remind myself.

But we are because he's exactly the kind of mate we want. My wolf pipes up.

It's embarrassing how obsessed we've been with him. All the way up to stalking him and learning all the little details of his schedule.

We're dating Nathan. We love Nathan. He takes care of us. The house and the car . . . All the things we didn't have when we left home. He cared.

But there's . . . something about Deacon.

But he's the —

I push my wolf away, cutting her off and focusing on climbing the stairs. Normally I'd take the elevator, but watching everyone else do the stairs all day makes me think maybe I'm being a wuss about it.

My calves are burning by the time I hit the third floor. Out of breath, I lean against the wall. I'm going to have to do stairs more often. Flat running outside is fine; stairs, however, need more work. *Why do all the other wolves make this stuff look easy? How can I possibly be the only out-of-shape wolf?*

Getting myself together, I walk the short distance across the hall to his door. I knock, unsure if he's going to be awake. Maybe I should have waited later in the day. But Deacon said 'see you tomorrow,' and tomorrow has arrived.

Cade made it clear there is no getting out of this.

For the first time in my, albeit short, professional career, I'm hoping an interaction with the public goes just sideways enough that similar future ventures aren't seen as beneficial to the pack's, and Cade's, long-term goals. Mostly because I don't want to be on the defense and have to explain to my boyfriend that traveling with Deacon is strictly work and that I'm not having an affair with him.

I get Nathan's concern though. Some of his past girlfriends have cheated on him, and it's not a good feeling. But I'm loyal, and I wish he'd trust me more.

All this runs through my head as I stand in front of the only occupied suite on the third floor. Aside from the cleaning staff, no one visits Deacon's floor.

The door opens a moment later, and Deacon's standing there without a shirt on in his boxers, his hair wet — I imagine from a shower.

Holy shit.

Wolves are runners and, by nature, are built of lean and deadly muscle. With how slouchy and effortless Deacon normally dresses, I'd forgotten that he's, well, wolf.

I've seen Deacon naked before . . . briefly, in passing, as we stripped down to shift for pack runs, but I'm usually so overwhelmed with getting myself shifted that I've never really *looked*. Up close and personal, it's a whole new experience.

Well-defined pecs, strong biceps, and defined abs. But he doesn't look bulky and ornamental like Nathan does after hours of lifting heavy weights. Deacon is a functional, deadly kind of beautiful.

"Good morning. I wasn't expecting you up here." Deacon abandons the shocked look on his face in favour of a panty melting smile.

Which I only notice because it's going to be helpful for the job. Women are going to love Deacon.

Yeah, only because of the job.

No other women, my wolf growls.

"Can I help?" he offers.

Deacon's smile and my wolf's excitement at seeing him are contagious.

21

I smile but feel it turning into an almost grimace. "We were meeting today about Cade's plan?"

"Yeah. That. Got it." The smile falls from his face, and he hangs his head, frustration clinging to his voice like the frost on the windshield of my car.

"Yeah. I guess I wanted to get started on discussing your comfort level." I trip over those last few words and clear my throat before gesturing back toward the stairs. "When you're dressed, want to meet me in my office?"

"No." Deacon opens the door. "Come on in. I'll grab a shirt. Lauren sent my breakfast up. I had asked her about some more towels, I thought you were her, but we can share breakfast."

CHAPTER 3

DEACON

She looks so beautiful with red cheeks from running up the stairs. Unlike me, Henri prefers the elevator. The three stories shouldn't be an issue for her, but I don't think Henri lets her wolf out outside of pack functions. Though that cute little wolf of hers flashed in her eyes when she saw me.

Not embracing our wolves makes us softer. I should know. I'm the king of stuffing him away and only letting him out either when required or to burn off the calories from the munchies.

I should have gotten dressed, grabbed my breakfast, and gone downstairs to meet with her, but instead I'm forcing my half hard-on into a pair of jeans. All because I want her scent to linger in my space. It'll mix with my own, and I can feel more connected to her.

I don't think Henri knows how beautiful she is. Since her eyes didn't drift lower than my stomach, she didn't notice that the sight of her had me wanting her in primal ways.

Avoiding Henri and trying to discipline myself to stay away

from her has been torture. I don't want to behave. I don't want to be the golden-retriever, good boy she deserves. I want to be the wolf she needs, the one to end anyone who looks at her funny.

Once I pull a graphic tee over my head, I get back to my study. Henri is looking at some of the specimens, rocks, and various trinkets I keep on a lower shelf. She's bent at the waist, and her round ass, clad in dress slacks, is popped out toward me.

I bite my bottom lip, sliding my bedroom door closed. The jeans are determined to stay tight today because I'm almost completely stiff with that view. *Cool it.*

Startled, she jumps and turns to look at me. "These things are really cool."

"Thanks." I walk closer but stop myself from going to her.

Instead, I pull out the rolling extension on my desk. It makes room for precisely two to sit.

I'm setting a place for her to eat with me when she starts to object. "Oh, I had breakfast earlier."

"Then humor me and sit with a fork in your hand." I offer her my desk chair. It's more comfortable than the folding chair I keep here for putting my feet on.

"Sure." Henri sits and slides the chair in, holding the fork like a weapon she might stab me with.

If she does it, I might even like it.

After taking my seat, I start opening the glass containers.

I laugh seeing the slice of Ms. Gertie's banana bread. It tastes so much sweeter knowing that a little bit of a lot of extra potassium is all it takes for it to be heart stopping.

"So, what's the plan?" I ask, taking a bite of the warm, doughy goodness.

"Well, I figured we could brainstorm a little bit about what sort of things you're interested in doing. Maybe find some good outreaches that interest you to make it easier for you."

"You come up with something, Henri, and I'll show up, put on a smile, and do what's asked of me." I nod, trying to make her job easier.

My reaction to Cade's proposal was childish yesterday. So I've got to do some digging to get myself out of that temper-tantrum hole.

Apparently, my attempt at appeasement is not what she wanted. She purses her lips and tries again to convince me. "I think it would be easier if it was something you didn't hate." She circles her hand, gesturing around my study. "For instance, it seems you've a unique, curated collection. Perhaps an event at the science museum or the historical society? Or I know you're a big reader and into the academics, so we could see about a library event, book club, or something?"

She glances at one of the bookshelves, where the large item in that display case is the articulated skeleton of the coyote Isabel LeFleur sent Cade. I can see where she'd get science museum out of what I did with that trophy. But it was a hyper-fixation to keep my brain occupied while I hunted down those associated with Isabel, who Cade might not have thought to.

Sometimes, people just go missing. Other times they turn up dead. I prefer if my prey goes missing, everything has to be perfect for someone to turn up dead. It's work. It's why Henri's boyfriend is still wasting oxygen.

She's loyal to her piece-of-shit abusive boyfriend, and Lena's problem stole my best idea for how to dispatch a human without drawing suspicion. A heart attack in one human connected to us is enough.

And try as I might, I can't deny the pull to her.

"Okay." I open another container and find bacon. "Science

museum could be cool. I don't love boring science like biology and the human body."

Henri laughs. "Okay, fair, especially since, like, our anatomy is only half human."

"What was it like being raised by humans?" I stuff a bite of bacon in my mouth so she feels like she has to answer.

I want to know more about her. Everything I couldn't learn from following her, really.

She shrugs. "They had no idea. I had no idea. I didn't shift until I was a teenager. It was terrifying. I was never one of those paranormal or fantasy reader kids. I liked real-world fiction, so I had no frame of reference."

"I can only imagine." I wait a moment and then offer something to connect further with her. "The people who raised me and my siblings were different from most other packs. It was a lot of old rules and intimidation tactics. I was often surprised when they did things like seek outside help for stuff. It broke the norm of isolationism."

"What do you mean?" Henri is quick to ask.

I open another glass container and find poached eggs in hollandaise.

Do I tell her? There really isn't a reason not to.

"They sometimes talked to human doctors about things. Progressive. Misguided. And then other times they would do things like public bondings." I try to keep things appropriate for breakfast, but the thought of stripping Henri down and fucking her, barely concealed by the tree line, wanders into the forefront of my mind.

Henri blushes. "Woah, I didn't think public bondings happened. I'd read about them when I did some studying in the pack's library. But it always seemed in severe retrospect."

I smile from my own discomfort but test the waters with

28

her. "Yeah, I was like ten when I first saw a bonding. That sort of thing stays with you."

Henri is pure and soft spoken. She used to get uncomfortable when Cade swore when he was pissed off. So my expectations of a reaction are low, and I don't have high hopes for her having any deviousness in her. Not that I should have any hope at all. We're just forced into spending time with each other. I'm just the job.

"You know, I always thought I was disadvantaged being raised by humans, but maybe not." Henri's words are in direct contrast to her physical reaction.

She claims disinterest, but she shifts in her seat, and the subtle smell of arousal wafts over the top of my breakfast.

Kinky. Henri surprises me yet again. *Fuck, I want to know what makes her tick. We could be compatible.*

I push the bacon over to her because I need her to stop smelling like that, or I'm going to do something that crosses a line. The line I cannot cross right now.

Or ever.

Henri picks up a piece of bacon and chews slowly.

I take a break from talking and push containers across the table. Henri gives in to the delicious food and eats with me.

I keep observing her carefully, watching as she eats. *Where is she bruised now?* None of her arm movements seem stiff, but I didn't really get a good look at her gait.

Last month, at the full moon run, Henri was hiding freshly broken ribs and a bruised hip.

When I confronted her about the bruising, she lied and stumbled through unfamiliar and uncomfortable words. She told me it was because she likes it rough. The time before, when there were deep purple welts all the way up the column of her slender neck, she told me it was boxes falling out of the closet on her.

I've seen through all her lies. Fuck, calling her out on them hasn't helped anything. But I should have known, from the day we went wedding dress shopping for Thalia and all the flippant text messages that came through on her phone, that asshole has his hooks so deep into her.

No matter how much I push, it very well could be that Henri won't leave Nathan. He has her believing so much bullshit that the truth is lost to her. It's evident in the excuses she makes for him.

It's why we're going to kill him. My wolf stretches out, waking up now that I've been fed and the dredges of last night's late-night binge reading and edibles session have faded.

The wolf isn't wrong. I'll kill Nathan if it's the last thing I do. But that doesn't mean I'll ever call Henri mine.

PROBABLY TWENTY MINUTES LATER, we finish off the last of the food. And as lost as I've been in my thoughts about Henri, she must have been thinking about me too because she breaks the silence. "Did you want to look at events for suici —"

The shake of my head cuts her off. "Hard pass."

Mistakes were made when I traded secrets with her at Cade's wedding. Telling her I've made plans to remove myself from the earth must have sunk into her psyche, doing just as much damage to her as seeing Nathan's abuse to her body has done to me.

"Okay, fair. I won't bring it up again." She looks at the shirt I'm wearing. "You have something other than one black suit and graphic tees to wear, right?"

"Uh." I look down. I'm wearing a concert T-shirt of a band I saw once. They were okay, I guess. "Not really? I own *a* collared shirt. It's also black."

"Okay." Henri's eyes widen. "You'll need to get a more sophisticated, casual look with some more formal pieces."

"Sure. Make a list, and I'll . . ." Out of the corner of my eye, I see Zachariah materializing. "Zachariah, go the fuck away. It's too early for your bullshit."

"I came to see the pretty secretary with the nice tush. If she'd worked for me, I'd have taken every opportunity to knock her pens on the floor." He wets his lips, and I reach over next to my computer and pull out the bottle of whiskey I'd set there.

Henri doesn't say anything when I take a pull straight out of the bottle. "Sorry. Guess I'm drinking before noon today."

"I didn't realize you had rules." The words are super judgmental, and she backpedals. "What I mean is, I assumed that you started early, in order to get ahead of your gift."

I nod and take another pull, knowing it'll take a lot more before Zachariah disappears entirely, but he gets the hint and fizzles away on his own. "I try to make it until at least noon. Some days it's easier than others."

"You can't be drinking or too drunk in public. Well, for most events." Henri starts setting rules, oblivious to my issue with the ancestor.

Henri looks at me and then looks back to the door, where my eyes keep flicking. "We should come up with a phrase or indicator that you're struggling. I've noticed you ask how many people are in a room. Could we come up with something more subtle?"

"Open to suggestions. And I promise to keep the drinking in public to a minimum."

When did I get to be so agreeable?

Since you decided to try to see if she's our mate. My wolf informs me of a decision I never made . . . Pretty sure I never made.

I ignore him and start stacking the dirty breakfast dishes.

"Sure, how about if you're struggling with ancestors . . ." Henri turns her attention back to me. "You ask me what the soup of the day is?"

"Soup of the day." I nod and accept her suggestion.

It's something easy for me to remember.

"Did you want to go today or another day?"

"I'm sorry, what?" She squints at me, trying to keep up.

"Clothes?"

"Oh, right." Henri looks at her watch. "I guess if you're open to going today. You seemed perhaps unenthusiastic about the arrangement. Kind of anticipated needing to butter you up to it."

"Butter me up?" I raise an eyebrow. The bad, dirty thoughts are back.

Bribe me with something fun, Henri. Something that doesn't require leaving this room. Fuck, I'd spend a day being your personal dress-up doll for a single lap of that . . .

I stand up from my chair and pick up the stack of breakfast dishes.

Get it together, Deacon, I remind myself. *She's never going to do that. She's never going to cheat. His manipulations won't let her leave, and he's not dead.*

My cock, not getting the message, gives a wicked throb.

"Well, I know Lena enjoys her mini-golf. I tried to find something you'd be interested in. Lena mentioned motorcycle or oddity related, which makes sense now seeing your shelves. But the only thing I found was a reptile show, and we're avoiding a whole 'wolves as pets' narrative. So, I kinda crossed that one out." Henri smiles at me, and it turns into a grimace as she stands from her chair. "But there are three events in December you can go to that I think would be pretty fun and safe for you to be a little inebriated, and no one would think it was strange. At least until we can figure out more of what you're interested in."

When she dusts off her lap, I try to brush away the thoughts of her thighs wrapped around my head. "What sort of fun?"

"Well, two of them are winter lights shows. One's at a garden where you can walk around and look at them, and the other one is kind of a sit-in-your-seat performance type." She bites her bottom lip, and I pause from leading her out of my bedroom. "I don't know what kind of substances you use, but I had a roommate in college who said the fairy lights on a low dose of MDMA is like the second-best thing in the world." Henri offers with a shrug as I continue to walk alongside her toward the stairs.

"What's the first best thing in the world?"

I don't correct Henri about the drugs I do or do not enjoy regularly. But from past experiences, I know she's not wrong. *Pretty lights on MDMA or shrooms would be amazing.*

Henri's eyes widen. "Uhm. Given the comment section on any social media post you're tagged in, I think you're familiar with the particular thing in question."

Oh, your thighs wrapped around my head. Of course.

In a perfect world, maybe she would reward me with the first best thing in the world? I'd even put up a small fuss so she'd want to reward me more.

I swallow hard, salivating at the thought. The desire to make her spell it out is so strong, but I fold. *Behave.*

I sigh. "Ahh. The kind of thing that perhaps isn't suitable for doing in public."

Heat flushing Henri's face accompanies her wide-eyed look, and the sweet smell of her arousal hits the air again. I opt to walk behind her down the stairs to revel in her scent through long inhales and exhales.

Sweet little exhibitionist or voyeur, I want to enjoy that with you.

With that smell, our discussion, and my lack of self-control, I'm one bad decision away from kissing her. Which is one tiny step away from getting the taste from someplace much lower.

Fuck. This arrangement is going to kill me, and not in the way I want it to.

CHAPTER 4
HENRI

"So, what brings you two in today?" The shopkeeper is way too chipper, and I immediately expect Deacon to go to his mostly stoic, more reserved self, letting me do the leading.

"I apparently need a new wardrobe as I've been informed that while black is suitable for any occasion, it's not suitable for all of the occasions." He smiles at her.

It's the casual and laid-back, mingling, personable version of Deacon, the one I need him to tap into regularly.

She gives him a once-over while clarifying. "Certainly, you're thinking four or five outfits for various occasions or . . . ?"

Deacon turns to me but doesn't take himself out of the conversation.

"Yes. Mostly business casual and smart casual. Pieces we can dress up or down," I answer, speaking the fashion lingo to help Deacon.

"Oh. My. Gawd." A woman from the back of the store comes rushing forward.

Deacon takes a step toward and in front of me, partially blocking my line of sight.

Is he protecting me? I can't rectify what's happening and ask my wolf, who is pretty much a swooning puddle and no help at all. *Ugh. Wolves.*

I step to the side to better see the interaction.

"You're James Alden." Her eyes are lustful and excited.

Deacon nods. "Last time I checked anyway."

"My girlfriends and I ran into you this summer." She tries to draw a connection to him.

The flirting is extremely obvious, and I think she's about to proposition him right here and now with the way she's pushing her tits toward him.

When he doesn't show any recognition toward her, she tucks her hair behind her ear. "I'm Cora?"

Deacon turns to me, completely dismissing her. "Sorry, but unfortunately, we're here on business. We'll have to catch up later."

"I could help you?" She steps, trying to get in front of the other sales associate again.

The first woman, older than the young woman flirting with Deacon, clicks her tongue, and I can't decipher it.

"Well, I'm so sorry, but I was really hoping to work with Bianca today." Deacon inclines his head toward the first woman and surprises me by reading her name tag for the discussion. He tucks his hands in his pocket, wobbling a bit with an appeasing shrug. "She's been super nice so far."

"Oh, well, I'm off at four thirty. If you're not in a hurry, we could maybe grab some drinks." She continues to push.

No means no, I want to growl.

My wolf is uncomfortable inside me. But Deacon seems to be handling it well. On the bright side, this is a good indicator of how he'll handle stress. There are worse trial runs to have.

38

"Sorry, we're on a time crunch. But thank you." Deacon rotates his body back toward Bianca and smiles at her. It's a bit larger, more engaged. "Alright, so not black, business and smart casual."

He's making a point to dismiss her. I don't give Cora a second look intentionally, but I catch her stunned, rejected face before she turns toward the back to lick her wounds.

"Yes, I've a couple great options for you." She puts her arm out, blocking Deacon's mega fan, and leads him toward a men's clothing rack.

Ten minutes in, Deacon's overwhelmed. His fingers twitch at his sides as the woman shows him another dress shirt, and he looks at me for guidance.

I pick up a few of the options she pulled for him — chinos and corduroy pants in dark colors, slightly brighter shirts, and two more neutral jackets in gray and brown. "Try these on to start."

He steps into a dressing room.

Bianca whispers, "Is he okay? He looks uncomfortable."

"His entire wardrobe is rock band T-shirts, dark wash and black denim, a leather jacket, and a black suit," I whisper back, knowing full well Deacon can hear us.

She makes an O with her mouth. "I'll step away for just a bit. Why don't you two try on some options and see what you think? Get a baseline for things that do and don't work."

I put my hands together in thanks and turn to the dressing room. Deacon exits and shrugs, turning around for me to get a good look.

I fight to keep my mouth from popping open. Deacon has always been attractive, but dressed up just a smidge? He's jaw-droppingly handsome.

The chinos hug him in all the right areas but a little too

well. The shirt he's wearing fits nicely, but his look of discomfort is accompanied by his fingers twitching.

"Okay, pants are too small. Size up." I immediately voice for him, trying to drag my eyes away from the bulge in front where the traitors had gone after checking out his chest. "How do you feel about the shirt?"

"I prefer more mobility. But after a wash, it'll probably loosen up a little bit." He runs his hand down his face.

"You okay?" I step toward him and ask quietly.

"Soup of the day." He nods. "Everyone's lack of concern tells me that the current flavor of woman and man arguing in the back of the store isn't living."

"Oh." I nod, agreeing with him. "They're not something I can see or hear. Do you want to go somewhere else and come back here? Maybe try another day?"

He shakes his head, letting it drop from its proud stance. "No. I just should have brought the fun flask."

"As opposed to the boring flask?" I narrow my eyes at him.

"Exactly." Deacon shrugs.

I reach into my purse hanging at my side and step closer to him. The metal is cool in my hand, and I pull it out and, below waist level, offer it to him.

"Didn't know you had it in you to carry." His surprise is punctuated with relief as he takes the flask from me.

My heart rate picks up at the look he gives me . . . approval maybe? "It's my job to manage you. If that means learning to carry a 'fun flask' for extended outings and urgent situations, then consider me the life of the party."

"You like this outfit enough?" Deacon asks before his head snaps over to the far side of the store. Whatever he sees has him shaking his head.

"I do. Let me get you a size up and try it again. Go and take a couple minutes in seclusion and come out in a different ensemble when you're ready." I look around the racks and the shop, wishing I could see what he could. If I could help him make this easier, I would. "I'll wander, maybe call Bianca over to give us a hand."

Deacon doesn't say anything and goes back into the changing room without further argument.

Drawing a breath, I look around and form a plan of attack for the fastest shopping trip I can come up with.

CHAPTER 5
DEACON

SITTING on the bench in the too-tight pants hurts, but I twist the cap off the flask before even bothering with the fly. I've played the idiot for so long that I'm actually becoming one. Method acting at its finest.

I sniff the flask before taking a swig. *Whiskey. Well, alright then.*

I've seen Henri manage Cade. She does so with ease and precision. The amount of stress she carried was alarming, but her intuitive nature of what he needed was always so intense. I thought it was something unique between the two of them. But the flask in my hand that pours sweet barrel-aged whiskey down my throat says it's all Henri. She knew to bring a flask in case I was too sober.

Which is strange since today is our first official day working together. But she's always been quick on the uptake.

The ancestor couple screaming across the shop are quieting now, but when he slapped her, I almost lost it. I can ignore screaming and yelling. I can ignore crying and begging. But violence isn't easily ignored.

With another swig, my wolf grumbles but gets the hint: he and his gift are not wanted here.

It's a temporary fix. Alcohol doesn't really work all that well. More like a gentleman's agreement. My wolf will disappear when I start drinking and give me a reprieve from the ancestors.

At last, when the world is brought to a more peaceful, insufferable existence, I stand and slide off the pants. They're way too fucking tight but damn the way Henri devoured me with her eyes. I'd happily be a little uncomfortable for more of her attention like that.

I know what the wolf would tell me. *She's probably our mate. The obsession makes it make sense. Get sober, get her off the suppressants, and live happily ever after.*

It's bullshit people like us don't get happily ever after. Henri might, but not me.

But what my wolf keeps forgetting is that sober me means more of this bullshit, seeing screaming, arguing dead people in stores. That sweet relief when Revecca took my gift last month? Fuck, I'd do anything to get that back. The peace I enjoyed in those days was so much easier to bear.

The other pair of pants is a size larger, and I pick them up to try them on. A soft knock comes on the dressing room door. In my boxers, decent enough, I undo the small metal closure and open the door a fraction.

Henri gasps and tries to push the door closed. "We're in public. Put some pants on."

I chuckle. "You've seen me naked before. It's nothing new."

"Not the point," she argues.

Curiously, her cheeks turn pink.

Closing her eyes, she hands me another few pairs of pants and a shirt. "Okay, come out when you're ready."

I was practically wearing the same thing this morning. *It's the public part.* My lip twitches, and this time the smile that comes with it is genuine. *We could have so much fun together.*

"I'm not straight. But I don't really care for labels." I goad her, and it gets a reaction, just not an anticipated one.

"You're open about it?" Her eyes fly open, and her lips remain parted at the end of her question.

Can you die from unfulfilled desires? I want to run my thumb across her lower lip. *What would it be like to kiss someone so innocent?*

"Yeah, Henri. I don't hide it any more than I hide being a wolf." Before I do something that Henri will regret, I raise the clothes and indicate with a nod that I'll try them on before closing the door.

I WILL ADMIT that other than feeling like Judah in his National Park Service uniform, I do look pretty good in earth tones. So, when we leave the first store with two bags of clothes, I don't feel awful about what my new wardrobe will look like.

"Had enough for today?" Henri asks before checking a quick message on her phone.

"I'd really like some lunch." I feel eyes on us as I say it.

"If you're open to it, like to go to one more store after we eat?" Henri seems oblivious or unconcerned if she does sense we're being watched.

"Then that's about all I can handle of human people for a day." I glance around, searching for who may be watching us.

Even through the alcohol, my wolf fights for alertness, and I let him know it's only a matter of minutes before that tiny bit of whiskey that I used to top off the buzz I had going burns off my system.

The predator stalking us shouts at the same time I target

the source of the glare. I've had the displeasure of meeting Nathan once when he tracked us down while we were shopping for Thalia's wedding dress. I'd recognize the top-heavy cartoon-gym-bro anywhere.

Nathan's bulked-out frame is only preceded by his annoying, artificially deep voice. "Henri, you're not where you're supposed to be! We don't have money for you to be out shopping! Why aren't you working? Clearly, I'm giving you too much of an allowance if you're spending time at a mall rather than working."

He's red in the face, a vein throbbing in his forehead, and talking so fast that even if Henri wanted to answer his questions, there isn't a chance for her to do so.

I squeeze the handles of the bags, trying to stop myself from intervening. *Come on, Henri, stand up for yourself.*

My internal begging does nothing because despite having a wolf from her pack at her back, Henri backs down from the fight. "Nathan, baby, calm down." She raises and lowers her hand, bringing him down. "I'm here because Deacon needs new clothes for events he's attending. You know how hard it is to shop for your clothes without you being there. I am working. It's just not the usual type of work."

At the mention of my name, Nathan turns his attention to me. "You fucking my girl?"

If I was fucking her, she wouldn't even be thinking about being your girl. I keep the snide remark to myself. "Henri, why don't you go home for the day. Take the afternoon off on me." I pull my wallet out of my front pocket and pull out a few hundred-dollar bills, then hand them to her. "Lunch on me. I'll go to the next store and show the lady the pictures you took of me and see if I can't find more of the same but slightly different."

"Oh." Henri freezes.

Nathan, however, doesn't have a problem taking my

money. He snatches it out of Henri's hand, "Come on. Let's go to that fancy place you've wanted to go for a long time. What's it called? Hare's Hearth?"

Henri glances backward one last time. Her eyes are sad, and she mouths 'sorry.'

I give her a tense smile and wave her off, then turn back toward the parking lot on the other end of the shopping complex where we came from.

My stomach is in knots. I don't feel good about letting her go with him. His anger ran deeper than it felt like it should. I shuffle my bags to my other hand and pull my phone out of my pocket.

Once I open the favorites contacts, I select one to dial.

The phone rings a few times, and I think he's sending me to voicemail, but then Finn picks up. "Hello?"

"Hey. I know your security-conscious ass activated the GPS tracking in the same system that Corinth uses. Can you lock on to Henri's phone? I think Nathan's taking her to Hare's Hearth. Let's get the bunnies acquainted."

I hate the idea of using Finn's hired assassins over doing it myself, but I need a backup plan for my backup plans.

"On it," Finn confirms. "You okay? I know you weren't looking at getting pets anytime soon."

"I may need to adopt, not shop." I don't bother lying but keep up with his extended metaphor.

"Want to talk to Lena?" Finn asks, and now I know why he took so long to answer.

If he and my sister are in the same room, I'm likely interrupting something. Most recently, a discussion about their upcoming nuptials. Even though Lena is not adopting his religious belief, she agreed, without arguments, to have a ceremony in his church back in Ireland despite the knowledge that it would be difficult to coordinate.

"Nope. I'm good. Have fun settling your differences about the mating ceremony." I hang up before there's any more discussion on the matter.

Back at Lena's SUV, which we took because shopping bags on a motorcycle aren't super fun, I slump into the driver's seat.

You let her go with him. You know what he can do to her, my wolf snarls at me.

I draw long, deep breaths.

She chooses him, I remind my wolf, trying to rationalize it all. *She knows what I think about him. She has to know there are other options.* I know Cade's offered many times to move her into a house on pack property.

"Fuck!" I shout, banging my palm on the upper portion of the steering wheel.

Nathan was so fucking angry that she was maybe spending money. Her money that he feels entitled to . . . *What is Nathan hiding in his finances?*

I drum my fingers on the steering wheel, trying to calm myself first and stopping myself from following them second.

It wouldn't be too hard to dig into his financials. While I have purposefully avoided stalking Nathan and what I'm sure is a filibuster-length list of values lacking any morals, ethical dilemmas, and legal crimes, it's time to move on the desire fully. I have to do it for Henri's future.

Lunch and one more store. I can do this.

I start the SUV and head to the nearest bar and grill, knowing they won't judge me for day drinking. Then, I'll go home and dig into Nathan. I just need a smoking gun, and I can figure out what nefarious shit he's up to.

Then I can frame whatever he's involved in for his death.

The dark part of me revels in the idea.

But the more I drive, with every mile between me and

Henri, the more a new darkness seeps in. The darkness that ruins me.

End this. No more stores, no more humans, no more worrying about people who aren't our problem. I'll never be what she wants, what she needs. It's all beyond me and my capabilities. Get it over with.

Everything becomes a temptation — overpasses, bridges, oncoming traffic. But they'd all be minor accidents. I'd survive.

I've noticed I don't think of suicide when Henri is in the same room. But fuck if these thoughts don't come back ten times harder once she leaves. When she leaves with him.

She wants someone like Nathan. Wants someone who can control her like that. The darkness blooms in the forefront of my brain. *You'll never be able to support a woman that thoroughly. Kill him or kill yourself.*

"You didn't tell me we were going shopping." Marielle, a ghost I've seen since I was ten, materializes into the seat Henri had occupied on the drive here.

She's in the same outfit she always wears. It's a housedress from the fifties.

"We." I emphasize the two of us, flicking my hand back and forth between us. It's bad enough I'm suicidal, but the pure rage and anger awoke my wolf and gift. "Are not going shopping. In fact, I am going home. No lunch, no shopping, so you could go the fuck away, or I'll get rid of us both."

"Well, I never."

And before I can really act on any further thoughts, Marielle dissipates with a huff.

CHAPTER 6
HENRI

NATHAN IS SQUEEZING my hand so tightly I'm worried he'll break my fingers. There's a sickly thick rage coming off him in droves. I knew I should have messaged him to let him know what was going on. It's fair to let him know when my plans change.

We get to the car across the parking lot, and Nathan speaks in long, hissing tones under his breath while holding the car door open for me. "I can't believe you were out shopping with that asshole."

I know better than to argue with him until he calms down. If I don't wait, it will only cause a scene. One that Deacon could see and escalate.

The door slams closed almost with my fingers in it. Nathan rounds to his side and yanks his door open, then slams it behind him when he gets in. The car rocks a little bit, and he turns my head to face him, fingers digging into my cheek.

"You don't talk to other guys." Nathan glares at me. "Especially. Not. Wolves."

My wolf rises inside me, pushing forward in the fight or flight response. He's so angry. I hold her down. He hates it when he can see her, any reminder that there's something different between us.

"He's my boss, Nathan." I reassure him, fawning to try and get him to calm down. "He really does want us to go to lunch on him. It's nothing but business."

"Yeah." Nathan roughly lets me go, the flat tone in his voice not giving me any indication to how he's feeling or what he's thinking.

Nathan drives in silence from the mall where we were shopping to Hare's Hearth. I don't dare open the conversation up. If I ask about his day when he's this mad, he'll say I'm taking him away from work because he was worried about me. It's logical and understandable.

We pull into the general parking lot nearest Hare's Hearth, and Nathan finds a spot.

"You know no one will love you as much as I love you," he says coolly before getting out of the car.

Those words strike a chord in the hollow of my heart. Without Nathan, I'm alone, and he's loved me all these years.

I take a fortifying breath and climb out of the passenger side, walking to where he waits by the trunk for me.

"Especially not one of those wolves. You said so yourself. You're more human than they are." Nathan leaves me with that information, stepping away from me.

He doesn't slow down, and I struggle to keep up with my shorter strides as he walks across the street.

I walk behind him, barely catching up just before the door to the restaurant closes.

I may be more human than Deacon, but I'm still less human than Nathan. I don't belong in either of their worlds.

"Table for two," Nathan commands the host at the stand.

"Reservation?" The host's accent holds a sharp undertone that reminds me of Finn's.

"We don't have one," Nathan says with a sneer.

"I'm sorry. We don't have any tables available until tomorrow afternoon." The host gives a curt nod.

Nathan pulls out one of the hundred dollar bills that Deacon gave us and tries to slip it to the host.

The host looks at it and raises his eyebrow. "We don't require deposits for reservations."

Nathan stumbles, clearly upset, and the tips of his ears go red.

I step up to the stand and flash the host a glimpse of my wolf through my eyes. "I'm Henri Greene. There should be a table reserved for the Aldens."

"Now. Why didn't you say so?" The host glares at Nathan before looking back at me with a Cheshire grin, and their eyes change from the green they once were to the hearty warm gold of a wolf. "That'll be this way."

We're led to the back of the restaurant, where it's quieter and booths of dark wood and soft seats are more private and a step above the regular dining level than the floor. Nathan slides into one side, the side facing away from the rest of the restaurant because 'no one can sneak up on him,' and I take my seat across from him.

"I'll send your server over right away. But can I start you with a pint?" The host speaks to me. Not Nathan.

I shake my head. "No, just water for me."

"Yeah, you serve anything other than imported shit?" Nathan runs his hand across the table like he expects there to be crumbs.

The strength it takes to not visibly cringe is something I have in spades after years of dating Nathan, but this time it falters. The host nods at me in some sort of understanding of my embarrassment.

He side-eyes Nathan and speaks with a really fake Southern

American accent. "I'll see if we can't rustle up something out of a can."

Nathan, if he recognizes it as an insult, says nothing. Without menus and sitting in the quieter section of the restaurant, it feels awkward.

"Well, I can see why you'd want to come here." Nathan scowls, his glare leveled on me. He seethes at a lower volume, "That wolf was practically all over you, and I'm right fuckin' here with you. No respect at all for humans."

"What?" The word comes out too fast for me to stop it. "Nathan, all I did was show him my eyes. It's just how we prove that we're pack."

"Mm."

He looks away from me, and I'm so frustrated with it all. I wish I had talked him out of coming here. Nathan wanted to do something nice, but I'm starting to forget the times when his thoughtful gestures felt genuine.

Thankfully, our server comes over quickly. Another wolf, but this one female, which historically makes Nathan less threatened.

"Hello, I'm O'Malley, I'll be taking care of you this evening." She sets a golden-colored beer in front of Nathan and water in front of me before pulling a set of simple paper menus from her apron. She gingerly sets them on the table.

They're not the same larger menus I saw on the tables while walking from the front of the house.

"Fancy." Nathan looks down his nose at the menu with his chin tilted up.

"This is the family menu today. If something isn't acceptable, I'd be glad to talk to the kitchen." O'Malley stands there for a brief second, shifting her eyes between the two of us. "I'll give you a minute and stop back."

Nathan checks out her ass as she walks away, which I ignore. If I criticize him for looking at other women, it'll just circle back to how I dress or that my boss is a man or any number of things that make Nathan nervous that I'd cheat on him.

He turns back to me. "This gonna be more expensive than the regular menu? Maybe we shouldn't have come here. Your boss was cheap and only gave us like three hundred."

"I'm sure it'll be more than enough."

I'm not completely sure it will or won't be, but from the conversation with Cade about taking client meetings here, I know there's an open tab. It really doesn't matter how much Deacon gave us because the pack will cover it.

Nathan immediately scrutinizes the menu. "This is all such heavy foods. I don't know that you should be eating all this. It's a lot of red meat."

My wolf presses forward, angry. She's used to being quiet when Nathan gets upset, but we both struggle with him controlling what we eat. Mostly because he forgets I need things, like red meat, for instance, to survive.

"It's a special menu. It would be rude to ask for substitutions." I try to cut this off before it begins. "It's just one meal anyway."

"Yeah, you're right. We can call it a cheat meal." Nathan nods.

I hate it so much. I feel so bad because if he knew all the food I eat at work, he'd be so angry. Trying not to panic, I push the thoughts from my mind.

Nathan changes the subject in an instant. "I just don't understand what you're doing out with him."

"Deacon is my boss." I reiterate what I told him last night. It was a difficult conversation, but I needed to tell him right away. "I'm doing a campaign to get him to be more forward facing with the media, and I need him to have a respectable wardrobe. It was strictly business."

"Hmm." Nathan seems more convinced than the last time I said these words. "The way he looks at you isn't appropriate."

How does he look at me? The urge to question him is strong, but I remain silent.

The dead air between us lasts just long enough for O'Malley to come back. A basket of bread and two soups on her tray. I'm salivating at the smell of fresh bread and the hearty beef stew.

"I'm just saying working for the gym would be a step up compared to working with them." Nathan spits at the last word.

O'Malley quickly retreats from the table.

"Them?" I ask softly, but I know what he's saying.

"Wolves." Nathan scoffs that I questioned it.

"I see."

Reminding him I'm a wolf will only start a fight. He's mad that I didn't tell him when we met. But it's not exactly something you tell a guy you just met, and then it got more serious. But then we moved to Minnesota, and I finished my degree and got an internship with the Aldens.

Wolves were never supposed to come out to the public. I was never going to come out to Nathan as a wolf, but it felt like only a matter of time for him to put it together. Explaining to Nathan that the Aldens only hire wolves and, therefore, I'm a wolf was excruciating. It was the most angry I'd ever seen him.

Putting myself in his shoes, I completely understand his anger. It's a big thing to hide from someone.

We don't have to hide from Deacon. My wolf recalls the pack run, being shifted and running alongside him. I'm a slow runner, but Deacon, even with his long legs, stayed back, jogging alongside me.

"Oh," Nathan pipes up, bread in his mouth as he talks. "The guys and I have plans for New Year's. We're going to go to Vegas for a fight. Leaving the twenty-seventh be back the third."

He'll be gone for almost an entire week. It makes my heart hurt that he doesn't want to spend it with me, but there's no point in arguing.

"Sure, I'm happy for you. That sounds like it'll be a great time."

"You don't mind, do you?" Nathan isn't exactly asking my opinion; He's looking for a fight.

"No, I don't mind at all." I smile, wishing for once he'd want to spend a holiday with me like we used to before. "I wish I could come, is all."

"You wouldn't have any fun." Nathan shakes his head. "It's gonna be a bunch of time in a bunch of different gyms and then the fights themselves. You'd hate it."

That's the final word on the subject.

Rather than argue, I try to make the most of the afternoon off and the meal at the restaurant I really have wanted to go to for years. On the bright side, his absence will make it a hell of a lot easier to coordinate all the New Year's Eve parties the Aldens have been invited to.

Mistletoe

Viscum album

DECEMBER

CHAPTER 7
DEACON

I<small>T</small>'s clear Nathan isn't used to being prey. He has no sense of awareness that a better predator is stalking him. But the girl he's with, the third one this week, senses my eyes on them. She looks around again, and I divert my gaze, digging into the empty center console of the rental car.

Since he interrupted my shopping trip with Henri two weeks ago, I've been lightly stalking Nathan. Mostly only when I can get away from Henri's lessons in dealing with the media. Or if she doesn't have a meeting for me to attend. In other words, all my other hobbies are gone.

I've learned so much.

The illegal activities I suspected Nathan was involved in were all correct. He has a gambling problem and owes, from what I could track down, at least four bookies a total of thirty grand. Plus, he's buying some sort of hormone therapy from a black-market pharmacy, which, from my understanding, is literally just ephedrine and vitamin D. Weird because I suspected testosterone. The rage must be a placebo effect, maybe, or someone else is getting it for him. A little more time and I'm sure I'll figure it out.

Morally, I already knew he was shit. Cheating on Henri is reprehensible. But in the time I've stalked him, I've found zero redeeming qualities. Every opportunity on his walk through life, Nathan chooses the road less traveled and the self-absorbed, what's-in-it-for-me quest instead. Parking like an asshole, not holding open doors, embezzling money from 'take a penny, leave a penny' jars.

But what did I truly expect from him? He's the epitome of the kind of person who would believe the birds are government spies and the earth is flat or some shit.

Feeling like I've given them enough time, I look back up at Nathan. The woman he's with looks uncomfortable. She's shifting her weight back and forth, and when she goes to leave, he grabs her forearm. My hand goes to the car door handle, but she rips her arm away from him, and he laughs but lets her go.

Like the two times before, the woman walks away and gets in her car, and Nathan takes off on foot. When he's sufficiently down the block, I start the car and follow him back to the dingy, rundown gym he's calling 'work.'

Nathan had a job opportunity with this 'weight lifting consulting company' a couple years ago, and he uprooted himself and Henri from their apartment in Ohio during her third year of college. But what the IRS and bank statements don't tell you is that he left behind a large sum of gambling debts.

The darkness inside me knows that culling him would be a blessing to this earth. It cries out for bloodshed in the same way that I'm thirsting for justice for Henri.

I'm parking around the corner from the gym when my phone rings.

"Hello?" I answer, not looking at the caller ID.

"Hey. Where are you?" Henri hisses.

"Where am I?" Pushing the question back, I try to remember if she had plans for me today.

I could have sworn I had the day off. *Where am I?*

"Deacon," Henri groans. "You have a meeting with the library to discuss a book reading with the children for next week. Please tell me you're close by."

Fuck. I close my eyes. "Stall. I'll be there in ten."

"What are you wearing?" Henri's question strikes me as odd.

Nothing if you're . . . Not what she's asking. I answer truthfully. "Dark wash jeans and a plain black T-shirt."

"Good enough. Just get here," she practically snarls.

It's adorable, and I'd tell her so if she wasn't angry.

"I'm on my way. I promise." I hang up and take one last look at Nathan.

He's talking with a couple of his gym bros. *Should I dig into them too?*

It doesn't make sense to. I don't *need* to go around killing people associated with Nathan. It's not like Isabel LeFleur's friends. Sure, Cade took his justice where he felt it was necessary. But I'm the one who hunted down literally every person she came into contact in her attempt to throw a coup.

Nathan's friends probably aren't squeaky clean, but that's someone else's problem. Without Nathan, they won't be a threat to Henri. What do humans need with one wolf? And really, she's all I care about.

She's mine. Even if I can't have her. I'll protect her until I'm not here on this earth anymore.

CHAPTER 8
DEACON

IT WAS stupid and I fucking know it. I could make a million excuses as to how I let this happen, but the long and short of it is the same: I mismanaged my inventory, and now I'm paying the price for it. This is the third — fifth? — event Henri has had me at this month, and I should know better by now how this goes. But I don't have a micro-dose to get through it.

Alcohol is only getting me so far today because my wolf is focused almost entirely on Henri. He won't simply agree to be quiet, and the alcohol's half-life keeping him under is negligible. Which wouldn't be bad except none of my dealers are texting me back.

I've even broken my rule to text Dealer 2 (Madison) and nothing. It's complete crickets.

Did I get iced out and not know it?

"Deacon," Henri groans. "Focus."

"I heard you." I snap at her and instantly regret it. I don't talk to her that way.

My wolf snarls, angry at me. *Don't be that way to her. You're a fucking asshole.*

I'm panicking about what will happen: first the wolf and then the ancestors.

It's not her fault.

Her head snaps up, and she mouths 'okay' before turning away from me.

This interaction isn't us. We haven't worked together all that long, but this isn't how it should be between us.

"Henri," I call, and she looks over her shoulder at me, waiting for more. "I'm sorry. It's just I . . ." Henri turns her body back to me at the same time a civilian takes interest, and I cut my excuse off but repeat the apology, making sure it's purposeful like when Finn does it. "I'm sorry, but I'm looking up what the soup of the day is."

"Fuck. Okay. I'm sorry, I didn't know. Let's get you through this panel. There are sixty-ish people here."

With that one phrase, Henri completely understands my current problem. Her body goes rigid, and she jumps into problem-solving.

She steps closer to me, turning her back to the room and bringing her voice down to wolf-ears-only volume. "Stay right by my side, and if someone approaches, just pretend, unless it's someone we're very familiar with, just pretend you've forgotten their name, and if they're real, I'll reintroduce you. During the Q and A, I'll moderate the questions and quietly restate the real ones to you."

I look down at her, hanging my head. "Thanks. I am sorry."

She's always so forgiving, but I've known that about her. She'd forgive me for practically anything. *Just like she'd forgive Nathan.* That's what makes this hurt worse.

"I know." She turns back to the room but steps into me just a little bit, leaning against me and drawing out some of the tension. "It'll be okay. Do I need to call Hare's Hearth to see what I can find?"

"I sent a text to my contact."

Getting from Hare's Hearth means that Finn is sure to find out about it. While I know he's trying to look out for me, having my little sister's mate meddle while I'm trying to survive is about as fun as it sounds.

My phone buzzes in my breast pocket. I pull it out and look at it.

FINN:

You put in an order at HH? Everything okay?

I knew this was coming, but it doesn't make it easier. Finn may have left the mafia, but he's still closely connected with Hare's Hearth. And they apparently started looping him in on everything that has to do with me simply because his mate is my sister.

At this point, I can't lie and back out of my attempt to buy. Alcohol alone hasn't kept my wolf fully at bay for years. Today is no exception. I need something stronger.

Or whatever Revecca did to my gift when she visited in October. But that probably isn't something I can order off a menu at an organized crime hub masquerading as a high-end restaurant.

ME:

It'll be fine. Is that an order confirmation? ETA?

FINN:

From what I know, there's an issue with the seafood. Menu is extremely limited.

Fuck. I close my eyes. But I'm in too deep to back down now. There's no putting the cat back in the bag of Finn knowing.

> Ahhh, well, I'm not exactly picky.

For family, I can always bring home leftovers.

With that sentence, I'm already feeling relief. Placebo effect, maybe? Or maybe it's just that Finn isn't judging?

"Deacon, are you ready?" Henri whispers.

"Just a sec." I nod. "Finn's telling me about the soup special."

She raises an eyebrow, suspicious of that. It's no secret that Finn and I have a delicate relationship.

> Any chance you'll bring some home and send a delivery over to the event center?

With chips?

I try to figure out what that might be other than french fries, but the worst that happens is I do, in fact, get french fries . . .

> Yes, please.

Finn doesn't answer, but my food delivery app pings, asking me to confirm my location. I do so before looking at Henri.

"I'm good." I give her a small smile and nod.

Henri gives me a once-over, her furrowed brow and pursed lips giving away the flurry of thoughts running through her head. But not once in her tabulation of risk for this event has she suggested we cancel.

With a nod, she steps aside, waiting for me to follow her. "Great. 'Cause it's time to mingle."

CHAPTER 9
HENRI

DEACON IS SUPER UNWELL. He's jumpy and has asked me a dozen times the name of the person in front of him. Of the dozen times, someone was only there twice.

My phone pings while Deacon's talking with a young fan. The kid was drawn to him from the science museum event we hosted in November.

FINN:

> I've got a delivery for Deacon outside. Send him out?

ME:

> Can I come get it instead? I don't want him to miss this interview.

> If you must. But it'd be best if he eats a little in the car with me instead of where everyone can see before going back into that interview.

Eat? Wait. What kind of delivery would Finn have for Deacon? I assumed drugs. Is this an extended code of some sort?

While I was looking at my phone, the young fan moved on

and the chairman of the program for the wolves-versus-bears sporting event started to speak with Deacon.

I cut in between them. "Excuse me, Chairman, I'll just borrow Deacon for a few moments."

"Of course." The chairman offers his hand out to Deacon. "Pleasure talking to you. Can't wait to have you in the box for a game."

"It'll be an honor." Deacon shakes his hand before turning to me.

Gripping his jacket sleeve, I pull him away.

I keep my voice down to barely a whisper. "What sort of delivery is Finn here with for you?"

"Soup," he answers softly. "And apparently french fries."

Yep. Delivery is code.

I nod toward the exit doors. "Please, hurry."

"I will." Deacon gives me a smile. "I want this to go just as smoothly as you do, Hen."

Less than five minutes later, Deacon returns, carrying a white takeout container, the lid flopping open as he lazily walks back toward me. The difference is night and day. He's back to being the calm, cool James the world loves, not the uptight mess he was before.

"French fry?" he offers.

I eye them suspiciously. "You had Finn bring you what, fish and chips?"

Deacon nods, chewing and swallowing before responding. "Yeah. Told him to tell the Hare's Hearth they could do way more business if this was a standard option."

"Oh-kay." I don't question it, opting instead to maneuver Deacon by the sleeve into the corner.

I'm no expert on drugs, handling Deacon is a crash course, but with how snacky and food motivated he gets, I can see the merit in that business proposal. Maybe Hare's Hearth will take it into consideration.

Deacon nails the discussion. Despite having no interest or working knowledge of sports, he brings excellent answers to questions and carefully, but playfully, ribs the bear representative on the panel.

Now, at the end, they all shake hands. The bear smiles wide, and it looks overall very diplomatic.

Deacon strolls over to me, hands in his pockets, and shrugs. "How'd I do?"

"Amazing," I answer truthfully.

"Cool, are we ready to get out of here?" He yawns, covering his mouth with his hand. "Had my snack, and now my brain is done for."

"Yeah, we can go."

This event could have gone so poorly. He should have told me he was struggling earlier than he did, but between the little yawn and shrugged shoulders, I can't be mad at him.

He's so tired, my wolf observes. *Comfort. Not scold,* she encourages.

Working with Cade and Thalia is always easy. They're both excellent at what they do. It's challenging because the people getting close to them are always trying to work an angle, but I don't have to coach them. It's a hands-off buffer.

Deacon is what I wanted when I started this line of work. I wanted to be someone's safe place. But maybe I should wonder about what that says about me.

We just want him in general. My wolf swoons.

I can't even argue with her. Especially not as I follow Deacon out into the crowd of paparazzi. The Corinth Security agents lead the way, and I follow up the rear, watching his back with the event security.

When we get into the Corinth Security SUV, Deacon pretty much deflates. He scrubs his hand down his face before wiggling out of his suit jacket and then unbuttoning his shirt. Tie hanging unknotted around his neck, he looks defeated.

"Sorry I couldn't handle today," he murmurs. "I'm trying to manage, but there's been a supply limitation, and yours truly was very bad at monitoring his stockpile."

"I'm worried about you." I'm battling my brain as the screaming urge to hold his hand or pat his shoulder or give him a hug overwhelms me.

My wolf pushes for it too. *Get close to him, love him.*

But that's the problem; no matter how much I want to love Deacon, he isn't mine to love. I'm just here to make sure he gets everything situated.

Thirty minutes down the road, Deacon still hasn't said anything. I look over, and he's watching the scenery pass by out the window, but his gaze is unfocused.

"What are you thinking about?" I ask, trying to keep my voice low.

"About how I don't think about suicide when you're in the same room," Deacon admits, his voice matching my quiet tone.

My mouth drops open. I'm not sure what I was expecting, but it was not that.

No, those are bad thoughts. My wolf and I are both anxious with his revelation.

I shuffle in my seat so I can look more closely at him. "I kind of assumed you had stopped. After . . ."

"All day, every day." Deacon blows a raspberry with his lips. "The thoughts are loud when I talk to an ancestor I've seen before. Louder when I find out I've been unknowingly talking to someone who is dead. Loudest when I remember how little

I've done and when I see the disappointment I am in someone else's eyes. But if you're in the room, even if just for a little while, the noise of ideation stops."

My heart breaks for Deacon, and I don't know what to say. "Oh."

"It's just, even today, when I was a complete wreck and couldn't tell the living from the dead, it wasn't that I wanted to die so much as I just wished I could be better." He's quick to add, "You're not responsible for what happens to me."

"I . . . I know." I try to grab something in any sort of capacity that'll help him.

"No, you're a people pleaser." Deacon laughs, his chest rising and falling with a huff. He looks over at me, rolling his head lackadaisically rather than turning it. "You're already trying to figure out how to spend all day every day with me, hoping it's enough to stop me from doing it. It's your turn."

I never would have guessed I was so obvious with how I thought about things. But Deacon seems to have broken me down on every level. "My turn?"

"Yup, I confessed that sin to you. Pay up." Deacon makes a game out of a simple conversation.

Then again, with Deacon, there are no such things as simple conversations. It's only deep thoughts laced with inspiration or dumb comedy.

It takes me far too long to come up with something, anything, that would make sense or feel anywhere near as weighty as Deacon's statements.

My voice trembles when I start. "Confession: I've always wanted to be loved. I wanted to be coveted. I guess not knowing my biological parents and finding out I'm not normal have made me so broken when it comes to love."

"You are loved and coveted. You're sought after, and I'm willing to kill for you. You will never be ordinary because you are the only one who possesses the power to destroy me. You are talented and capable and everything I am not worthy to be in the presence of. Broken is not a word that applies to you, you don't see yourself how I see you."

His words bring tears to my eyes.

What do you even say to that? I try and scramble to form words.

Deacon, however, changes the conversation without missing a beat, like he didn't just take a sledgehammer to every belief I've lived with as truth — the ones no one's ever been able to convince me of otherwise. "Michael, any chance we can get tacos at that one place?"

"Didn't you just have fries?" Michael Tate, today's assigned security agent, is already changing lanes toward an exit ramp.

"Mm-hmm, but you know those tacos will haunt you all day if you don't get them now." Deacon laughs at his own joke.

English Yew
Taxus baccata

NEW YEARS EVE

CHAPTER 10
HENRI

"Cade?" I say for the fourth time, calling up the stairs of the rental house. "We're almost late."

I check the time on my phone again. We really need to leave within the next five minutes to get everyone where they need to be and only be 'casually' late.

Thalia giggles from the bedroom.

Their door is open, so I hope they're being a little modest. With Cade's cousins, Ezra and Dinah, here, I would think that'd be a deterrent.

"Time is a social construct. They'll wait," Thalia shouts.

Ezra snorts from the couch. "A human social construct. No wolf in their right mind would have ever tied us to a schedule. It's not like wolves could even wear watches."

"But what if we could?" Deacon smiles as he ties his hunter-green tie.

The earth-tone suit complements his laid-back nature and matches the New Year's Eve party I reserved for him of the options from the Aldens' invite list.

"Besides, if we're supposed to lean into this 'I'm the King' nonsense, then I might as well get to set the time of our arrivals." Cade smiles with Thalia on his arm as they come down the hallway toward us.

Dinah yawns. "I'm really glad you rented a house in town. Good idea, Henri."

"It just made the most sense given the forecast." I smile, taking credit for this, per her advice, from the phone call when she advised me that driving home from New Year's Eve events in sixteen inches of snow overnight was 'not the vibe.' Instead, she thought renting a house best suited the plan.

Snow is already falling, and we're expecting sixteen inches overnight. I have a feeling this has to do with her gift of future sight, but I'm not in the business of asking. It's common knowledge, even among non-Ardelean packs, that you do not ask an Ardelean about their gift.

I look around the room at the Ardeleans. "Alright, your drivers all have the addresses of where you're going, and you were provided a list of who is who in your emails."

"Yes," Dinah sighs, standing up from the sofa.

The floor-length red dress with a high slit in the side elongates her legs further and makes her look like a model.

"You're not dressed though." Deacon cocks his head at me.

I look down at the pants and sweater I opted to wear. It's formal and appropriate for the event I'm accompanying him to in the official capacity as pack publicist.

"Yeah, Henri." Ezra scoffs in a mocking tone. "Holding everyone up."

"This is what I was going to wear?" I look between Deacon and his counterpart in the Cousins Grimm.

I couldn't say where or when the title originated, but pretty much every sighting of them posted on social media is accompanied by that hashtag. There's even a Cousins Grimm group dedicated to them. From my cursory search, it's because they both mostly wear black, give off bad-boy vibes, and it's a play on the original dark version of the classic fairytales. I'm not quite sure I get it, but I don't need to. It's that sort of attention I'm trying to squash. Making Deacon an upstanding citizen is the first and only goal I've truly set for the next six months.

"Mmmm, no." Dinah shakes her head and offers her hand out to me.

"This is the fanciest clothing I brought," I argue. "I don't have time to change, we're going to be late."

Dinah sighs. "Social construct, they'll wait."

The 'social construct' and 'they'll wait' are becoming more and more of a theme. One I'd rather they not all embrace.

"We'll go. It'll make you feel better knowing the governor and senators are covered." Thalia shoos me with her hand toward Dinah.

Apprehensively, I let Dinah take my hand, and she leads me back to the smallest bedroom in the house that I kept for myself. Hanging up in the closet is a garment bag.

After opening it, Dinah pulls the gown out and hands it to me. "It'll fit."

"How do you know my measurements?" I ask, holding the velvet material in my hand. It's so soft.

"Really?" Dinah rolls her eyes. "I know everything, comes with the gift."

I take the dress and move to step around her to the bathroom in the hallway to change.

"Henri," Dinah says, "You don't have to change in the . . ." She stops herself. "Deacon can help you with the zipper. We'll go and get the University Gala and media taken care of."

"Thank you." I smile at her and then look at the dress. "For everything. I guess."

Dinah makes her way back down the hallway, and I tuck

myself into the bathroom. There isn't a price tag on this dress, but the velvet damask fabric and designer label in the back say it all. This dress costs more than my monthly salary.

It's not worth arguing about. Dinah won't ever return it, and I'm sure she probably even had it tailored to fit me. But her reputation online is high fashion and elegance, so it's not super surprising the floor-length gown is here and waiting.

Changing into the dress feels so foreign. I don't wear dresses a lot because Nathan doesn't think they're modest enough or professional enough looking. If I want to be taken seriously by men, I need to dress like them. This dress with a sweetheart neckline and capped sleeves is feminine and soft. Dressing up like this is kind of fun . . . and it's only for a night.

I open the door to the bathroom and jump. Deacon's standing there, leaning against the wall, hands in his pants pockets.

"I heard you needed a zip up." He smiles.

"Please." I turn and show him the open back of the dress.

His fingers skate up the inside as he protects my body from the sliding metal. It's the smallest touch, and I shiver.

"Mmm," Deacon says, letting go. "Let me see?"

I turn around for him and note his goofy smile. "Good enough?"

"Almost." Deacon pulls a jewelry box out of his coat pocket and hands it to me. "Now, don't go reading too far into it, it's not asking for an intention on you, I'm trying to respect your ab–" He swallows a growl and then continues. "Relationship with Nathan, but after I picked out the dress, Dinah said the gown would look better worn with a necklace."

"Oh." My heart rate picks up. *He picked it out? The dress and the necklace?*

My wolf perks her ears forward. *He bought us jewelry. A collar to show he wants us.*

It's not a collar. He's not collaring us. This isn't an engagement. He isn't asking for an intention. We're not going on a date. This is a social event for work. I'm not supposed to stand out. I remind her and myself as I open the box. There's a necklace comprised of a double golden chain of diamonds.

"Whooo." I draw a short breath. "Please tell me these are fake."

"I think you and I both know they're not fake." He does not do as I ask. "Nor are they zirconia, nor are they lab grown."

"Deacon, this has to be a few grand of diamonds," I argue.

He lifts the box from my hand and starts removing the necklace from where it sits. "And?"

"And? I can't wear a diamond necklace that costs more than my car." I try to object, but he puts the box in the crook of his arm and tilts his head down, giving me an authoritarian look.

Under his gaze, my wolf takes a step back, bowing down to the subtle air of authority.

I turn for him, and he loops the necklace around my neck. He clasps it, and I feel his breath against the top of my head.

"It costs more than my bike, and before you object and say that it's too much, consider it part of your new wardrobe for work. If you and I must go to these events, you need appropriate work attire. It's like a really fancy uniform."

The evidence that Deacon knows nothing about uniforms is all here in front of me, but I don't push the issue. He steps away, and I follow him down the hallway to the living room. There's a mirror by the door, and I get a glimpse of myself.

I do look pretty.

"Which one?" I turn to look at Deacon.

He's looking at his phone.

"Hmm?" Deacon looks back up at me, pocketing his phone.

"Which of your bikes does this cost more than?" My fingers touch where the necklace rests on my collarbone.

"Does it matter, Henri?" He cocks his head to the side.

"Well, I mean, the one that's pretty much pieces on your workstation is probably not very expensive." The more words I speak, the more amusing Deacon seems to think I am because a smile creeps across his face.

"I'm super wrong because apparently, the pieces are more expensive, so let's go before we're any later than we already are." My face heats, and my fingers go absently to the collar — *no* — the necklace he draped around my neck.

He gets a look in his eye, and then he licks his lips before clearing his throat and offering his arm out to me. "Let's go. My social media manager will be pissed if I'm late, and the pack publicist will slaughter me if I miss the opportunity to schmooze with the commissioner for the DNR."

I'm self-conscious. *Should I take it off?*

With his arm around my shoulder, Deacon leads me outdoors. These little possessive gestures, even if it's only a few quick steps across the threshold, are screwing with my feelings.

Boyfriend, Henri. Boyfriend. I urge myself to let it go.

But he feels so right. My wolf pushes. *Come off the suppressants. Let's see to be sure.*

Those thoughts are much easier for me to quell. My first heat was hell, and never ever again.

CHAPTER 11
DEACON

"James!"

I turn my head, and a flash of a camera goes off. I pop a smirk and let them take another one.

Henri reserved, as she called it, 'the most fun' event for us. And I'd love to agree since it's an event geared toward human kids learning about conservation and the environment, but there are a lot more cameras here than I anticipated.

I've lost track of Henri again, and I'm getting exhausted. The large clock projected on the wall shows almost two hours until the ball drops at midnight.

Swirling the champagne around in the flute I picked up off a passing tray, I start looking for Henri. My wolf is tucked under deep enough that, at this point, I'm actually getting to enjoy the buzz of the alcohol.

I can't help but search for her in any room when I know she's nearby. With a cursory scan, I find her examining the silent auction items. She's squinting at an item listed for auction.

"Hey." I try not to startle her.

She looks at me, then back at the item, and whispers, "What is it?"

It's some sort of taxidermy. But it's seemingly different pieces of animals put together to form some sort of new creature from the depths of some child's imagination. The base, though, seems to be a badger.

"I have no idea. But if I come across one of them alive, I'm most certainly running the other way. Don't mess with a scarier predator." I shudder.

She snorts. "You think it's a predator?"

I point to the head, which I believe to be a porcupine with owl feathers for quills. "Yeah. Because there's no way something like that gets eaten by anything else. The bare minimum reason is because it would taste terrible."

Henri giggles.

Even though I know I shouldn't, I wrap my arm around her shoulder. "Come on, I want to see if I'm still winning the brewery tours."

"You bid on the brewery tours?" She shakes her head.

I shrug, leading the way down the auction lineup. "Well, it was either that or I bid on the tour of the Pack House and property."

"The item you donated?"

I get the 'really, Deacon' look that comes with a scolding head shake from Henri, but I'm smiling like an idiot at my own amusement.

"Well, I was actually planning on demanding that Cade show up, dressed all nice, and walk me around the house and talk about the pack while I take pictures and 'oooh' and 'ahhh,' but that seemed like too much of a time commitment. Our house and pack property is a lot bigger when you think about it in a tour sense." I look down at her, and fuck, if I don't want to kiss her, to taste the single glass of champagne she allowed herself on her lips.

I force myself to take my arm off her shoulder. The space is the only way I'll stop myself.

Then the collar glints in one of the special lights meant to illuminate the auction items. *Boundaries Deacon. It's not really a collar. It's not really staking a claim. She's hot, not your mate.*

When we go around and look at the various items, Henri giggles at the prices on some of the bids. Yearly season tickets to the hockey team, shooting lessons, hunting excursions, all priced in the thousands. While we walk down the row, I double the bids on all the brewery tours before moving on to the next, and by the time we get to the end of the row, it's only killed another twenty minutes.

"Ahh, James. Man of the hour." I recognize the woman but can't place her.

"Commissioner Alise Mitchell for the Department of Natural Resources, she's the guest of honor," Henri says behind her champagne glass before pretending to take a small sip.

"Alise, I was telling my associate how excellent it is that the media is finally recognizing the hard work the DNR does for the state." I lie with a smile.

"Bullshit," Alise says with a smirk. "You were probably talking about outbidding me on those brewery tours. Answer this for me: how do wolves feel about the wolves . . ." She stops and rephrases. "How do wolf shifters feel about the wolves released into Northern Minnesota as conservation efforts?"

Thank fuck Henri told me to prepare for this question. "Well, I can honestly say we think it's excellent to see wolves being returned to their natural habitat as part of the work to restore the conservation of the north woods."

"Right. But aren't they your direct competition? You're all out there acting like wolves aren't killing deer all times of the year while shifters still need to go through the proper legal channels." A man stumbles over his words, and it doesn't take a certified rocket surgeon to know where this conversation is headed.

Henri stands behind me a bit and puts her hand on the flat of my back. She's trying to warn me away; it's part of the system she devised over the last month to communicate when to disengage, but I think I have this okay, at least for now.

I shrug and relax a bit, trying to appear less intimidating by slouching. "While we do not necessarily hunt using a gun, we always apply for the proper tags from the DNR. Wolf shifters" — I make the direct separation between us and our permanently four-legged family — "have always been highly dedicated to the natural resources. The DNR has proven they're very good with tracking data, and cooperating has always been our priority. I'm sure Commissioner Alise can more eloquently speak to the conversations she and Cade have been engaging in."

"See!" The Commissioner pats me on the shoulder. "The packs are on our side. I really do think that ultimately, those who spend that much time in the woods really are our best resources for furthering the discussions of conservation."

"Well, folks, if you'll excuse me." I dismiss myself with a head bob and turn toward Henri, rolling my eyes and offering her my elbow.

Picking our way through the crowd, I find an open table in a quiet corner of the event hall. Henri takes a seat as I drop into a chair and pull the fun flask out of my jacket.

"Deacon. There's literally a bar here. An open bar," Henri hisses and gestures to the flask. "Put it away."

I tuck the flask back in my pocket and sigh. "Dancing?"

"Aren't you tired?" Henri yawns.

"Bored. Not tired. I didn't have the heart to tell them I

haven't gone on a stag hunt since I was forced as a teenager as part of the 'coming of age' nonsense." I use air quotes for her.

She shakes her head and looks at the same clock I've been eyeing. "Okay. This event is not as fun as I anticipated."

"Is that code for we can get out of here?" I look at her.

She pulls her phone out of the clutch she's been carrying. "Ugh. If we go back now, the others will know we didn't stay for our whole event."

"Who said anything about going back?" I start thinking of last year's New Year's Eve parties and try to run down the best one to take her to.

"Where else would we go? It's snowing, remember?" Henri looks toward the giant windows as if they're evidence.

"Always so practical." I stand up and offer her my hand. "We've got ninety minutes before the ball drops. I know a place."

Henri stands but doesn't accept my hand. She tucks her phone in her clutch. "Are we overdressed?"

"Absurdly." I nod, thinking about the warehouse rave. "It'll make it more fun."

I can see the gears turning in her head as she contemplates making us stay, but Henri finally slips her hand in mine. Wrapping it around my forearm, I start leading her toward the coatroom.

Bundled up and in the security detail's SUV, I give him the address. He hesitates but doesn't question it.

Four miles away, we pull up in front of a warehouse. Mechanical hums, thumps, and beeps come from inside the building, but it's eerily quiet outside. Cars line the streets in all directions around us.

"Phone stays here." I show Henri, tossing it into the back seat of the SUV.

"What?" She shakes her head. "What if we need to call someone?"

"Agreed. Not safe," the security detail pipes up.

I shake my head before grabbing her clutch and tossing it in the back seat. "Live a little, Henri."

Slamming the door closed, I choose to wrap an arm around her, the excitement thrumming in my chest.

"I didn't think you liked spending time with people," Henri says as we get closer to the door.

"My Man! Deacon!" The bouncer smiles at me. "Who is this fine thing? Hot damn, mama, you look good."

I growl at him.

"Deacon," Henri whispers, scolding me.

But I'm too busy putting myself between him and her. "None of your concern. You've got room for us?"

"For you, they always make exceptions. Ezra and Dinah said you were comin'. Cousin's Grimm getting rowdy tonight?" He picks up the metal detector wand off the table beside him and runs it over our bodies before nodding and opening the door.

"Hadn't quite decided. But the night is young." I smile.

No way I'm having any additional party favors with Henri here. The 'fun flask' was enough to keep my problems at bay.

The music spills out around us, the rave blaring.

When I turn to look at Henri, she's wide eyed, but it's not a look of fear. A smile pulls at the corners of her lips, and her hips have already started subtly swinging.

There's no hesitation this time as I pull her in from the cold night air and toward the dance floor.

There's a digital clock on the wall, but it shows the countdown instead of the regular time, and I plan to get lost in every minute until midnight when this secret party with Henri ends.

CHAPTER 12
HENRI

Does Deacon know I love EDM? I can't imagine how he would. I don't get to listen to it a lot. Nathan thinks it's noise, and some wolves can't stand all the squeaky sounds.

Yet we're in a full-on rave. The DJ is amazing.

Deacon leads us to a person standing by a long line of coat racks.

This is a very classy rave.

Deacon motions to me, and I shrug. I don't have anything to give the guy. But while Deacon takes off his coat and tie, the man goes down the line and comes back with a plastic bag with something in it. He hands it to me, and I fail to read his lips over the sound of the music.

Shaking his head, Deacon takes the bag and opens it. He shakes out the contents and shows me that it's a shorter white dress. I look around for a place to change, which gets me an eye roll before he drapes his jacket around my shoulders. I try to object, but Deacon doesn't stop moving. As he drops to his knees in front of me, his hands adeptly slide the zipper down the back of my dress.

It's almost innocent the way his hands slide the white dress up my calves and then my thighs. Slowly he bunches the velvet fabric around my thighs while trailing the shorter dress in its place. He gets close to the top of my hips, and I shuffle uncomfortably.

Deacon, on his knees before me, looks up, checking in on me. His eyes are fixated on me, waiting and asking for permission. I hold his jacket tighter together and nod.

He slides it up, the white dress covering me. Deacon rises to his feet and runs his nose against my cheek, reassuring me. An intimate gesture that sends my pulse racing.

The attention Deacon pays to the unhurried movements, adjusting his hands and the fabric to keep me covered, settles the uncertainty of changing in a crowded space.

He's so close, and despite how many people surround us in this proximity, I can still pull a breath of his whiskey and cedar scent. I gasp, fighting the excitement running through my body.

So close to him, my wolf whispers and pushes me forward, loving everything about the two of us together.

She's not alone. It feels so good to have someone care for me in the most thoughtful of ways.

Deacon's hands have effectively slid up around my bust. He stills his hands against my upper rib cage, thumbs resting on the outside of my breasts where my bralette is thinnest. His touch is so intimate yet familiar. Calm and steady like we've done this together a hundred times before.

Is this what being with Deacon would be like? It's a fleeting thought while I lift my arms.

He raises both the velvet dress and his jacket off me while pulling the white dress in place. My chest, not all that big, doesn't require a bra, so I reach behind me for the clasp. But Deacon sees and beats me to it and, in one careful movement, unhooks it. Still blocking me from the view of the club, he also diverts his gaze while I pull the undergarment from the dress.

The space between us is electrified with a tension that makes my pussy clench.

I try to ignore it and push the thoughts out of my mind, but the wanting is there all the same.

After placing the velvet dress in the garment bag, he taps on my necklace. I go to remove it, and he nods. Once I get it off, he puts it in his pocket and hands the rest of our items to the coat check guy. With a hand guiding me on my lower back, Deacon leads us out on the floor.

In the black light, I discover the dress isn't just white. The patterning, somehow pushed into the levels of the fabric, glows in a vibrant pattern.

Deacon nods knowingly and spins me around like he's drinking me in. A dark, needy look crosses his face, and damn if it doesn't feel good being the object of his desire. Even if it's not something I should . . . it's just for one night, and it's not like I've kissed him or anything.

At Cade and Thalia's wedding, I waltzed with Deacon. While I'm not an expert on dancing, I was positive he was good at waltzing. But now, as Deacon leads me onto the floor, I'm certain the truth is that Deacon can dance. Plain and simple, he can dance. Out on the floor and moving to the music, his rhythm is effortless and sensual.

We start apart but are slowly lost in the crowd's energy and movements, subconsciously working ourselves together. Our bodies press closer together, his hands on my hips. We're in and out of each other's space.

When he's behind me, Deacon grinds up against me, and it's not unwelcome. It's so good. No, not good. Better than good.

Need. My wolf demands more.

As if Deacon can hear my wolf, he wraps his arms around my waist, my ass pressing firmly against him. When the next bass drops, Deacon brings me low before we're into the next hype and he spins me.

Deacon's pupils are blown wide. I know he's mostly sober. The fun flask from his coat pocket isn't anything more than whiskey. It only leaves the excuse of low light to pretend it isn't lust of the deepest level.

Rolling my hips, I grind against his leg, dancing myself farther into him. I rest a wrist on his shoulder, my other hand finding his upper arm.

My eyes fall closed, unable to handle the flashing lights from the way my arousal has blown my pupils wide. I may regret this later, being so close to him, yet I can't make myself care.

He runs his hand from my low back down to my ass, caressing it before running back up into my hair. I suck in a breath and open my eyes, locking onto Deacon's gaze. His eyes are dark with his wolf rising to the surface.

I didn't expect to see his wolf. Not on a night like tonight.

The sensual way we move together sends desire coursing through my whole body. The sexy beat of the song dragging us into the movements. Not unaffected, Deacon smirks and shifts his hips, rubbing against my core. I gasp and throw my head back, lost to what a little more friction between us could do.

That is until the song changes, and we part to match the energy of the crowd around us.

It's been ten minutes, I swear, but when I look at the clock on the wall, it's been so much longer.

The countdown is starting to flash in time with the music. Thirty seconds until midnight.

"This has been amazing, Minneapolis!" The DJ cuts in.

Howls, wolves' and humans', go up over the sounds of the thundering beat. Deacon's joins the chorus, and mine comes out so effortlessly with his.

I've never enjoyed howling; it's too wolf, weird and abnormal, but right now it feels so . . . right.

"Get ready to count it down with me," the DJ instructs. "Then you know what to do. Grab a partner and kiss your way into a new year full of love."

"One life!" the crowd chants with the music.

"One love!" the DJ calls back as he cranks the music.

The soundtrack he cuts on starts counting down from twenty.

The whole crowd shifts, going back to dancing, the thundering bass matching the seconds of time ticking down on the wall.

Deacon and I dance right along with them.

"Ten," Deacon shouts with the crowd.

"Nine."

He pulls me into him until there's no room between us.

"Eight."

The bass thuds in my bones.

"Seven."

My heart is thundering in my head.

"Six."

My wolf is howling inside with the excitement and the crowd.

"Five!"

Deacon's eyes glow from one of the stage lights flickering around us.

"Four!"

I'm so close to Deacon I can smell the fur of his wolf.

"Three!"

Our eyes lock.

"Two!"

I'm practically wrapped around him.

"One!"

I grab hold of Deacon's collar and kiss him.

Big mistake, Henri.

I try to pull away, expecting rejection, but Deacon brings his hands to either side of my head, and he kisses me back. His mouth moves over mine like we're running out of time rather than starting a new year.

And I've never been kissed this good.

The crowd cheering around us is the only thing that seems to break Deacon and me out of our embrace.

Taking a few steps back, I cover my mouth, touching where our lips had just been locked together. *That was amazing.*

I'm lost in his eyes, wanting and desire pooling through me.

He licks his bottom lip but smiles, and the lust drops from his gaze, his features relaxing.

Deacon offers me his hand, and I'm starting to think our relationship is reversed today. Instead of me leading him through the media and the world of being active with the public, Deacon's leading me through life.

I place my hand in his, and Deacon pulls me closer. Bringing his mouth to mine, he kisses me again. He moves against me, and we're dancing together, kissing, and I don't want to stop.

My wolf is howling inside, feeling so good and so right, caught up in this moment with him.

My hands drift into his hair, and I tug, drawing a moan from him. He opens his mouth, and my tongue plays with his.

The beats of the music are sensual, long and short beats intermingling, and it's like the DJ is taking the energy shift in the room and using it as permission. I half expect orgies to be breaking out on the floor around us.

It isn't until we're panting that Deacon and I stop kissing.

With my forehead against his, I try to get my breathing under control.

What did I just do? Why did it feel so good?

Wild Parsnip

Pastinaca sativa

JANUARY

CHAPTER 13
DEACON

ONCE OUTSIDE, the cold is quick to sober me up to what just happened. But Henri, drunk on exhaustion, wobbled on her feet while I got her and the items from the coat check back into the SUV.

Our driver navigates slowly, and in no time, Henri is fast asleep next to me.

But the slow pace and the falling snow only give my brain time to process. The few drinks I had at the formal event are nearly worked out of my system from the sweating and moving. And instead of the quiet hum of my own thoughts in my brain, the wolf emerges. Pulling at the memories of Henri working her body against mine, he approves, wanting to take it further. My cock pulses against my zipper, and it's only made worse by the memory of the kiss.

It doesn't change anything in this moment. Even though I want it to.

I still have the intense desire to possess her, only it's stronger now. And she's still tied to Nathan. The urge to kill

Nathan is there and loud as my wolf works to weasel us between them, but the problem is Henri.

Henri has to make the choice to step away. If she can't do that to keep herself safe, I'll have to step in and remove the choice for her by force. Lena's offered Henri a place to stay. I know Cade's offered for both her and Nathan to move to pack property.

She isn't ready to let him go.

Would she forgive me if I killed him? *If . . . she found out?* Would it matter if she was safe?

The SUV pulls up in front of our rental shortly after one. And poor Henri, used to going to bed early and being responsible, is practically dead to the world. I want to carry her and put her to bed, but the part of me that harbors some morals bars me from scooping her up into my arms.

Instead, I wake her up with a gentle brush of my knuckles against her hair. Her beautiful blue eyes flutter open, and in a quick second, she gathers her surroundings and understands where we are.

Had I not woken her up, I probably could have carried her into the house and brought her to bed. But awake enough to know where she is and how to get there, Henri navigates the snowy sidewalk straight into the house. I lose my chance to keep her for the night as she closes the door to the smallest bedroom with the single twin bed at the back of the house.

"Good night, Henri," I whisper. "I love you."

I'D LOVE to say that, waking up this morning, I don't know what to expect. But I've come to understand Henri well over the last forty-five days. So, to save her from facing my family, I insist, heavily, that we let her sleep in while the others go out to brunch. I, of course, stay so she doesn't wake up alone and afraid.

They've been gone for half an hour before I decide to wake Henri up. I give her door a couple soft knocks, and her feet are on the floor a little quicker than I anticipated. When she opens the door, she's fully dressed.

"Oh, did you want to go to brunch? I guess I assumed you'd be sleeping." I puff out my lips.

How did I not know she was awake?

"No, I appreciate you getting me some time this morning." She refuses to look at me.

Great job, Deacon. You officially fucked this up, you fucked this all up.

I step back, not wanting her to feel caged in. When Henri doesn't step to follow me, I walk away.

This is probably worse than I expected.

If I regretted kissing her back, this might be easier.

But that medium-sized part of me that likes being an asshole is hoping that this is the wake-up call she needed. Nathan will never satisfy her. She doesn't have to take his beatings, the assaults, and who the fuck knows what else she's suffered through.

Unfortunately, I don't have my cousin Ansel's optimism. I don't see the world through his call to hope.

Plopping down on the couch, I look at my phone notifications.

> EZRA:
>
> What happened with you and Henri last night?
>
> Also, do you want biscuits and gravy?
>
> THALIA:
>
> I love youuu. Did you know that sloths can hold their breath longer than dolphins?

And then completely unrelated to breakfast, comes a message from Finn.

FINN:

> Lena saw that you may need to discuss adopting some Hares. It is the new year, after all.

Finn's message isn't out of the ordinary, considering my little sister sees the past. Lena is so attuned to my life that I probably kissed Henri, and five minutes later, she had a vision about it. Which, of course, the next logical step is to have the Hare's Hearth's assassins intervene.

I only answer one of them back because, by now, Ezra should know I always want biscuits and gravy.

ME:

> I did know about the sloths, but did you know that crocodiles can't stick their tongues out?

"Can we talk?" Henri sits down in one of the chairs across from me.

"Of course." I put my phone down on the couch next to me, face down.

"Last night," Henri starts slowly.

Immediately the polite Midwesterner kicks in, and I want to apologize.

Maybe it's not negative. Maybe she wants me. I try hope on for size.

"That shouldn't happen again." Henri meets my expectation and confirms that hope only has a place in Ansel's house.

Yeah. Not a great feeling to have it crushed.

Hanging my head, I try to come up with a response to her statement.

"I have a boyfriend."

I'm so sick of this asshole being in her life. Maybe I should hand him over to the hares. Finn already put them on the radar for me when Henri and Nathan ate there for lunch. It would be easier. What's the point of having a brother-in-law who is ex-mafia if you don't get to use the perks?

My darkness disagrees. The hares are easier but less fulfilling.

I can't tell Henri what she wants to hear. I should but I can't help but throw out one last-ditch effort. "It wasn't me who kissed you first. Some part of you wanted that."

Henri nods. "It wasn't a super conscious decision. I own that. But that doesn't make what happened last night right."

"Understood." I look at her, and her face matches how I feel.

A furrowed brow and soft mouth, we're both crushed by the weight of the circumstance.

I'm not a fool enough to believe I'm the 'right' choice for Henri. But even if I have to be the 'wrong' temporary choice to get her away from Nathan, I'd be willing to accept it.

My wolf scoffs at that thought. *If we get her, no way in fuck will we let her go. You'll just have to learn how to be a better person.*

A better person wouldn't kiss someone else's girlfriend because the voice in his head wants him to. I lash out at my wolf, thinking of all the times the human therapists called him a figment of my overactive imagination. I threaten him. *Maybe today I'll drink before noon.*

He goes silent while we wait for the conversation to move on.

Henri is the first to break the silence. She uses her PR-representative voice, the one of facts, sans independent personality. "We shouldn't touch like that. I appreciate you helping me change, but we're not in that sort of relationship.

We need to maintain a professional relationship. No touching. No kissing. No being too close to each other. This must be aboveboard."

"Got it. Aboveboard. We'll keep our personal space bubbles big." I agree with her only because I know the argument won't get me anywhere.

Tell her she's probably our mate, and this is why we feel this way. She'll have to stop her meds and see. My wolf combats my decision, trying to get what we want.

Drinking. Before. Noon. I threaten him again. He grumbles but sulks to the back of my brain.

"Did you want me to have them bring breakfast back for you?" I offer, trying to clear the uncomfortable tension out of the room.

"Sure. Pancakes, French toast, or something." She shrugs. "I'm not picky about breakfast foods."

A message is already on my phone.

DINAH:

I ordered you biscuits and gravy and Henri strawberry stuffed French toast. Be back in like twenty minutes. Be decent.

Evidently Dinah saw our conversation going in a different direction.

CHAPTER 14
HENRI

"Henri, I told you that you didn't need to come pick me up," Nathan says, throwing his duffle bag in the back seat of my car, which is running surprisingly well.

This time of year it rarely ever turns over without a fight, but don't look a gift horse in the mouth and all that.

"I know. I just really missed you." Standing next to the car, I hold my arms out for a hug.

After a week of him being gone and . . . well, what shouldn't have happened with Deacon, I'm ready to get back to normal.

Nathan gives me a half hug and then lets me go, ushering me into the passenger seat of my car.

My wolf immediately jumps to feeling rejected. She paces inside me.

No. Of course he's not ready to be cuddly; he had a long week away. I argue with myself, that feeling, and her.

"What the fuck is wrong with your car?" Nathan mutters as we pull away from the airport pickup zone.

"Uh, I don't know? It seemed to be running really well."

What the fuck? After a week away, all he cares about is how my car is running? I bite back the frustration of him being more concerned for my car than me and curb my expectations. It's Nathan. He's not one for public displays of affection or sweet sentiments. My expectation was too high.

"I don't like that your boss is handling your oil changes and maintenance. How do we know they're taking care of it right?" Nathan taps on the steering wheel as he floors it onto the freeway ramp, but not the one that leads home.

"Well, the fact that I'm their employee and they'd like me to come to work is probably a good indicator." I joke with him. "Besides, it just means more money for our savings."

"True." Nathan seems like he'll be less prickly.

"Are we grabbing lunch?" I ask, trying to clarify why we're not heading home.

"Uh. No? It's after noon." Nathan indicates to my clock but then changes lanes to get around another car. "You know I don't eat from one until seven."

I squint, wondering when this became a rule. Never once has he said that to me before. It didn't stop us from going to Hare's Hearth a couple months ago. I struggle but let it go.

"So, where are we going?"

My phone dings, and I'm quick to pull it out.

"I thought you'd drop me off at the gym, and then I could get a little workout in before home tonight. You're making dinner, right?" He takes the next exit ramp headed toward the gym.

The notification on my phone for a published article about Deacon doesn't need any of my attention, so I put it back in my purse.

"Yeah. I thought we'd do dinner in and maybe cuddle and watch a movie." I push a little bit more. "I really missed you. It's hard when you're not home."

"Well, I've an early morning. We probably won't get to

watch the movie." Nathan runs a yellow light, and I grip the door handle with how erratic he's driving in traffic.

But I don't dare criticize him.

"Well, maybe we don't . . ." I try to get him to pick up on the subtext. "Don't watch the movie."

"Right. I said we won't get to watch a movie. I've got to go to bed." Nathan parks in the lot at an angle despite it being perpendicular parking, per usual.

"Okay." I concede, my heart sinking by the minute.

My wolf and I deflate. She takes the opportunity to remind me, *Someone else wants us.*

"So, I'll pick you up then? A couple hours?" I try to push the feelings of unworthiness out of my brain.

"No, I'll have someone drop me off." Nathan is practically in a frenzy to get out of the car. "Just go home and make dinner."

I climb out slowly and wait for a goodbye kiss after he grabs his duffle bag. I get a peck on the cheek as he jogs to the door, leaving the car door open.

Well, that went well. I don't stay outside the gym licking my wounds. *Maybe when he's not jet-lagged, it'll be better.*

CHAPTER 15
HENRI

DEACON SIGHS, coming out of the busy meeting room to see me and the Corinth Security agents Cade sent over from the main DC office. "Ooo, another death threat? What did it say this time?"

"Don't worry about it." I smile at him, hoping to appease any nerves he may have. "Cade isn't worried, but with it being our last day here, there was no harm in making sure."

"Spoilsport. I'm starting to think the death threats are funny." He steps closer to me, ready to be led off.

It's the closest he's been to me in the last two and a half weeks. I mean, not that I've been measuring, but after New Year's Day, since I told him we had to be professional, Deacon has been a complete gentleman, if not entirely indifferent to my existence. Which, well, being what I wanted, is good. It's not . . . it doesn't feel right.

This six-day trip has been filled with so many awkward interactions between us, and there's only one more night before we're home and can spend less time with each other. Again, another thing that doesn't feel right.

"Henri." The event coordinator calls my name, walking over in a hurry.

He's been on my ass, adamant about what events he wants the Aldens here for, like he can demand we make an appearance, but I can't get him to understand I'm calling the shots.

"I really appreciate you both coming today. It's been great getting to know the Aldens better. I wish you could have made the journey and brought Finn and Lena for the Wolves in Film and Literature feature."

Even though it's not an audible thing, I'm pretty sure I hear Deacon's eyes rolling. He voiced massive distaste for that event, citing that if they were throwing an event about 'Wolves in Film and Literature,' one of them in each category, at the bare minimum, should be created or written by wolves. And he's not wrong. Plus Lena and Finn were in Ireland, so it was physically impossible to get them there even if I wanted to.

"Yes, well, it didn't quite fit our schedules. We best be going." I smile at him and gesture to the security agents, bringing them forward with us and ending the conversation.

"Oh, of course. Thank you again." He gives me a tight smile, which is super fake.

Deacon doesn't even bother saying goodbye, but as we take steps toward the door, he groans, "I hate feeling judged by pompous assholes like that."

"Same. It feels like everyone's always judging me," I tell him, being even more unprofessional than before the kiss.

It's like I can't find my usual buttoned-up self with him. He's so disarming.

After two months of spending at least four days a week together, it's become so natural. Like now, I know I shouldn't be tucked in close to him, but away from the flashing cameras and press that would read into everything, it's nice to pretend.

"I'm never judging you. I already did. All it took was one time. I judged you, and I fell in love with you." He says to me, pulling me in for a hug. "Today was a hard day, but you did so good."

Deacon's reassurances have absolutely no business being this good.

He's perfect, my wolf coos. *Kiss him again. He loves us. You heard it, right? You heard it.*

He doesn't mean it like that. I correct her, nipping all the bubbly feelings she's trying to make out of a friendly, platonic interaction between us.

Looking up at Deacon though . . . it almost feels like an option. The closeness of our bodies pushed together brings dizzying memories of New Year's Eve back into my brain.

"In a platonic way." I echo my thoughts, hoping that offering him those words and removing myself from the hug will stop the warmth of desire settling within me. Desire for him.

My wolf wags her tail. Her encouragement for us to be together sends panic slamming into me like a wrecking ball.

We can't be more, I remind us both. *Besides, he might not have realized what he just said. It could be the liquor talking or God knows what he got from the impromptu meeting in a café this morning.*

Deacon doesn't contradict me and lets me go without a fuss. But his eyes hold a deep desire, and I'm not sure how to handle it.

He didn't say it wasn't platonic. That means it is. I try to cling to that logic.

"So."

"So."

He and I try to change the subject at the same time.

I gesture to the doors that will lead us out of this private space and back out in front of the press, keeping myself quiet to let him talk.

Deacon smiles and rubs his hands together. "There's that cake place on TV. Think we could swing by and try?"

"I don't see why not. We've got to get dinner anyway," I answer and shrug. "It would be good for filler posts for your social media."

"Excellent. Cake and making you happy." Deacon smiles down at me.

He doesn't mean happy in anything other than our working relationship. I try to squash down these feelings. *I love Nathan. I can be friends with Deacon.*

The reminders are hard to keep up while the memory of that look, how he looks at me, is burning its way into my brain.

CHAPTER 16
DEACON

DESPITE MY NEW personal stack of death threats, which warrants a four-person security team, I receive no calls or objections from Cade, or his business partner, Peter Corinth, as I convince the team to take us all over the place. The first couple threats were funny, but evidently my response to them was not, and now they don't like to tell me why people want to kill me, only that I need to be careful and watch my back. Which means I'll be doing exactly not that.

Four of my favorite takeout restaurants, scattered across DC, and the cupcake place seemed like a good reward for not being a dick to the event coordinator who talked down to Henri.

I let Henri spend a half hour taking pictures of me while I impromptu shake hands and sign autographs with patrons and bakery staff before I make it obvious that I'm overstimulated and my wolf is starting to come back.

But back on the sofa of the hotel suite, I can't think of a better evening. I sure as fuck can't think of a better way to spend the last evening in DC, given the circumstances.

This is a date. **My** wolf decides. He's barely conscious after the prescription pills I bought this morning, but he's loud enough to give me words like that. The ones that send an ache to my heart.

I try to dismiss the feeling because Henri is adamant about staying with the asshole boyfriend. But this would be a unique and enjoyable date. If only I could end it with another one of those kisses. It's been about three weeks since New Year's Eve, and I've fallen asleep to the thought of her tongue in my mouth every single night.

Her phone buzzes on the sofa between us, and the asshole's name lights up the screen.

NATHAN:

You having a good time? I hope (. . .)

I growl. I don't want to, but it starts in my chest before I can help it.

Henri picks up her phone, and then she lies to me. "He's hoping I'm having a good time and says that he misses me."

I should be good and let her lie. But I'm no good for her, and I'm no good as a person. "That's not what that text says."

She bites her lips together but doesn't contradict me.

"You haven't texted him enough this trip. So, when you get home, he'll probably accuse you of cheating on him." I run my tongue over my teeth before I finish. "And then he'll beat on you, trying to make you remember your place, or maybe it's in some sort of fugue state or fake hormone-induced rage. You'll come back to the house wearing long sleeves or, overall, a little tender from something and pretend you're fine. Because sure, by the next day, you will be . . . physically at least."

"He's not a bad guy." Henri isn't lying. She believes that.

"No, he's a fucking terrible human being," I assert.

I move the bao takeout container back to the coffee table and shift on the sofa to look at her.

Henri shakes her head and plays with her food. "He's been cheated on, and I don't do enough to show him how loyal I am. He feels ostracized since I started to work with wolves. Me being more in human culture than wolf culture made it easier for us to connect. Now he's worried that I'll forget what it's like to be human."

"You were never human to start with," I argue. A ball of ice cools me from the inside out. My fingers ache to touch her. "He's trying to make you compliant and held to this ideal that won't ever exist. He tries to isolate you from the people you have the most connection to."

"I don't have a connection to other wolves." She puts her takeout container on the coffee table. "I don't, Deacon. I know you all think I should. I don't miss the slight insistences from Cade and Finn and Lena . . . to do wolf things. But I *was* human until one day I just went into heat. Then I was supposed to be different." She draws a deep breath. Letting anger fall out of her words, Henri adopts a more somber tone. "He's so good to me. No one seems to see that part of him." She defends him and then looks away from me. "Like for my birthday, he'll book us a nice weekend away. We'll really get to reconnect."

Her phone pings again, and Henri lifts it, lighting up the screen. She winces slightly with whatever she just received.

"Don't tell me he's your boyfriend and that he loves you. He's cheating on you, Henri." I say those words less gently than I wanted to.

Fuck, I'm an asshole. That's not how she should have heard that information.

"He's cheating on me?" She shakes her head once. Then her shoulders drop. "You're sure they're not just his clients? He goes to people's houses sometimes." Despite questioning it,

Henri holds tight to the rigid belief that her relationship is 'good.'

"I'm positive." I nod and behave against the thought of spelling out how many and when.

Henri's lack of questioning comes from a suspected knowing. She doesn't argue with me or defend him. This information isn't new to her, but my presentation of it . . . wasn't the greatest.

"But you kinda knew that, didn't you?"

She drops her head into her hands, covering her face. There's one small nod. If it were any smaller, I'd have missed it.

All the details locked away in my head of his schedule could destroy her. As much as I want to rip her out of his arms and be selfish, using this information to do so would hurt her. It's bad enough I told her like this.

I let myself put my hand on her knee, violating the 'no touching' rule, and it stops some of the tension in my voice. "I'm not asking you to pick me or choose me. I'm not asking that you live with us, with me, because I'm being selfish. This isn't about me."

Mmm, kinda is, my wolf snarks at me.

"I'm not asking you to pick me," I reiterate. Henri isn't looking at me, so I take two fingers and, as gently as I can, turn her head toward me. "I'm asking you to not pick him. I'm asking you to do what's right and safest for yourself because he isn't it."

We lock eyes, and I can see her turmoil. The eyes are a portal to the soul and Henri's is tortured. I'm all too familiar with being tortured, but knowing Henri is experiencing it is a different kind of pain.

I run my fingers along her jaw into her hair, and she parts her lips.

I'm not sure it's an invitation, but I move on instinct,

kissing her anyway. My lips press against hers, and she kisses back.

That is until her phone pings again.

It kills me to let her go.

Neither of us needs her to look at the screen to know who it is.

But Henri's silence, after that kiss, is an answer in itself. I'm not asking her to pick me, but even if I was . . . she wouldn't.

"Answer him again before it gets worse." I shake my head. My patience with being the voice of reason didn't last long. "Why don't you call him, give him some extra attention."

"Are you sure?" She cocks her head, examining me.

"Positive. Wasn't kidding, Henri, it kills me inside that he hurts you because of me." I hang my head and pick up a cupcake. "I'll go to my room so you can show him that you've lots of privacy and I'm nowhere near you at all."

I don't stick around for her to argue with me. I've given her the information. At some point, something will give. My patience, probably.

CHAPTER 17

DEACON

I'VE BEEN CAMPED out at the Wisconsin house on a bender. After almost three weeks of people-ing nonstop, Henri scheduled me a break. A break that, after a week in close quarters with her, I had no choice but to take, or I'd keep pushing more of those 'no touch' boundaries like I already did in DC.

I don't usually get high just to get high. It's a secret I've guarded close to my heart for a long time. These 'benders' I send myself on aren't even all that dramatic so much as they're a vacation from everyone else's problems, being free of the responsibility of answering when someone calls. This time, I did thoroughly enjoy recreational drug use to take the edge off and distract myself.

But this morning, the alarm for the calendar on my phone says that it's been four days since we returned home from Washington, DC, and that means I've got three days to get myself 'presentable' for pretty much anything else Henri can come up for me to do.

Sober adjacent, I've spent the day digging into Henri's past. Adam, Cade's favorite keyboard warrior, may have accidentally gotten her passwords, stored in her online computer profile, for her personal social media profiles loaded onto my laptop. *Best 'accident' ever.*

Henri's personal profile has her adopted parents completely muted. They're still 'friends,' but they don't see updates or anything about her.

I read the conversations where the messages said they weren't treating Nathan fairly. But I've made myself a Henri communications expert, and those words weren't from her, not entirely, that's for sure. Word choice and comma usage are all off. Sure, it could be that she's grown as a writer, but it doesn't feel like her.

The messages from her account go on to say that if they can't support her with him, then she can't talk to them.

Henri's adoptive parents still haven't given up. If they've sent her a hundred messages, they've sent her twenty thousand, asking to talk with her. They've sent life updates and pictures of the two of them together. They made it incredibly easy for me to track and store their address and telephone numbers.

Maybe she just needs a new voice of reason? Someone Nathan can't shut out.

It's now almost eight in the evening, and my wolf is finally perking back up. I'm pretty sure I've drank more water than I ever have. The refrigerator, stocked when I was putting an online grocery order in while stoned, is full of delicious and surprisingly rather nutritious items.

But I don't argue with myself on it. Stoned Deacon making responsible choices is a first.

Pulling out a flank steak and some peppers, I start debating fajita bowls or burritos.

My phone dings.

Saw you're doing all the socialite shit now. Are
you still partying too?

I groan looking at his message. I'd been avoiding that dealer's particular style of suppressing my wolf. My usual micro-dosing has been a cocktail of a variety of substances that I've tested, measured, and experimented with to determine my tolerance.

But maybe getting back into opioids would be better for my time in isolation, my retreats, where I let everything purge out of my system and give my brain a full break. Opioids make him the easiest to suppress entirely. There aren't any accidental breakthroughs of my wolf and gift. When I'm micro-dosing and with opioids, it's the closest to feeling like I did when Revecca borrowed my wolf and gift. My wolf snarls at the idea.

Well, if you'd pull your weight and keep the ancestors at bay, this wouldn't be a problem, I remind him, to which there is no snarky reply.

We can't protect her if you put me away. He thinks of Henri and the rave before going into a montage of all the times she's looked adorable.

Setting my phone down, I vow to revisit the discussion when I'm fed and not making rash decisions hangry.

There's a knock on the front door, and I leave the kitchen island to look at the view screen of the security system. Should probably turn the notification sounds back on or at least route them to my phone. Pushing the buttons, I turn on the volume first before looking at the door.

A knock comes again as I flick the camera over to the right one.

Henri's on the other side of the door with her arm around herself. Something doesn't look right.

Abandoning the security panel, I run to the front door and yank it open. "Henri, what's wrong?"

"I just. I'm." She starts and stops.

Putting my hand on her shoulder, I pull her inside and close the door behind her.

The scent of copper hits me.

Henri's bleeding. Actively bleeding.

I feel like I look the way Cade did when they told him Thalia was missing. That frenzied, heartbeat-in-my-ears-and-eyes-wide, panicked look.

Gently, but no less frantically, I drag her into the kitchen. I walk backward, trying to see if she limps or anything. There's a slight hitch in her step, but nothing screaming she needs a doctor.

She's a wolf. She's a wolf, I remind myself again and again. There's nothing he could do to her that her body can't heal on its own.

Fear gets the memo and leaves the forefront of my brain. Anger, however . . . he's here to stay.

I pull her flowy shirt off the top of her head. *Bruising, no blood.* I turn her around in a full circle. *No blood.*

She objects. "Deacon."

I toss the shirt on the floor and strip her dress pants off. Where I find the source of the bleeding. The snarl coming from me echoes in the house. It's not a lot of blood, but it's my sensitivity to it because it's hers.

Henri flinches, turning her head away from me and squeezing her eyes shut. I stifle the growl that continued to take up residence in my throat and respectfully, but begrudgingly, take a few steps away from her.

I try drawing a deep breath, but it doesn't calm me down. You can't inhale, exhale this sort of anger out of your system. Homicide can't be stopped with therapeutic breaths.

134

He fucking hurt her. My wolf slams against my surface, trying to get out. *He hurt her. She is pack, we have to fix this.*

It shouldn't come as a surprise that he hurt her like this. It's probably because of me. It's been one abuse after another, and I anticipated that this could happen after DC and . . . And what? She would have gone home to him every night, no matter what I said.

What am I supposed to do? Sleep outside their house in the event he hurts her?

I stalk back across the house to my bedroom, into the adjoining bath, and open the first aid kit. Closing it, I walk back to the kitchen with it. Anger and rage brewing in my mind make it hard to sort ideas. The wolf, loud and demanding to take and kill, isn't helping.

When I return, Henri is trying to pull her dress pants on. My snarl stops her dead in her tracks. The smell of her fear has permeated the house, and it stops me.

"Fuck," I hiss, forcing everything brewing inside me deep down.

Everything gets shoved down until all that's left is the snarling wolf.

I set the kit on the counter near Henri and walk past her to the refrigerator.

Pulling open the sliding drawer to the freezer, I take out the bottle of vodka, and by the time I take my third swallow, my wolf stops. I'm not 'calm' by any definition of the word, but I won't fly off the handle and kill someone in a blind rage, again.

"I'm sorry" are the first words out of my mouth.

Henri's still fearful. She's still not looking at me.

It's for the best. She doesn't need to like me. I shouldn't want her to like me.

I don't know why I bothered grabbing the first aid kit. I can't tend that kind of wound. There's nothing in that kit that will help how brutally he took her. But I left it out for her anyway if she wants it.

"I will kill him, Henri," I tell her.

"You can't. Deacon, promise me you won't." Henri draws a deep breath.

Shaking my head, I answer, "I can't promise that, Henri."

"I can go. I've a little money set aside. I just felt safe coming here. I'll go to a hotel tonight. I'm sorry to have bothered you. But you can't kill him."

"You're not going anywhere, Henri." I hate that I sound like a possessive Alpha wolf, but the truth hurts. "If you leave, I'll go kill him, and I don't have the perfect way figured out yet."

"Deacon, he's human." She sits on the stool, and the grimace that accompanies the movement indicates she's still in some sort of pain.

That face stays with her long after she's settled. Emotional wounds from that sort of violence last longer.

I manage to refrain from asking what Nathan did so I can avenge her properly, but apparently I can't refrain from being an asshole. "Henri, I don't have any problems killing humans. I don't have any problem killing wolves. The moral compass that guides most people does not guide me. I don't see the world as this magical place where life is sacred or precious."

Henri's eyes are watering again, and it's clear she's hurting. Sitting here telling her how I'm going to slaughter him won't help her.

"After the first time you came here, to be safe away from him, I assumed that if it got bad, you'd come back. In Lena's bedroom, there's a bunch of new clothes. I washed them. There are fresh towels in her bathroom." I fight back my rage that's boiling again and keep my voice level. "Go get yourself cleaned up."

Fuck. I sound like an asshole.

I focus, trying to be softer. "I'll make some food for us."

Henri walks away with her head down and shoulders slumped.

The rage is almost choking me. After the door to Lena's suite closes, I go into the utility room and close the door. It's one of the few rooms with total soundproofing. I grab one of the spare sheet sets off the shelf before turning off the light and screaming into the abyss.

I scream until my chest heaves and I'm not sure I can make any more noise. Now I know what Ezra means when he says that the worst part of standing there through Dinah's abuse was knowing he could have fixed it but was asked not to.

How do I balance the pain she's in right now with the guilt she'll feel when I kill him? Is there a mathematical equation I can apply to this? Is there some sort of law of diminishing return that will make this all . . . make sense?

I throw the sheets into the washing machine and start it before going back to the kitchen. I'm not quite at the level of numbness I need to have to hold it together for her. So, I pour vodka over ice and add a splash of orange juice for color.

How many times can I do this before I finally snap?

CHAPTER 18

DEACON

LAST SEPTEMBER

I was supposed to have today, and the better part of this week, alone out here at the Wisconsin house.

I'm sober. Because you're not supposed to make any big decisions under the influence.

A distinctive engine clank comes from outside, and it sounds oddly similar to Henri's shit-box car. I haven't been able to work out the cause of that sound in the time I've had to investigate it.

I'm hearing things surely.

A minute later, keys rattle in the doorknob. Impractical heels click across the floors, and finally, Henri says the passcode to the alarm aloud as she enters it into the panel.

Her purse finds the countertop with a clunk, and, uncharacteristically, there's a poof of the sofa as she sits on it. The fabric rustles as it embraces her body before she's settled.

I'm way too sober to see her. I had to pretend to be normal through weeks of wedding bullshit, and it's drained every fiber of my being.

And now that I'm sober, the wolf starts. *I'm pretty sure she's our mate. Get her to stop the suppressants.*

I'm pretty sure I never asked for your opinion on anything other than getting rid of the fucking ancestors, I clip back.

The last thing we need is for him to be so sure that the blonde wolf is ours.

He rolls his eyes. *You're mad you can't figure out how to get rid of me and keep your life.*

Ignoring him, I stalk around the corner of my bedroom to the living room. Henri's head is in her hands, and it seems like she could probably use a little bit of time believing she's alone.

A massive sniffle does me in. I can't pretend I'm not here if she's crying.

"Henri?" I call and lean against the wall.

"Fuck. Deacon, I thought you were out. I'm sorry." Her voice cracks, and she draws a deep breath and moves to get off the couch.

I'm too sober to resist her.

The space across the house has never felt shorter. I cross the living room and pull her up off the couch and into a hug.

"Talk to me, Henri. What's going on?" I squeeze my arms tighter around her.

Henri falls apart, deep heaving sobs quaking her body.

I hold her until the scent of her hair and the feeling of her in my arms becomes entrenched deep in my mind. Swaying back and forth, I try to soothe her.

Finally, the crying stops, and I break our embrace.

She wipes tears from her eyes. "I'll leave."

"Don't go," I tell her, but my words come out more like begging.

Because if she leaves, I might do it. I don't believe in signs, but if I did, she's as good as any.

"No. No." Henri waves her hand, trying to stop me. "This is . . . so unprofessional. I can't."

"I know you pride yourself on being a professional, but you're in no shape to drive." I start with the truth and move right into a lie. "I'm not sober enough to drive you anywhere myself."

"I'm so sorry. I can sleep in my car. You don't need me to be here and bug you." She keeps trying to argue with me.

"Henri, I know Cade and Lena's rooms would feel weird with their smells, but you're here enough . . ." I sigh, scrubbing my hand down my face.

We had the foresight to not build a guest room under the principle that if you don't have a guest room, you don't have guests and they don't feel welcome in your den. *I guess the three of us have always been antisocial.*

"There's a perfectly good couch right there." I indicate to where she was just sitting. *Or we can sleep on the same half of my king-size bed.*

Offer that! My wolf interjects, wanting to be closer to her.

"No, no. I couldn't possibly. It was a mistake. I just didn't know where to go and . . ." She draws a deep breath.

"He kicked you out?" It doesn't surprise me, but I let my question hang with as little judgment as I can.

Which, arguably, is still a lot of judgment.

Abusive narcissistic asshole. I'd put money on him calling before noon tomorrow to apologize and gaslight her into coming back.

"He doesn't mean it. We were both tired." As expected, she goes on the defense for him. "I have to give him some time to cool off. It's just a misunderstanding. I didn't explain the plans for the wedding well enough."

"A misunderstanding is both of you trying to pick up the same dry cleaning or being at the wrong restaurant for dinner

SARAH JAEGER

reservations." I try to be gentle. "You being unable to stay in your home because he's mad at you is not a misunderstanding."

"I'm —" She lets out a slow breath but doesn't finish her sentence.

"It's fine, Henri," I assure her, walking toward the kitchen. "Let me make you some snacks, and we can figure out what to do."

"Oh, no." She shakes her head, insisting. "You just . . . seriously. You don't have to. I'll —"

"Henri. You're not sleeping in your car. You're not sitting out here on the couch and probably working." I cut her off as politely as I can.

She interrupts me right back. "I don't want to ruin your plans. I'll stay quiet, and you do what you were doing."

That makes me laugh, and I chew on my bottom lip. *Corrupting little Henri could be fun.* "Henri, I don't think you want to sit out here and listen to me masturbate for a few hours before I pass out."

Immediately, Henri's eyes widen, and she spins away from me. "Oh. God. Okay. Yeah. I'm going to go."

"Stay." I press out those words, pleading with her. "I don't want you to go. You're here, and you're pretty much the only person I don't mind changing plans for this week."

Henri turns back to look at me. Her face is red, but she seems to respond to me being soft for her. Why wouldn't she? Henri's dying for someone to be good to her. But forcing her to stay, if she doesn't want to, is just as bad as trapping her like he's done.

Be the bigger person, Deacon, I remind myself and extend the invitational exit plan for her. "If you really don't want to stay, let me get you a hotel in town. You deserve to feel safe."

142

"I feel safe here." Her words come out at a whisper, and she seems surprised by them. "With you."

Each word is true.

What else can I do but let whatever's happening right now happen? "It's settled then. We stay."

With the 'decision' made, we stand here, staring, within reach of each other.

"You're not . . ." She seems to dig through words that are professional enough but not so stuffy that they're sterile. "Here alone because you're planning on uhm . . .?"

I snort and shake my head, immediately dismissing it. "No. No suicide plans tonight, Hen."

How is it fair, though, to hide this from her? We talked about my plans and how there are dates saved in my phone's calendar, during a break away from the chaos of Cade's wedding, in a closet of all places when she needed a break from the world.

I look straight up at the ceiling and then back to her, telling the truth myself this time. "I don't really believe in signs or a higher power or fate. But your arrival here, today, now." I stumble over my words. "I can't exactly go killing myself while you're here or after you leave. Wouldn't be fair."

"Please don't," she whispers. "I don't want you to die."

"That makes one of us." I match her volume.

Tears well in her eyes. "I don't understand how that feels. I've never met someone like you, and if I have, they've never been this honest. The silent suffering must be horrible. I wish I knew how to help you."

"I appreciate you, Henri. But today isn't about me." I give her a soft smile and change the subject, looking around the house for an idea. "Well, there aren't a ton of options."

She shrugs, looking around the house in the same manner I did, but then her voice becomes firmer and more assured. "I was planning on lying on the couch until I fall asleep or maybe getting some work done if I get too anxious."

At her instructions, I flop down on the couch without another word, then look up at her expectantly. "Oh, is couch lying a solitary activity?"

Henri follows my lead, lying on the other wing of the sectional, our heads in the center together. Staring at the ceiling with someone there next to you, doing it too, feels less lonely. I'd expected to wallow alone, but fuck, Henri makes everything better.

It's because she could be our mate, my wolf growls.

Rolling my head, I watch as tears well in her eyes. Henri blinks them away, but they run down her cheek toward her ear. In a can't-even-be-bothered fashion, Henri just lets them go, not wiping them clear.

"Do you want to talk about him, or do you want to be distracted?" I want to fix this, and distracting us both from how I *want* to fix this is the best thing for us all, for now.

"I know you're not the biggest Nathan fan," she groans. "It's probably best if we don't talk about him. But what about you? No wedding date, no hooking up, no significant other?"

"Nah. I hook up now and then, but I'm one of those 'project' types girls think they can take on and change." I snort before continuing. "Ezra and I even have a whole point system for our hookups and all the different ways they try to get us to hang around. It's how the 'Cousin's Grimm' thing started, the two of us out partying together. It's really pathetic when you think about us keeping a tally, but at some point, you've got to find joy somewhere."

When I roll over toward her, I can't handle watching her look up at the ceiling, so sad and lost. She arches to face me, and as gently as I can, I brush a lock of hair out of her face. "No guy is worth crying about, Henri."

CHAPTER 19
HENRI

WHEN I EMERGE from the bathroom in what was Lena's suite, Deacon is scrolling through his phone. He stops before clicking the burner on the stove and starting the steaks in the pan with the peppers.

Deacon is quiet, and I understand why.

Everything is all my fault. I shouldn't have come here. But the more time I spend with Deacon, the more like he feels like a place I can call home. It's a warm and fuzzy feeling in my heart that I don't feel with anyone else. I've never felt this close with anyone. Yet, I've fucked it all up.

"I'm sorry," I whisper.

"Don't be sorry, Henri." Deacon stirs the steak slices and coats them in a seasoning. "Did you want tortilla or rice bowls or both?"

"Rice in the tortilla?" I hope that means he's dropping the conversation because 'be smarter, leave him' is what I'm guessing comes after 'don't be sorry, Henri.'

As kind and caring as Deacon is, he just can't possibly understand. He has people who love and support him no matter what. Deacon won't understand that at the end of the day . . . without Nathan, I'll have no one and nothing. Even if I take the pack up on all their offers, I'll just be at someone else's mercy.

"Rice in the tortilla it is," Deacon confirms.

He heats tortillas on the stove, tossing them in a fancy tortilla keeper. Once he's done, he takes his bowl to the giant sofa and comes back for mine.

I'm quick to object. "Oh, it's fine, we can . . ."

"Henri, let me take care of you." His eyes are soft, and his attitude has changed.

I nod and accept his help off the stool. It's strange for someone to help me. Sure, I remember my adoptive parents caring for me, like making dinner and such, but nothing like this. But that's because I've never needed someone to care for me.

I'm a wolf, and being a wolf means no sickness or sick days, and even now, Deacon is here physically supporting me, but time is making the pain fade.

Deacon sets my bowl down on one side of the coffee table and his on the other, giving me the space we usually take from each other.

The cozy couch in DC where we shared a meal is what I want. But it's not right. Nathan is right, maybe I'm having an emotional affair with Deacon.

"I don't trust you, Henri. You're always fucking with him. Why can't you get someone else to be his wrangler? What is he, some sort of giant man-child?" Nathan shouts at me.

"It's not like that at all." I shake my head. "He's a decent guy. He's just different and needs someone more in tune with handling someone more complex."

"*I can't believe you're standing up for him!*" Nathan screams, his face turning red. "*You know he wants to fuck you, right?*"

"*No. I promise he doesn't.*" I put my hand on Nathan's chest, trying to calm him down. I keep my voice soft. "*He doesn't want to fuck me. I'm not his type at all.*"

He laughs. "*Ha. Henri, you're so naive. Has he even fucked someone else in all the time you've known him? I bet you even get one hotel room so he doesn't pick up any randos.*"

"*We get a suite with multiple rooms because then we can control the security better and —*"

I don't get to finish my sentence before Nathan pushes me back against the wall.

"Henri." Deacon sits next to me on the sofa. "Come on, Henri, come back."

Safe. My wolf reassures me, pushing me into him.

I'm trembling, and I don't know how to stop. I draw a long, deep breath, but it gets stuck in my throat, and I choke. I can't even breathe.

I can't breathe.

Deacon pushes my shoulders back from where I've hunched in around myself, and the air comes easier. He squeezes my hand and whispers, "Slow breaths. Focus on steady not deep."

It's not that easy. But I try to do what he says. I follow him through breathing exercises just like Cade does for Thalia.

Are they all masters of therapeutic techniques? Surely not. Because the only way I've seen Finn handle Lena is disappearing for twenty minutes, and she comes back with an attitude adjustment.

These thoughts, of normalcy, of the people I see daily, settle the panic in my wolf. This is what belonging is.

This is pack, my wolf offers. Then she insists, *He is ours. No matter how it feels off the stupid suppressants, we're never letting him go.*

When the shaking stops, Deacon moves to separate us.

My fingers cling to his shirt. "Stay?"

He reaches for his food before cozying in next to me and my plate of fajitas.

"You'll be okay, Henri." Deacon's wolf comes to the surface despite what I assumed was a full glass of a screwdriver nearly emptied on the counter.

"Are you sure?"

Deacon wraps his arm around me while still eating with his other hand, stabbing into his bowl. "I'm sure. Let's eat, and then if you wanna talk, we can." He pulls the TV remote out from under a pillow. "Trashy housewives of some god-awful city, trashy boat peoples, or humans trying to survive in the wilderness."

"Trashy boat peoples." I nod, knowing exactly what show he's talking about.

ONE EPISODE IN, and I've all but licked my plate clean when Deacon turns the television off and rotates on the couch next to me. "I'll tell Cade to assign someone else to me. We've proven I can behave and do this whole public appearance thing as long as I keep myself the right level of inebriated. So, it's time you go back to managing your staff and Cade's appearances full time. I'll promise to only run off the employees I think are assholes."

I don't know what to say. Tears prick my eyes, and I blink them back, forcing myself to see the logic in this. A whine rises inside me like sick bile, betraying the understanding and professional nature I know I need to put forward. "Okay."

Deacon is right. Until I can figure out my next move, it

would be easier if I could tell Nathan I'm not managing Deacon full time.

But the way Deacon is pulling away from me confirms that the Aldens' hospitality is just another crutch for me to hold onto in life. They don't want me so much as they want me safe. It would be some sort of indebted feeling all over again. I need to find my own way without their help.

Monkshood
Aconitum napellus

FEBRUARY
LUNAR NEW YEAR

CHAPTER 20
HENRI

THE AGENDA for the Lunar New Year pack run was set. Per my request, the wolves would run first, with members of the press and early arriving guests able to watch and snap candid pictures from the deck as we departed. Once we ended our run, the vetted members of the press would be invited onto the snowy lawn for closer pictures. Then there would be time for everyone to get ready before formal dinner and mingling.

And I'm stalling with every intention of trying to get out of it.

"You coming, Henri?" Cade waits at the top of the stairs for the family to descend to the dressing and shifting room.

"Me?" I'm caught in my attempt to escape the pack run I said I would be here for.

It was heavily implied that since I've missed a few . . . all . . . of the pack runs since the one in October, my running tonight was mandatory.

And, based on the look in Cade's eyes, The Leviathan won't let me out of it.

"Yeah." Deacon's voice comes from behind me. "Henri and I are running tail."

"Sounds good." Cade takes Deacon at his word with a nod before descending the stairs.

I feel Deacon so close behind me, and when I look over my shoulder, he's right there. Tilting my head up, I see clearly into his eyes.

"I tried to get you out of it earlier, but we're both on his shit list for skipping a bunch. But it's okay, I'll hang back with you, and we can come in at the end of the run when the schmoozing is almost over."

Fuck. No getting out of this.

My wolf is pressed up against my skin, and then I see the barely there dark-brown flicker of Deacon's wolf in his eyes.

It's been three weeks since Cade and I assigned Deacon to one of my team members, but not spending time with Deacon has felt weirder than I thought it would. I only worked with him for almost two months. I have no business missing that. But standing here and feeling vulnerable but comforted by his presence really feels like I've been missing him.

"It'll be okay," he reassures me.

It's strange having Deacon comfort me, and he does it without even putting a single hand on me. With a nod toward the stairs, I follow his suggestion and descend to the basement.

When Cade and Thalia finished the original basement build, the changing room was built on the smaller side based on the average number of people who attended the pack runs on holidays per the pack registrar's account.

Within two months of the house being done, the number of those in attendance quickly tripled. A quick renovation was done to increase the space's size. Cade said it was a good problem to have, that more people feeling comfortable to come to the main house to shift and to be together was the sign of a healthy pack.

I questioned then why Finn had challengers while Thalia was in heat, but the answer surprised me. According to Cade, a healthy pack will test the leadership, not always out of malice but for proof they're strong enough to be dependable. Like children learning to respect authority, it's learned and only gained through consistent dependability.

It's poetic. That even if it feels rocky and unstable, the group is working to be stronger rather than falling apart.

Trying to remember the positives, though, while stripping down in a room with a bunch of other people is impossible. The bigger room and space with more people inside gives me this awful feeling of being under a microscope. I'm instantly back in high school gym class and being awkwardly looked at and scrutinized by a bunch of mean girls.

That's never been my experience here, but feelings aren't always logical, and this social norm feels like one I'll never adapt to.

Deacon ushers me into the changing room and past a small group of people stripping.

His voice is barely audible over the excited chatter of the room. "I'm between you and the rest of the room. I'm facing away from you, and we'll be the last ones out the door. Everything is just fine. Relax so you'll be able to find your wolf and shift."

"Is it that obvious?" I whisper back.

He takes a beat before answering. "To someone who doesn't watch you the way I do, probably not."

Is that cute, or is that creepy? I squint, looking at his back. If I could see his face, maybe I'd know for sure.

Barely two minutes later, most of the people have left the room.

"Come on, Henri," Deacon beckons. "Time for our mandatory athletics."

"You should really get some pictures with the press though." I urge. *Has Kyle been reminding him of that?*

"Mmm, pass." Deacon's voice is muffled as he must pull his shirt off over the top of his head. "The problem about being a white and cream wolf during the winter is I pretty much just look like a splotch of dirty snow. Not attractive and doesn't photograph well."

"Nothing about you is unattractive." The words spill out my mouth, and I clamp my hand over it. *Fuck.* I draw a deep breath. "It's why the media is obsessed with you."

"Yeah." Deacon doesn't say anything.

Everything between us is so fucking awkward. It's hot and cold.

Kyle does the best he can to monitor Deacon, yet I find myself stepping in. It's been a month since that kiss in DC and then again when we got back home, and it isn't getting easier to maintain distance between us.

A chorus of howls starts outside, and my wolf presses to the surface. The telltale electric hum runs through my body. Similar to what I felt when I kissed Deacon.

When I turn around, Deacon is already walking away from me, naked. His ass flexes with each footfall, and he pauses at the door. "If you want to shift in here, I'll open the door for you."

My wolf takes my body faster than normal. It's not pained or laborious, and I settle into my four-footed form. Deacon opens the door and steps out of my way. We keep our head low to the ground, submitting to him. He's not an Alpha wolf, nor is he even all that dominant as a person, but he's royalty and we respect that.

The door closes behind us, and a groan comes from Deacon

before he brushes up against us, from our hip to our shoulder, even placing a lick on our muzzle, praising our shift.

One final howl echoes out, and Deacon adds his call to it, but we don't.

The humans on the deck above us are being surprisingly agreeable. They don't shout or try to call for our attention at all. It's good to see they're following directions. The electric whir of cameras and shutters snapping can be heard, but it's not overwhelming.

At the back of the pack, we trot slowly, waiting to get to the wood line to run. Deacon hangs back, walking and openly watching the back of the pack. When the pack is engulfed in the woods, everyone takes off running, except for Deacon, who stays right alongside us as we trot across the frozen earth.

CHAPTER 21
HENRI

THE RUN TAKES OVER AN HOUR. It's a long trek around the property. I know for most wolves, it's quick, but Deacon and I stay at a comfortable pace, following more of the older wolves and those with children and keeping everyone together. It's fantastic. Then when we come into the clearing, Deacon knows exactly what to do, which is to go to the assigned 'human-handler' — someone designated to stop humans from getting too close — for pictures with the press.

In his wolf form, he sits next to The Leviathan and Thalia. I watch them for a little bit but then know it's better if I have thumbs and am universally understood when directing the media.

Knowing I have to shift back and do so in a space with other shifters brings the heated feeling of self-consciousness. I peek my head into the room, but people and wolves fill the space from wall to wall, leaving me no room to shift back. *It's okay. I can just wait. No one needs me right this second.*

"Has anyone seen Henri Greene?"

Of course they do.

Despite being incredibly exposed while standing just outside the door to the changing room, I focus on my human form and work to tuck my wolf away. It feels like I'm in the limbo between forms for forever, but finally I push up into standing on two legs and can duck into the changing room, dodging between families wrangling children into clothes and teenagers horsing around and flirting.

There's plenty of room in the back corner, where Deacon and I left our things, for me to dress while being out of the way. When I'm finished, ease settles over me with the warming accomplishment, knowing I made the right choice as the changing room hasn't thinned out at all.

Once I'm out of the changing room and leave behind the joyous laughter and lighthearted fun, I head upstairs, where the difference in the atmosphere inside the house is palpable. Tension fills the air as if one misstep could lead to an eruption, but why?

My wolf raises her hackles, and the hair on the back of my neck stands on end. Head on a swivel, as Cade would say, I'm on edge and looking for the problem to defuse. Someone asked if they had seen me, so it's clearly something I'll need to handle. The press and pack members are mingling in the formal dining room, the living room, and out on the large deck.

As I greet people, I keep waiting for more information, but nothing seems to come out of the woodwork. There's seemingly no rhyme or reason for the unease polluting the energy of the gathering nor any explanation for who was looking for me or why.

"Henri."

I turn in the direction of my name being snarled.

Nathan is bright red in the face. People, humans and wolves, step away, putting distance between themselves and us.

The anger rolling off him is the source of the problem.

"Nathan, you're here early." I step toward him quickly, as if getting to him faster will immediately change his mood. "Let's go to my office."

His lip curling in a form of disgust, Nathan shakes his head. The look alone has panic flooding my system, and I'm sure fear is wafting off me. Arms crossed in front of his chest, Nathan holds his head high, glowering down at me.

Trying to comfort him, I put my hand on his forearm.

We were doing so good after I got back from the Wisconsin house. It's been weeks without incident.

He shrugs me off with a shift of his shoulders. Malice spikes his words. "I can't believe you."

"Come on." I walk past him, beckoning him with a small wave of my hand. *It's a misunderstanding. Surely, he'll calm down if he gets a minute.* "We can go speak in my office about what's upsetting you."

"Like that'll make it better?" Nathan raises his voice.

"Nathan." I lower my voice, trying to get him to meet my volume, but eyes are finding us in the crowd. "I'm not sure what's wrong, but we can talk and figure out a way to make it better."

"Unbelievable." Nathan scoffs, moving in the opposite direction of my office, toward the front door.

Relieved it's not toward the back deck where majority of the media and onlookers are, I follow behind him. But Nathan doesn't go all the way outside. In the front entryway of the house, he spins to look at me.

"I can't believe you did that in front of people." Nathan isn't shouting, but it's close, the harsh anger cutting through.

"Nathan, please lower your voice." My face and neck are heating.

We can't do this here. Humans attending the event will see

163

this as a tense moment between lovers, but my employers won't see it so simply. It's unprofessional at best. But I'm not the reason people are here; it's not the scandal they're looking for, nor should it be. I need to get him out of here.

Before Deacon sees.

I grip his forearm and try to pull him back past the wall that blocks some of the main living space from the front entry.

"You fucking shifted, in front of everyone, you let them see . . ." Nathan is seething. His chest rises and falls in short inhales and slow hissing exhales.

"I'm a wolf, I had to shift. And it's not like I was mid-yard. It was off to the side, and no one was focused on what I was doing. I was only outside for a few seconds." My shoulders push upward toward my ears, but a sickly frozen ball of dread settles in my stomach.

"You shouldn't be shifting at all!" Nathan shouts as we reach the front door. "You're not fucking one of them, Henri!"

"Nathan." I reach for the doorknob, trying to usher him outside and hopefully out to his car so we can talk.

"No!" He screams at the top of his lungs and directly into my face.

Tears burn my eyes, and I'm not sure what to do. I can barely breathe. "I —"

"Excuse me." Cade pulls both of our attention.

He's dressed in sweats rather than the clothing Lunar New Year would warrant. Someone told him something was going on, and he rushed to get here.

"I'm talking with Henri." Nathan glares, clearly oblivious to the gravity of who he's speaking with despite having met Cade before. "It's got nothing to do with you."

"Anything that happens on this property is of my direct concern." Cade's using his 'you're in deep shit' Alpha voice as he stalks toward Nathan with silent footsteps.

He's easily six inches taller than Nathan, and while he shares the same leaner athletic build as Deacon rather than the thick, dense muscle like Finn, Cade is an intimidating person.

"I'm having a conversation with my girlfriend." Nathan turns away from Cade.

The Leviathan rises in Cade's eyes, and he turns his attention to me. "Henri, please go to your office."

The word 'please' is simply to be polite because Cade's words hit hard with an Alpha command. My feet move of their own accord, and Cade directs me to the secret closet passageway rather than going back through the main portion of the house.

"Where the fuck are you going?" Nathan snaps at me, and I struggle to keep going, trying to follow Cade's command. He wraps his hand around my wrist and holds me in place.

"It doesn't matter where she's going. You're leaving, and if Henri would like to leave later, she's welcome to, but you'll be leaving now." Cade growls, laying down the law.

I look behind me as I stand before the door.

"I'm not fucking leaving without her." Nathan squares up with Cade.

"Nathan, stop. Please." I draw a deep breath and try not to focus on the ache in my bones from his fingers digging into my arm. "I'll go with you. Let me grab my purse and keys, and we can go."

My wolf whines, upset, trying to crawl out of my skin from not following Cade's orders, her whole being needing to comply.

When I pull my arm away from him, Nathan lets me go. "I'll be here. Go get your purse."

I'm through the closet passageway and on the other side when I come face to face with Deacon. My stomach drops seeing him. He steps to the side, allowing me to walk down the hall toward my office. But I don't make the walk alone.

Deacon speaks in a low volume, low enough to avoid eavesdropping from the wolves in and around the house. "If you go with him, he's going to hurt you."

"I'll be fine. He's just mad. By the time we get home, we'll have talked it out and everything will be okay." My voice is shaking.

Why did he have to be early? I squeeze my eyes shut, glad the hallway is straight and that I only have a few more feet before my office door.

I open my eyes a few steps before my door, and Deacon leans on the wall next to it. A place I'm so used to seeing him, and it's comforting.

It'll be fine.

I unlock my door and step inside.

"You shouldn't go with him, Henri." Deacon sighs, following me into my office.

"I appreciate your concern —" I immediately go to defend Nathan.

"Henri." Deacon's voice is stronger, commanding my attention.

"Nathan just needs a minute to calm down. It'll be fine." I can't spare a glance at him as I quickly load my purse with my laptop, keys, and lunch box, gathering everything I would normally have left for tomorrow.

I'm doing it quickly to appease Nathan, yet I find myself stalling to give Deacon the time to talk.

Deacon shakes his head. "I don't think it will be."

His words are overwhelmingly solemn. If I think about them too long, I won't be able to leave. Finally, I'm able to face Deacon, and the pain in his eyes doesn't match what I was expecting.

"Henri, I'm worried about you leaving with him." He steps closer to me and places his hand on my shoulder. "I really don't want you to go, Hen."

Picking up my bags, I gesture for Deacon to leave the space.

We lock eyes, standing in the low light of my office, illuminated only by the hallway lights. But Deacon doesn't say anything else. Instead, following my silent directive, Deacon leaves my office, allowing me to follow behind him and lock the door.

Dread fills me as I walk alone back down the hallway to the entryway.

Deacon doesn't know him as well as I do. It's going to be fine.

CHAPTER 22

DEACON

I CAN'T FUCKING JUST SIT by and watch her go, and Cade knows it. He's seconds away from commanding her to stay to protect her. He could. Then she'd have no choice.

The other option is simply commanding Nathan to leave. But there's no way, with a house full of humans, he would risk it getting out that, since having embraced The Leviathan, his gift has grown, and he could simply command Nathan. The power imbalance with Cade being able to command humans would scare them.

Standing in the snow, Cade catches a glimpse of me from his view out the front door.

My brother and I haven't been close in a long time, but he understands what I'm telling him without question. I move out of sight of the small-dicked meathead taking Henri home and head over to the garage down by the gate. I ignore Marielle as she shouts something about cookies while I jog past her. Bud and Zachariah are hanging out in front of the doors. They wave but go back to whatever debate they're having.

Making Henri stay against her will would make her resent

us and drive a wedge between her and the pack. It's what happened with her parents, but I can't, I won't, let her be separated from a pack that loves her.

Not taking away her power to make the decision to leave with him and save some face is the compromise she felt she needed. But my concern for her well-being doesn't end at the front gate, and I can't help but act on that concern.

Not like it's a hardship to get out of Lunar New Year celebrations and playing nice with the press. While Kyle babbles on. No, this is better. Nathan is due for his date with death. If he tries to hurt her tonight, then he'll be on the receiving end of the pain he's inflicted on her in the past.

I grab the keys to one of Cade's blacked-out SUVs. I've stalked Nathan in various cars we keep in the garage, but if this gets nasty, a fully equipped, tactical vehicle will be better than a vintage muscle car. Besides, be a shame to get road salt on a classic and risk rust in the time it takes for it to be warm enough to give it a bath.

From the safety of the garage, I watch the cars come down the hill. First Nathan's and then Henri's. They're not driving together. It further proves my point that this won't de-escalate while driving.

She can't talk him down if they're not in the same car. But it also leaves me with opportunities.

He could never make it home, my wolf offers.

The darkness inside me has already pushed the idea into my brain. It would be too easy for him to get into an 'accident,' and wouldn't that be 'a shame.'

DESPITE AMPLE OPPORTUNITIES, I don't run Nathan off the road, nor do I jump him at the gas station. But I follow, always watching. There are too many witnesses, and I don't want to kill him in front of Henri if I don't have to.

Thankfully, by the time we get to Nathan's house, night has fallen, and there's plenty of cover for me to lurk in the bushes, staying close if something goes badly.

Just end him now. My wolf demands. *Quit wasting our time.*

Henri needs to leave him. She needs to feel that power.

In the last month, on more than one occasion, I stopped myself midway on the hunt to kill Nathan. Henri's pain that night at the Wisconsin house altered my brain, making me prone to rash decisions in the name of her safety. But there's too much on the line for me to go off half-cocked. I could accidentally undo all of Cade's work to improve the shifter image or, worse, implicate Henri in his death. Everything with Nathan's death must be perfectly calculated. No mistakes.

Sitting outside the house, I close my eyes and focus on the sounds from inside. It's nowhere near as soundproofed as the pack house, but most homes aren't built for wolves.

One thing Henri was right about is that the car ride did de-escalate Nathan's yelling and shouting.

"I'm so pissed off." His voice is at regular speaking volume. "You fucking shifted where the entire world could see that you're a wolf."

"I am a wolf." Henri is calm. "I shifted because I have to, it's a rule. I made sure to not shift in view of everyone, but I needed to do my job."

The end of her sentence slows, and guilt and shame blanket her words, enraging my wolf.

No one should make her ashamed of her wolf, he snarls, drawing memories of how beautiful she was trotting along the trail.

Henri is stunning, but I shut out memories of her for better focus.

"It's like you're one of them." Nathan speaks over the sounds of cupboard doors opening and closing.

Cooking supplies moving, maybe?

"Nathan," Henri says softly, "we talked about this. I am one of them. I'm a wolf, and I have to do wolf things."

"You don't go into heat. You take the pills. You can't, I don't know, take something to stop your wolf?" Nathan's question is not out of curiosity.

"The heat pills are different. It's like birth control. It's just so that I don't go into heat. It's not like it's doing anything other than stopping me from being miserable," Henri explains.

More kitchen clanging sounds, and then a blender starts up.

Conversation is halted, and when the blender stops, Nathan speaks. "Well, come off the pills then. I won't let you be miserable."

"Nathan, it's really bad. I don't know that —"

"Are you saying I'm not man enough for it, Henri? That I'm not enough for you?" Nathan jumps in.

"Hello." A woman's voice pulls my attention away from their exchange.

Fuck. I turn to look, afraid I've been caught eavesdropping, but the voice belongs to an ancestor. She's faint and so hollow I can see the streetlight from down the block through her form.

"Hi." I give her a small wave and keep my voice down. "Sorry, I've gotta keep tabs on this."

The woman steps through the foliage and sits on the ground facing me.

"Wolves aren't all that great," Nathan says, and I know I've missed something.

"Nathan is nowhere near as angry with her as he was with me." The woman says, and now my curiosity is piqued.

Ancestors talk to me all the time, but very rarely is it something more useful than not.

Keeping my voice low, I try to split my attention between the ancestor and the terse conversation in the house. "Tell me about him?"

"You know what you know. But what you don't know is how I know he won't kill her. Not here," the ancestor starts. She brushes her hair out of her face, a nervous tick, and it's a reminder that she's not alive. It hurts my heart. "Nathan won't kill her at home. He made a big deal out of this trip he took me on, a big week-long vacation. The promises that everything would be okay and that we would talk about us. We didn't talk about us."

A vacation? Like the one Henri says he has planned for her birthday? I didn't think I could feel any more unpleasant emotions about this situation, but suspicion joins the party.

"Nathan killed you?" I ask softly, double-checking the information she's giving me. Grief digs into my stomach.

Do I bust in there and take her away from here?

"I'm just saying, Henri, it's a good way for you to prove that you love me." Nathan raises his voice. "I'm going to game with the guys. Do whatever you want."

The ancestor leaves me, fading into the house. I want to follow, but not being dead like her, I can't.

Anger and panic flood my system.

They're done fighting, but that doesn't mean Henri is safe. I came here to make sure she didn't get hurt. And now . . . now I know it could be way worse.

A few minutes of silence pass, and I'm about to leave when she comes back and sits down. "They say it was an accident. That I died in a car accident. Which, I guess, isn't wrong. I remember being put in the car."

"What did he do?" Whatever she says will make me furious. But I need to know.

The ancestor shakes her head, not wanting to talk about it. It was insensitive to ask.

"Do you think I've some time before he tries it?" I don't know how I can even ask her to predict that. How can I expect an ancestor who died by his hand to predict the rage? *She did say that Nathan wouldn't kill Henri here.*

My fingers itch, and I debate calling Dinah and Ansel from right here. *I would know for sure. Well, mostly for sure.*

"Yes." The ancestor nods. "I've been here, watching him and trying to warn her. You can convince her to leave. There's still time."

"What's your name?" I keep my voice as quiet as I can.

"Grace," she answers.

"He'll suffer for hurting you too." I promise her.

Staying low, I slink away from the house. I trust Grace. Maybe it's misplaced, but ancestors are very rarely wrong about these sorts of things.

Tomorrow I'll talk to Henri. She didn't listen . . . care . . . react really when I told her Nathan was cheating. But tonight, I'll comb through everything I can turn up on Grace. I don't know if I'll be able to prove that he killed her, but maybe I can make a compelling enough argument. People don't respond well to 'a ghost told me.' Henri, having witnessed my gift firsthand, would be more accepting of the notion, but previous rejection of something so tied to my base person stings.

Then we'll hunt him down and kill him? My wolf gets excited at the prospect.

Then we'll hunt him down and get justice for Grace and retribution for Henri, I agree.

Sometimes it's favorable to be a monster.

Foxglove
Digitalis purpurea

FEBRUARY

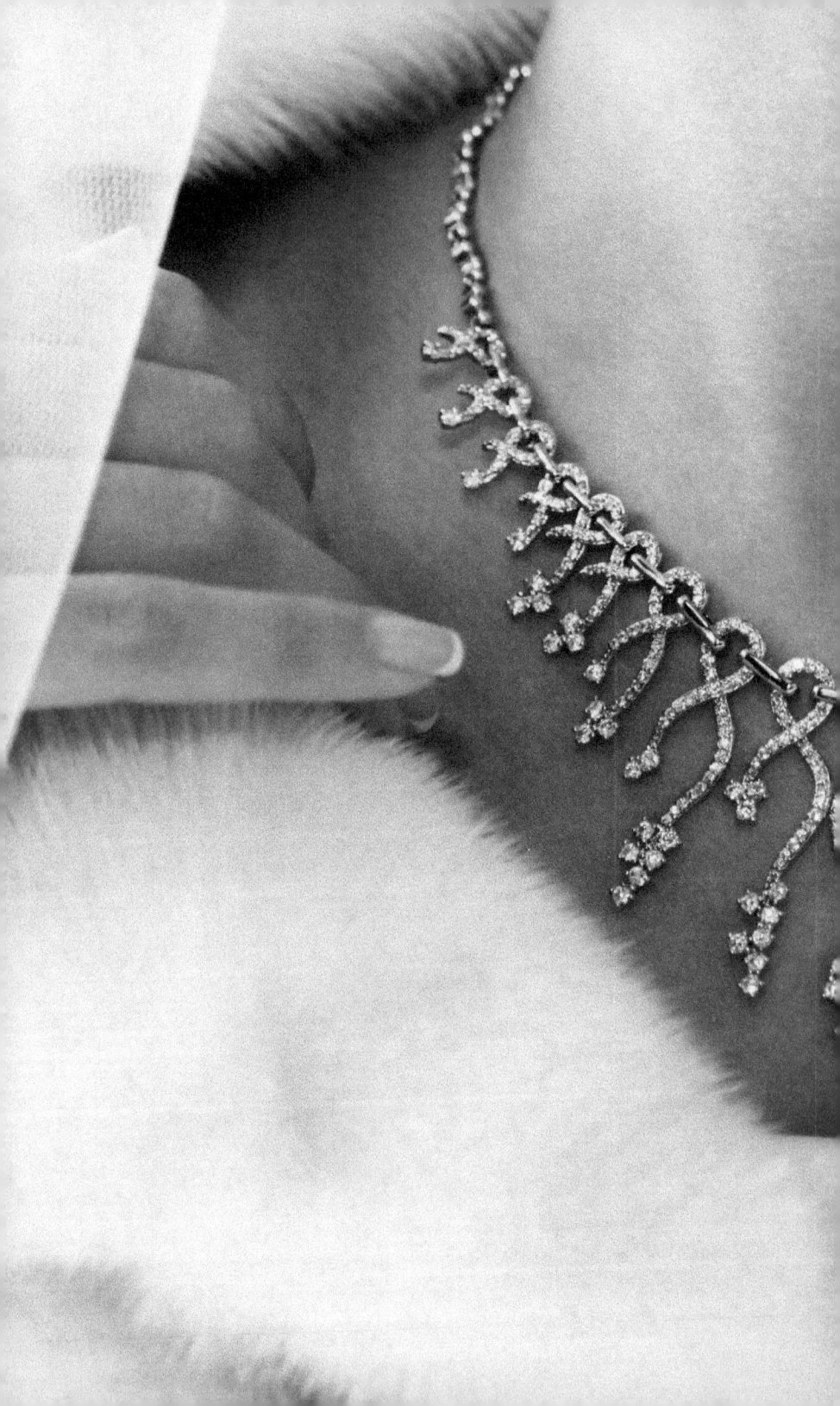

CHAPTER 23
DEACON
LAST DECEMBER

Lena and Finn's mating ceremony ended without anything eventful happening. My little sister looked radiant in her dress, and when Finn clasped the diamond collar around her neck, the news media finally realized and accepted that a 'collar' is not strictly reserved for kinky things but is a deep part of wolf culture.

In interviews following the ceremony, I may have said, 'Exactly, dogs are like wolves and dogs wear collars,' as well as, 'Why would anyone want Finn?' but I managed to stop myself from saying 'She shot his last ex.'

After that near miss, I was banished to the Pack house's event space on the bottom floor, where I've spent the last almost two hours having drinks and fancy snacks. As daylight transitions to nightfall, it becomes less of a public affair and more of a family one. Finally, people I want to spend time with begin to come down the stairs. The first being Henri. It's unfortunate, though, that she brought the human equivalent of three koala bears in a trench coat with her.

As expected, after changing out of her 'work attire' for

something more 'casual,' Henri is wearing an oversized dress. It's belted at her waist but does nothing for her lithe figure. She looks like she's hiding in the clothes.

Nathan, on the other hand, looks like he couldn't find anything in his size. Dress shirt too small, it clings to his biceps, and if he reaches too far for something, it'll probably split across the back like a superhero in a children's movie. He's no superhero, but I'll be the villain of his story.

It's hard not to notice the way people look at him. It's a mix of lust-filled glances and skeptical eyebrow raises, and wolves attuned to other predators around them move protectively around the space.

Cade walks up behind me before turning from the room to face me, his voice barely audible. "He's gotta go. I knew he wasn't treating her right, but I didn't realize he's . . ." Cade makes a breaking motion with his hands, saying through actions what I've been thinking.

"If humans could," I agree.

Even whispering the word 'fracture' in a room packed like this . . . rumors could start to fly.

I shake my head and look away. "I've tried to get her to leave him. She's . . ."

"Attached?" Cade offers quickly.

It's not simple attachment, but if there's a word for this, I don't know it. What is it called when a victim bonds to their abuser? Surely a word or phrase exists to describe it, but without it, all I can answer is with a shrug. "Worse."

I clear my throat, and Cade immediately moves from protective Alpha to the charismatic Cade everyone loves.

"Cade. Where is that lovely bride of yours? I was just telling the wife that Thalia's been working on the historical society's new installment, and she's dying to hear about it," the governor interjects.

"She'll be down in a few moments. I'm positive Thalia would be glad to talk about the new installment." Cade tucks his hand into his pocket, where he's started to carry at least one tactile toy to fidget with when talking to people he can't stand.

The number of people mingling, pups running about underfoot, and human adults and children who were invited and turned up is a testament to how well Cade and Lena are doing running things. Seeing how well they're finally adjusting to it all brings me a sense of peace, like maybe it's finally time. Cade and Lena are happy and mated, and they have a pack that supports them. I don't have to be here anymore.

My eyes rove the room, taking in the scene, checking if maybe I'm right and this could be the end of it all.

My eyes keep going back to her.

Henri, standing by one of the seven banquet tables full of food, glances around the room before nearly shoving a Russian tea cake into her mouth and turning back to the banquet line. The behavior is odd. Why would anyone care that she's eating a cookie?

The longer I watch, the more obvious it becomes.

Henri adds an obscene amount of spring mix salad to her plate before adding fresh fruit next. Anything that isn't whole foods gets overlooked: stuffing, buns, casseroles and hot dishes, puddings and desserts. I'm stalking her from across the room, and she makes her way down the buffet line and, finally, picks up a protein. It's a small chicken breast intended for one of the pups. Not that anyone would care that she has one, but my suspicion is quickly confirmed.

Nathan, done flirting with a couple of wolves, comes up to Henri and starts examining her plate.

I can't hear them over the sound of the room, but I can see his scrutinizing pointing and Henri lowering her head and putting it aside in submissive behavior. I wish I was naive enough to believe he was scolding her because she wasn't eating enough, but I'm not.

She smiles with appeasement and lets herself be led away to a table.

Curiosity hits, and I watch as Nathan goes through the line. He carries two plates and picks up a wider variety of foods. As anticipated, he takes his plates back to the table and begins to dig in.

I'm simmering with rage.

THE NUMBER of people giving Nathan the stink eye increases exponentially as the evening progresses. To keep an eye on him, I take to playing paper football with two of the older pups in the pack and let my peripheral vision do some of the work.

I'm about to win when Finn taps me on the shoulder. "We're taking a walk before Lena and I catch our flight."

"We're taking a walk." I nod and then flick the football through the kid's upright fingers, scoring the points I needed. "Good game, friends."

Finn leads me out of the pack's gathering space in the basement, outside around the far side of the house to the side stairs. Lena's tucked into the alcove, and I immediately freeze, drawing a small breath. She seems fine, but what's going on that Finn would have the three of us talk?

"If you don't kill him, I will," Lena says quietly.

Ahh. My little sister is feeling murderous.

I tuck my hands in my pockets to hide my clenching fists. "I'm working on some options that will satisfy my desire and, at the same time, keep us safe."

"Do it faster," Lena growls, the sound rising above the level we were talking.

"Faolan." Finn scolds with an underlying growl.

She shoots him a murderous look, and Finn, to my surprise, falls quiet.

"I'm serious, Deacon. He needs to, at the very least, get the fuck out of her life. But I've seen what he's done. . ." Lena shakes her head, and when her gaze meets mine, my darkness is reflected in her eyes.

Done to whom? My little sister's gift of past sight, as much as she hates it, comes in very useful when trying to hold someone's sins against them.

Her words stir my darkest corners, lifting the hollowness from within me and focusing on him. "What are you suggesting I do?"

"Kill him."

"Offer her an out."

Lena and Finn speak at the same time, and it's my little sister who knows I want the bloodshed.

I look to Finn. "The fact that you think I haven't offered her an out is really telling of your thoughts on me."

He may be amazing for Lena but fuck if he doesn't get on every one of my last nerves sometimes.

"Before you go jumpin' to conclusions" — Finn keeps a level tone — "offer her one last out, and then, if not, we take care of the threat."

The way he includes himself in the 'we' of taking care of the threat is both frustrating and kind. Finn wants to be family, and he is. His heart is in the right place. But I kill alone. This is my fight. My scum of the earth to torture and kill. My mat . . . I want to claim her, but it's impossible. I'm just acting in someone-I-care-about's best interests.

CHAPTER 24
HENRI

I'M TOTALLY GETTING FIRED. There's a new meeting on my agenda with Cade before the recap meeting we originally had scheduled. Nothing good will come from this.

Last night I could barely sleep. Tossing and turning, I couldn't get Nathan's behavior out of my mind. What on earth did he say or do before I got there? I can only imagine that the person asking for me did so because of Nathan.

There were so many people to offend. My face is heating, and that tight, tingling feeling of embarrassment starts in my shoulders all over again.

But two minutes before our meeting, I knock on Cade's office door.

It takes forty-five seconds before someone turns the doorknob. Seconds that I count out in my head, hoping to drop dead before this conversation can happen.

The door opens, but it's not Cade who lets me in.

It's Deacon.

Fuck. I really am getting fired. I close my eyes for a second and then cross the threshold.

"Hey, Henri." Cade doesn't look up from his computer. "Come on in, have a seat."

Out of habit, I plant my butt in the chair I've sat in hundreds of times before. It's almost comforting that something so familiar is here for me.

"I don't know where to start." Cade shrugs, looking at me as he closes his laptop.

Deacon closes the door with a soft thud, slowly twisting the handle so it doesn't click so loudly. He crosses behind me, and my hackles rise with how tense he feels. I know those feelings from our time together. When he's on edge like this he's hurting and sober. I almost ask if he needs to know the soup of the day, but now's clearly not the time. Deacon isn't my responsibility anymore.

"Am I fired?" I whisper.

Cade snorts. "No. You're not fired."

Even Deacon gives a small laugh and a shake of his head.

There's only a niggle of relief from those words. I'm not dumb enough to think this is going in a different direction than talking about Nathan. *At least I still have my job.*

"I've turned a blind eye for a long time, Henri. But that's ending now. Nathan is no longer welcome on pack property. As much as I would love to just issue the Alpha command that you need to break up with him and come to live on pack property, it would be an abuse of my gift." Cade draws a deep breath and lets it out, but it does nothing for the tension radiating from his side of the desk. "Henri, I know I don't have to tell you this isn't a healthy relationship."

Guilt and shame cool the fiery heat of embarrassment previously coursing through my body. I try and fail not to shuffle in my chair, but instinct makes me slouch down from the force of his presence.

"There's nothing I won't do to help you out of your

situation. I can send the sheriff's department with movers and members of Corinth Security to help you pack up and get your possessions. We can put you up in the extra suites in the house, or there's an extra cottage down with the pack if you'd like some separation and your own space." Cade's offer isn't unexpected.

"I —" The argument doesn't come.

I tilt my head back up to look at him rather than the desk in front of him.

"Henri, if you don't leave him, Nathan will kill you." His words are so assured, ringing with the truth in his conviction. "I called Dinah last night, and she saw it."

The gift of future sight, the polar opposite of Lena's gift, is wrong on occasion, and I don't want to believe it's the truth.

"I spoke with Nathan's last girlfriend." Deacon's voice is cold and concise.

My eyes flick to him. I didn't forget he was in the room, but I didn't expect him to speak.

"Then, with the rest of the night, I tracked down everything about Grace Morelli that I could find, and while the coroner's office wrote it off as an accident . . ." Deacon looks at me, his wolf's deep brown eyes calling to my wolf. "After seeing the bruises that Nathan's left on you, there's no fuckin' way that's true."

My wolf rises to the surface. *He's afraid. Deacon is afraid.*

Nathan's last girlfriend. She's dead. And Deacon spoke to her.

Beyond that, I could have sworn I smelled him outside the front door this morning. It was just a faint scent, so I figured I was crossing scents. *Did he stalk me . . . at home?*

Cade opens his laptop and spins his second monitor so that it's visible to me. He pulls up a small news article.

Local Woman Dies in Tragic Accident

It's maybe two paragraphs long without a picture, nondescript, and it would almost go without notice. A tragic yet uneventful news experience except to the loved ones involved.

Cade taps his track pad, and the screen refreshes to pictures of the automobile. Pictures from a police report and not the newspaper.

"Best guess." Deacon steps over and points to a picture of the driver's seat. "He swapped out the floor mat."

I lean in to get a better look at what he's pointing to. The car's interior is a cream color, and the floor mat is gray.

"The mat got hung up in the brake pedal, so it couldn't be depressed. Without the ability to brake when she went around a curve, there was no way for her to navigate safely, and the car went over the embankment." Cade navigates to the next photo. The car sits mangled among rocks at the bottom of a steep hill. "The car flipped at least once, probably twice, before it ended up at the bottom."

Before hitting the button again, he warns me, "The rest of what Deacon found is a little graphic."

A blonde woman is lying on a steel table. Bruising mars her face and neck.

Cade zooms in on a portion by her neck and ear. "This is fingerprint bruising." The next picture is of her side and arm. "Broken ribs, unlikely sustained during the crash. She was wearing her seat belt, but these were on her left side."

"The coroner conveniently did not take photos." Deacon's voice is harsh with an undercurrent of a frustrated snarl. "But he noted unrelated bruising on her inner thigh."

The implication of that last statement takes me back to our time at the Wisconsin house when I ran there for safety. But Deacon spares me the disgrace of drawing comparisons out loud.

"A wolf might have survived this." Cade pauses as he closes out the files. "But I doubt it. Grace was half dead before the curve."

If I hadn't been speechless before, I am now.

Nathan told me his last girlfriend cheated on him and that he blocked her on social media. I didn't even do my due diligence and check into that story.

Who would lie about that sort of thing? Who lies and says they blocked their girlfriend on social media when she's dead instead? *Nathan? No . . .*

I shake my head in disbelief.

The other alternative is that . . . Cade and Deacon are lying. What motive would they have . . . *Because Deacon wants me for himself? No.* I brush a flyaway hair out of my face, trying to keep some semblance of calm.

"I need to think about it." For the first time in the conversation, I pull a coherent sentence together. *There's got to be some rationale here.* "This is a lot."

Cade purses his lips, then pulls them into a thin line, and his nostrils flare. "Don't wait too long, Henri. He was vocal yesterday about how much he disliked wolves and that we'd host an event like this."

"I'm so sorry that happened." The apology comes out second nature. "Obviously, I completely respect you not wanting him here anymore."

Deacon steps back from the desk and returns to the window.

Silence between the three of us is tense, but Cade breaks it.

"Why don't you go get ready for this morning's debrief. Think it over. I won't let this be you, Henri."

"I understand." I can't flee Cade's office fast enough. My heart hammers in my chest, and I nearly run to my office.

I have twenty minutes to pull myself together after our meeting, and I take it to organize my things and stare off into space, trying to center myself and focus on the task at hand.

I'm not fired. It's going to be okay. That doesn't stop the images of Grace haunting my mind. *Could Nathan have done that?*

Those twenty minutes pass in an instant, and the five-minute reminder on my meeting app reminds me that I've got to go be the pack publicist.

Fear of being late drives me across the hall and into the library, where we handle our group meetings. I sit in my usual space as the teams filter into the room and take their chairs. No one says anything or looks any different than any other day. Last night is seemingly not a topic of concern.

I draw a slow, calming breath. *At least I've got that going for me.*

"Good morning, everyone," Meaghan says, walking into the library with her usual folders and tablet keyboard setup. She takes her normal seat next to where Cade will sit when he arrives, Finn already seated at his other side. "Cade is running a bit late today. He told us to cover some of the basic items that quote: 'he doesn't know anything about anyway.'"

A chorus of laughter rises around the room.

"Okay, so Cade obviously wants to handle the thank-you and appreciations himself. Finn, did you want to start with the talk about the security updates?"

"No, we need to hold on that." Finn shakes his head. "The electronic component makes this awful fuckin' high-pitched dog whistle noise the humans didn't know about because they can't hear it."

"Oh no." I cringe just thinking about the pain that must have put him through.

Meaghan goes down the meeting agenda. "That means we can discuss clean up and prep for March Equinox."

The discussion is straightforward, and I'm following along taking notes, knowing there isn't anything I need to do for this part because I have a whole person on staff for events like this.

Cade strolls through the door, and in the silence between topics, he greets us. "Thank you for starting the meeting without me. I appreciate your flexibility in my arrival."

"Excellent timing." Meaghan smiles. "We were just about to start the next line item."

"Well, I'll have to cut this meeting short, but let's cover the important bits, and we can make the rest of the meeting, that probably could have been some emails, into an email." Cade laughs.

"Fuckin' Christ," Finn mutters under his breath.

"Thank you all for your work in making yesterday flow without any issues. Obviously, I was concerned about the potential of a mauling, but the only one who got even a little dinged up was my ego when the one article called TL 'cute.'" Cade wrinkles his nose.

"In my team's defense, they did catch the attempt to misgender and misidentify TL and Thalia." I laugh and cover my mouth with my hand. "Apparently there's a notion that all black wolves are male."

Cade rolls his eyes, and Finn snickers. The rest of the table takes the cue, and we all give it a little laugh, easing off some tension.

"Food and beverages were delicious. I probably ate a pan of lasagna all by myself. But we should make sure that every kitchen that contributed to the event receives extra thanks, maybe some sort of gift card because we all know they're not going to accept cash, and getting receipts is already like pulling teeth." Cade laughs and looks at the group. "Somethings never change." He runs his hand back through his hair. "On less positive news, Deacon is taking a leave of absence effective immediately. Henri and Meaghan, coordinate to figure out how to transition his appointments to myself and Thalia. Last resort, please push things to Finn's and Lena's calendars."

Kyle clears his throat next to me, and I shoot him a glare. The mystery of what just happened is a bigger deal than him feeling slighted that Cade didn't address him for this.

No reason or timeline is given for Deacon taking leave, and I don't ask.

"Let's adjourn there. Email Meaghan, please, any meeting things that we all need to be aware of. We'll get everything regrouped and hashed out. But I've got to move on with my day, or I won't get to see my mate for dinner." Cade smiles and gestures toward the door.

We all rise to leave him at the table, and Cade says lowly, "Meaghan and Henri, stay, please."

Finn follows the other meeting participants to the door and closes it behind them before returning to the table with us.

"Deacon needs some downtime. He's not doing awesome. I'm hoping a week and he'll be back to normal, but let's go ahead and give him a bit more than that just to be safe." Cade scrubs his hands down his face.

What happened after I left last night? Or is this because of the meeting we just had? Guilt wiggles against the back of my brain. I bite my lip against the desire to ask all the questions. *I could go up and talk to him.*

No. My wolf stops me. *Don't question the Alpha.*

"It's been a long time coming." He breathes out a heavy

sigh. "I shouldn't have asked him for so much so fast." Cade pauses but looks between me and Meaghan. "Are there any major issues that we need to hash out right away? Large events that have overlap?"

My fingers are shaking as I open my tablet to Deacon's calendar. The screen refreshes slowly, and I then overlay Cade's schedule on top of it.

"Henri." Finn speaks lowly to me. "This was coming long before last night and the interaction with Nathan. Don't feel responsible for this."

I knew everyone knew about last night. Hell, Finn was there to stand behind Cade as his Second, but why did I think maybe no one noticed? I fight back whatever sting is making my eyes want to water.

My lack of belief in his words is monumental. Deacon was fine until yesterday evening. But I just nod and pretend to accept his words because he wasn't there in the hallway. All Finn saw was Nathan. He has no way of knowing. He didn't see the pain in Deacon's eyes when he begged me not to go.

How isn't this all my fault?

CHAPTER 25
HENRI

WHERE THE FUCK are my suppressants? I know I picked up a bottle. I'm positive I had the shipment sent to the pack house for delivery and I brought half of them home like always.

They weren't in the bathroom cupboard with Nathan's aspirin stuff. Not in the kitchen cupboard where I had the last bottle. Drawing a deep breath, I dump my purse out on the dining room table and look at the contents. Maybe I hadn't put them away yet?

But I'm positive I did. It doesn't make sense that I wouldn't have, at least by now.

The purse definitely does not contain the amber bottle they come in. I open all the side pockets, even though they're too small for the bottle, just to be sure.

Maybe I left them in the car?

Grabbing my car keys, I head to the garage. Today was a clusterfuck with my meetings with Cade and Deacon, and then Deacon taking a week off. Now this?

Could today get worse?

"Henri, where you going?" Nathan calls.

"I'm just looking for something." I leave the door open behind me so he can hear that I'm, in fact, not leaving for a random excursion he didn't get advanced notice of. I learned that lesson.

I check under the driver's seat and am walking around to the passenger side of my car when I see him standing in the door. I give him a small smile.

"What are you looking for?" He leans against the doorframe, crossing his arms in front of his broad chest.

There's a dark look in his eye. The look he gets before things get bad.

My wolf cowers.

"My heat suppressants." I shrug, trying to brush off his dark gaze, and open the passenger side door. "I know I picked up a bottle. But I can't find it."

"I tossed them." Nathan's nonchalant words stop me cold.

Standing here, with the door to my car open, all I can do is look at him. Dread coils inside me, and I stare at him, hoping it's a lie.

"Why would you do that?"

Nathan sighs and rolls his eyes. "You don't need them. Remember?"

I draw a deep breath. "Uhm, could you remind me why I wouldn't need them?"

"Well." He pushes off the doorframe and steps toward me. "We talked about this last night. I'm going to service you through heat. You don't need a wolf to help you through them, baby. I'm man enough for you."

I shake my head. This isn't about him. Maybe if I reassure him, then it'll be okay, and he'll give them back. "Nathan, this doesn't have anything to do with you being able to service me through heat. My heat doesn't make you any less good enough for me."

Nothing can stop the panicked beating of my heart. My wolf thrashes inside me, upset by the fear flooding my system.

"It's not natural to be on those things. Who knows how they affect your body? Maybe it's why you're not feeling good enough to come to the gym with me." He keeps advancing toward me.

He closes the car door. We're nearly chest to chest.

"Nathan, I need suppressants so I can work." I shake my head, looking up at him. I soften, trying to give him puppy eyes. "Heat is a little over a week of unproductive time. You wanted to be saving for a vacation, for my birthday next month, remember? If we take that time off now, that could mess with the trip."

"You said we could go away for the weekend now that your job is settling down again. You said your boss is giving you time off. Now's the perfect time to do this." His hand comes to the side of my face. "You want to have fun with me, don't you, baby?"

"Of course I do, but heat isn't just a long weekend." I try to explain. "I'm going to start having symptoms, and it's going to make other wolves want me. It's going to make it hard to work for a few days until I go fully into heat, and then it's a week of heat and a few days of recovery afterward. Not just a couple of days where I'm going to be horny. It's not simply a weekend in bed. I would need someone to be with me all the time."

"I trust you, baby," he says. "You wouldn't let anyone sweet talk you into bed. It's like you've said, you'd never cheat on me. Especially not with your boss."

My wolf pushes a picture of Deacon forward. His beautiful wolf. *Oh, yes, we would.*

"It doesn't work like that. This isn't something I can push

through. I don't need to be around people. I would need to be with you, my partner, the entire time from when I started having symptoms until I was done." I draw a deep breath, pushing her wants out of the way. "Nathan, this isn't safe. I need those meds."

Instantly I know those words didn't come out appeasing enough. My frustration and fear bled into my tone, and I offended him.

Nathan shoves his hands in his pockets and works his jaw. "They're gone, Henri. I flushed them."

My wolf's thrashing in moments like these has always been driven by her anger, and my reaction has always been fear. But for the first time, that's flicked off like a light switch. Rage replaces fear.

"No." I shake my head, jaw clenched together.

He's gone too far.

Cade and Deacon's concern slams into the forefront of my mind. Cade warned me not to wait too long before making a decision.

Nathan killed her. Cade and Deacon weren't lying. He killed her, and I sure as fuck won't let him kill me.

Retreating away from him, I walk the long way around the car. Nathan's heavy footsteps follow me, but I barely hear him over the pounding of my pulse. I practically sprint into the house and slam the door in his face between us. With shaking hands, I scoop my purse off the table and haphazardly throw everything in it just as Nathan comes through the door.

"What are you doing?" Nathan's voice rises and falls with the question.

I can't answer him. I'm too angry to even open my mouth. I storm to the bedroom and pull out an overnight bag. Grabbing things from hangers and drawers, I stuff clothes in until the bag is full.

When I snatch it off the bed to storm past him, Nathan grabs the bag, trying to stop me. "Henri! What the fuck are you doing?"

"Leaving!" I snarl back.

My wolf rises to the surface, and despite shifting yesterday, she could almost burst from within.

Seeing her in my eyes causes Nathan to drop the bag.

I grab my purse and work bag and head out to my car as quickly as I can without running. I shove everything in through the driver's door, not wanting to take any more time.

"You can't fucking leave me!" Nathan screams. "You don't get to leave me."

He's almost caught up with me, almost. But I slam the car door and manage to shove the key into the ignition despite the tremors racking my body. When I crank it, the beater purrs to life like it has for the last six months, and I back it out of the garage as fast as I dare.

Nathan bangs on the hood, screaming at me.

I make it down the block before tears pour from my eyes. I wipe them away, alternating hands on the steering wheel as I navigate out of our neighborhood. I attempt to take a steadying breath, but it doesn't do much to soothe me.

The photos Cade showed me barrel into my mind.

Fuck, should I even be driving this car? My hands are still shaking when I look at the steering wheel. But I'd only been home for like five minutes. The car got me home . . . it'll get me wherever I need to go.

Where am I going to go?

My wolf instantly brings up the Wisconsin house. The living room chats with Deacon, lying on the couch, looking at the ceiling.

Deacon doesn't want to be bothered. I shut that idea down. *No. His bike was in the garage when I left work. He's not there anyway.*

Going there without him no longer feels right either.

Back to the Pack house? A hotel?

I draw a ragged breath and head north back to the Pack house, back to work, and back to Cade's offer. Subsequently, back to where Deacon is too.

Embarrassment heats my face again as I relive yesterday evening and the shame from this morning. It washes over me, sending shivers throughout my body and blurring my vision.

My phone is blowing up with dozens of message notifications and phone calls. The incessant buzzing in my purse is driving me nuts but also has me pressing the gas pedal harder as I pass exit after exit.

By the time I get to the front gate of Pack Alden's property, my phone has either died, or Nathan has given up. It's a welcome reprieve.

"Henri, you're back?" the guard at the front gate questions. "Are you okay?"

"I'm . . ." I shake my head, feeling incredibly awkward. Clearly, I look like I've been crying. My voice trembles. "I'll be fine. I'm just, I've gotta meet with Cade."

"Absolutely. Sorry!" He jogs away from my car to open the gate in a hurry.

The guard ratted me out. I know he did because by the time I make the short two-minute drive to the main house, Cade is leaning against the garage.

I pull my car off to the side space in front of the house, where I usually park during the daytime. It's not like I've never been afraid of Cade. I was terrified of him in the beginning, but in the almost year I've worked with him, I've come to learn that Cade's 'intimidating presence' is really the work of me meddling with the media to get him to appear larger than life, along with wolf traditions and lore working in my favor.

That doesn't stop me from feeling like a disappointment to

my superior. I draw a deep breath, my shaking finally subsiding. Forcing down all the negative personal feelings, I put forward my best professional self before opening the door and walking around the car.

With his hands tucked in his pockets and a soft smile, he doesn't seem so intimidating. There isn't an 'I told you so' look of superiority.

Thankfully Cade doesn't make me say it.

He gestures to the car with his elbow. "Can I help you carry anything in?"

"I can get it." My voice cracks pathetically, and I brush more tears out of my eyes.

I'm trying so hard to hold it together. But . . . I'm alone.

The suddenness of that thought setting in stings. All the people — friends and my adoptive parents — I've lost touch with over the years catch up to me at once.

Cade steps forward and unexpectedly wraps his arms around me.

My muscles lose some of their tension, and my wolf settles. I don't feel completely better, but I don't feel so alone.

"You're gonna be okay." Cade's voice rumbles through his chest. "It's been a shitty twenty-four hours, but we'll get you settled in for the weekend, and come Monday, it'll be better."

I nod, stepping away from him, and wrap my arms around my middle.

Cade heads to my car and looks in the windows. He opens the passenger door and grabs my bags from the front seat.

"I'll coordinate with security and the sheriff. Don't go get your stuff without them." Cade warns me. "Lauren's making up a suite on the second floor."

"He's going to want the car back." I look at the silver car behind me.

"Good." Cade smiles, and I almost swear he laughs.

"Deacon's gonna be so fuckin' glad this thing is gone. I'll get a vehicle on order for you tomorrow. You can use Lena's red one in the meantime."

I manage a small laugh. It's not like Deacon's distaste for my little car has been a secret, but I think Cade probably heard more about it than I did.

When we walk into the house, it's alive with activity.

"We're about to have dinner," Cade says, kicking his shoes off and setting my bags down. "If you'd like to eat with us, you're more than welcome to."

Shame heats my face, and I feel conflicted. I'm starving, not having eaten since lunch, but what is everyone going to think?

"Henri!" Lena shouts from the kitchen. "Finn is making that thing with the sauce that you like."

"So descriptive." Thalia giggles.

Cade leads me around the corner, and I see the two of them sitting at the countertop, watching as Finn commands the pans on the stove.

There will be perks to being single. I can make whatever I want, I lament, watching Finn.

Then hope flutters in. *I can find someone who cooks for me now.*

My wolf looks for Deacon in the opposite way I am. She longs for him, but I'm dreading facing him. I know it'll come sooner or later.

"Stay with us and eat," Finn says as he starts dishing up five plates. "Deacon isn't coming down anytime soon. I saw him cart what I'm pretty sure equates to seven days' worth of junk food up to his room this afternoon like he's some sort of rodent."

Thalia snorts. "I think we should probably send up some actual food over the weekend."

"If we don't, it makes him come out when he's really

hungry." Lena disagrees. She pats the stool next to me. "Come on. If you don't sit and eat, I'll eat your portion for you."

Part of me wants to decline the offer, but the normalcy of them all together feels good, and my empty stomach demands food. There's all weekend to mope.

Yellow Sage
Lantana camara

MARCH

CHAPTER 26
HENRI

By the time dinner rolls around, I've had enough of today, and I'm just ready to go upstairs, curl up in my bed, and stare at the ceiling until I fall asleep. Except the kitchen is full, and there's no way I'm just going to be able to casually steal my ice cream out of the freezer and dart off to my room.

"Well, I spun around on that tabletop so fast and, being more than a little tipsy, fell right into that handsome man's lap. It wasn't even six months later, and he was askin' my momma for my hand in marriage." Ms. Gertie, the elderly human adopted by Pack Alden, tells a story.

Her eyes are lit up, and everyone's laughing.

"Ms. Gertie, so scandalous, dancing on a table like a floozy." Lena laughs, and Ms. Gertie shakes her tea towel at her.

"There she is!" Ms. Gertie sees me, and I get a megawatt smile. "Cade told me I just got myself a new neighbor. He also said that, unlike himself and Thalia, you fancy yourself a morning tea drinker. I may be able to convince you to sit on the front porch and share a cup with me every morning."

That sounds so comforting.

I nod. "I'd like that very much."

It's no wonder they all love her. Ms. Gertie has this 'mom vibe' I can't quite figure out.

"Well, come on now, sit down. I gave Lauren the night off. She's got a date." Ms. Gertie wiggles her shoulders excitedly. "I made chicken and waffles because ya'll don't seem to have any place here that serves it worth its salt."

Despite how exhausted I feel and how low my energy level is, I sit at the counter next to Lena and watch Ms. Gertie finish cooking. Not even five minutes later, Cade and Thalia walk in the back doors, and then two minutes after that, Finn comes down the hallway from the offices.

Deacon? I want to ask. But it's been a week since Cade told me he needed some time off. And I haven't seen or smelled him.

"Alright, before we get too far into relaxing for the evening." Finn pauses and waits until I'm looking at him. "I'm going with you and the sheriff's department to get your things from Nathan's house tomorrow. I've set aside four hours, and we're bringing two of the sentries. So, if you've any furniture or anything, we've got enough hands to move it. If you'd like, we can have the sheriff's office send a notice to Nathan and let him know, asking him not to be there during that time. However." Finn shakes his head. "I don't think that's a good idea. If we make him aware we're coming, it may escalate things further. I want to be sure we get everything in one go."

With a nod, I struggle to come up with anything to say. My shoulders tighten, and I try to think through where everything of mine is in the house so we can get it all at once and not miss anything, but I can hardly breathe.

Lena rests her hand on my shoulder. "Don't stress out about it. Finn told me I couldn't come because apparently you shoot an ex and can't be trusted."

Thalia snorts. "According to Finn, it was two."

She jumps off her stool, almost toppling over, and Cade mutters something under his breath as he reaches for her. He guides Thalia around the counter and starts the assembly line to make plates from the dishes Ms. Gertie stacked her hard work on.

"Listen . . . The first one pissed me off, and the second one knew that and still chose to be stupid. It's different." Lena rubs her back and picks up a plate.

"I'm sorry, you shot two of Finn's exes?" Cade sounds outraged, turning around in the line to look at Lena. "Are you trying to —"

"It wasn't Finn's ex." Lena cuts him off with a sharp snap. "And again, they were stupid."

Finn pats my shoulder and gestures for me to follow Lena rather than him through the line. The break from protocol makes me uneasy, but he hands me a plate and insists.

"Well, I guess we're even then for the burnt grilled cheese." Cade sighs.

"Accidental arson, attempted murder, potato, tomato," Thalia adds.

I cannot believe what I'm hearing. I'm just grateful none of this made it to social media.

Drawing deep breaths, I force my shoulders down from around my ears and unclench my jaw.

"And you all thought me dancing on a table was scandalous." Ms. Gertie's voice is right behind me.

Finn put Ms. Gertie before him in line, completely throwing off the whole traditional hierarchy I've been learning from the pack.

"Ms. Gertie." Cade, waiting at the end of the line for the rest of us to fill our plates, puts a hand on his chest and feigns indignation. "The impropriety. We draw the line at public indecency."

"Oh, okay." Lena rolls her eyes. "I guess it depends on what you call public, then. Shall I remind you there's a trail camera at the gun range?"

"Cade!" Thalia gasps.

"Like you could even see anything." Cade snorts but looks at Thalia adoringly. "There's no way she or Deacon could see anything."

Thalia shakes her head, her face bright pink.

I feel secondhand embarrassment on her behalf.

There are so many cameras . . . Lots of opportunities to be kind of caught.

Fuck. That shouldn't be hot.

Rather than eating in a long line at the counter on the stools, the six of us sit at one of the big round event tables in the formal dining room.

Butter, syrup, and jam are on the table already. Cade and Finn take trips back to the kitchen and return with decanters of milk, juice, and water.

"I was promised a mimosa." Lena eyes Finn as he sits down.

"Yes, you were." Finn smiles at her. "I figured you'd like that with the rest of your reward tomorrow morning after church."

Lena raises an eyebrow but picks up her fork.

It's been fascinating to watch their relationship. Looking at them, it's hard to reconcile the way they are now and the early days of their relationship. Sometimes they communicate almost entirely without words. But then there are times when I'm fairly certain Lena might shoot him.

Deacon should be here. My wolf looks at his family, and we can't help but miss him. It's strange spending time with his family without him.

They're my employers, and I've been with them less than a year, but with how much time I've spent with them, sometimes I feel like I belong.

But in a couple days, I'll be moved into a cabin and have that separation of work and . . . well, a life, I guess. For now, though, the hospitality and the fun family dynamic are a good distraction from the hollow of loneliness carved in my heart.

CHAPTER 27
HENRI

"So . . ." Kyle quickly sits in the chair across from my desk like he's been commanded to do so.

He and I didn't have a meeting scheduled, but I set aside what I was working on because having Kyle manage Deacon has come with a bunch of impromptu meetings I can't ignore.

It's been over a month, and Kyle isn't getting any better in his role. And that's with Deacon behaving himself. The one time I let Kyle try to handle something on his own, Deacon nearly missed a flight.

Worse than that, Deacon's been on sabbatical for nearly three weeks. All Kyle has to do is manage Deacon's social media. It's literally pictures that have been taken and curated over the last six months. He just needs to add captions and load them into the scheduler with some base engagement like commenting back . . . He's just not great at this.

Kyle chews on the bottom of his lip, broadcasting his nerves. You can read him far too easily. It's why he can't be forward facing with the public by handling any of Cade's meetings. The sharks that circle Cade would eat him alive.

Realistically, I know he couldn't handle Finn and Lena either. Especially now that there's a general knowledge and murmuring that they're tied back to Ireland and subsequently may have connections to organized crime, which, weirdly, Cade isn't concerned about.

With a deep breath, Kyle rushes his words out. "See, you told me to give Deacon two or three weeks off. But the last time I saw him, he was a little checked out. It's been more than almost two and a half weeks, and I can't pin him down. He stopped answering his phone a few days ago. I'm wondering if maybe we need to ask Cade for some help?"

At the mention of Deacon, my wolf perks up. It's been a long week, and she's been completely fried with the pack meetings for planning the coming Equinox.

I didn't know Kyle was talking to and seeing Deacon?

Sure, I moved into the cabin over a week ago, but I still haven't seen or smelled Deacon on the main floors while I'm at the house for work.

"He, uh." Kyle fishes for words. "He . . ."

I shake my head, not sure I'm understanding what he's even trying to begin to communicate. I circle my wrist, trying to encourage him to talk to me. But unsettledness roils in my stomach.

Kyle finally spits it out. "I haven't seen him in five days. I've gone upstairs, but his door is locked. Neither the keycode I have nor the key works."

My heart stops. I'm pretty sure it stops dead.

I grab my phone out of my desk drawer and run to Cade's office. He's in a meeting with Finn, but it's not super important. I push the door open without knocking, which gets me two guns drawn on me.

"Have you seen Deacon in the last forty-eight hours?" I

snap, trying to draw a deep breath. Neither of them moves. "Seventy-two hours?"

Cade's furrowed brow and Finn's shrug tell me everything I need to know.

"I need the master override to Deacon's door," I order, snapping my fingers, and what I'm saying finally sinks in.

Up and out of his chair, Cade pushes past me and takes the stairs two and three at a time. Running, I try to keep up but nearly fall. Finn follows me rather than overtaking me on the stairs. He doesn't bother telling me it's going to be okay.

Cade's fist on Deacon's door rattles the pictures hanging in the hallway, and he panics waiting for a response.

It doesn't come.

Cade punches in a code on the keypad, and the door opens for him without effort.

"Are you fucking kidding me?" Cade shouts.

"What the fuck?" Deacon snarls, and only then do I breathe.

Approaching Deacon's door, I don't know what to expect. It's black-out dark in his room, and I hesitate to cross the threshold.

The blinds get yanked open, and Cade shakes his head, looking at Deacon's mess.

"We talked about this." Cade starts scolding. "You told me you were done with this shit."

I look to where Cade's pointing on the desk, and drug paraphernalia litter the surface. I haven't even seen Deacon yet, but based on the syringe, I'm not sure I want to.

Finn tugs on my hand. "Come on, Henri. Let's let the boys have their minute."

CHAPTER 28

DEACON

CADE KNOWS how to kill a buzz faster than anyone else. The Leviathan rises to the surface, and all the fluffy feelings that were finally taking hold start to evaporate. I grab a pen and paper off my desk to write myself a note.

Pulling the pen out of my hand, Cade snaps, "No one's heard from you in days."

"And that's my problem?" I laugh, running a hand back through my hair. It's gotten long and tangles a bit around my fingers. "I told you what I was doing. You asked me to do it here rather than go to the Wisconsin house. You don't get to be upset that I did exactly what I told you I was going to do."

Cade grabs my wrist and rolls my arm over, revealing the injection sights in my arm. As quickly as he grabbed me, he lets go, shaking his head with a grimace.

I wince, pulling away from him. My lip curls up into a snarl, and I force it down. "Skip the fucking lecture. It's just going to piss us both off more than we already are. What do you want? I thought I had a couple days before I was back to being your lap dog."

I clench and unclench my fists. Drawing deep, ragged breaths, I hold everything back, struggling against every fiber of my being that demands to lash out and release some of the emotions I've kept bottled up about him, about this, locked away.

In the silence of my struggle, there's a shift in the room.

Cade's anger fizzles out as he tucks The Leviathan away. It leaves us with cold, sharp fear and sweet sorrow, not putrid pity.

Even his voice changes as it drops in volume and tone. "What can I do, Deacon?" He pulls me into a hug. "I'm sorry. Fuck. I'm sorry."

I hadn't realized how long I'd been isolating until Cade's touch grounds me.

It's like he's remembered I'm a person.

"I can't keep doing this anymore," I murmur into his hug. "I've tried so fucking hard with the ancestors and now with her. I'm sick of spending my days questioning what's real and waiting for some intervention."

He nods against my head. "What do you need, Dea?"

"I . . ." Pushing away from him, I draw a deep breath.

Cade lets me go but watches, interested, focusing on me.

I pace, trying to keep myself focused on the present situation above the thrum of other thoughts running through the back of my mind. "I don't want you to think this is just something I came up with one night and thought, ah, fuck it, why not?"

"Okay. Walk me through it." He encourages.

Who is this guy? I know it's my brother because I've seen him before. I've seen Cade be this person before, but never toward me.

"Revecca made the ancestors stop when she was here." I

look away from him. "It's been months of thinking about what she did to me and how good it felt. Cade, she cut open my hand, and it was days before I saw them again. It was . . ." I scrub my hand down my face, yawning, jaw creaking as I release the tension. "I've spent weeks trying to figure out how to ask you about this." I laugh because what else can you do in a situation like this? "High Deacon has run through every single scenario of how this conversation could pan out between us."

Panic quickens my heart rate again as I try to push down the thoughts, feelings, and emotions in anticipation of how Cade might respond to what I'm about to say.

"I don't want to be a wolf anymore." I let the words drop. "I don't want the gift, and if the gift comes with the wolf, then I'm okay giving up the wolf too."

Cade's eyebrows shoot up in surprise. He waits for more information cocking his head to the side.

But my words end there. There's no more for me to say.

"Well, I don't want to be unsupportive, but while you were" — Cade gestures to me from head to toe — "busy. Your mate broke up with her boyfriend. So, maybe don't ditch the wolf as the first-choice option, maybe hold that for after a conversation with Revecca about how to possibly make your gift more manageable?"

In the thousands of scenarios I've run through my head about this conversation, not once was this a potential outcome. I come to a full stop, standing there looking at him as he watches me.

"Shit," I hiss.

"Changes some things, huh?" Cade runs his hand back through his hair.

The wolf is still numb inside me. Awake, alive, but numb. It'll be a while before he truly comprehends.

It's weird leaning on Cade for answers, but I try. "What do I do?"

He pulls out his phone and checks the time.

There's daylight outside and it's March, so chances are it's an acceptable hour for him to make the call. Assuming he's dialing Revecca.

Revecca's voicemail picks up with information on how to contact her staff in Romania.

"Put me on a plane. I'll figure it out when I get there. How hard can it be right?" I blow out a raspberry, feeling more like maybe I should sleep it off before I make any big decisions.

But some impulsivity might be the answer to the calculated approach I've had to everything.

Henri broke up with Nathan. Should I talk to her first?

Cade rolls his eyes but continues this weird dynamic of support in an unexpected direction. "To be honest, I'm only saying yes to that plan because she waltzes in here like she owns the place, so it's only fair one of us does the same. And you're probably the best man for the job to cause equal amounts of chaos."

He's not wrong.

"Go get washed up." Cade wrinkles his nose.

I look down and catch a whiff of my scent. Lena's voice echoes with the thought, *ew.*

"What day is it?"

"Saturday. It's been almost three weeks since Lunar New Year," Cade answers, giving me a frame of reference.

"Nice." I nod, getting my bearings. Some things don't change, though, so I cock my head toward my desk. "Since I know you're going to invade my privacy and toss out the heroin. The stash is in the top desk drawer, and my sharps container is behind the door. Don't yell at Dinah. She's trying to be a good nurse."

I turn to leave to do what will make him feel better.

"Can I —" Cade stops himself from calling me back. "Nah, go get washed up."

"Ask." I stop and turn back to face him.

"Sometimes you're not the same." He pauses and scrubs a hand down his face. "I should call Henri and have her give me a lesson on how to behave correctly with my own brother."

"I think you're asking why I don't always use heroin." I don't give him a lot of room to interject. "Cade, I haven't been as high as you think I have been for a very long time. I've been micro-dosing to keep things under control at the very least enough that I could function to be here if you ever really *needed* me." I gesture to the desk. "Throw it out, things are going to change. I just don't know how yet. Okay?"

"Deacon." Cade sighs. "All this time, you've been, what?"

"Well, not all the time." I smile at him, watching agitation and confusion cross his expression. "But yeah, there have been times I let you think I was in way worse shape than I was just so you'd deal with shit."

"Why am I not surprised?" Cade laughs, and the tension breaks again. "Go, you smell. I'll book your ticket."

Stripping out of my sweats and T-shirt, I toss them into the trash can. After you live in a pair of clothes for an extended period, they never seem to get clean enough to lose that lived-in stench. I've tried.

Despite Lena's disbelief in my laundry competency, I am quite good at getting stains and stench out of fabric, but sometimes it's not worth the effort. *I'm not worth the effort.*

I walk out of my bedroom after a shower, dressed in a fresh pair of jeans and T-shirt, heading to Cade's office to face the music of a stern but caring older brother. But my older brother did not leave my room. As expected, he cleaned up my desk, all drug paraphernalia out of sight and, I'm guessing, on its way to being destroyed.

He's gone above and beyond, all the way to sanitizing the surface of my desk based on the smell of disinfecting cleaner.

Now, in true control-freak, older-brother mode, he's going through my computer. Best guess, he's scrolling through my history, but after a few more clicks, he locks the computer and looks at me. "Booked you a ticket, first class, to Romania. Do I need to remind you of our international incident rules?"

"Don't get arrested. If I do get arrested, don't confess to anything. Call Peter." I list off the important rules.

There are others about not taking drugs from strangers and not taking something if I don't know what it is, but this isn't that kind of trip.

"Do you want me to go with you?" Cade offers, leaning back in my desk chair.

I wait for one of his tells, something to give me an idea of what he's thinking. He sits there neutral with a genuine offer.

"You'd really go with me?" I quirk an eyebrow, testing his resolve.

"Believe me or not, you are worth risking being trapped in Romania forever." Cade smiles. "I love you. You're my brother, and I only want you to be happy and healthy."

"Blood —"

"Fuck the fucking blood tests. I wish I had killed Robert more slowly for all this. You have always been, and will always be, my little brother." He locks eyes with me. "I know I fucked up putting too much on your shoulders. You were already drowning with trying to exist. You handling all the shit I left behind? I owe you more than you'll ever hold me accountable for."

"You aren't responsible for me being a fuckup." I try owning my actions, but that little part of me, the dark part, likes hearing Cade tell me I'm not responsible for everything I've done.

"You're not a fuckup, Deacon." Cade shakes his head. "The choices you've made haven't always been fantastic, but everything you do, you do because you're trying to survive."

We don't talk about me.

Cade and I haven't ever talked about me.

He's talked at me.

We've set ground rules that I walk right past ninety percent of the time.

But for the first time, I feel seen.

"If it turns out that being human is the only option, I get it if, like, that means I need to figure out how to get my mechanic's license and move out. A human living with wolves is a liability, and it's not like I'd be entitled to the fund." The hours of math I did the other day — week? Month? — start to sink in. Between the odd jobs and cash in my tins would sustain me for probably six months.

"I'm not throwing you out or taking away what's rightfully yours because you might not be a wolf anymore." Cade draws my attention back with a sigh. "But if you give up your wolf, and you get and stay clean and then decide you don't want to live here, or you feel this need to try and support yourself and do whatever you think it is you need to do in life . . . I'm not going to stop you as long as you're safe."

"Cade?" Thalia's voice comes from the door, and we turn to look at her.

She's trying to keep the panic to a minimum, but I hear her heart beating way too fast.

"I'm okay, little red." I reassure her. "It's just time for me to take a trip to dish out some payback to Revecca." I plaster on a smile for her. "Did you know that Romania has the most bears in all of Europe?"

"I didn't know that." Thalia's eyes are watering, and she does the little squirming of her toes against the floor when she's uncomfortable.

The high fades further, and guilt sinks in its place.

You hurt our friend. My wolf finds his way back to the surface. *And now we won't be here for our mate.*

CHAPTER 29
HENRI

NOTHING good ever comes from talking to Kyle. I've moved past the beginning stages of second-guessing and into complete, deep, sinking regret over hiring him and fear of firing him.

I can't even escape him when working from home. His name flashes on my caller ID, and before I even say hello, Kyle's voice chimes in.

"Hey, Henri."

"Hey Kyle, what's going on?" I answer, trying to keep the panic to a minimum.

Deacon was fine yesterday.

My wolf joins in on the panic I wasn't doing an awesome job containing. *What if he's not fine today?*

"I hate to bother you, but I sent you an email this morning and haven't heard back. I get it if this is too last minute and you want me to take up some slack somewhere else, but . . ." He pauses, clearing his throat. The tense silence makes me want to rush him or tell him to spit it out. "With Deacon in . . . on his way to . . . Romania? I guess I don't quite know the flight timelines. But I was thinking this is probably as good a time as any for me to take that vacation."

"Oh." I scroll through my inbox. The first email this morning is from Kyle. I look at the time-off calendar. "Wait, Deacon is in Romania?"

"Yeah? Cade told me it was fine. He didn't need a handler because if Deacon had an issue, it would be Revecca's problem as part of the royal family." Kyle pitches that sentence as a question like I'm going to dispute it.

Cade didn't run it by me. *Which means I wasn't supposed to know?* I correct that thought. *They didn't tell me because it's not my responsibility.*

I look over the extra workload, and anything I could give Kyle, he'd mess up. "I'll go ahead and approve that time off for you. Enjoy your week. I'll handle anything Deacon related in the event he returns while you're gone. Be sure to set up your out of office to go to the main inbox."

"Will do. Thanks, Henri." Kyle is quick to get off the phone, and I don't blame him.

Everyone likes some good time off.

I look from my 'workstation,' a stack of boxes supporting my laptop, to where I'm curled up on the couch with a water bottle and a mountain of sugary snacks. I should take some time off today to unpack and try to make the place homier.

The cabin Cade provided is quaint, and while starkly furnished, it's cozy. Even if I wanted to complain about it . . . I couldn't. It's everything you'd want in the cottage-core vibe waiting to be brought to life.

Lonely, my wolf notes.

But we've been living out here for a while, and we get companionship with Ms. Gertie every morning at 7:00 a.m. for tea and whatever baked goods she made the previous afternoon. I also do lunch every day with the Aldens. We're adjusting.

I'm cozied in, ready to get back to work, when a knock comes to my cabin door.

Closing my eyes, I debate ignoring it . . . but I can't. It would be rude because we're wolves, and besides hearing me, smelling me, and probably seeing me through the open blinds . . . everyone who would look for me knows I'm in my cabin today.

With a sigh, I push the boxes supporting my laptop to the side so I can get up. I leave my phone on the couch and cross the small space to the door. When I open it, Ms. Gertie is on my porch with a little tray in her hand.

She brushes past me, entering my cabin. "Now, I know you're going to object, but I won't hear anything of it. I didn't know your favorite, so I just went with what the good Lord said we were feeling today."

"What?" I turn and follow, letting the door fall closed behind me.

She sets the tray down on the counter and looks around my place. "Child, we need to move you in. It's not good to live in so much unkemptness. I've got a work order to paint your porch ceiling blue too. Deacon said it doesn't make a difference, but he's never seen a bad spirit in my house, so that makes me think maybe it does."

The words are fired a hundred miles an hour as she digs around in my kitchen drawers and then starts looking at the boxes on the ground around the kitchen.

"Ms. Gertie, what's going on?" I lean up against the kitchen island, studying her.

"Here we go!" She picks up a crock of utensils I took from Nathan's and sets them on the counter by the stove.

Then, grabbing a serving spatula, she pulls plates out of the cupboard she'd previously opened and closed and then forks out of the drawer. Ms. Gertie doesn't answer me but opens the box in the center of the tray.

She carefully lifts a little round cake out of the box. It's maybe four inches across, and on top is a little H decoration with green flowers.

No. I bite my lips together. Hot tears well in my eyes.

"Deacon said your birthday wasn't on the pack registry, and he told me it must be an oversight." Ms. Gertie turns the cake to face me. "But since it was today and rather last minute, we figured maybe you just didn't want a big fuss about it."

I swallow. I was the one in charge of putting the staff birthdays on the pack registry, and I purposefully omitted mine.

"Must be somethin' you don't like talkin' about, but there was no way I was going to break my record and not bake everyone a cake for their birthday." Ms. Gertie pulls the H off the top and quickly cuts into it. "Besides, I made a small one, no pictures, no singing songs. Just cake."

"Just cake," I whisper. *The first birthday cake I've ever had.*

Not because I never wanted one or because my parents never thought to get me one, but because I insisted on never having a cake as part of a long-standing history of not making a big deal out of it. But I guess at twenty-four years old, maybe I can start a new tradition.

CHAPTER 30
DEACON

It's not like Revecca said, 'Hey, when you're in Romania, look me up,' but it's also not like she said I couldn't visit. Cade made it a point not to tell Revecca I was coming as payback for her unsolicited visits. Neither of us was sure how this was going to work.

Off the airplane and ushered into customs with the rest of the passengers, I get flagged by one of the agents. He takes my passport, and with one quick look between it and me, he gives a curt nod. I'm then guided off to the side and into a secluded room.

I've got nothing to hide. I know way better than to take a flight to another country carrying anything illegal. That knowledge doesn't stop my heart from beating a little faster. I'm here for answers, and I sure as fuck don't want to be turned away before I get them.

Inside the more secluded room, another agent is reading something on a computer. The agent with me hands her my passport, and they both do the back-and-forth, double-checking my picture with the documentation silently before the woman pulls the phone off the hook.

The second customs agent, standing with the phone pressed against her ear, says nothing, and the faint sounds of hold music come from the receiver.

The first, holding my passport hostage, thrusts his chin toward me. "What is the reason for your visit?"

"Seeing family," I answer calmly.

I've been through the United States customs as a drug mule before, but something about this, doing absolutely nothing wrong, is making me significantly more antsy. There wasn't a security threat for me outside of the United States. Finn looked, Cade's people looked, I looked. There's no reason there should be any interrogations happening.

"And who is your family?" The agent on the phone raises a brow in my direction.

"Revecca Ardelean," I answer, flashing them my wolf.

God, that's got to sound ridiculous. Ah, yes. Here to see the queen.

Flying into the country in business class like a peasant and not a private jet is probably my first mistake, but I should have seen this coming.

Maybe I should have just said Vex O'Brien?

The woman on the phone starts speaking in, what an educated guess says is, Romanian.

"You'll come this way, sir." The man doesn't wait for whatever answers the woman on the phone is going to get.

Whatever she said was enough that he hands me back my passport. He leads me through another door, away from the main section of the airport.

It's not suicide if you're killed in a foreign prison when your honest intention is to just visit family, I remind myself, thinking about how angry Lena will be if this is me being led to my execution. But the longer we walk through back rooms and various hallways, the more nervousness starts creeping up the back of my neck.

I don't get nervous. I don't have the same healthy sense of fear the rest of the world has because I'm not afraid of dying. There's nothing for me to be afraid of because the 'worst' thing that someone can do is kill me. I already live in a hellscape of my mind, and dying would be an escape.

But the longer we go without seeing a single other person, the more my hackles rise. *What will Henri think if I don't come home?* That's the feeling. That's the worry.

No doors open. No break rooms or alcoves. It's just hundreds of feet of hallways before we're in a stairwell. I follow them down, and when I'm pretty sure this is the dark hole I'm going to get shoved in, forgotten about, and waste away and die in — if only I could be so lucky — the door opens to an underground parking garage, where a black town car is waiting.

Two men in black suits stand by the car and execute steep bows toward me.

The first opens the car door. "This way, Your Highness."

Not a fan of the title. I force down a grimace and instead give them a curt nod, mimicking Cade when someone treats him like royalty, before climbing in the vehicle.

Rotting in prison inside the royal palace is better than rotting away in one inside an airport. Probably. It sounds better, anyway.

"If you'd have given us notice, we could have been waiting for you at customs and gathered your bag. We did not know of your arrival." One of the men seems to be both chastising me and fishing for information at the same time.

As we drive through the city streets, I note the heavy traffic and turn on my cell phone. The time, early morning, gives me reason to believe this is Romanian rush hour.

The driver and, presumably, the guard — or security personnel or knight? I don't fucking know — talk in Romanian on the way to what I'm assuming is the royal palace. I open the map app on my phone, watching as we drive past landmarks.

Exactly forty-six minutes later, we pull up to expensive wrought iron gates, and the car rolls through with ease. It looks a lot like a mansion and a larger, grander-scale version of the sort of home the not-parents tried to recreate for our pack. It's pretty if you're into white exteriors and buildings with too many rooms and not enough occupants.

When the car pulls to a stop in front of the house, I'm not expecting a lot, but four people rush about, trying to figure out why I only brought a duffle bag. They ask me questions in Romanian, which I don't understand and, therefore, don't know the answers, and everyone seems to be suffering the same frustrations. We're seemingly paused halfway up the stairs leading to a door.

The flight of stairs is either full of some sort of reenactment or ancestors. Given that no one seems to pay them any attention other than me, I'm going with the latter. Just so long as none of them speak English, I should be safe.

I'm about to start saying Revecca's name on repeat, trying to figure out if I'm being brought into the house or thrown out of it, when a friendly face comes into view at the top of the stairs.

Well, friendly as in, he's been in my home before. Patrick, an acquaintance or friend of Finn's, has evidently been placed in Revecca's royal guard by Magnus O'Brien. And from what Ansel told me, Magnus and Revecca were married in some sort of secret union, and an Irishman as part of the Romanian royal guard is his compromise. Regardless of the circumstances, I'm happy to see someone who at least will be able to tell me some of what's going on.

"Deacon, Revecca wasn't expecting you." His voice booms, and his thick Irish accent makes me reconsider my ability to understand what's going on.

But the four men arguing around me stop and turn to look at him.

I laugh. "Payback is a bitch."

"So, your brother didn't send you?" He examines me, brows pulling together.

He looks at one of the men holding my sole duffle bag before tossing his head toward the house.

The man with the bag carries it up the stairs toward him.

"Definitely not." I nod and wholly embellish the conversation I had with him. "Distinctively, he told me that if I got stuck over here, he wasn't coming to rescue me. The fact that he loves me very much doesn't outweigh the belief he'd never escape Romania if he stepped foot in the country."

Patrick snorts a quick laugh. "She's holding court right now." He waves me up the stairs. "Let's get you cleaned up and presentable to her standards, and then I'll see if I can't pull her away."

With care, I navigate around the ancestors sitting on the stairs and allow myself to be led into the castle, down corridors and upstairs. I land in a massive bedroom.

"Wash the airport smell off you. I'll have a suit brought up. Any idea of your measurements?" He extends a business card. It seems like a weird accessory for a royal guard to carry and even weirder for someone who's a member of the Irish mob, but I take it anyway. "Text them to me."

The bustle of staff and guards is gone, and I'm left alone. Scoping out the place, I find a bathroom stocked with toiletries and a wardrobe consisting of a robe, cleaned, steamed, and hung pajamas in various sizes, and slippers also in various sizes. *Efficient.*

With the phone number off the card, I text the suit measurements, which I only know from working so closely with Henri. I wonder how on earth they're going to get one here so fast.

I at least brought a button-down shirt to go with my jeans. I'm not a complete heathen.

The bathroom door, thankfully, locks, and I don't waste time getting clean.

I have a mission for my time here in Romania: get in, get Revecca to do something about the wolf, get out.

THE WHITE LINEN shirt and Ardelean-blue vest are too bright for my taste, but when in Romania, so to speak. Deemed presentable now that I'm in a suit, I follow a staff member who speaks English and refers to themselves as similar to a concierge. They lead me to the throne room evidently.

Revecca's floor-length dress hides her delicate frame, and the crown on her head glistens in the light coming through the window. Revecca has never been what I considered comfortable when she comes to visit. She was normally stiff in demeanor and dressed in business casual. I now understand that was relaxed for her. Her current situation isn't 'her' as I'm familiar with, but it is 'her' at the same time.

Tension radiates from her like it does from Cade when he's crabby and needs to get laid.

The person she's speaking to bows and leaves.

I'm ushered forward to the long carpet that leads toward her. This feels like a scene from a movie rather than something that happens in real life.

"His Royal Highness, James D. Alden of the Harbinger Bloodline." A man in a black suit announces me.

Huh. Maybe I should have Revecca give me a title breakdown. I didn't expect to have one.

The fact that I'm being called Harbinger's Bloodline makes sense though. I'm not really Cade's brother — we were just raised together. I've said before that it's convenient for the only two Ardeleans who can't figure out where they came from at least have the decency to be blood related.

Revecca's lips twitch as she fights a smile, and she eyes a spot on the floor, indicating for me to approach. I do, walking slowly, hands in my pockets, until I'm standing before her while whispers flutter around the room.

"Is this the part where I'm supposed to bow?" I wrinkle my nose at her.

"Traditionally, yes. You're also supposed to wait until I address you." She corrects me, her voice low.

Pinching my fingers together, I mime running a zipper across my lips and bow. The etiquette lessons that Ebenezer and Karina beat into us slowly start to come back.

A woman dressed in a fluffy white dress and a black apron comes running forward, screaming at the top of her lungs, and flings herself down on the floor between me and Revecca. The lack of movement from the royal guards is a good indicator that I'm the only witness to this. It's heart wrenching.

"What brings you to the home country?" Revecca sighs.

I'm not her favorite person. And I admit I've done plenty of things to specifically provoke her, half in fun and half for the betterment of Cade's arguments. It's understandable.

"I want you to take my wolf."

A gasp comes from the people behind me.

Poker face intact, Revecca does and says nothing, but for the tiniest fraction of a second, there's a glint of something in her eye. If I hadn't seen her fight with Cade, I wouldn't have noticed it. Their snarling matches are legendary.

"No wolf, no gift, no problem," I explain as the silence, from the living, ticks by. I fight to keep my voice at normal speaking volume. Instinct is to raise it over the wailing woman, but I've had to learn throughout my life how to act as though the ancestors aren't there. "I'm being tortured by it. Enough is enough. I'm chasing the bliss of those days when you borrowed it."

"Toți afară," she says to the room, but her eyes don't leave mine.

Footsteps, shuffling bodies, and not-so-hushed murmurs file out around us through various doors.

"I can't believe he'd even dare to ask that of her," I catch one of the voices 'whispering.'

Well, if I do nothing else skillfully, I've got a knack for upsetting people.

I assume they're not an Ardelean and don't know what it's like to have a curse like this.

Even Cade, with The Leviathan, struggles on many levels. It would be too easy for him to slip into a dictatorship, which would go against what he believes, but The Leviathan is a monster craving blood and control. He's a machine built for a violent war in an era of civility and political games.

None of us are gifted, all of us are cursed.

Revecca stands from her throne and walks down the three short stairs, stepping through the ancestor and dissipating her, until she's standing before me. Her eyes lock on mine. *This is what she did to Lena. Maybe it'll be quick and painless.*

Revecca pulls her eyes from mine and then scrutinizes the rest of me.

"Why do you want to be rid of him? He's more than perfectly acceptable for you." She folds her arms in front of her chest and adopts the less-formal Revecca I'm more familiar with.

"Remember when you borrowed my gift without asking?" I level with her. *Was it as life changing to her as it was to me?*

"I recall." Her statement is short and unapologetic.

"It was the best four days of my fucking life." I make my plea, explaining the dream I've been chasing. "I slept for more than two hours, food had taste, and I could think and feel. It was better than any high I've ever had. More exhilarating than any toy or partner I've ever fucked."

She scoffs and holds her hand up. "You fully understand what you'd be giving up?"

Henri crosses through my thoughts. It's a montage of every smile she's ever given me and those little moments I've stalked her where she didn't know. The peaceful silences within her presence that quiet the roar of the thoughts in my brain.

I try to keep my resolve, and even though everything inside me is screaming not to, I answer her. "I understand."

"You're a bigger idiot than Cade." She walks a few small steps before she turns from me and begins pacing. "You've figured out she's your mate."

"Assuming. She hasn't been off suppressants since I met her, and I've been keeping myself more than a little blitzed," I answer and then turn on the offense. "But how would you know that anyway?"

How much did she see of Henri when she visited? Is this a Mother of Wolves thing or just an intuition thing? I decide against voicing those questions because the resulting overwhelm of information wouldn't be necessary given my ask of her.

"Do none of you know anything? I'm the Mother of Wolves. I know all wolves and their mates. I know every Ardelean and assign their gifts." Revecca scoffs. "Furthermore, don't be ridiculous. Of course she's your mate, suppressants or not.

Why wouldn't you be able to recognize her as such?" Revecca shakes her head like I'm being childish. "Given how long it's taken for you to bring your wolf to power claiming her may help you."

"I would rather give her up and give her a chance at a better life, a better mate, than go through life trying to get through each minute of every hour feeling like this," I tell her, fighting back the obstruction clogging my throat. I clench my fists and stare at the ceiling, trying to regain my composure. I told myself a hundred times I'd leave emotions out of this, but here we are. Returning my gaze to Revecca, I continue. "I know it sounds selfish. No, I know it is selfish, but if anyone is going to understand what it's like to want to do one thing for yourself for once, it's going to be you."

Revecca sets her jaw, and the thick, dense feelings of an Alpha wolf about to boil over permeate the room.

Brace for impact.

Coming to a standstill, Revecca turns to face me. Where I expected deadly calm, fury contorts her features. "Excuse me?"

"Oh, come on. Not too hard to figure it out." I raise an eyebrow at her. "Cade returns to Romania and to his rightful place on the throne, and that leaves you as . . . duchess, princess, or whichever, and Mother of Wolves. You wouldn't be tied to Bucharest and could be with Magnus."

"Lena?" Revecca narrows her eyes at me.

I shake my head. "Deductive reasoning. You're familiar enough with Finn that you screamed at him, but not in the awkward familiar way that you were fucking him at one point. So, most likely siblings. Finn has an older brother. Not too far of a jump." I can't help but smile. *I love being right.* "Then Lena confirmed it for me after the wedding."

"How is it you can figure that out but are completely

oblivious when it comes to your wolf?" Revecca draws a deep breath and begins walking again. "Come with me."

She leads me out of the throne room and into a courtyard. It's packed with people.

I hesitate, looking over the crowd. There aren't enough clues for me to be sure how many people are here. But Revecca starts walking through the crowd, and they dissipate.

"Is there a problem?" Despite the short question and direct phrasing, Revecca speaks with kindness.

She's an Ardelean. She understands my gift.

I try to fight down the embarrassment and disappointment that comes with freezing. "This part of your home is pretty haunted."

"Ah, at one point they held executions here." She nods knowingly and turns toward another door on a different wall from where we entered the courtyard. "This way."

Down several hallways, through doors, and past guards, who I know are real based on the clothing, we finally come to a chamber with a desk.

"As I did not receive advance notice of your arrival, I have a packed schedule for today. I would love to work with you and speak a bit more before I grant your request." Revecca stops at the desk.

"I don't have any plans. I'm guessing I'm on castle arrest?" I gesture to the giant house we're in.

She shakes her head. "Not necessary. You've been assigned royal guards. I encourage you to visit the city."

The tension in Revecca's face, the twitch in her jaw, and the stiffness in her shoulders are more obvious versions of Cade's 'I need to ask you something' pause.

"Is there something you'd like to ask me?" I try to handle her more carefully than I do Cade.

"It's just that I could perhaps have you . . ." Revecca gets a glint in her eye. "Crea un dezastru at dinner tonight?"

"Assuming that means what it sounds like." I snort before falling into a laugh. "There is one thing I'm good at, and it's being a near disaster."

Revecca bites her lips together before saying, "There are some other Ardeleans from out of town who could perhaps use a bit of the . . . *charm* you bring to a room."

"You want someone to tell them where to shove their bullshit?" I pause, waiting for more.

"If it isn't a bother." Revecca slightly backtracks. "We don't need to bother with anyone from the afterlife who may be connected to them, but just perhaps speriem?"

"Sounds dirty. I love finding exactly which buttons to push." I shrug and look back to the hallway. "Maybe I can get a nap in before dinner. Point me back to my suite?"

"Patrick will take you." She doesn't even get the words out before he's standing in the doorway.

CHAPTER 31
HENRI

I LET his calls go to voicemail. It's safer. I think. Part of me doesn't trust that I won't go back to him. Even after Ms. Gertie and I talked during our tea dates a few days ago about what keeps her from feeling lonely, it hasn't stopped me from having small regrets.

Things were good sometimes.

Good with Nathan is still worse than bad with Deacon. My wolf protests.

Glutton for punishment, I read the transcript of Nathan's voicemail again.

NATHAN:

> Hey, Henri, it's me. I wish you'd return my calls. I've been thinking about you. A lot. I miss you. I don't care what the guys said about you. I think you're probably the best woman for me.

It started out so sweet. I always thought it didn't bother me that Nathan's friends didn't like me, but I should have known. My friends, when we were still speaking, didn't like him. His friends have never liked me. If I had been strong enough then to know and realize . . .

Opening the photo gallery on my phone, I look back at the memories of Nathan and me. There aren't many. He always was so stubborn about taking pictures with me. With his friends, he has dozens of them.

My wolf points out the obvious with a sharp bite in my inner thoughts. *It's because he didn't want to be seen with us.*

If that's true, though, why is he working so hard to get me back? Why does he keep calling?

CHAPTER 32
DEACON

C<small>ADE</small>, Lena, and I have had our fair share of troubles, and the Alloways have had full-out brawls. But when I casually walk in late to the predinner drinks, it's absolutely unmistakable that everyone in the royal family has years beyond their wisdom. That's saying something since I'm not the youngest at the table.

Side-eyed glances and whispers start the moment I cross the threshold. *Maybe I should download one of those language-learning apps.*

Revecca eyes me, and fuck if she and Cade don't have that weird genetic predisposition to having the same behaviors bullshit. In the slight flare of her nostrils and a side-eye glance, I know where I'm supposed to sit and, in another glance, who it's about to piss off.

He's Hugo Ardelean, if the 'who's who' crash course Patrick gave me is anything to be believed. Robust in an uncharacteristically wolf way with a large barrel chest.

"Shall we join the table?" Revecca asks in English, which I'm sure is for my benefit.

Hugo Ardelean practically sprints ahead of the group headed to the dining table and gets to the chair that my ass is supposed to occupy. Normally, I'd say fuck it and grab a chair farther down. I'm not concerned so long as there's food served in that seat as well.

But there's fuckery to spread.

I stalk up quietly, hands tucked in my pockets, and slouch back on my heels. "I believe you're in my chair."

Hugo huffs. "You can't be serious."

Casually I rotate to Revecca and shake my head, giving her a rough shrug of my shoulders. I get the tiniest of nods before turning back to Hugo. I pull my hand out of my pocket and extend it to him. "His Royal Highness, James Deacon Alden, of the Harbinger line. You can call me James."

"Your Majesty," Hugo sputters.

I cringe on his behalf. "See, that is the problem, isn't it? She's not Your Majesty the Queen. She's Your Highness the Queen." The room goes deathly still. *Please don't be wrong.* I draw a slow breath. "The woman, who, from my understanding, has been doing an excellent job caring for the people of Romania," I lean forward and whisper yell, "despite your best efforts to undermine that." I lean back and sigh. "She's only Your Highness like the rest of us. His Majesty is at home with his mate."

"You can't possibly —"

"Can't possibly what?" I cock my head to the side, kind of wishing I had drugged my wolf as ancestors materialize through the walls. "Can't possibly be implying that he or his future children return to Romania?"

"Well," Hugo huffs.

"Hate to break it to you, but despite Revecca's best efforts, she can't get Cade to come here. Sorry, she can't get *Alexandru* to return to Romania to fully abdicate the throne of Romania, which means The Leviathan rules from the United States." I turn on my heels, making a big show of it to look at Revecca. "That about covers it? More or less?"

She gives a curt nod. "More or less."

She swallows, and it seems difficult.

"So, if The Leviathan isn't abdicating, then Revecca is still Your Royal Highness, not Majesty, and that means that all the power is still in their bloodline, and because my half-brother is The Harbinger, then . . . whatever the fuck my wolf is qualifies as his successor, and Harbinger is the successor of The Pricolici, so I'm the successor of Harbinger, so therefore would you fuckin' move."

A gasp comes from somewhere down the table, and I'm not exactly sure if it was the use of the word fuck or something else.

Hugo Ardelean steps away from my chair and walks around to the other side of the table.

"And before anyone fuckin' asks, yeah, the bloodwork's been done." I look down at the ten other people flanking the table.

Revecca takes her seat, and I follow her lead, sinking into the large wooden chair. Remarkably comfortable for being an antique. With a careful nod from Revecca, service staff enters the dining hall and begins dropping the first course.

"So, James," a woman to the left of Hugo pipes up, "what is it you do?"

"I'm a venture capitalist," I say confidently.

"A freeloader," Hugo grumbles.

"From my conversations with the director of the Ardelean Fund, Deacon is very good at putting money into the right hands for a profitable reinvestment."

Revecca shocks me, mostly because I didn't realize she could see our finances.

"Oh, and your gift?" A man's voice comes from down the table.

"It's not polite to ask about an Ardelean gift." I'm quick to push back.

Laughter erupts down the table.

Of course, it's a dinner with a room full of Ardeleans.

I look over at Revecca, and she takes a sip of her soup.

Fuck me. Wrong answer.

"I see and speak with the ancestors." The minute I say it, the ancestors in the room start getting loud.

I scrub my hand down my face, ignoring them all to pick up a spoonful of soup.

"It must be lovely being able to see your loved ones after they've died," a woman muses.

"I've been blessed with never having lost a loved one." I let those words out quickly and effortlessly. I don't miss the shifting eyes in the room and pauses in the casual eating. "Not having parents I've cared about, no grandparents to speak of, and all the close calls have ended on our side of lucky."

"Grigore," Revecca cuts in, and even the ancestors in the room go silent, "tell me about the expectations for the sunflower crop this year."

I FOLLOW Revecca's lead for the rest of dinner, throwing out soft jabs here and there, saying the cutting words that usually go unsaid in polite conversation. When Revecca finally dismisses the rest of the company, she and I leave in the opposite direction down the hallway. We're probably on the other side of the home when she leans against a wall, breaking out laughing. The royal guards stop and look at her, confusion and fear rippling off them in waves of concern.

"What on earth" — she gasps for air — "is an earth-vexing varlet?"

"No idea, but it sure sounded good." I laugh along with her.

"I haven't had that much fun at a family dinner in years. How did you know that about the royal family?" She wipes a wayward tear from laughing so hard out of the corner of her eye.

I steady my breathing before answering. "A lot of time in the archives with Thalia, a lot of time on the internet, and a lot of deductive reasoning."

"Do you really believe Cade or one of his children will want the throne someday?" she muses, and we're nearly back to where she spends most of her time.

"Cade? Personally? No." I shake my head. "He's loyal to his people, and they're not here. And I don't mean that to sound like your people are lesser."

"But there's a connection to familiarity." Revecca gives a solemn nod.

"I know you and him are struggling to find a new relationship path." I wince thinking about the last yelling match and the comments he's made about having a sister. "But I don't think Cade's problems are with you as a person so much as how you approach him and your insistence that he returns to Romania. If all you want from him is for him to return home, then take this as a 'stand down,' so to speak. But if what you're looking for is connection to your sibling, he responds well to genuinely expressed interest and conversation."

Silently contemplating that, Revecca bobs her head. "How long do I have to wait for him to tell me his mate is expecting?"

"They're planning to announce it once they tell the family at Equinox. Thalia is nervous with the first trimester." It's not worth lying to her or pretending I don't know.

"Okay, but I'm brimming with excitement." Revecca's words don't match her body posturing. "Can I please at least tell you what they're having and their gift?"

"The fact that you get to pick gifts pisses me off." I finally have someone to voice my frustrations to. "Your mother? Grandmother? Knew I was coming into this world and gave me this hell to deal with."

"It's not exactly as straightforward as you make it seem. Certain gifts can only be relegated in certain scenarios. Your gift is only available if Harbinger and The Leviathan come forth. As much as I'm sure you'll hate the idea, Deacon, you are correct in that you are above Hugo Ardelean for the throne. I could abdicate to you." Revecca places her hand on my shoulder.

That thought sinks into me like hot lava falling into a frozen lake. Things inside me crack and sizzle while I try to comprehend what she's saying.

Fuck. I'm going to die in Romania with a crown on my head. Maybe I should call Cade.

Revecca turns to go. "Tomorrow, there's someone you need to meet."

"So." Calling her back, I shake off my impending dread, not ready to give up whatever peace we've found between us just yet. "If a guy was about to start a betting pool on the gender of Cade's child and the due date?"

When Revecca turns back, she's smiling. It's something I wasn't so sure she could do but seems to do a lot here. "Girl. Strong like her sire and fair like her mother. I would guess before her due date."

"Give her a hellish gift, and I'll make your life hell," I warn her.

"The gift of —"

256

"No. Don't tell me." I shake my head. "I don't want to be culpable for your crimes of bad gifts."

"Fair enough, given your current take of the situation." Revecca nods.

This time when she leaves, I don't argue with her going.

CHAPTER 33
HENRI

NOTHING IS EVER GOING to be okay again, and it's all your fault. My wolf berates me. *We need to see Deacon, and you won't go to him.*

There's nothing I can say to her that I haven't already said, and arguing with her gets me nowhere. Instead, I flop down on the couch, pull a pillow over my head, and scream.

I scream until the air is gone from my lungs, and I leave myself suffocating under the pillow, wishing to hide here forever.

No boy like that is worth crying over, Henri. Deacon's voice is in my head, and I pull the pillow off my face. Instinct takes over, and my body expands, my lungs sucking in a breath of life.

Today has been just another exhausting day. Deacon's been gone for twenty-four hours, and it's last-minute RSVP to Equinox after last-minute RSVP to Equinox, and something I didn't take into consideration when hiring staff is that some wolves go into heat. I can't even blame them for it, but damn the timing is inconvenient.

We could go into heat with Deacon if you'd just fucking go to him. My wolf pushes forward, wanting Deacon.

There is no peace and quiet in my head.

She thinks about his brown hair, messy after a long conference when he finally shakes off the professional demeanor to be his more laid-back self.

Going to Romania for absolutely no reason at all doesn't make sense. He didn't want to see me. He said it himself. I didn't have to pick him, so long as I wasn't with Nathan. If that isn't a nice way of saying 'let's just be friends,' I don't know what is.

Nathan's been texting me on and off. The messages go from 'I want you back' to 'you're such a whore,' and I know I should block him, but I just can't make myself.

I can't make myself because part of me wants to go back to him. Which is absolutely absurd. There's no way I should go back to him. But part of me is so lonely that I wonder if being on edge and trying to anticipate what he's thinking or doing could really be all that worse than being alone. Logically, I know it can.

Cade and Deacon showed me that it can.

I can't even call and tell Mom and Dad because how, after all these years, do I just open communication like that? 'Oh, hey do you remember me, your adopted daughter, who just ghosted you?' And then what? What happens then? They'll probably say they don't want to talk to me.

Go find our maybe mate. He'll take care of us, my wolf snarls at me.

I'm not going to Romania. He's gone, and we don't know for how long. It's not worth it.

I groan. Closing my eyes, I try to block her out. Can you completely close off from your wolf? Just make her go away?

From my understanding no . . . But Deacon . . . The Ardelean gifts come from their wolves.

Deacon drank and used God knows what drugs to keep his wolf quiet. It wouldn't have to be for long, just some peace before bed.

I push myself off the couch and nearly run to the kitchen for the bottle of wine in the chiller. I dig through the drawers until I find the corkscrew and then the cupboards until I find my thermal wine tumbler. Deftly, my hands move through getting it open, and I pour a usual serving size. Then I pour a lot more. The only time, since having found her, I didn't feel my wolf was when I was drinking at this party. Coincidentally where I met Nathan, and I was sloshed. *Better safe than sorry.*

Television and I haven't spent any time together lately, but I find the remote in the ornamental bowl on the table and turn it on. Before flicking through the streaming services, I set an out-of-office email, telling everyone I'll answer their messages tomorrow morning. I might be drinking away my wolf, but that doesn't mean I can neglect my job. A break for one night, though? Well, no one will fault me for that. Cade knows where I am if he needs me.

THE COUCH HAS NEVER BEEN my favorite place to wake up, but damn if that wasn't the best night's sleep I've had in a long time. My phone's almost dead, but it's only five thirty, meaning the light coming in the windows, not the alarm, woke me up.

I can sleep for three more hours before I have to get up for the day, and thankfully, no wolf to be found. After a trip to the bathroom and changing into my pajamas, I climb into the big fluffy bed and snuggle in among the covers.

It's one thirty in the afternoon in Bucharest. Closing my eyes, I try to push the thought out of my mind. *I could just text him and make sure he got there okay. It's still part of my job to make sure he has the right social media coverage.*

I roll to my side, facing the nightstand, and pick my phone up. I pull up his number from my favorites and hover over the keys in a new message. *No. Fuck it. He's Revecca's problem. I'm sure she has social media people who can handle him.*

Phone back down on the table, I stare up at the ceiling for a few moments before forcing my eyes closed.

My wolf stirs inside. Groggy and uncoordinated in my mind, she thinks about Deacon again.

I have three hours . . . I shuffle to the chiller and pull out the bottle of wine. After pouring a smaller serving than last night, but still substantial enough, I down it. *It's just a few hours of sleep.*

CHAPTER 34
DEACON

Revecca's friendly demeanor last night is long gone. This afternoon she steps out of the throne room, rage ready, and snaps an order. "Come."

Not quite ready to take her on when she's mad, I dutifully fall into step behind her. My wolf is no stranger to her and Cade's tempers. He doesn't even rise at the aggression.

She leads me through the palace. As we walk, people bow their heads and wait. Some go the full traditional route of tipping their heads aside and exposing their neck entirely. The air around her is completely uncomfortable for a wolf, and going so far to submit so completely, nearly ready to die with their throats exposed, is telling of the fear she strikes in those around her, me excluded.

Ten minutes later we've reached the far end of the castle, and Revecca stops, hand resting on the door handle. "It's quite possible that this will be a bit of a shock to your system. Just know that what has happened to her is not entirely her fault."

Her ominous warning doesn't sit well with me, and my stomach churns.

Revecca leads me inside and crosses the room, coming to stand beside a woman sitting in a wheelchair.

"Deacon, this is your mother." Revecca pauses. "Your and Ansel's mother. Though, I don't believe the blood work results came to you with any shock."

I can't come up with anything to say.

The woman has long graying brown hair and piercing green eyes that are lost in a thousand-yard stare. She's little more than a hollow shell staring out the window. I should have feelings about this, but shock is taking over.

"Does she speak English?" I ask, turning toward Revecca.

"A couple years ago, when she last spoke, it was in English," Revecca answers. She strokes the woman's hair. "We were called by Robert, perhaps six years ago now, and told there was an Ardelean in distress. He did not feel comfortable caring for her." Revecca's distaste of Robert is evident in the venom dripping from those words. "So, we brought her home. Unfortunately, it's been a slow decline in her health. She gets trapped a lot within her gift. With yours, you shouldn't have any issue speaking with her."

Still too shocked to really know what to say, I nod in response.

A couple years ago. Trapped in her gift. Fan-fucking-tastic.

"What is her gift?"

"She walks in the astral realm," Revecca answers like I should know what that means.

Then she leaves me alone with this woman without another word, closing the door behind her.

I move to the wall with the window and slide down to sit facing her. Her vacant expression, staring off into the ether, is a damn near perfect reflection of how I feel inside when I'm not in the same room as Henri.

"I'm Deacon. I guess."

She doesn't move. I don't expect her to.

Is this my fate, slipping away into a meager existence within my own head?

I draw a breath and start talking because what else am I supposed to do? "From my understanding this might be the longest amount of time we've ever spent together." My voice falls flat, but I keep talking. "Allora and Elliot Alloway, my sister's biological parents, say that Ebenezer and Karina Alden announced my birth just a few days after I had been born, but there wasn't a lot of certainty that Karina had ever been pregnant. Revecca confirmed that the Aldens, whoever they really were, were never her or Cade's parents. That sibling set seemed to be wrapped up with the Ardelean royal family's disappearance. I personally never witnessed Ebenezer and Karina having a gift. It didn't seem plausible that I was their son being cursed like this. People, children, don't materialize out of nowhere. It's clear I had parents out there somewhere."

I force myself to quit rambling over nothing, to stop drawing conclusions and passing off my deductive reasoning as facts. I hang my head and sit in silence for a long time, looking at her stocking feet on the floor. The blanket they've draped across her lap ends just below her knees, and her hands rest in her lap with her long hair draped over her shoulder.

"I guess." I start again. "Maybe, sitting here with you is answer enough. If a hollow shell is my destiny, I'm well on the way to that. Ansel's gift is easier, but his life has been more fucked up. Yet somehow, I'm the one at the end of my rope."

She says nothing. I think her fingers move, threatening to twitch to life, but I'm probably seeing things.

"Revecca can take my wolf. And my gift." The words come out easier this time.

You'd be lost without me. My wolf interjects.

I don't need to speak Romanian to find something strong enough to make you disappear. Don't push your luck. I warn him. He slowly sinks back in my consciousness.

Revecca wanted me to talk to her, so I guess this is as good of a conversation as any. "I'm useless. Not exactly the child you should be proud of. That's Ansel because there's an enigma. He's a fucking genius with wolves who need help and well, want help. I don't fall into that category, I don't think. No one is better for me being in their life."

Especially not Henri. That thought dampens the fire that had sparked in my rant but doesn't put it out.

"Anyway, if Revecca takes my wolf and gift, then I don't have to deal with seeing them — the ancestors, old dead people, spirits, ghosts, whatever it is. They won't be able to talk to me, I won't have to talk back, and it'll finally be peaceful." I push my head against the brick wall and thump it softly again and again, trying to push intrusive thoughts from my brain only to spark ones of bashing my head against it until that's the end.

I look at her sitting in the chair. She looks more like me than Ansel. Except for the high cheekbones we all share.

"But if I give up my wolf, I lose the possibility of finding my mate." The world is blurry, and I wipe the moisture out of my eyes. *So much for anger.* "I've been purposefully so stoned or drunk that I can't feel my wolf when the person I like the most is around. If you can't feel your wolf, you can't feel your mate, and it's not fair to her."

Silence blankets the room, and I swear our heartbeats echo.

"It's not fair to her that she ties herself to me if this is how I end up. Fuck, how old are you, even? I'm thirty. So, what . . . I've maybe twenty years left before I'm completely useless to the world? That's hardly fair because really, it's only fifteen when you think about how long it must have taken for you to deteriorate to this. Wolves heal fast, so what happened that you're like this?"

I didn't realize my words turned sharp again until the feeling of my nails digging into my palm startles me. My hands shake as I uncurl them from fists and try to steady myself.

"Fifteen years isn't long enough to be happy." I sniffle and wipe my nose on my sleeve. "I don't want this for me. The only thing I can do is give up my wolf. I'm glad to just be human. It's not so bad. I've known a lot of nice humans, most of them living. I could make a really good husband to someone. But not a mate. Not for her."

If I could though . . . I look at the first biological parent I've ever located. My thought sours. *I'd only bring Henri more heartbreak.*

"Fuck!" I shout to break the silence.

The shell of my genetic match doesn't even flinch.

"If I could control it. If I could just find a way to shut it off." I shake my head, thinking of all the times I've tried. "There's no controlling it. There's no learning to deal with it. There's no relief except to live as a human. Even then . . . I'll lose her. There's no winning in this end game. There's no point."

Pressing my head against the brick again, I look at her. I wait for answers that I know won't come.

The door doesn't open or click close, so when I hear a voice, I know it's not someone alive in the room.

"Deacon."

Of fucking course the ghosts here have all learned my name.

I turn my head to look at the ghost, ready to tell them to fuck off.

The sight takes my breath away. The woman in the wheelchair hasn't moved but her spitting image, younger but definitely her, stands halfway across the room.

She walks forward, and I scramble to my feet.

269

"You are so beautiful. Just like your brother. How did they give you that name, Deacon?"

My hand goes to my chest, and my heart is pounding behind my ribs.

"I know you can see me, Deacon," she prompts, tilting her head to the side. "I also know you can hear me."

"I —" What do you even say to that?

"You were brought here to see me, and I'm here," she says, expecting something from me. Something more than shock apparently.

Vague statements and a divine knowing must be a key trait among females in our bloodline.

I have millions of questions, but the beginning feels most logical. It's where the pain started. "Why did you give me to them?"

"I didn't want to. But I was no better off than you are now." She gestures for me to follow her. "The men who were . . . keeping me . . . wouldn't let me have suppressants. They wanted another one of our bloodline. They told me they needed one more son to protect the spare heir of The Pricolici. If I made one more son, just one more son, they said they found a family who could keep you, in my place, that you'd be safe, and they'd let me go. They told me that these people wanted a baby more than anything. I could help, and then when I was done helping, I could go home."

I follow her to a sitting area by the fireplace, with one more look back at the shell sitting in the wheelchair.

"Did they?" I don't even know what to ask.

In the end, this is where she ended up. Help or not, this was her fate.

"It was a lie. There was something not right about the oldest boy. It was too late before . . ." She swallows and then changes her train of thought. "Not home, no," she answers softly. "I cleaned myself up and retraced my tracks, trying to find your brother first. I wanted us to be a family. I always knew you were safe and would continue to be."

"But?" *Isn't there always a but?*

"You must know how hard it is." She trails off, looking at me with a raised eyebrow and a cocked head. It's somehow judgmental and understanding at the same time. "It's hard to stop doing anything that stops the gift. I didn't have skills or a pack. Your father and your brother's father weren't my mates. They were chosen for their distinctive traits. I had no mate, no pack, no home, and my gift . . ."

My empathy wiggles free from the tight grip I've kept on my emotions. How many times have I thought about how much easier life would be without a pack or a family? I could just let go and be free. She was alone, and it didn't make it easier for her. Maybe life with my idiots is better than without them.

"You should spend time with your brother. Perhaps he can help you, the bond between you could strengthen you." She offers this without knowing anything beyond this conversation.

It's not like Ms. Gertie when she mothers me. She, at least, doesn't come across as sounding entitled.

I dismiss her since it's something I've already tried. "Ansel has his plate full already."

"Where did he end up? I always hoped it was with kind people. How did he come to have that name?" She rests back, lounging effortlessly and unburdened, asking questions. Her nonchalance hurts the inner child in me who wondered if there was a parent out there who would have loved me. "I wasn't allowed to name either of you. I would have liked to. Maybe."

It doesn't feel like my story to tell. But in the same breath, I'm never going to tell Ansel she's here, so he won't be telling her his story either. There's no need for him to relive the nightmares of his past more than he already does.

"They found him in Montana. Victim of severe neglect, child abuse, and sex trafficking." I cut off that he's the most intelligent person I know and that he's so much stronger than any of us.

I want to hurt her in the way Ansel and I have been hurting by showing her what she missed out on, but it doesn't feel like this is supposed to be her fight. Yet, that anger is there.

She shakes her head and clenches her fists. "He was born when I was in a dark place. I hadn't seen the light of day since my heat. They took him from me. I assumed he was dead."

And when she weeps, I want to be the bigger person. I want to have Ansel's strength and ability to forgive. But I have no compassion. My anger, disappointment, and frustration with myself and the world are bigger than her and her sorrows.

"How many of us did you curse with the irreparable damage of growing up without loving homes? How many —" I fight back the snarl.

I want to blame her for our gifts because while Revecca's grandmother had control of assigning them, I know they run in bloodlines. They'd all be related somehow. All of us would be cursed with seeing the dead or astral plane, but I leave it out of this conversation.

"There may have been one more of you," she answers, shaking her head. "I don't know. There was a time when reality, my gift, and . . . and the drugs blended."

I've never been so messed up that I didn't know what was real. Keeping a level head for Lena was always the most important part of my life.

What a blessing my mother had that so effortlessly . . . I stop the judgmental thoughts. *She didn't ask for this any more than I did.*

"Ansel must see when death is coming. Since you can see the astral plane." She makes it sound like I have a choice.

"That's the gist of it."

How is it fair she just has all this information? But the answer is evident: ancestors.

I look back over at the hollow shell. "Is that what I can look forward to?"

"Embrace who you are and lean into your gift. Quit running from it." She has the audacity to scold me with a sharp and snappy tone. "I only wanted happiness for you. I thought for sure Ebenezer and Karina would coach you to find your mate and accept them. Here you are hiding from love and what can make you stable. All you had to do was do better than me."

"So, you're saying all I have to do is sober up and magically, my gift will be manageable?" *Tall fucking tale if I've ever heard one before.* It's not even something she did for herself.

She shakes her head. "It's never going to be that easy."

"Ditch the wolf, save the world." *Get up the courage to finally end all this suffering.*

Or, let me do my job? My wolf rises to argue with me. Apparently he's forgotten the chances he's had to prove he can.

"If you're so dead set on being miserable for the rest of your life, then do it. Let Revecca release your wolf." The woman challenges me like reverse psychology or some bullshit has ever worked on me.

I'm miserable now. Misery is subjective.

"I don't think you have any room to talk." I stand and start across the room.

I hope her spirit is tied to her body so she can't follow me.

It's time to end this.

Out in the hall Revecca isn't there, but Patrick is. He smiles. "Her Royal Highness had some additional matters to attend to, but she sent me. Figured it would be beneficial to have someone who speaks Romanian with you."

"That's fantastic." I try to leave off the sarcasm, but I'm rattled.

Patrick snorts. "I can't imagine that was an easy visit."

I deflect. "Any place one can get black-out drunk?"

"Well." Patrick starts walking, and I follow because he's right. Probably will help to have someone who speaks Romanian, even if I've got to find a way to bribe him to get what I want. Halfway down the hall, he finishes his statement. "Finn called."

"Of course, he fucking did. Has he always been this meddlesome?" I growl.

"Yes. Only worse." Patrick laughs. "But only for those of us he cares about. If Finn doesn't give two fucks about you, then it's a completely different relationship."

"How do I get him to not give two fucks?" I ask, knowing there isn't an answer for that, but it feels good to at least have someone who understands that my sister's mate is overbearing.

"If you figure that out, let me know." Patrick smiles and opens a door to the hallway on our left, leading me into it.

A wall of windows lets in the midday light, and it's surprisingly serene if castles are your thing.

"I had our doctor cut you a script. I wasn't sure what dosage, so I went mid-range." Patrick pulls a bottle of pills out of his pants pocket.

"Thank you." I look at the amber bottle, shocked by what I find.

HRH Deacon Alden, Morphine.

"Collect the script before you fly out, and you can take what's left with you." Patrick continues down the hall.

I shrug, pocketing the pills without checking how many there are. "You're assuming I'm not here to stay."

Patrick snorts. "Right. And I'm only here as a goodwill ambassador."

"Never know. Romania is a beautiful country, perhaps I enjoy being here." I look at the courtyard. *There are worse places to die.*

"Then you won't be needing those at all. Revecca won't allow an Ardelean to keep their wolf as far under as you normally do. She can't stand to know they're hurting." Patrick holds his hand out to take the pill bottle back. "Revecca wants you mostly sober to work with her and your wolf. However, she can't meet with you right now, this afternoon, or tomorrow. This way you have some time to avoid the ancestors, if you want to."

I put my hand in my pocket, thumbing the lid. But I can't bring myself to hand them back over. It's pointless to even bluff that I'm staying. I want to go home, and I want to be buried at Ansel's in the desert. Someplace this nice doesn't need me tainting their soil.

But that little part of me that's attached to Henri wants to see what Revecca has to say and if she really can make this better. The single donor of genetic material I've met isn't exactly the greatest encouragement that life is going to get better.

"Let's go see the sights." I bring the pill bottle out of my pocket, thumb off the lid, swallow a pill dry, and then put it back in my pocket. "I'll talk to Revecca when her calendar allows. Today, I want to see why she's obsessed with this country."

CHAPTER 35
HENRI

MY PHONE VIBRATES on the dresser, and I tap on the screen, revealing the nearly dozen messages from Nathan since I got in the shower.

I skim down the list. Some of them are longer than others. They're all cutesy reminders of the things we used to do together, how much he loved spending time with me, and how we'd go out and have fun when we first started dating.

Responding will only encourage him to text me back. It'll start a cycle I don't want to engage in.

He cheated on me. He threw out my pills. He killed his last girlfriend . . .

I still haven't been able to reconcile that last one.

The thought of my slowly dwindling pills makes me nervous.

Ignoring my phone, I go back to drying off. But the movements aren't very soothing. I have another headache this morning, and it's making me crabby, but beyond that, the reminders of what he did heighten the anxiety of my new reality.

I'm going to go into heat.

I can't even ask for more pills because they don't allow for replacement prescriptions. You sign a disclosure every time you pick them up, and there are strict rules about suppressants. Never double dose. Keep tabs on your symptoms. If at any time you have symptoms of estrus contact the lab. If you miss a dose, take it as soon as possible, and if over twelve hours late, contact the lab. Never take less than a full dose, unless directed by the lab.

If those aren't enough to warn us away, there are warnings about the possibility of becoming sterile with long-term use and that it sometimes takes a full heat or more for your body to be able to conceive again.

They've always seemed worth it. But maybe going through heat won't be so bad this time.

Maybe it won't be like the last time.

I proceed to my bedroom and ruffle through my boxes of clothes, still not unpacked, looking for the proper undergarments for today. Digging through the boxes does me no favors. The act of searching only elevates my uncertainty. I'm not even unpacked here. It's not a home that someone would want to go into heat in.

But if I clean up my space and settle in, it could be homey and safe. Plus, I'm older and more experienced with sex. There are plenty of cute sentries I could —

Absolutely not. My wolf stops that thought dead. *No. No way. Deacon and no one else.*

She refuses to believe or consider that he's not a possibility. He's not even in the country, and no one knows when he's coming home. If he even comes home, there isn't a guarantee he'll be home in time for my heat. And more than that, there's no way to know for sure that he'd even want to do that with me. It's a big ask.

My wolf pushes forward the kiss. New Year's Eve and how hot it was. The way his hands burned against my skin and the gasoline he poured on my desire.

But that could have been from being caught up in the moment. He doesn't necessarily still feel that way.

You're being stubborn. My wolf then brings up the soft, tender kiss at the Wisconsin house. *You're just brushing him off because you're scared.* She huffs. *If you messaged him right now, he'd come home for us.*

Her certainty, even without a way of knowing we're mates, is so firm that I feel it branding my heart. But I've twenty-four pills left.

I should tell Cade sooner rather than later that I'm going to need this time off. That way he can approve my arrangements for it. My face heats at the thought. Telling him something so shameful and violating feels heavy.

How did I ever let it get this far?

In the silence of my cabin, the feeling of being alone kicks in.

After dressing quickly, I grab my tea cup and work bag and head across the way to Ms. Gertie's. I'd planned to work from home today, but the familiarity and hustle and bustle of the main house will be better.

"You're early this morning!" Ms. Gertie is all smiles.

Ushered through the doors, I'm treated to the fragrant smells of hot coffee and baked goods.

"I hope not too early." There's something so comforting about Ms. Gertie that I spill. "I just feel so lonely."

"Mmmm. Child." Ms. Gertie gestures for me to sit at my normal seat at the table. "Sometimes being alone isn't so bad. Not so bad at all. Especially if you've got people who love you nearby."

She pours hot water into my cup and opens her tea box. I flip through and grab an orange blossom one.

"What do you do when you get lonely?" I place the tea bag in the water and let it steep.

Ms. Gertie's chuckle isn't condescending, but it does seem like she's about to impart some massive life lesson on me. "I don't have time to be lonely. I've got bridge, church, the Aldens. I've also got the pack ladies and book club. Then I babysit some of the youngins when their parents are busy. Deacon meant it when he said he'd bring me to a place that I'd have a family to love all over again."

Deacon. My wolf swoons thinking about him. *Could we go to Romania to be with him?*

No. I don't argue beyond that.

Absolutely no way can I track Deacon down like that, even if I want to.

"So, just work and have a social life?" *Why is that such a foreign concept?*

Ms. Gertie puts a slice of her fresh zucchini bread in front of me. It's warm and steaming, with melting butter on top of it.

"Well, it's either that or doing something completely outrageous like Deacon would do. Maybe you could start running an illegal poker game or something like that." Ms. Gertie laughs and winks at me. "Though, I hear there may already be one among some of the college kids in the pack if you wanted an invite."

"Ms. Gertie, are you being a little bit devious?" I cut off some of the bread with my fork.

"Well, idle hands and all. If I don't do something on Friday nights, I might just get myself in bigger trouble than takin' those rascals to the cleaners," she muses, finally sitting across from me with a slice of bread and a cup of black coffee.

As I finish my bread, Ms. Gertie beguiles me with some of

the pack gossip and a story of her and her husband getting into a big batch of trouble when they accidentally ran into moonshine makers. Then how they started selling moonshine themselves and how they ended up being the only ones not caught by the police because she was in labor.

The craziness Ms. Gertie got herself into and out of truly shows how she never let herself sit still and embraced a full life. It feels familiar in that sense. It's easier to be constantly moving rather than enjoy the stillness of solitude.

CHAPTER 36
DEACON

Bucharest is beautiful. As much as I'd like to say it's just another city, there is something magical about it. Aside from the scenery, wolves freely greet me here, eyes flashing to golden tones to pay respects.

While I did take one of the pills Patrick gave me, they're near the dose I'd take back home. It's just enough to keep the wolf quiet, but I might be able to shift if a fight breaks out. However, tagging along with the royal guard, I doubt there's even reason to think about that. Probably rules about it anyway.

I'm talking with a little kid who is practicing his English when Patrick pats me on the back, his phone extended toward me. "Her Royal Highness is ready to meet with you. I'll take you to her."

"Sure thing." I nod but look back at the kid. "Thank you for talking with me today. I've got to go see the queen. Keep up the hard work."

"Goodbye!" He waves before running back to his mother.

Patrick gives me a weird look, eyebrow cocked in the same direction as his head.

"Don't tell me that kid wasn't real, and you just let me talk to no one for ten minutes." I look back, but the woman and child are still there.

"Not at all." Patrick is quick to affirm. "They're very much alive. With your reputation, I wouldn't have assumed kids would be your forte."

"Nah, kids are easy after they're potty-trained until they become teenagers. Then I'm cool because I'm not a narc." I shrug and look around. "Lead the way."

We walk a few blocks with more haste than the wandering we had done to get here. "Hey, Patrick," I ask, looking around at the city streets. "Have you ever wondered what it'd be like to be human?"

He laughs and pulls up his jacket sleeve just enough that I can see the start of scarring. "I was bitten in."

"So, do you miss being human?" I change the question.

"No." Patrick shakes his head as the castle comes into view, "But my situation is different from yours. I don't miss how fucked my life was before I became wolf and before I became pack. Had more in common with you now than what I suspect you'd be like as a human."

I don't comment on that. The implication of his words is enough that I don't need to.

The front gate lets us through like it isn't even a security stop. The guards at the front entrance open the doors for us, and we waltz in, unlike when I first arrived and thought I might be turned away.

Two minutes pass before Patrick stops in front of a room with a guard on either side of the door. They nod him through, but he knocks first.

"Open." Revecca's voice comes from the other side.

Patrick twists the knob, pushing the door open a fraction, but he doesn't enter. Waving me in, he leaves me to find my way.

Revecca is seated at the large ornate desk, typing on a laptop.

"How was your visit with your mother?" Revecca doesn't look up from her computer.

"It was bias confirming. I have the same ask of you as when I started, just a greater conviction for it," I answer, sitting in one of the chairs in front of her desk.

It feels no different than sitting across from Cade.

"I was afraid you would say that." She sighs, closing her laptop.

The blue eyes staring at me hold pity.

Making this so fucking easy. The sarcasm in my own brain causes an eye roll. "Listen, if you don't want to take my wolf, that's fine. But do some sort of ancient magic to fix Henri with another mate. Don't punish her to a life with me because I'm fucked and you won't fix it."

"I am not some benevolent dictator you all seem to think I am." Revecca shakes her head. "I was afraid you would say that because this isn't as easy as you're hoping it will be."

She's not wrong. I did think she was a dictator.

I bow my head, submitting to her power for a minute.

"You were born for greatness." Revecca's gaze bores into mine. "Born to make a difference in people's lives."

"I wasn't born," I tell her flatly. "I was bred. The people who stole Cade and killed your parents used that woman to have me created for them."

Revecca confirms with a small nod. *Did Revecca find this information out when she borrowed my gift?* That thought changes in my mind with the realization that I can only pick out the image of the woman in my brain. *I don't even know her name.*

"She may have thought she had no choice in the matter, but she had two sons, and both of us ended up alone in the world." I find myself raising my voice and force it back to speaking volume, but it doesn't change my coarse words. "I don't know what county in the state of delusion she lives in. I was not born but brought into this world as a sick guarantee that no one would look too closely at Robert's lack of a gift."

Revecca is eerily silent. She tips her head ever so slightly to the side, watching me.

With a shake of my head, I dismiss it all. "It doesn't matter."

"It does matter." Revecca corrects in an uncharacteristically sweet and caring way.

I lean back into the chair. "With all due respect, it doesn't. I can't be this person everyone wants me to be."

"What did they do to you that made you so resentful of your gift and stopped your wolf from developing?" Revecca's words don't match anything anyone has ever said to me, and it hits me hard.

No one has ever asked.

I can't stand feeling like I'm this big of a fuckup. That I'm the one who made this happen. *Didn't I though? I could have left. Couldn't I?*

"Tell me about them." Revecca is more forceful; it's coated with some sort of gift. Pressure maybe? Like Cade's Alpha command, I can't not comply.

"Ebenezer and Karina took me to human doctors." I close my eyes, not able to look at her, at anyone, when I talk about this. "They started me on antipsychotics despite proving to the doctor that I really do see dead people. They kept upping the dosage until the dead people stopped showing up. But then I couldn't be a wolf anymore."

Revecca is snarling before I finish speaking. "And Karina is dead, yes? Through a conversation with Robert, I know Cade executed Ebenezer. Though Robert was convinced Ebenezer was The Leviathan." She seems genuinely concerned and slightly hangs her head. "I should have visited America sooner. So much could have changed."

Revecca's somber tone tugs on my heartstrings. Normally, I wouldn't share so much of the darkness I keep locked inside, but the guilt conveyed through her frown draws it from me. "I hunted her down myself. Everyone says she died of a broken heart from losing her mate. She died from an overdose, but that's what happens when you're force-fed pills."

Revecca doesn't even flinch at my words. "Impressive. Don't let Magnus hear of your darkness, or he'll recruit you."

After confessing to murder, there isn't really anything more to say. So I shrug and chuckle only slightly awkwardly with the hope she leads the conversation.

"I can't take your wolf back until you've let him fully develop. You're an Alpha wolf and haven't come into your strength yet. It has to do with what they've done to you, but I'm sure it's continued with your self-medicating behavior." Revecca sighs, pushing her hair back in a move that suggests Cade's tell is biological rather than learned. "I failed you. I knew there were wolves in America, aside from the Alloways, and that they were claiming ties to Romania. I should have come to have a better look once I was coronated. This could have been stopped."

Her repetition of this idea is telling. *I wish she and Cade could put aside some differences. They could be really useful to each other.*

"Everyone is so quick to take the blame for this." I gesture up and down my body, then shake my head and slouch in the chair. "All I'm asking for is help out of it. You keep saying my wolf isn't at his full power and not developed, but I don't know what you're trying to tell me."

"Get yourself sober and let your wolf develop into his full strength." Revecca drums her fingers on her desk. "If you do that, you should get control of your gift. And if that proves to have been the worst of your problems, maybe life will be more manageable."

Access denied. I nod, "And if it isn't?"

"If it isn't, then I'll come and pull your wolf for you." Revecca shrugs. "It's a waste. But I would rather release him than see you dead. For what it's worth, you're equally entertaining and aggravating."

I'm pretty sure that was a compliment. If not, I'm taking it as one anyway. "Thank you."

"Why are you so set on abandoning your mate?" Revecca cocks her head, and I'm not sure what she thinks she'll find by squinting at me.

"I'm not." I try to keep the growl suppressed, but it doesn't happen. I clear my throat. "I'm not. Until recently, like apparently right before I came here, she was with a human. She's had no interest in being with me."

"She doesn't?" Revecca furrows her brow and squints. "Pe bune? A human?" Revecca tsks dismissively. "How does he even handle her heats?"

"Suppressants." I shrug.

Revecca rolls her eyes. "Your sister makes more problems than she solves."

"And she takes great pride in that."

Revecca's small smile proves that with every passing interaction between her and Lena, their disdain for each other seems to be waning.

"Are you leaving now, then?" Revecca traces shapes with her fingers on her desk.

"I guess. I don't need anything else. I got my denial of services, so I'll book a return flight." Taking her words as a dismissal, I stand.

"There's a possibility I can help you with your wolf and that we can make this a bit better for you. If you'd stay a few more days, a week even, it might give you a jumpstart on control, if you're truly going to attempt life for her." Revecca purses her lips.

"I think you may be my favorite." I let my jaw go slack. "New plan: I'll convince Cade to rule in Romania if you come to rule in the States."

"Absolutely not." Revecca shakes her head. "It's far too . . . what's the word . . ."

"Uncivilized?" I offer.

"That would be one fitting word." Revecca sighs. "I can work with you tomorrow morning if you're interested. I really would like the opportunity to see you try to gain control. I hate you least."

CHAPTER 37
HENRI

HE'S NOT GOING to come back, my wolf complains.

It's been barely five days, and the house seems quieter. It's not like his presence is normally very loud; he mostly keeps to himself, but without him, there's a lack of something. I can hardly stand working here with how strange the feelings are.

I'm stuck looking longingly down the hallway toward the staircase that leads upstairs to his bedroom.

A rogue thought crosses my mind. *I highly doubt Revecca is going to kill him. Right? He wouldn't be going there to die.*

"He's on a flight, not tomorrow but the next day." Finn's deep Irish voice comes from behind me, startling me.

"Oh." I find him carrying two steaming cups.

"Thought you and I could have a chat?" He raises a cup he prepared for me.

Begrudgingly, I agree to his offer, feeling like there's a choice in this but not knowing for sure. "Your office or mine?"

"I was thinking the back deck?" Finn cants his head back in the direction he came.

"Oh-okay."

As I make my way down the hallway, my stomach isn't settled. While the back deck is significantly less formal, it doesn't ease my mind that this isn't a business chat.

Did I screw something up?

Being mid-morning, the only people at the main house are the cleaning staff and various support staff members — fulfilling one of their two mandatory in-office days a month — so it's private enough that we won't be bothered.

Through the glass doors and on to the deck, Finn sits at one of the tables.

"Henri," Finn says in the soothing voice he uses on Lena, and it's ridiculously comforting. "This isn't meant to be a stressful conversation. I want to know how to best support you."

"I'm not sure I understand." I take a sip of my tea, forcing my hand steady.

"Well, as Lena would say, I'm being an 'overprotective arse' and 'not letting her fight her own battles,' but I've sent away a few shipments of flowers from Nathan on your behalf, telling the florists he's used there's no one here by that name." Finn looks a little guilty as he ducks his head, but he's quick to carry on. "I also know he's been calling and texting you more than a little regularly."

I don't have to ask how he knows. I've started switching my phone to silent because of the incessant buzzing during meetings.

"I'm worried about your well-being. Not because you can't handle him, but because I think you feel like you need to handle it alone."

Finn's words give me pause.

My shoulders drop only slightly. "I know I should block him, but if I block him . . ." *How do you explain this?*

"If you block him, he'll call from different numbers. He'll text you with new phones. You won't know what is or isn't him." Finn eloquently puts words to my feelings.

I nod and find words for the other thought that's been weighing on me. "And it's not like we can change my number because of the people who need to get ahold of me on a daily basis."

"There are options, Henri." Finn takes a sip from his cup before he sets it on the table between us. "There are options to make this stop."

"Why does that sound like you're planning on killing him?" I shake my head. "Why do wolves always make quick jumps to murder?"

"You're the one who went to murder, I was thinking restraining order." Finn's lip twitches with a smile, but he schools it back. "I can have it filed the minute you say the word."

"Can I . . ." I chew my bottom lip. *Why? Why am I even thinking about this?* The logical thoughts don't mesh with my emotional ones. "Have some time to think about it? Maybe he'll stop if I just answer him."

"The offer doesn't have an expiration date." Finn eyes his cup for a moment before picking it up and bringing it to his mouth.

"I appreciate it." I sip more of my tea. Pretending this isn't an awkward conversation between the two of us, I change subjects. "How's married life?"

"With Lena?" Finn laughs, and it lightens the dark, somber mood between us. "An adventure, but I wouldn't have it any other way. Finding my mate has been everything I'd hoped it would be. And as much as she drives me mad, I get how Ma and Da have always said there's no explaining it."

I want that, my wolf tells me. *That's not Nathan.* She pushes back New Year's Eve, and I cross my legs immediately, feeling the memory of Deacon's body clinging to mine.

Deacon might not be our mate. I'm sick of arguing with her. It's this same old song and dance. Finn's 'warning' about Nathan is quite literally telling me someone loves me and wants me back. *Deacon didn't even seem all that thrilled about me. Remember?*

You're. Wrong. She's adamant.

"I'll let you get back to your day. I've got to rip some teenagers new arseholes over being respectful to other people's property." Finn seems far too cheerful for that task.

"Good luck." I smile.

The fun flask is in my desk, left over from when I was working with Deacon. Maybe I just tuck her away and get the rest of my work done. I can go home early and watch a movie or something.

"Thanks." Finn laughs and stands from his chair, taking his cup with him. "This is gonna be fun."

CHAPTER 38
DEACON

"We need to talk," Finn says, sticking his head out of Cade's office as I make my way down the hall.

We *don't need to talk, you do.* I bite back the smart-ass remark and walk my ass into Cade's office before I piss off the Alpha wolves used to running the show.

Following Revecca's instructions is going to kill me. My head is throbbing, and I'm strongly considering the opioids tucked away upstairs in my suite, just to use as painkillers. As soon as the last pill wore off that I took at the airport in Romania and my wolf came back, ancestors started bombarding me nonstop. Their lack of courtesy in not even allowing me to sleep proves that the phrase 'I'll sleep when I'm dead' is the biggest load of shit ever.

Finn doesn't lead the way into the room. Instead, he closes and locks the door behind us. *Apparently, I'm in trouble.* Weird since I didn't start an international incident. *Fuck, just get this over with.*

Instantly my wolf goes on edge, taking in the situation and readying for the defense. *Fight.*

He's been weird inside me. It's been exhausting trying to fight him back and silence him as he breaks through almost every single one of my thoughts with calls to violence. His uncharacteristic, near-constant need for brutality is starting to feel normal.

Fight back.

I shake my head, brushing off his ideas, and advance to the chairs in front of Cade's desk. My older brother is resting his head on his palms, pressing the heels against his eyes. It's not one of his usual stress indicators. I've only seen it once before, and that was when Lena was possibly dying.

A pit forms in my stomach, and I tilt my head. "Cade?"

The gravel in my voice hides the fear, kinda, mostly, not at all.

Finn sits next to me, and after a few long seconds, Cade lifts his head from his hands.

"Henri." Cade says her name. and my jaw twitches. Despite having my full attention already, he still pauses a second longer. "She's . . ."

"Henri's in her office, and it seems she's been drinking." Finn keeps his voice low with misplaced concern that it may escape the soundproofing of Cade's office.

I furrow my eyebrows at them and frown. "That's not usual."

"Not usual?" Cade mutters before making his voice clearer. "Fuck, nothing fazes you, does it?"

"I don't know why you're still surprised about that." I answer his rhetorical question but keep myself neutral despite the throbbing in my head, which now matches the thundering of my heart with worry over Henri. "Has anyone talked to her?"

Finn shakes his head.

Blind leading the blind. Why wouldn't we just speak to the person we're worried about?

When I move to stand, Cade's Alpha command hits me. "Sit down."

My ass becomes glued to the chair. This is wholly unfair, but I take it, then throw my hand up, gesturing to the door behind me. "If the two of you aren't going to talk to her, then I will."

Slumping back in his chair, Cade shakes his head. "She sent me an email stating she'll keep managing her team remotely, but she would like to work from home for a few weeks."

Speechless is usually a response I intentionally adopt rather than one I fall into accidentally, but I'm down the rabbit hole, looking for Alice so I can get out of here and storm Nathan's home like the beaches of Normandy, invading his life to ruin it like he's done to hers. It doesn't matter that she no longer lives there. He seems to still have control over her, even after she saved herself and got out.

Grasping at straws, I try calculating why Henri would behave this way while also catching up to where Cade is in the scenario. He's always one step ahead of most people, and I try to be two steps ahead of him. "Did you approve it?"

Cade shakes his head. "I haven't answered her request."

"We obviously don't want to go that route," Finn states. "I know she's upset about leaving Nathan, but from conversations with her and others, this seems to be more than just a breaking-up issue."

Right, like escaping the years of domestic violence as the main contributing factor. I leave the snark unsaid. Finn's trying.

"What do you think?" Cade looks for my opinion.

It's not that he never does, but the only time Cade consults me is when he's truly out of his depth and is looking for a new perspective.

"You know her best," Finn affirms.

My wolf thinks about Henri and brings all the happy memories to the surface. *She's ours now.*

Drawing a deep breath, I speak past his question. "Let me talk to her first."

"I'm worried about you." Cade's worrying and honesty about it isn't my favorite thing. "I can feel a difference between you and your wolf. It's only been a few days you've been home, but The Leviathan even . . ." Cade lets that linger before continuing. "The Leviathan isn't unsteady about you and what to do with you. It's the first time since, before . . ." He struggles to communicate his worries.

"Before I was drugged with the human shit that made me numb but did nothing for my wolf?" I offer, knowing he's talking about the antipsychotics our 'father' shoved down my throat.

My wolf growls at the memories of how it all started. The way I figured out how to silence him.

Finn tenses in his chair as the room crackles with the energy between us.

"I'm sober. I'm trying to stay sober even though it hurts like fucking hell. Revecca says it's possible to make it easier. She and I worked on getting my wolf under control. But I have bad days. There are even more ancestors here than there were before." I look over my shoulder at the door where Marielle is watching us. "I don't think I should have to tell you how hard I'm willing to fight for her."

Finn nods. "Tell us what you need. We'll make it happen."

"Be prepared to have her team work without a lot of supervision for a couple weeks. But I'll get her cleaned up as fast as I can." I bob my head in time to the throbbing behind my eyes as I start formulating a plan.

It's okay. I'm used to holding other people together.

Cade runs his hand back through his hair. "Anything you

need. I'm serious, Deacon. If she's just done and needs a change of jobs or to retire entirely, the fund will cover it."

Giving her money, a roof over her head, food on the table, and a cozy life isn't going to fix her problem. But Cade's generosity is endless, and it makes him a good leader.

"Let me see what I can do." I don't make him a promise because I can't be sure I can fix it.

I've never seen Henri drink more than a single glass of champagne at any event.

We need to see her. My wolf and I agree about that, at least.

I spent the first day home jet-lagged and trying to adjust to the massive time difference. It's not that I didn't want to see her, but I wasn't in any shape to do so. She deserves me at my best, more than I am now, but if what they're saying is true, Henri's problem is bigger than mine.

Time to get our mate. My wolf gets antsy, pushing me to leave the room and get closer to her.

I don't blame him. We can't do anything for her sitting here in Cade's office.

I toss my head over my shoulder toward the door. "May I?"

Cade purses his lips but gives me a single, tight nod.

Leaving Cade's office, I head upstairs to pack some things before heading to Henri's office. There's a male child playing jacks in the stairwell, and I sigh at seeing yet another ancestor.

CHAPTER 39
HENRI

SHAKING MY HEAD, I look at my laptop screen, but it's still fuzzy. The door to my office opens.

"It's customary to knock on a closed door. The occupant —"

"Get up," Deacon growls.

"Excuse me?" I push back.

When did Deacon get home? Finn mentioned it, but has it really been that many days?

"Get up," Deacon says firmly as he pulls my purse off the hook near my spring coat.

My heart flutters in my chest.

"I'm working." I retort, pointing to the laptop.

Why is it so hot that he's trying to order me around?

"Your eyes are swimming. You smell like cheap whiskey, and you haven't washed your hair in three days. I can see the dry shampoo." He argues with me, pointing out everything I've done wrong today. "You're not working, you're looking at the computer, trying to get it to make sense."

Oh fuck, do Cade and Finn know I've been drinking?

I go back to staring at the screen, pretending I can read it, embarrassment flushing my cheeks.

Deacon draws a deep breath. "Get up."

An Alpha command hits me, and I rise to my feet. *When did that happen?* My heart pounds in my chest. The room sways.

"Take those ridiculous heels off before you break an ankle." The alpha command has passed, but the firmness is still there.

I slip out of my heels begrudgingly.

"Come on." Deacon turns around and starts walking out of my office. "Don't think I won't pull a Finn and carry your ass out of here."

I pocket my phone and follow Deacon to wherever it is he thinks is more important than work.

He leads me back down the hall and through the house until he opens the mudroom door.

Obediently, I walk through it. "What do you possibly need me in the coatroom for?"

Deacon walks past me and pulls his backpack off a hook. "Come on."

He opens the door to the garage, and my stomach drops. "I'm not getting on your bike barefoot. I'm not going anywhere with you. Period."

"I am not joking. I'll pick your ass up. Move."

I've never seen Deacon like this before.

Still confused, I walk out the door, willing to humor him that much. My shoulder bumps against the doorframe. *Pull it together, Henri.*

He wraps his arm around me, steadying me, and involuntarily, I melt into him.

"Come on, Hen. Let's get you home," he whispers.

Home? The mood swing he's got going on irritates my last nerve.

"You can't be such an asshole and then all sweet to me." I try to snarl and push myself up out of his arms.

He huffs. "Don't be so sure about that."

Deacon opens the passenger door to Lena's red SUV and walks around to the driver's side before I can even climb in.

Closing my eyes while Deacon backs out of the garage is a bad idea because once they're shut, it's impossible to open them again.

For the first time in weeks, it feels like I can rest.

Waking up disoriented is never fun. Waking up disoriented, with the man your wolf believes to be your mate in the driver's seat of your employer's vehicle, in front of their very remote second home, with a hangover, is significantly less fun.

I'm reminded of the times I've come here, semi-uninvited, looking to feel safe and finding Deacon instead of solitude. Now he's brought me here on purpose.

The SUV is stopped just before the garage as Deacon waits for the door to finish rolling up.

"Welcome to the land of the living." He keeps his voice low as if he knows I'm hungover.

The world spins.

"I thought wolves don't get sick." I groan and bring my hand to my head.

Deacon laughs softly. "As Lena would like to point out to me regularly." He adopts a huffy, light tone, mimicking the way her voice sounds when she's irritated. "It's not sick, it's a side effect."

I grumble at him as he drives into the garage and closes the door behind us.

"I don't know why I went anywhere with you when you

said home and a vehicle was involved." I start being contrary with him, hoping he understands my frustration. "This isn't where I live."

"Home isn't where you sleep at night, Henri, it's where you feel safe enough to let go."

Deacon doesn't seem to notice my shock at his words.

Home. It feels more right than anything else.

He unclips his seat belt and gets out of the SUV. "I also had an uncomfortable talk with my brother and sister's mate, and it seems they don't appreciate their PR professional drunk on the job."

He closes his door before I can respond.

Shit. Shit. Shit. Shit. I cannot lose this job. I draw a deep breath, trying to stop myself from hyperventilating.

But breathing hurts my head.

Deacon pulls the backpack out of the back seat and leaves me to get out of the car myself and into the house.

I grab my phone out of the well on the door and check for messages.

There aren't any. Zero. Zilch. Nada.

I flip to the text messages to see if maybe Deacon cleared the notifications.

Nothing at all today. Nothing new in my emails either.

I refresh the boxes and look at them again. It has to be broken.

Maybe Deacon will let me borrow his. This can't be right.

I get out of the SUV and head toward the house.

The concrete floor is cool under my feet, so I scurry across it at the risk of aggravating the pain in my head. The room whirls as I come through the door, and I sag against the wall to make everything stop spinning.

Okay. I'm way more drunk than I expected.

Deacon is in the kitchen, writing something down on a notepad.

"What are you doing?" I try to distract myself from the pain.

"Grocery list." Deacon doesn't look at me.

"So, I'm fired, and Cade's exiled me out here with you?" I mope, setting my phone on the counter.

"Nope." Deacon pops the *p*.

I slouch against the countertop. *Did I even eat today?*

Deacon looks up at me from the list. "You were dead to the world, but I called Cade on the drive here. I've got two weeks to get you back together, or Cade's going to retire you to a nice cottage on the property."

My heart starts going a hundred miles a minute. "I'm fine. I can work just fine."

"You're not," Deacon says without breaking eye contact. "You haven't been fine because no one goes from almost completely sober to intoxicated on the job overnight."

"It's fine. I'll pull myself together." I say those words again, but his expression doesn't change.

"Henri, quit saying 'it's fine' or I'm about to get mad." His voice is level despite the threat of anger.

It's too much. It's just all too much.

I draw a deep breath, trying to hold it together, but between the hangover and the emotions of failing at my job, I let the tears fall. "I'm sorry."

Deacon sets down the pen and walks around the counter. Wrapping his arms around me from behind, he kisses the top of my head fifteen million times — or twelve, whichever comes first.

"Let's get you fed and hydrated. I can imagine how that hangover feels. You smell like you drank your weight in cheap whiskey."

He gets me a glass of water and pulls a bottle of unmarked pills from his backpack. He slides it to me. "Take this."

I put the pill in my mouth and swallow it down.

Deacon brings his hand to his forehead, smacking himself lightly, before pulling it away. "You'll just do anything anyone says without questioning it, won't you?"

"Well, I didn't get up earlier by choice in my office when you used an alpha command on me. That's not something you did before Romania. So, seems like I'm lost to the pack hierarchy, and asking questions is frowned upon." I snap back.

"Never, not even once, have any of us thought we're better or above anyone else in our pack. Especially you." Deacon's mouth presses into a thin line, brow drawn together, the look screaming disappointment.

He takes a picture of the list he wrote and sends it off to someone, if the whooshing sound of a text being sent is any indication.

"Hey, can I use your phone? Mine's not working or something. It won't get any updates or emails or texts." My phone is suspiciously quiet, not even Nathan's texted me today. And I'll do anything to change the subject.

Deacon goes back to his phone, but instead of giving it to me, he does something on it.

He tucks it back into his pocket, and mine dings.

DEACON:

It works, Hen, you're on timeout. Cade and I
are your only allowed contacts.

"Who. Gave. You. The. Right," I snarl and throw my phone.

He narrowly catches it before it slams into the cupboard to his right.

I pop off the stool and storm around the island to where I know Deacon keeps the alcohol.

He still doesn't say anything when I grab a bottle and take a pull right from it.

"Henri." Deacon stops me about two swallows in.

He tips the bottom of the bottle down so that I don't make a mess of it.

"I left Nathan. I'm completely alone." I spit the words at him as if any of this is his fault when we both know it's not.

Between leaving Nathan and battling my wolf's obsession with Deacon — and mine if I'm being honest — I have way too many feelings to process. I don't even know where to begin.

This is easier. For now.

Deacon takes a minute, setting the whiskey bottle on the countertop. He grabs my chin, forcing me to look at him and not the bottle of booze.

"You are better off without him. You are not alone." He battles my statement with his absolute certainty, and the conviction in his tone makes the belief I've had for weeks falter just a little bit. "When was the last time you were sober?" Deacon lets my chin go to run his fingers back through my hair, which he knows is too-many-days dirty.

"How can you say that? Outside of work, I don't have anyone." I try to level with him. At least the headache is going away. "And what is it to you what I do with my free time? You aren't really one to judge."

"I'm here, aren't I?" Deacon laughs and shakes his head like what I'm saying is ridiculous.

"What does that have to do with any of it?" My jaw drops. "You're technically still work."

My heart squeezes with those last words because I don't want them to be true. *How can I feel this way about him even when the wolf isn't here to say the ridiculous words?*

"Come on, Hen." Deacon offers me his hand. "Let's get you washed up, and then we can talk."

CHAPTER 40
DEACON

HENRI GOES toward my and Lena's bedrooms, but I stop her. "I took the liberty of moving into the primary. It has nicer amenities. No one else comes here." I selfishly sweeten the pot so her scent might linger where I spend a lot of time in my secondary home. "Thalia loved the shower and tub here so much she had the Alpha bedroom at the main house constructed similarly."

Henri redirects herself back to the primary bedroom without further objections.

I thought I could stay away from Henri. I could keep my distance and get my wolf together, and if I couldn't get my gift together enough to be a good mate for her, I'd give up the wolf. Henri wouldn't have to suffer for me.

She feels alone. That no one is here for her. *How could I ever let her live that way?*

My wolf laughs at that. He doesn't have to say it, and he knows it. The 'I told you so' air is evident. Since I laid eyes on her after coming back from Romania, everything is different.

Revecca made a lot of sense. Embracing the fluffy asshole

and trying to figure out my gift is working — *ish*. The truth is that the darkness within me has become even more toxic. It whispers, *Maybe for her I can figure it out . . . I'll hang every hope of life on her. No matter what that means for her.*

Leaving her to shower or take a bath, I start the task of taking inventory and putting the home together for the next week. The pantry has enough random odds and ends left over from my past weeks of decompression that I can make a pretty decent meal for tonight.

In the freezer, I find peas and heat them in the saucepan on the stove. I try to remember what weird eating things Henri has.

Surely there's something she doesn't like.

Nothing, other than Nathan practically starving her, comes to mind.

I can't do this. I don't even know her.

Although I imagine that'll change being in close quarters with her for however long we're here for.

The door to the primary bedroom opens, and Henri walks out in one of my T-shirts and a pair of my sweatpants.

Seeing her in my clothes elicits a physiological response I wasn't expecting. *Fuck. I'm getting as bad as Cade and Finn.*

"Can you at least have some of my clothes sent over if I'm going to be held here as a prisoner indefinitely?" Henri snarls.

Maybe I should have shown her where I have clothes in her size? Nah. This cute little angry thing she's got going on is fun. *Finn and Lena's bickering makes sense now.*

"So hostile." I shake my head and move on. "You like peas, right?"

"Yeah?" Henri pauses, drawing her eyebrows together. "Why?"

"I don't know," I answer with an offhanded shrug. "Lena

312

has a bunch of stuff she doesn't like. Thalia is less particular but still kind of a picky eater."

"Not all women are the same," she grumbles, but the stool slides out across the floor, and she sits on it.

I hang my head. When did she get to be so combative? Or was it that I was too messed up to notice?

She's hurting. My wolf is focused on her.

I pull down two bowls and start plating the penne pasta with alfredo sauce, chicken breasts, bacon, and peas. Pulling the parmesan and asiago, which spoil slower and are fridge safe for a long time, out of the fridge, I turn back to her with the bowls.

Her eyebrows rise seeing the dishes.

"What? You just told me women aren't all the same and that you like peas." I set the bowls down, drawing a deep breath, trying to check myself against the frustration.

"No, it's not that." Henri softens. She draws a deep breath. "I just don't remember the last time someone personally cooked for me, not a group meal, without some devious intention behind it."

I roll my eyes. "Well, a few minutes ago you were accusing me of keeping you prisoner. So, assuming that this battle between us is going to continue, then truly the reason to provide you a meal is that the Geneva convention states I have to feed you."

Henri rolls her eyes. She takes a fork from me and stabs it into a slice of chicken.

"Jeez." I gasp in false shock. "What did that chicken do to you?"

With a shake of her head, Henri pops the chicken into her mouth. She chews and swallows and then looks at me. "You're not eating?"

"No, I am." I look away from her and turn back to the food.

For being a hodgepodge of premade ingredients like canned sauce and slightly freezer-burned peas, it's not bad. By the time I've finished, Henri, the slowest eater in the world, is halfway done with her food.

I rinse my bowl and put it in the dishwasher, and Henri slides her bowl toward me.

"Eat." I slide it back.

"But . . ." She tries to argue with me, but she relents and takes the bowl back.

"You can be the only one eating. It's okay." I encourage her.

I forgot to eat slowly so she didn't feel pressured to be done.

"Fine, but while I eat, you have to tell me how you've come to the conclusion that I'm not alone," Henri demands.

"Henri, we've been dancing around each other for months. You were the best kiss of my entire life. The only thing that's stopped us all this time is that you've had a boyfriend." I'm jumping all over the place and doing a shit job of explaining my feelings.

Henri cocks a brow but keeps eating. She doesn't interrupt my silent struggle.

Closing my eyes, I draw a deep breath and start again. "I talked to Revecca about us, and a number of other things, but about us in part. She confirmed we're a match from fate itself and fuck . . . it's the only . . ." I shake my head, clenching my fist, trying to hold back the words, but it's got to be honesty.

My words give Henri pause. She closes her eyes and sets her fork on the counter beside her bowl.

I can't stand to lose her when the opportunity is right here in front of me. "It's the only thing that has me committed to trying to work with my wolf."

Henri's eyes pop open. Then she squints at me. "I'm what, the reason you're going to try and get sober?"

"No." I shake my head quickly, taking that pressure, that blame, off her. "I'm committed to getting more sober and letting my wolf become strong, but, on the off chance you and I can't seem to get along together . . . I can have him removed and set you free to find a better mate."

"How is that any better?" she pushes out through gritted teeth.

You don't get stuck with a mate who's barely functioning. That doesn't seem like a smart answer though. It's certainly not one that will convince her of anything.

"It's the least selfish thing I can do for you, Hen. If you love someone set them free and all that. Better to let the wolf and you go rather than hurt you." I go quiet for a minute, debating saying this. *Ah, fuck it.* "It's either that or I kill Nathan so there's no chance he'll hurt you again. Though, realistically, there's no reason I can't do both."

"You don't have to kill him. Why do you keep casually admitting to plotting murder?" She rubs her temple, frustration overflowing from what I'm guessing is an ingrained portion of her job.

"Because I can." I wrinkle my nose. "I'll confess to a few if it'll make you feel better."

Henri pulls her hand away from her face and looks me dead in the eye. "What?"

"Brayden Bachman? His 'heart attack'" — I use air quotes — "was potassium induced." I shrug as she slowly shakes her head. "The wolves and humans Cade didn't kill in relationship to Thalia being kidnapped and turned, most of them will never turn up from the missing person reports." I draw a deep breath and let the air out. This next one is getting easier to confess with the more people I tell. "Karina 'Alden,' or whatever her real name was, died of an accidental drug overdose, which was really done at gunpoint."

"Deacon." Henri shakes her head, but there isn't any fear wafting off her, it isn't her trying to escape from any of it. "Please, for the love of anything at all in this world, do not ever mention this outside of this room ever again."

I laugh. "Okay, Henri."

I admire her form. Her blonde hair, clean and hanging around her face, makes her look more normal, better, despite sallow skin and the dark circles under her eyes.

She would be so accepting of this.

Why wouldn't she be? She's fucking perfect. My wolf sees those things, the weariness of her body, the same way I do, but we're both looking past it to the inner beauty that no amount of alcohol or sleep deprivation can wash away.

CHAPTER 41
HENRI

DEACON'S asleep within twenty minutes of whatever the fuck is playing on the television.

I finished the drink he poured me. It seemed like he was taunting me. Begging me almost to keep drinking. I didn't even want it. I don't even want to drink when he's in the same room as me.

But then he said those things, and I couldn't believe it anymore. Deacon has always been aloof — eccentric, as Cade and Finn call him. But never, not even for a minute, did I ever consider that Deacon was dangerous.

Seductive, sure. Charming, most definitely. And everyone knows he's got a great sense of humor. But that doesn't coincide with what he admitted to today.

My wolf is too far under the influence of alcohol to weigh in. And quite frankly, I don't want to hear what she has to say on the matter. It's all her fault anyway. She encouraged me to start this mess with Deacon, encouraged me to stalk him.

"Fuck, Henri." Deacon moans, but he doesn't sound like he's awake.

I don't answer him.

"Henri!" Deacon gasps, sitting bolt upright, panting.

His wolf's eyes shine through in the low light. Drawing a deep breath, he steadies himself.

"You okay?" I don't know what else or what more to ask. I just sit there staring at him.

My heart hasn't gotten the memo that he's dangerous, that he's a killer, that he's . . . Deacon.

"Yeah. I'm fine. Sorry." He shakes his head, the movement in stark contrast to his words.

"What was your dream about?" *Why did I even ask?*

He hangs his head. "Nathan was killing you."

Sorrow drapes over Deacon's words like a sheet covering a dead body.

Pushing himself off the couch, he eyes the bottle on the table.

"Go away, Marielle," he growls and walks past me and the bottle of whiskey. "Fuck off, Zachariah. The two of you are perfect together. You'd make excellent spouses for each other."

I hear a cupboard door open and close in the kitchen. Then the electric whir of the ice machine, and cubes clank into the bottom of a glass. Most unexpected is the gurgle of the water as it comes through the spigot on the door.

"Zachariah," Deacon snarls, "get the fuck out of my house." Deacon keeps talking. "Great, all three of you, it's a fucking party."

Normally when I've witnessed Deacon dealing with the ancestors, he doesn't engage with them openly. He notes their presence and gets tense, but I've never seen him have a full-on conversation.

He's not even trying to hide them from me.

Looking over my shoulder, I see Deacon clutching the glass.

His eyes are closed, and the skin on his fingers turns white with his grip.

"Fuck. Off," Deacon says more firmly.

Seconds tick by, and he opens his eyes. They're completely dark black.

"Get out!" Deacon shouts.

The glass cracks in his hands, and glistening shards fall to the floor.

A shiver runs down my spine, but Deacon draws a deep breath and hangs his head. "Sorry, Hen."

Deacon proceeds toward the back door. I head to the kitchen and pull a dishrag out of the drawer.

"I've got it." Deacon approaches with a broom, dustpan, and bucket.

"Let me help." I crouch down on the floor, using the rag to soak up the water.

Deacon doesn't argue with me. He stoops down and starts picking shards of glass out of the puddle of water, tossing them into the bucket.

Once done, Deacon takes the cleaning supplies back to the entry.

Busying myself, I make him another glass of water, trying to remember how many ice cubes I heard hit the bottom of the glass before I switch it over to water.

"I'm sorry." Deacon's voice, nearer than expected, startles me.

The glass slips from my hand, but Deacon catches it.

"Wouldn't that have been something? Cleaning up two. I'd have to give up drinking water then too. Would be some sort of sign."

"Sorry, I just didn't hear you." My face heats.

"You don't have to apologize. I'm the one with the outbursts. You were simply here to witness it." Deacon takes a sip from the cup, and his face falls like the taste disappoints him.

I don't know what to do. Turning away feels like the right thing but I'm enamored by him. His darkness calls to me. "They're gone, right?"

Deacon nods. "For now. I probably have sixty to ninety minutes before someone dares to come back. If I focus on not seeing them, sometimes they stay away longer? Or stay invisible."

Shaking his head, he looks at where the clock used to hang on the wall. It isn't there, and he groans, switching his glass to his other hand to pull his phone out of his back pocket. "I suppose it's late enough to be bedtime."

I don't know if it's the power of suggestion or something else, but my eyes become so heavy I can barely keep them open.

Deacon drinks all his water, leaving the ice cubes behind. He looks disgusted with himself but sets it on the counter by the sink.

"You can sleep in the primary bedroom. I'll go crash in my old room." Deacon tosses his head, indicating to the bedroom that used to be Cade and Thalia's.

The one that smells like him.

"No." My voice wavers.

"It's too late to drive you back, Henri. You can sleep on the couch if you'd prefer, but the bed is much more comfort —"

"No." I cut him off more forcefully.

His shoulders tense, and he raises his eyes to the ceiling, seemingly looking for answers.

"I'm not sleeping alone." I elaborate more firmly. "I'm not going to lie in bed while my wolf seeps back in as the alcohol burns off and listen to her rant about how you're within seventy feet of me, and all I have to do is get out of bed and find you."

"What do you want me to do?" Either Deacon is playing dumb or I'm not making sense, and I'm positive it's the former.

"Come to bed." I glare at him, waiting for him to lower his eyes to me.

The longer I wait, the more aware I become of his active avoidance.

His Adam's apple bobs as he swallows. "Don't —"

"Don't what?"

"Don't play with me like this, Henri. You're drunk. You're upset. Don't give me one more thing to try to work through." His words are pained.

Leaning to the side, I look up and see that his eyes are closed.

"I'm not that drunk. I'm not that upset." I argue with him. "I don't know how to feel about what you've told me tonight, but I'm not playing with you. I don't know how I feel, but I know that I don't... that I didn't do the right things sooner."

That I didn't leave him when you were right there asking me to.

"You are that drunk. You are that upset." Deacon shakes his head and runs his hand down his face. He looks jet-lagged, dark circles under his sleepy eyes. "I can't let this go any further than it has. If tomorrow, in the light of day, you're sober, and you still feel like this is what you want, then we can talk, but not tonight."

"It can be just sleep." I don't bother hiding the frustration in my voice.

I'm pouting and being childish.

"Oh, Hen," Deacon coos. He closes his eyes, and despite hanging his head, I can see they're squeezed shut. "Not tonight. Tonight, you've got to sleep alone. I know you don't understand it now, but you will tomorrow, and I've got to be the responsible one right now."

CHAPTER 42
HENRI

HEAD POUNDING AND BODY FREEZING, I wake up looking for warmth. *How drunk was I?*

The night comes back, starting with the fact that I'm not in my bed. The bed, larger than I'm used to, is cold, and I'm missing blankets. I force my eyes open, and light filters in from the shade drawn over the window.

It's the Aldens' Wisconsin house. Which tracks against my memory of Deacon driving us here.

Deacon.

I squeeze my eyes shut again as bits and pieces of what we talked about come to mind.

Oh no.

Offering to take him to bed. And I was doing that without my wolf. Well, I mean alcohol lowers inhibitions.

This is so bad.

My face heats, but then my stomach swirls, and I hurry out of bed despite the protest of my pounding head. At least I make it to the toilet before I throw up.

On the counter in the bathroom, a new toothbrush and

toothpaste, along with some other toiletries, are left out for me.

This is going to be so fucking awkward. I cringe, hoping Deacon is kind and lets it go.

My wolf is starting to rise, but not enough that she comments. Just enough that I'm not alone in my own skin again. Maybe that's the solution. Deacon said Revecca can take his wolf, so why couldn't she just take mine? *Then I'd be really alone.*

I head back through the bedroom and into the kitchen, where Deacon's standing over a pot of boiling water, glaring at it.

"Watched pots don't boil." I crack the joke before I think better of it.

"Good. I'm trying to poach eggs, and if I take my eyes off them, then they have the audacity to overcook." Deacon doesn't break focus.

Without looking, he picks up a slotted spoon off the counter next to him. First one and then another gets carefully wiggled and shaken and placed on top of English muffins with steak slices.

My mouth is watering.

He does another plate. Then he turns off the boiling water and moves to another pan, where he ladles out hollandaise sauce and pours it over the eggs.

Deacon sets the plates on the counter. "I was going to bring you breakfast in bed. But you braved the bright kitchen, so I'm guessing you're feeling a little better."

"Well, I just got acquainted with the toilet, so yeah. I guess," I blabber.

Deacon doesn't comment. "Eat what you can. But tell Lena I made you eggs Benny, and she'll probably murder me."

"She really likes eggs Benny?" I guess.

He slices into his stack with a knife and fork. "She has no patience when it comes to food and cooking for herself. Super picky but none of the desire to focus that long on something that doesn't interest her."

"I get that though. She's so fucking smart. Anytime I'm around any of you, but especially her, it's like I'm playing out of my league. You're all brilliant," I admit, pushing my hair back out of my face and taking a bite.

It's divine. The steak is fall-apart tender. Steak, muffin, spinach, egg, and sauce. It's a work of art. We eat for a long time, Deacon done before I finish.

"You don't give yourself enough credit." Deacon turns on his stool and looks at me, his hands resting in his lap. It's so genuine. "You have no idea how many people would have given up in your situation. Cade is an amazing team lead, but if someone doesn't stand up for themselves or speak up, Cade just assumes everything is okay until you make a mistake."

"Like drinking on the job?" I scrub my hands down my face.

"Like drinking on the job." Deacon agrees with me. "Or working so many days in a row without a break. Or being constantly available twenty-four seven."

When Deacon lists out all my shortcomings, it just reminds me exactly how fucked I am.

"I just want to do a good job," I defend.

Deacon puts his hand in my lap. "You are extraordinary. What I'm trying to say is that what you see — Lena being a dedicated student and scientist, Cade being a half-decent king and pack alpha, Thalia effortlessly stepping into role as Luna, mate, and wolf, Finn seems to be everywhere, nowhere, and doing twenty things at once — it's not something that came naturally overnight. Nor is it as easy as they all make it seem. I mean, you just saw Lena's entire life fall apart in front of her."

"I guess I don't understand." I shake my head.

"No one with your experience would have ever been able to put up with us for this long. That makes you extraordinary." He sighs with his whole body, shoulders and stomach stretching with the inhale and then a stuttered exhale. "Can we talk about how you got to doing a really good impersonation of me in my absence?"

"Can we not?" I push back, trying to stop the ache in my chest that comes with admitting all the terrible things.

Deacon nods, but it quickly turns into a headshake. "We do have to talk about it before we leave here. I told Cade I'd do what I could to get you back together, and that means talking about it. I figure if you get talking about it out of the way, you can be in your feels about it, and then we figure out how to fix it."

"In my feels?" I question. The use of slang doesn't seem normal for Deacon, but it makes me smile.

"What? Would you rather I say have an emotional breakdown and be catatonic on the couch disassociating?" He gives me the most blank expression, accompanied by a slow blink.

Even being silly, I can't stop myself from opening up. "I feel like I'm battling a monster all on my own. Nathan is all over the place. Calls, texts, and I guess even sending flowers to the house." More words start coming like the floodgates have been opened. "And now I don't know what to do with everything. Obviously, I want to keep working, I can't believe I fucked that up. I'm so going to get fired."

"You're not getting fired." Deacon interjects. "Cade literally couldn't replace you if he tried, and he knows it. Meaghan, as good of a job as she's doing, isn't you. Let that worry go."

I sit with those words. Deacon seems so sure.

"Has Cade ever personally expressed any displeasure with your work?" Deacon raises an eyebrow. When I shake my head, he smiles. "Then your status as his favorite employee remains intact." He reaches over and squeezes my leg. "You're not alone."

"But I don't have any friends, I chose Nathan over them. It's not like I can go back to my adoptive parents, and I don't want to even try finding the missing ones." I brush past that pain and onto the next thing. "Nathan is hot and cold. In one breath, he wants to get back together, and in the next, I'm some whore. I'm afraid to block him or change my number because what if he just starts calling from another number? Plus, the contacts for Cade's media have my phone number already, and changing it would be a logistical nightmare."

Deacon's grin is lopsided. It's a devious smirk, and I can almost hear the offer.

Beating him to the suggestion, I cut him off. "You can't just kill people. That's not a solution to a problem. Seriously, why are wolves so murderous? Even Finn and Lena so easily think of murder as an option."

"Shhh." Deacon puts a hand on my shoulder and rubs it.

That's when I notice the silence of the house and how loud my voice was.

"Sorry," I whisper.

"I'll have Cade's lackey, Adam, see what we can do about your phone." Deacon trails his hand down my arm to my hand.

"Then there's you, and we're hot and cold and back and forth. I just don't understand what we are and what we're doing. My wolf is utterly obsessed. She's dead set that we're mates. It's so bad that I just had to shut her out. I couldn't stand listening to it anymore because I'm pretty sure you don't feel the same way. You told me I didn't have to pick you, that you just wanted me not to pick him. And even if we are and you do, it's not like we can do this because you're my boss."

Leaning forward, Deacon presses his lips to mine, silencing me.

My tension melts away as he lays claim to my mouth with a firm kiss. A kiss I return, opening my mouth for him.

It's not hot and heavy like New Year's, but it's just as all-consuming. I soften, yielding to him, and he directs the kiss. He slides his hand into my hair, but he doesn't grab or pull. He supports my head, kissing me breathless.

A blissful minute passes before Deacon pulls back, but he doesn't go far. He keeps his fingers entwined in my hair. The physical connection solidifies my body and eases my mind.

"I am not your boss." Deacon waits for a moment, a small smile pulling the corners of his lips up, and it's obvious he's watching my brain catch up with my body. "Let's not put pressure on us and whatever this is between us, okay? Let's just see where this goes."

"Yeah. I can do that." The lack of commitment makes it feel better.

How does he always know how to make things better?

He places another soft, chaste kiss on my lips. "And for the record, my wolf is also obsessed with you."

We're quiet, and Deacon moves his hand from my hair, snaking it back down my shoulder to rest in my lap. I squeeze his fingers.

"You're one of us, Hen. Regardless of us seeing where things go, you're Pack Alden and you're family. Like Lauren and Ms. Gertie, it's nonnegotiable you belong with us in our weird little family." There's a firm decision in Deacon's words.

"Okay." That's so hard to accept, but I trust him. "But I don't know how to be pack. My wolf is trying, but I feel so awkward."

Deacon rolls his eyes. "You're doing just fine being pack. Give yourself more credit than that. The only thing is you've gotta not be so set on being secluded. Wolves, regardless of our feelings on it, thrive on connection. They need us to make an effort to be there."

"I am my own worst enemy, aren't I?" I brush my hair out of my face. "I've been so hung up on being alone that I've failed to try and make new connections."

"Sometimes the obvious answer is hard to see," Deacon confirms. "Making new friends is hard, but it's not impossible. I've got faith in you."

Deacon shifts on his stool and squeezes the hand he hasn't let go of.

"About last night." Deacon winces. "I think we need to talk about that."

"Do we have to?" I also wince, and we both look at each other, squinting.

It makes Deacon laugh, and the tension breaks. "Henri, I'm insanely attracted to you. You're in charge of anything that happens between us as long as you're sober enough to consent."

CHAPTER 43
DEACON

"I WANT YOU, but I'm scared."

Henri's response stops my heart.

Those two little words — 'I'm scared' — are the exact reason I didn't accept her offer to go to bed together last night.

I'm frozen, waiting for more.

"I'm sorry." Henri's heart is fluttering like a hummingbird.

"Don't be sorry, Hen." I slide off the stool, trying to give her space like that's going to help her overcome whatever fear she has.

"It's just. I can't get the bad memories out of my head." She runs her hand back through her hair, tousling it, and it catches the low light. "It's not that I haven't thought about being with you. Because I have. And last night, my mind didn't get in the way of what my body wanted. Which was probably the alcohol, but . . . what if I can't?"

"I am not going to make you tell me what those memories are." *Because my gut feeling tells me I already know.* "But I need to know how I can help you."

"I swear it's nothing you've done. I'm trying so hard to get

333

past it. It's so stupid because it's not like it's ever been that bad. It's not like I've really had it bad. But there's just these jolts, and I feel so fucking helpless." She stumbles over her words as she rushes them out, wringing her hands in her lap.

Henri's wolf is pushed forward in her eyes. It's certainly a wildling look. So wounded and afraid that she's . . . *helpless*. That word echoes in my brain, bouncing around the inner curvature of my skull, waiting for processing. The chaotic energy in my head matches the look of her wolf.

Fix it, Deacon. I focus as hard as I can on a solution, the echo not subsiding.

Make her safe, my wolf offers with no actual plan.

"I've an idea." I move slowly away from her, keeping my body turned toward her. Anything to show her she's still my focus.

I get to the kitchen drawer with the sharp implements, and I pull out one of the paring knives.

Henri flinches, and something inside me squeezes. Knowing that her fear of me is linked to him doesn't really sting. What does hurt is that she feels so powerless because, to me, she's a queen I'll serve until my dying breath.

"It's for you." I set the knife on the counter, not approaching her with it.

We're going to make a mess of that asshole's body. We're going to filet him slowly like roast pork. My wolf grows more and more violent with thoughts about Nathan.

The agreement between us growing stronger.

"And what am I supposed to do with it?" Henri eyes the knife.

"Well." I pause and draw a breath. "I propose that, when you're ready for more, you arm yourself with said knife. Take control of the situation. I wouldn't hurt you, and your logical brain knows that. But there's a wounded soul tucked inside you that's been holding its breath for so long. Now that it's able to breathe again, it can't be ignored."

Henri hangs her head.

"It doesn't have to be right now. I'm offering you something for when you're ready," I explain.

My cock throbs, not getting the memo that this isn't going to happen right this minute.

"What if I want it now?" Henri raises her eyes to me. "What if I'm sick of fighting my wolf all the time?"

"Then take the knife," I encourage her. "Put it anywhere you want. My throat, my chest, my cock. And if I hurt you, then hurt me back."

She tilts her head as she looks at the knife and then flicks her eyes back at me. "What if I hurt you?"

"On accident?" I ask for clarification, hoping she knows I won't ever hurt her on purpose.

She chews on her bottom lip.

"Then it's a little pain. You feeling safe is more important than the risk of accidentally cutting me." I don't tell her that I'm pretty sure it'd be fucking hot if she cut me, period.

My wolf presses forward, trying to call hers back to the surface.

And, fuck, do I want to end the uncertainty in this for her. I know I can give her what she needs, but not at the expense of her mental health. I won't do what she's afraid to talk about. He's used her and mistreated her, and I would never.

Her feelings aren't about me. But they're hers to sort through.

I try to slow things down between us. "I want you, Henri. I've wanted you for a long time. When I told you that you didn't have to pick me, it wasn't because I didn't want you. It's because I respect you enough to give you room to make the decisions you need to when you're ready."

She reaches for the knife but hesitates.

My cock and heart throb in unison, and I'm about to go toss myself into a cold shower for being too eager.

Our mate wants us. My wolf argues with me. *Just give her a little push.*

"You're in charge, Henri. I'm at your mercy." I slide the knife a little closer to her. "This offer isn't going away. No expiration."

Why won't she accept us? My wolf whines.

I don't like the honest answer. *Because we're no good for her. Nothing that pure can ever truly desire someone as dark as us.*

So, it's your fault? He huffs but doesn't retreat, his focus returning to Henri.

I expect Henri won't pick up the knife. That it's not the right solution or it's not something she can live with doing.

But hesitantly, she touches the handle, just her index and middle finger coming to rest on it.

With pursed lips and tensed shoulders, she asks timidly, "I want this, but are you sure?"

A silent exhale rushes out of me, and my muscles lose some of their tension.

"I promise." Those words feel right.

I'm not sure if she fully understands how much I mean them. The weight of the promises I make is sometimes a deep burden on my soul, but I gladly take that weight for her.

"How?" She pulls the knife toward her.

"On a flat, stable surface probably best." I make the leap, assuming she's asking how to fuck with a knife between us.

"Valid." Henri nods and lifts her gaze from the knife to me.

"Dare I say, Henri." I smile at her. "Is that mischief in your eyes?"

The sparkle in her eye as she pulls her top lip between her teeth gives away that she's embarrassed.

"We'll take it slow, okay?" I hesitate. *I'm not pushing her too fast, am I?*

"Deacon." She looks at me, and there's a steady resolve in her expression that wasn't there before. "Like you said, we've been dancing around each other for almost a year. I'm single. You're single. The kiss on New Year's. Everything we've done here. At what point do we just say fuck it and try?"

The change makes me uneasy.

"Hen, we've been dancing around each other for almost a year." I repeat those words back to her before choosing my own direction with it. "When I said that, it was to try and express my feelings for you, but that doesn't mean we have to jump into something. That was not the intent."

Henri growls, and it's the first time I've truly heard her embrace her wolf. The feral sound has me dead on arrival. Her eyes are gold with the presence of her wolf, meaning the alcohol must have completely left her system.

Quit trying to talk the smokin' hot blonde out of bed, Deacon. What a first.

"I want this. Quit telling me I might not." She clutches the knife with a white-knuckle grip.

"I think it might be safer if you're on top." I don't have a frame of reference for this, but the logic makes sense. "That way, you can control the speed and move any way you want."

The gears work behind her eyes. When her wolf pulls away, I stuff mine down. He growls but goes . . . mostly willingly.

Bedroom feels too intimate. But is the living room too public? No. Henri got excited when we talked about public bondings. It wouldn't be too public.

"Wait here? Let me get some things?"

"Sure." Henri looks at the knife, and I head to the laundry room.

Through there, I go back through the closet, the primary

bathroom, and into the bedroom. Along the way, I pick up and force as many fluffy bed things I can into my arms.

When I get back to the main living space, Henri is still by the kitchen counter, eye fucking the knife, and my cock throbs with the way she's looking at it.

Fuck. It's not like Henri is dangerous. She's small and unassuming, but seeing her armed and potentially slightly more deadly awakens my dark lust. I try to shake off those thoughts in the same way I shake out the blankets over the ground. If I don't, there's no way I'll be able to satisfy her. I'll be done the second she sinks onto me.

The coffee table in the living room is easy enough to move, so I lift it up and put it in the empty space where Lena's painting supplies used to be. Then I move on to making some sort of makeshift bed on the stable floor, positioning the pillows and bedding around the space with a low level of padding in the middle to make it comfortable but not dangerous.

"Come on, Henri, your living room glamping site awaits." I offer my hand out to her.

She almost tries to extend the hand holding the knife before realizing it and swapping them.

"Can . . ." Henri sits on the floor with me and groans. "Why does this feel so juvenile?"

I look around at my very flat blanket fort. "Well, I mean, if you're up for danger, I've got other ideas."

"No." She shakes her head. "This is probably the nicest thing someone's done for me. But ugh." Henri tries to relax, but something's rattling around in her brain. "Could we make out for a minute first?"

"I'm going to need to raise the bar for the nicest things people do for you." I shake my head. *Fuck it's a blanket on a floor. The bar is so low I couldn't dig a grave under it.* "But don't ever feel embarrassed about what you want or need. No matter how silly you think it is, ask for it because I'm not judging you, Henri. I already did."

"And you'll love me anyway?" Henri smirks.

It's almost patronizing, but I let it go.

"I didn't think you caught it in DC." I smile at her, dying to kiss her again. I reiterate, enunciating the important part. "And I *love* you anyway."

Mindful of the knife's position in my peripheral vision, I move in and tip her chin up. I kiss her, gently placing my lips on hers, then I let her choose how this is going to go.

She chooses to go slow. Her hesitant kisses test my resolve to truly let her take the lead.

Henri guides me down into our blankets and pillows until we're horizontal, lying on our sides. It's the beginning of her guiding me through it all. I'm completely at ease because I'd follow her anywhere, and getting to follow her to bed, or floor nest anyway, is a bonus.

She pushes against me, rolling me to my back.

The power she has over me like this . . . My cock throbs, begging for her to touch me, use me, and make me hers. But I wait, maybe not so patiently because a small whine escapes between her kisses.

Her lips on mine vary between soft and sweet and damn near trying to get me to come without even touching me. I knew Nathan was an idiot, but to fuck around on a woman who plays this well? Stupid doesn't begin to cover it.

I become putty in her hands, letting her move me and mold me to what she needs. The soft kisses grow more insistent, and she straddles my thigh, grinding against me. The layers of fabric between us are too many too much. I want her riding my thigh, to feel her wetness, to have skin-on-skin connection, but I've been gratifying my own desires for a long time.

This is about Henri, and I'm going to indulge her and, from that experience, draw my own pleasure.

"Fuck," she gasps, moving her hands between us.

The knife scratches lightly against my skin as she tries to pull my shirt up.

I lean up into her and help her pull it off, the knife's blade pushing against my flesh.

My shirt's barely off over the top of my head, and she moves to the band of my sweatpants.

The knife barely knicks the skin across my pelvis, and I gasp.

Not ready to have a blood bath just yet, I tilt her head up with one finger. "Let me help."

Henri's breath is ragged, and she looks from my torso to the knife. "Shit, you're bleeding."

"It'll stop," I assure her.

With Henri still straddling my thigh, I lie back and lift my hips to slide my pants down.

Henri squeaks, grasping my chest to keep herself from falling off. I laugh, but she stands, the pommel of the knife sliding down my thigh as she strips my sweatpants off.

I'm fully naked before her, just waiting, and my breaths come faster. I've been patient and good. I've controlled myself this long, waiting to have her as my own. I can wait just a little longer and let her decide she's ready for the next step.

She moves her gaze over my body, and she shudders from head to toe, the knife twitching in her hand. I can see desire spiking in the way her pupils take over the irises of her eyes.

Then she starts to strip, and I'm fucking dying inside.

We haven't even started fucking, but the excitement has her skin glistening with sweat, and when her shirt pulls up over her tits, exposing her pebbled nipples, I want to suck them one at a time into my mouth and taste her skin on my tongue.

I don't know if I've ever seen something so hot, and I want to stroke myself as I enjoy the view. I'm squirming, trying to keep my hands neutral. It's insanely difficult to deny myself. We didn't make any sort of rule that I couldn't, but yielding to her desire and neglecting my own is a learning experience. One I'm definitely trying to master.

The knife isn't sharp enough to destroy the shirt, but it definitely makes her pause, and she passes it between hands as she pulls herself free of the shirt sleeves.

Knife in hand, Henri smirks, and it's a look I know she doesn't do regularly, but it's full of hot mischief. "You know, one thing I haven't figured out is if you're an ass man or a tits guy?"

I laugh, watching her run the thumb of her free hand into the waistband of her pants.

She quirks an eyebrow and looks slightly confused.

"Henri, if it's yours, I'm into it. There isn't anything about you I'm not dying to touch, lick, or fuck. You could walk around in snow gear, and I'd be drooling over you." Her fingers pull on that band of elastic just a little bit farther, and a very wolfish whine comes out of me. "Fuck. Henri."

"You mean that. Don't you?" She furrows her brow and tilts her head, almost like she's skeptical.

To further my point, I wrap my hand around my cock. "You're in charge, Hen. But one thing you'll never be able to convince me of is that you're anything but perfect."

Henri's face softens, and she turns around but swivels her head to keep her eyes on me.

I keep my gaze trained on her, wondering where her thoughts have gone until she slowly bends at the waist and pushes the sweatpants down her thighs. Her underwear drags down with the pants, and I'm gifted a perfect view of her pussy. Her slick glistens in the light, and I squeeze my shaft, giving it a few strokes as I admire her.

She straightens and kicks her pants aside.

But when they're gone, and she turns back to face me, she sucks in a sharp breath, clutching the knife a little tighter. Some of her bravado seems to have faded, and the scent of fear hangs in the air.

Denying the throbbing, raging desire pulsing through my body, I release my cock. Tucking one hand behind my head and reaching for her with the other, I welcome her back to me.

"Come here," I encourage her, curling my fingers like I'd grab her if I could. "I want to feel you threaten me with that knife."

She freezes.

Come on, Hen. Don't shut me out. I know I'm pushing her a little bit with this. Is it a little bit too much? I meant for this to be baby steps, letting her take her power back.

CHAPTER 44
HENRI

I TAKE Deacon's hand when I step over the mound of pillows. Excitement pulses through me, and I can feel how wet I am.

Yet I struggle to sink down next to him.

He isn't going to hurt us. My wolf reassures me. Her gentle nudging to go to Deacon is genuinely helpful. *He called us his mate.*

Down on my knees in the little blanket and pillow pile on the ground, I put the knife flat on his sternum before lying next to him.

I know Deacon isn't afraid of the knife. It's a tool to make me feel better. A placebo effect. But fuck if it doesn't make me feel like I've got control.

I push myself up, holding my weight with one hand while the other goes to the knife resting on his sternum.

His breathing is ragged, and tension radiates from him. The laid-back man I'm used to is damn near rigid. His wolf rises in his eyes, and it feels warm and welcoming . . . like we're connecting for the first time.

Sure, at the rave, there was an undeniable spark that drew

me to Deacon. But it's only brightened and lit all the pathways leading to this moment.

I kiss him deeply, pushing my tongue into his mouth, and while Deacon kisses me back, he doesn't move to touch me.

It's amazing. Deacon doesn't push or demand more. He barely even breathes when I move the knife from his chest, rising up to climb on top of him.

But then the panic sets in.

I don't know what to do. My brain goes blank.

I want him. With every fiber of my being, I want him, but I don't know how to move. I don't know how to do this.

Deacon shifts beneath me. He brings a hand up to my face and brushes his fingers against my cheek. "You look so perfect like this."

Because I'm awkward as fuck I nod.

"Stop focusing on what you think you should be doing," Deacon advises, brushing the soft pad of his thumb against my bottom lip. "Focus on what you're feeling and how to make yourself feel good."

I've never asked, but now I wonder if mind reading is part of his gift.

Or he's just that dialed into us, my wolf smugly suggests.

He leans up and kisses me, barely moving his hand out of the way. Tender kisses fuel the fire inside me, and his encouragement to toss the match and let myself feel works.

I lean forward, deepening the kiss until he lies back.

With his head resting on a pillow, Deacon watches me, and his cock throbs when I push back. I raise my hips and slide myself lower. His cock presses against my warm center, and the ragged breath he takes is encouragement.

I've got Deacon completely at my mercy, but it's not a dark or heavy feeling. My fingers wrap tighter around the handle of the knife, which is between us, keeping me upright rather than coming to rest chest to chest where I could kiss him more.

"Henri, if this is too much —"

A snarl comes from me, and I didn't know I had it in me to make those noises.

"Fuck." Deacon blows out a breath. "Raised by humans but damn, Henri. You and that wolf might be scarier than Thalia."

He respects us. My wolf relishes in the way Deacon's wolf is forward, looking at us.

I feel so seen.

Holding Deacon's gaze, I rock backward until his cock enters me.

He draws a sharp inhale, holding himself almost perfectly still. The throbbing of his cock and clenching of his abdominals are completely involuntary, and I shudder at the feeling of fullness and the connection between us.

Closing my eyes, I embrace this wildness that's overtaking me. Rather than thinking, I just let my body do.

I grind down and slowly move on and off Deacon's cock. The movements take every bit of my fear away. Every time I grind down, my arousal heightens. Slack jawed, I roll my head back, feeling so close to the edge. Never have I felt this free.

"That's it, Hen," Deacon praises. "You're close. Just let go."

And he's right.

My pussy locks around Deacon's cock, and I almost double over from the force of the orgasm. It's exhilarating. My movements falter, and Deacon gently keeps me rocking forward and back with his hands on my hips, maintaining the stimulation just like I had been doing until I'm nearly falling over.

Apparently, I do fall over because Deacon's stroking my hair, our chests pressed together.

He whispers in my ear, "You did so good. I'm so proud of you."

His praise cloaks me in an intimate warmth. And then a physical warmth covers me as Deacon curls us up with a blanket into a cozy burrito inside the nest-like fort he built.

"I left him," I whisper. "If it matters. He didn't break up with me. I left him."

Deacon is quiet, but he rubs the tip of his nose against mine. I take it to mean 'no, it doesn't matter,' and it feels like 'as long as you're safe, I'm happy,' which makes so much sense.

"You were right. Cade was right." I sigh and curl up closer to Deacon, and he tightens his arms around me. "I can't believe I couldn't see or face it. I just lived that way and accepted it. Deep down, I had suspicions he was cheating. But you really think he killed his last girlfriend?"

"I wasn't lying to you, Henri. I spoke to her." His words are whisper soft, and he tips his head to plant a kiss to my forehead. "I really wish it wasn't true. She was probably an amazing woman. Strong like you. It's unfortunate that vermin like Nathan have a way of weaseling themselves in where they don't belong and gnawing away at all the good parts of life until you're isolated with one shitty tether to the world."

Deacon's words resonate with that wounded part of my soul. He so easily defines the isolation I felt but couldn't name, nor did I see it until I was drowning in it.

"I wouldn't normally press. But the last time we talked, before I was a completely selfish asshole, you were dead set on staying with him." Deacon pauses, glossing over the self-deprecation. "What changed? I'm not believing it was the outburst at Lunar New Year."

My body freezes before I can convince it not to act suspiciously. I was too relaxed after a mind-blowing orgasm otherwise I could have seen this coming. *He doesn't have to know everything. I don't have to tell him now. We'll talk about it later. It'll be fine.*

Embarrassment warms my face, and I dance around it carefully. "I was never human enough. He was so adamant that I go into heat so he could prove that being a wolf didn't make me different or special."

"It doesn't." Deacon shocks me. "What makes you different and special is how you approach the world. Experiencing heat with you is something he would have to prove himself worthy of, not that it's right."

"But it's over now." I kiss his nose, trying to change the subject. "He doesn't control me anymore. I can get on with my life. If I can figure out how."

I don't recognize those words from the thoughts I've had. The hope in them is foreign, feeling as weird as an invasion from outer space.

CHAPTER 45

DEACON

HOPE GLINTS in Henri's eyes, and it startles her. I can see it. Plain as day. I'm not dumb enough to believe that, just like that, with the snap of her fingers, she's going to be free of the trauma from the years of being with him. But the hope, a lightness of relief beyond the cage she was trapped in, is a brilliant thing to see.

Henri's always been pretty easy to read, and it was subtle, but she froze when I asked about the catalyst of the breakup, which leads me to believe there's something she's not telling me. But hopefully, someday — when she's ready — she'll feel comfortable enough to share it with me.

The glint and gleam of hope in her eyes changes to wide-eyed fear in the space between breaths. "Oh, my god. Deacon. Did Cade remember the meeting with New York by the Hour was today?"

"Was it on his calendar?" seems to be the right question.

"Of course it was on his calendar." She scolds me, furrowing her brow as she squirms out of my grasp, pushing off the blanket and leaving my perfectly good little fort.

351

So much for a time-out. I find the knife cast aside and pick that up before I start moving the blankets to the couch.

"Deacon." Henri glares at me, having gone from worry to rage. "Why is my phone not calling out?"

"Because you're on time-out." I remind her.

My phone, over by the stove, is her next target. She picks it up and draws the pattern I showed her the last time I let her play with it.

"You changed your passcode?" She looks at me suspiciously, raising an eyebrow.

"Yes. Because you knew it, and you're on a time-out." I put the knife in the dishwasher and then step over to her, wrapping my arms around her. She deflates a little with the skin-on-skin contact. "Cade is a big kid now. Take the training wheels off. It's not like we left him alone. He's got Meaghan, and she's doing a fantastic job."

The massive sigh she lets out is Lena-level dramatic. *This'll be harder than I thought.* "What do you do for fun when you're not working?"

Henri sets my phone back down and turns in my arms, looking up at me. She shakes her head. "I don't really have any hobbies. I never had time. I was working and then taking care of the house and cooking. Then we'd go out with Nathan's friends. Or, when I was still in school, my days consisted of studying."

"Alright, go back as far as you can. When was the last time you didn't have a million responsibilities? What did you like doing then?" I take big leaps.

I probably shouldn't rush her into the healing process. But I have a feeling she's gonna need a major distraction to stop her from thinking about whatever it is that she would normally struggle to delegate.

"Well, I guess high school?" She pulls her hair up in her hands and fans her face but still stays leaning up against me.

Begrudgingly I let her go. "Alright, high school. What did you like to do? Sports, reading, trivia, cheerleading."

My wolf and I immediately think of her in a cute little cheerleading uniform. *Focus.*

"Not athletic." Henri shakes her head. "Oh god. I'm so not athletic. Haven't you seen me at pack runs? That's the most I've ever 'sported.'"

Cheerleading uniform pushed aside, I try again, "Fair enough. So, reading? Writing? Binging television shows? Crafting? Photography?"

Henri steps away from me, but I catch her face turning pink. "You'll laugh. I'm sure we can find some new hobby or something if you're so insistent."

"Oh. No. No. No." I follow her back to our fort so she can track down her clothes, walking backward to face her. "What has you all embarrassed?"

She bites her lips together, which has me tipping my head to the side.

"I liked to crochet. I made a bunch of granny squares and turned them into blankets." She sighs and picks up the shirt.

"Well, Henri . . . you little hooker." I give her the never-fails devil-may-care smirk.

"Deacon!" she gasps. Looking up at me, she's about ready to smack me with the shirt, but then she catches my expression. "Oh no, that face doesn't work on me. I'm immune to your charms."

"Mm-hmm." I roll my eyes and start looking for my clothes. "Well, it's just your luck. Thalia is a stitch. As you may know, that is someone who practices knit craft, and it has made me an absolute yarn snob."

"I don't think those . . . That's not how that goes." Henri starts to correct my completely made-up terms.

"Tomato, potato." I ignore her. "Just call me your sommelier of yarn. Let's get cleaned up. There's still time today to make it to a couple yarn stores if we hurry."

"I don't get paid until tomorrow," Henri blurts out in a hurry.

"And?" I shake my head at her. "Listen, I know we're not exactly having the talk of what we are or who we are to each other beyond our wolves being positive we're mates, but, Henri, in case you haven't noticed . . . money really isn't something I worry about."

"It just feels so weird." She draws a deep breath but pulls my T-shirt over her head. "Cade's already insisted I don't pay for rent nor the SUV. Or fuel for the SUV or any maintenance on it. I feel like such a freeloader."

If Henri isn't paying for a car or rent and she doesn't exactly eat a ton . . . assuming she has student loans . . . "Henri, I know it's not polite to talk about money, but what happened to your paycheck?"

Her lips bitten together, staring at the floor and not looking at me, says it all.

I pull my sweatpants on and try not to storm to the kitchen. I stay cool as I cross the space.

After a few taps on my screen, my phone starts to ring out.

"Deacon, how's Henri?" Cade doesn't mince words.

"Good. Remember your interview with the newspaper." I give Henri a thumbs-up, not turning around to face her and knowing her well enough to know that she would have watched me walk away even if she couldn't meet my eyes. "Freeze Henri's paycheck."

"Okay." Cade pauses. "Why?"

"Think that through and ask the question again." I pause, trying not to be angry with him.

How the fuck did he not think of this?

It takes him a minute, the metaphorical gears whirring in his mind, but the overthinker finally gets it. "I have her information on file. I'll get her an account with the pack's credit union because she's going to insist on using her own money."

"Mm-hmm." I don't argue with him.

Henri's footsteps announce her approach behind me as she stalks closer.

Money doesn't matter when she's our mate. My wolf acknowledges.

I don't bother arguing with him either.

"Alright. I'll use her paycheck and a bonus for putting up with your ass to get it opened." Cade finishes typing out something, keyboards clicking in the background.

"Would be really nice if you would take care of your staff's student loans too." I offhandedly mention.

"Good call. I'll get Meaghan on that. No reason for the government to get any more interest than they need to." Cade agrees, and I'm surprised by his very anti-nationalistic comment. It's more of a me statement than something that would come from him. "Anything else?"

"The meeting tomorrow with Alise Mitchell from the DNR," Henri whispers.

"Meeting tomorrow with Alise Mitchell, the DNR commissioner." I sigh. *She's supposed to be on time out.*

"Rescheduled. She wants me to go up with her to the boundary waters. Thalia and I are going to make it a whole excursion. I've already got one of Henri's staff on it." Cade is quick to answer.

"That'll do it. Henri will be back to work in a couple days." I inform him before hanging up without saying goodbye.

"You didn't have to do that." Henri's blue eyes are a little glassy.

I put my phone back down and turn to face her. "I didn't. But I did anyway. I don't want anyone to control you. And if that means being a little, tiny bit assertive from time to time, I will."

"Well, if you don't let people know you're assertive, I can probably live with that. It would change how the media sees you, and I can't possibly have that. I just got them to think of you as slightly responsible and intelligent, not just a playboy." Henri's brain is officially in work mode. It's like a light turned on in the house and you can't find the switch.

If she posted us together, there'd be no question we're not fucking others. Everyone would see it, my wolf explains.

While his concept of social media isn't quite there, he's not wrong.

But I don't voice his ideas. I don't know what the 'order' of the world is like between us, and I'm afraid to ask.

CHAPTER 46
HENRI

DEACON and I took turns in the shower. It seemed like he wanted to join me, but something stopped him, and I'm not sure if I'm happy or sad about that. It's a battle between jumping into another relationship, which my wolf wholly supports, or taking things slow and trying to date Deacon, whatever that might mean.

Whatever I choose, though, based on Deacon's behavior, he's not in a hurry to rush me. Which I appreciate.

Then why does it feel like he doesn't want us? my wolf argues.

I try telling her to shut up again, my own thoughts getting ahead of me.

I'm finishing drying my hair when Deacon emerges from the closet, completely dressed and ready to go. He's wearing the same band T-shirt from the first day that we worked together. The difference is he swapped out black skinny jeans for dark blue bootcuts today.

He leans against the doorframe, watching me, but it's not the menacing glare that Nathan would wear as he rushed me.

Deacon's just watching, his gaze contented with a curious head tilt.

I finish at my own pace before turning to look at him and gesturing to the clothes he brought me. "I look okay? It's not my usual style."

"More than okay." Deacon nods.

The clothes don't smell like anyone else. They're too small to be Thalia's, and while they seem like something Lena might casually wear, I'm still not certain they're hers. The colors are lighter, more neutrals and pastels.

"You bought these for me, didn't you?"

"Yeah, Hen." He rubs his hand across the back of his neck. "After the second time you came here, I got some stuff for you to keep here. While I wouldn't want you to be back here under the same circumstances, it was wishful thinking that you'd ever wear them."

"Are you . . ." His face is turning a little pink. "Are you embarrassed?"

"Yeah, I kinda am. It's like being caught with your hand in the cookie jar. I hoped you'd be here, and you are. Busted. Didn't think it'd ever go quite like this though." I step toward him, and Deacon offers me his hand. "Come on, the yarn places wait for no one."

"We don't —"

"I want to. Please don't fight me." Deacon tips his head. "We're in this super awkward place where we don't know what we're doing and how to define what we are to each other. But one thing is for sure, I'd really like to spoil you more than a little bit. Besides, I didn't get you a birthday present while I was out of the country."

With a sigh, I accept, putting my hand in his. "Okay. But let's not go over the top?"

Deacon just smiles. "I have no idea what you're talking

about. I'm the criteria by which all over-the-topness is measured."

He leads me out the door to the garage, grabbing our jackets on the way, and into the heated garage. I climb in when he opens the passenger door for me. Once I'm buckled, he drapes my jacket over my lap and closes the door.

After tossing his coat in the back seat, Deacon climbs into the driver's seat and starts the car. "Okay, so there are two farms nearby, and then I figure we'd grab dinner and come back home. You can spend all night showing me how good of a hooker you are."

"You're not gonna let the hooker thing drop, are you?" I groan.

Deacon laughs. "Only because you asked so nicely."

After ten minutes of comfortable silence, Deacon pulls us off the road and into a driveway with a sign that says 'alpaca crossing.'

There are fields of what I'm guessing are alpacas — because of the sign. They're all happy out and about, munching with little sheep friends.

"They're so cute!"

"Just wait until you see the shop." Deacon encourages my excitement, his chaotic nature building.

The shop is a whole experience, not simply a yarn store. Deacon buys little cups of feed to take out to the alpacas. And thankfully it's not too cold with the sun in the sky.

Once outside, little signs are displayed, telling us the alpaca's names. They all get in as close to us as the fence between us allows.

"Who's your favorite?" Deacon asks over my giggles when an alpaca licks my hand, their tongue leaving a wet, slimy trail behind.

"Well, I think Bertrand likes me the most, but look at how cute Willow is." I sigh in lamentation.

Animals are so much work to care for, but I could easily come back and do this regularly.

"Alright, let's go inside and buy Bertrand and Willow yarn." Deacon ushers me back to the shop.

And sure enough, inside and out of the cold are little fiber art models of each alpaca on displays around the room. Skeins of yarn dyed in fun colors are all twisted up with labels and tags.

Pretty much any yarn I touch, Deacon picks up and holds in his arms, sometimes picking up multiple bundles of the same ones.

"You don't have to —" I start to argue.

"I'm spoiling you. Plus, there's a competition to see which alpaca sells the most yarn. We wouldn't want the favorites to lose." He grins.

They even have stitch counters and crochet hooks in sizes that match the spun-out yarn. And Deacon makes sure I get the cute alpaca charms and counters rather than the plain ones.

Our skeins push both Willow and Bertrand to the top of the alpaca contest charts, and we walk out the door with two packed bags of supplies.

On the way out the door, Deacon wraps his arm around my shoulder. It's warm and comforting. He places a kiss on my hair, and I swoon. Physically swoon at the touch. It feels . . .

Right? my wolf offers.

Scary, I correct.

It's sweet and cute, and I like it, but I feel equal parts anxiety. *What if this doesn't work out?*

CHAPTER 47
DEACON

BY THE TIME day six rolls around, Henri is a little stir-crazy, asking more and more about Cade's work schedule and if he's making his meetings. I've enjoyed the quiet peace of our routine. Me reading and her crocheting into the afternoons, then watching movies and relaxing together. Since the first time we had sex, neither of us has initiated anything. Sure, we've flirted, but it never went anywhere.

Touching her has seemed taboo. I want her, but she's dodged it a little. Not one to push, I've let it go. Whatever she's working through isn't ready to be solved. That's not for me to heal but for her to find in introspection.

But this drive home is killing me, anticipation on every breath.

There's this awkward moment when you can just feel a breakup coming. I've only been through it twice before, and it was enough for me to stick up the 'not relationship material' sign on the front lawn and call a spade a spade. I'm only built for one-night or one-weekend commitments.

Henri is giving off epic there's-a-breakup-coming energy.

We turn off the main highway, onto the road that'll lead to the pack property, when she finally pulls up the conversation. "You said earlier that we don't know what we're doing or how to define what we are to each other." Her hesitation is apparent in the pauses between her words.

"I did." *Come on, Henri. This doesn't have to go this way.* I watch her in my peripheral vision.

She fiddles with her hair. "Is it okay with you if we stay this way for a while? Not defined but not nothing?"

"We are something," I answer quickly.

My wolf snarls in frustration, demanding I fight for her. But I won't, not right this minute. I know Henri and all the things going on in her head. She can't just jump into this. Fuck, I can't promise to be perfect for her either.

"Oh." Henri laughs, nervous tension bleeding from her side of the car.

She's our fucking mate, you numb nuts. My wolf berates me. *You can't let her walk.*

I ignore him. "We just watched Lena's life explode when she and Finn were outed. I'm not opposed to just being 'us' while we figure out who 'we' are." I use one-handed air quotes, hoping she hears how I don't want to really separate but am open to keeping us quiet without being disrespectful toward her. She doesn't deserve to feel like a secret.

Fuck, relationships are hard.

"Uhm." Henri doesn't drop it.

My stomach roils like I'm on a jet doing a nosedive. The breakup still on course. *Can't be broken up if it was just sex one time, Deacon.* I chastise myself, but it doesn't help the feeling.

"Just say it, Henri."

"I'm just not ready to really be anything." She winces as she says it.

You fucking scared her, my wolf snaps. He immediately wants to fawn over her, to kiss her and make her feel better.

"It's just that . . . I need to prove to Cade that I can still do my job and be trusted. I really fucked up, and I know you're going to say it's fine, but it doesn't feel fine." She picks at a loose thread on her sweater.

I don't know how to respond to what she's saying, but saying nothing feels rude. Reassuring her that Cade won't fire her isn't going to ease her worry. Having Cade fire her to get her to chill out will breed animosity. There's no win in this situation.

So, I lie. "I get it. You need some time."

I turn the blinker on and pull up to the gate. We're waved through instantly.

"You sure?" Henri draws a deep breath.

"Positive." I fight the disappointment out of my voice. "It's all good. Which cabin is yours?"

"The one directly across from Ms. Gertie." Henri perks up thinking about her.

How could anyone not? She's most certainly one of the sweetest women in the world.

I drop Henri off and loop back up to the house.

I'm not even all the way into the mudroom before Cade's breathing down my throat. "How's our girl?"

"She's back on the wagon and nervous as fuck you're going to fire her." I scrub my hand down my face. "Not like I need to say this, but you're not allowed to fire her."

Cade laughs, but it's a nervous one. The stress hiding in it is telling. "I don't know that I could replace Henri. I will double her salary if she signs a work contract for a minimum of five years. It was fucking awful without her."

"Well, that might be necessary." I kick my shoes off and shoulder past him into the house.

"What?" Cade follows me to the kitchen.

I open the refrigerator and start digging through leftovers. We missed Equinox, and the fridge is loaded with extra food. *There's got to be something munchies worthy in here.*

"Deacon," he snaps.

"Yeah?" I don't want to elaborate on what I just said.

I lean into playing the 'I'm more messed up than I appear' version of Deacon. Except I'm not micro-dosed. Yet. Hopefully, but unlikely, he won't notice I'm painfully sober.

"What do you mean that might be necessary?" He crosses his arms in front of his chest as if he can intimidate me.

I've never been afraid of Cade.

My wolf snarls and snaps at the challenge. I fight him back down. *This is why you're getting punished. We're going upstairs, and you're taking a nap.*

He retreats within me.

"Dea, I put you and Henri together because anyone with a single brain cell bouncing around in their head, like that computer screen saver, can see you two belong to each other. It's why Ezra wasn't the primary choice for playing nice with the humans."

"Well, your hopes of pushing us together weren't worth it. I hate to break it to you, but she's not interested." *Not one fucking bit.*

I toss one of the containers of food in the microwave. Steak with roasted vegetables.

Cade doesn't deny his meddling. "How is that even possible?"

I shrug, holding my arms out at ninety-degree angles and raising and lowering them.

Pursing my lips and raising my eyebrows, I try to drive the point home. "I'm not exactly the top candidate in the mate-material category." I sigh and pull a fork out of the drawer, ready to stir my meal. "Henri isn't on board. I don't blame her."

"Fuck, Dea."

The pity in Cade's voice hurts about as bad as being put in this limbo. Because I'm not sure we were even really dating to consider it a breakup.

The microwave beeps before either of us speak again, and I stir the contents before tossing it back in. "I don't want to talk about it, Cade. I got your publicist back up and working. That's what the ask was. That's what I did."

"I'm done letting you tell me we're not talking about something," Cade presses.

He runs his hand back through his hair, and I feel the tension of The Leviathan coming forward.

Command me all you want, fucker. You won't like what I have to say.

"Revecca gave me some pretty good instructions on what I need to do before she'll consider removing my problem from me. You said so yourself, there's a difference." I change the subject before I break down over Henri.

"Yeah, she and I had a chat." He rolls his eyes. "Nah, I shouldn't say it that way. She's quickly becoming my third favorite sibling."

"You only have three," I grumble as the microwave beeps again. "Unless you're still counting Robert, and in that case, I'm questioning my ranking."

On autopilot, I pull the food out and stir again. It's steaming now and ready to eat.

"Deacon." Cade makes me look at him with a firm bite in that word.

"Cade?" I get cocky with him.

Provoke him and fight until he kills me? No. Thalia will be sad.

"You are my favorite sibling."

The container and fork slip out of my hands. Instantly I try to stop them but am a fraction of a second too slow. The plastic container flips as it falls, and my now-hot dinner is dumped out on the floor. I miss the guilt-free days when I'd leave it for the staff to clean up. But a decade of being the responsible one means I can't force myself to text Lauren to send someone to fix my mess.

Cade beats me to it, bringing the roll of paper towels and wet rag while I just stare at what feels like a good analogy for my life. So close I could taste it, yet it slipped through my fingers.

"You're my favorite because you don't take my shit, and you give me perspective," Cade explains.

I finally move, pulling out the trash can from its place at the end of the counter by the sink.

"You're also the one I can talk to about getting the job done, and you don't judge me when I want to do it in less politically correct ways."

The conversation has taken an unexpected turn, so I take advantage and follow it. "How many times did Nathan call and text?"

"The contents are more alarming than the quantity," Cade confirms. "I was hoping we could warn him off before things escalate."

"I'll get it done." I run the wet rag over the floor after he throws the last of the food in the trash.

CHAPTER 48

DEACON

CADE:

> Come down to the garage, I brought you a present.

Like I don't have enough going on? I know it's not a present. It's a classic car he wants restored. But at least it'll be fun to make faces at him and complain loudly, insulting whatever piece of shit he dragged into my garage.

It's not like I'm not already leaving the house anyway. Cade asked me to warn Nathan off two days ago, and with the ancestors suppressed for the rest of the day, it's time.

As Revecca would say, I'm excellent at crea un dezastru. Nathan needs a healthy dose.

When I get to the garage, Cade smiles at me and cocks his head to the side, The Leviathan peeking through. The car is clearly forgotten about as he reads my face and body language. "What fuckery are we spreading?"

"The kind that involves things you shouldn't be involved

in." I keep walking closer to him and the garage, trying to look past him at the grill.

"Mm-hmm." Cade nods.

I ignore his attempt to meddle in what doesn't concern him and look more at my 'present' that I'm equally intrigued and disgusted by.

It's a '64 or '65 Mercury Comet, which looks like it was most likely grazed by a comet if the first glimpse at the damage is anything to go by. In addition to major body dents, the paint is flaking and the dash seems to have melted a little inside.

Who tortured you, baby girl?

I make the most incredulous face I can come up with. "I see you found me the second-to-worst Comet in existence."

Cade tosses me the keys and answers. "It was a gift from Thalia, and she's quite proud of her find."

"Awww." My tone reminds me of when Lena sees someone's pup for the first time.

Thalia picking this baby out immediately means I can no longer judge the little Comet harshly.

"Did it drive here or get towed?" I hold up my hands and cross my fingers on both hands, hoping he throws me a tiny bone.

"It runs fantastic. Only backfires now and again. Sticks from third to fourth." He shrugs noncommittally.

It's got good bones, and he drove it here, so it's fine. I can fix it.

I move to the driver's side and open the door. Once I'm in the car, the inside doesn't smell very barn-like. Though there's a slight scent of furry woodland creatures having been in here at one point.

The engine comes to life without protest, and I nod along to the hum of it. When I give it some gas, there's no way to hide my pleasure. I give him a thumbs-up but manage to contain the smile.

He's right. Despite it being a mess this feels like a present. Besides . . . if little red liked it, I could make some time.

He climbs into the passenger seat. "So, where are we going?"

I drum my fingers on the dash. There are so many things that could go wrong involving him. But then again, bringing Cade means this can't escalate too far. He won't be an accomplice to murder. It'll be a heavy-handed hint, also known as a tiny threat.

I finally answer. "Gym down in Edina."

"Ohhhkay." Cade purses his lips, trying to wait me out for information.

I pull the Comet out of the garage and head toward the front gate.

He makes it until we pass the guard shack, which is probably a personal record for him. "And why are we going there?"

"Remember when I was like fourteen, and you told me I'd need to learn how to defend myself? I smarted off saying that you're Pack Second, so what the fuck do I need to know how to fight for?"

Did that day put as big of a blip on his radar as it did mine?

Cade hangs his head. "Yeah. Sorry."

"Don't be. Made me tougher for when Ezra and I sometimes intentionally start bar fights." I laugh, and that gets Cade to run his hand back through his hair.

"Okay, but we're going to a gym. This isn't quite a bar fight. You think you're capable of —" He lets that hang.

"Don't worry. You're not fighting my fight for me. You weren't supposed to be coming. Bigger they are, the harder they fall. I'm quick and surprisingly good." I smirk over at him, trying to ease his mind, but I don't pull over to let him out.

"Why am I starting to think you've been . . ." Cade looks over at me.

"Underground fighting?" I finish the question for him but don't bother following it up with a confession.

"Is there anything you do for fun that's legal?" Cade shakes his head, settling into the drive, resting one arm on the door and drumming his fingers against his leg with the other.

"Lots of things. I can't think of any off the top of my head. Probably something Henri made me do that didn't suck." When Cade does nothing more than shake his head, I continue. "Besides it's not like I'm running an underground poker ring or one of those cult MLMs."

"No, but you bought some sort of business in South Dakota?" Cade looks over at me. "I got the paperwork while you were gone."

"Yeah. Favor to a friend. It's good money. Should have earned back its purchase price by now." I squint, trying to remember how many days ago that was.

"Oh, it has. You've a knack for finding businesses turning profits." He chuckles. "You'd think that with all the investments the pack has, the little business deals you make wouldn't matter. But a few of your deals are now key assets in our portfolio."

"Well, this one was a fluke." I start to confess. "I really just wanted —"

"Don't tell me." Cade shakes his head. "I don't think I'll like what you're about to say."

I mime zipping my lips and pretend to throw the key out the window.

THE GYM, built in part of a strip mall, isn't even close to pleasant. The dimly lit space and worn-out equipment have me questioning my decision to come and kick his ass here. It's clear that not a single shifter works here because the stench alone almost has my eyes watering.

Cade coughs. "Fuck, it's putrid."

But I push through the smell of wet socks and body odor, seeing my target leaning against the boxing ring set up toward the back.

Nathan encourages a fighter. Unironically, he speaks to the fighter nicer than I've ever seen him speak to Henri.

Stopping next to me at the opposite side of the ring, Cade looks at the fighters, giving his assessment at a volume designed to be heard. "I don't know. You sure you want to take one of these two? You'll mop the floor with them. Not fair at all."

Fuck. I love it when Cade understands the assignment.

"No." I tilt my head and indicate to Nathan, who has now seen us. "That big slow thug."

"Deacon," Cade groans, adopting a good caricature of an asshole further aggravating the situation on purpose. "What did I tell you about beating losers?"

It was rude enough.

Nathan comes storming around the ring. "What? You two think you're tough shit? Fuckin' wolves coming in here like you own the place."

"Oh. Trust us, this isn't the kind of business we'd buy." Cade snorts, and I'm sure he's thinking about our conversation on the ride over here.

It's easy for me to forget how much fun Cade can be.

Nathan tries to step around me to Cade, but I don't let it happen.

"We don't need your kind here," one of the men from the

ring sneers, his thick Southern drawl making him an easy target.

Lacing my words with a thick Minnesotan accent, I throw an easy insult, "It's Minne-snow-tah. Why dontcha go back to all your swamps and leave the ice fishin' to us."

"You're just a coupla overgrown dogs." He cackles like what he said was funny.

"All I've come here to say is fuckin' leave Henri alone. You weren't loyal to her. You don't need her. Move on." I don't lower my voice entirely, but I do drop it down to give Nathan what could be privacy if his 'friends' had enough brain cells left between them to keep their mouths shut.

Nathan hasn't broken my gaze. He shakes his head. "You think you can tell me what to do?" He looks me over and smirks. "Get in the ring."

Cade snorts.

This is too fucking easy.

I kick my shoes and socks off while Nathan walks back around to the other side of the ring.

"Don't kill him with witnesses," Cade warns in the softest tone we've used yet, normal speaking volume.

"Nah, I just plan on makin' him think twice about what'll happen if he keeps upsetting our girl," I reply before pretending to badly climb into the ring.

Nathan's stripped down to his shorts and is stretching out.

In my T-shirt and surprisingly formal-looking sweatpants, I wait for him to finish intimidating me.

There are some advantages to being a wolf. I still have quickish healing and muscle recovery.

It doesn't matter if I take a minute to warm up or not. In the end, Nathan's going to walk out of here with bruises, and I'll be mostly healed by the time we get home. Tomorrow morning at the latest.

When Nathan begins to circle, I keep an eye on his footwork. Slow and uncoordinated. *Is he trying to do this professionally?* I pretend to stumble, and that's when he makes the first move, striking out with his fist, trying to collide with my face as I fall.

Instead, my foot connects with his lower ribs.

He coughs, but there's no satisfying wheeze.

"Little harder." Cade coaches under his breath.

The silence from Nathan's friends is interesting. Not a single encouragement as he steps back, squaring up again.

He makes the cataclysmic mistake of rushing me. He tries to push me down to the mat, but I do the same thing my brother would have done. I knock one foot out from under him with a sweep, putting him off balance before thrusting my hand into his face and breaking his nose, then kneeing his ribs.

Nathan crashes onto the mat with a pathetic human yelp. This time he releases a satisfying wheeze, a telltale sign I broke his ribs. Well, it's satisfying for me.

I crouch down just out of reach. "I can kick your pathetic roid-rage ass in my human form. I sure as fuck can tear it apart in my wolf form. Send another bouquet of flowers, another text, or place another call to Henri, and I will show you that this was nothing."

I stand and look at his friends staring dumbly at us. I've got a bunch of witty things I could say to them, but you can't have a battle of wits with an unarmed person, and it's not fun if you have to explain the joke.

When I turn back to Cade, he yawns. "Well, that was boring."

"Right?" I sigh but turn back to Rosencrantz and Guildenstern, Nathan's ridiculous friends. "If he tries to hurt her, it won't be just him I kill. Decide if the two of you value your lives, then figure out how to keep him in line."

Cade turns away and whispers, "Not enough gray matter, Deacon. Asking for too much."

I slide into my shoes, not bothering with my socks, and follow Cade back out the door.

When we're almost back at the car, Cade ruffles my hair. "I taught you good, Dea."

"Yeah. Sure, take credit for that." I laugh, but it's tainted with my darkness.

I don't believe this will be the last time I have to pay Nathan a visit. At the very least, I've given him a chance to leave her alone. It's more than most hunters give their prey.

Oleander

Nerium oleander

APRIL

CHAPTER 49

DEACON

I'VE GIVEN Henri all the space I possibly can. At the cost of being back to square one with my wolf.

The ancestors are back to being nosy and judgmental. It's too much on a daily basis. I'm not strong enough for it. I'm back to micro-dosing and hiding the usage from my siblings.

Henri, however, has taken all the space between us and gone one step further, having left with Cade and Thalia on to Louisiana to meet up with another pack Alpha and discuss who the fuck knows what. I didn't finish reading Thalia's text. Instead I sent her an article on how a bunch of grannies knitting sweaters has saved some penguins.

Ms. Gertie tells me I need to give her time and that she'll see what she's missing. But it's not like I've given her anything to miss.

Sobriety is too hard. Finding strength to fix the dumb wolf and the stupid gift is pointless. His rioting every time I put him under is getting tiring, and the more I push, the more violent he gets.

I'll go feral. Problem solved.

CHAPTER 50
HENRI

EVERY DAY I wait for Cade to think he's made a mistake in hiring me. But he keeps treating me like nothing happened. It's been business as usual.

It's like I never drank on the job and took an irresponsible last-minute week off for no reason.

I've been working overtime trying to make up for the massive bonus he put into a checking account he opened in my name. The debit card is barely used with how little I go anywhere. Working it off seems like the right move.

Where is Deacon? My wolf complains about missing him for the umpteenth time while I sit in business class on our flight back from New Orleans.

He's at home where he belongs, I remind her.

The sniffs and smells we've gotten of him around the house have been keeping her steady. Just knowing he's nearby is a significant improvement over when he was gone to Romania. She's manageable.

Not great, but I don't feel like crawling out of my skin to escape her. Not right now, anyway.

Maybe soon I'll work up the courage to ask if Deacon will spend some time with me. A weekend, maybe? But as it is, I'm so tired by the time I get home that I collapse into bed each night, ignoring how empty and vacant my still unpacked cabin is.

My alarm goes off on my phone.

Suppressant.

The notification pops up on my screen, and I reach into their designated pocket in my bag. I'm nearly out. The elephant is in the room with a foot on my chest. I'm the only one who can see him, and I'm completely ignoring it as an issue. Every day a little more weight is pressed down on me, and for five minutes while I take the damn pill, I have a micro freakout session.

My fingers shake as I fish one of the pills out, and I struggle to twist the lid off the water bottle. But eventually I get it in my mouth and swallow.

Telling Cade I need leave feels so wrong given my major breach of trust. But it's unavoidable. Short of an act of God, I'll go into heat, and just like the first time, I'm going to suffer through it alone, locked in a cabin, fucking myself, wholly unsatisfied until it's over. Hopefully it'll be short.

If we tell Deacon, my wolf growls, baring her teeth in anger, *he will care for us.*

We can't tell Deacon. I discourage her. *We're not ready to figure things out between us yet.*

But now I'm not sure if that's true or not.

I add a meeting to Cade's calendar and start dividing out my workload into preplanned emails to send to the team.

I only have five pills left.

CHAPTER 51
DEACON

MY PHONE BUZZES.

Something's unsettled in my gut, like a too-quiet moment in the woods.

Picking it up, I see Ezra's name on the screen. There's nothing abnormal about him calling. Especially since we had just talked about taking some time off from our brothers' agendas to go gallivanting for a weekend.

"Hey, Ez."

"Get on the next plane to Moab or Salt Lake or fuck anywhere in Utah. Hell, Denver. Whatever. Now," he orders, his voice pitching and forceful.

"What's going on?"

A bang rattles my door.

It opens before I can even get there.

Cade meets my eyes. "Ansel's been arrested. I put us on a flight to Provo. It leaves in two hours. Take Henri. Move it."

A pit forms in my stomach.

I nod and put my phone on the desk, then run to my closet and pick up the go bag I keep packed.

By the time I get back to the desk and pick up my phone, Ezra disconnected the call.

I jump down the flights of stairs, trying to get to Henri's office as fast as possible. She's packing her big purse with her laptop, tablet, and a binder of some nature.

"Ready?" I drum my fingers on my thigh.

Giving me a curt nod, she follows me.

After slipping on my tennis shoes, I run to the locker and start pulling out gear and a duffle.

There's no way we'll make it through TSA before the plane takes off unless we take something fast. I don't know what Cade's plans are, but I'm guessing it involves lights and sirens.

"Deacon, we can't take that." Henri argues with me.

"We don't have time for anything else. I get that you've only met Ansel once, but if he dies, none of us are going to be okay." I keep putting on my chaps.

Henri doesn't argue again and takes the gear.

I put our things into the duffle and secure it to the back of the bike. Before kicking it to life, I offer my hand to Henri.

She takes my hand and climbs on, wrapping her arms around me.

If Ansel's life wasn't on the line, I might have taken a moment to relish in my proximity to her.

The gate is open before we get there, and I buzz off the property as fast as I can.

What could Ansel have been arrested for?

I push the bike to 150 miles per hour, only slowing down when we get to the winding parts of the road.

When we're through the last of the curves, I remember Henri is behind me. So I only accelerate to ninety when we get on the freeway. Fast enough that cops won't bother chasing me but slow enough that we've got a chance of surviving if we crash.

CHAPTER 52
HENRI

I COUNTED the pills in my desk four times this morning. Not that it was hard, but because I don't want to believe it's true. I have exactly three days left before I could start going into heat. Sometimes they say that if you've been on suppressants for a while, it takes time for your body to flush all the suppressants out of your system. So maybe I get an extra day or two? Surely we'll be home by then.

On the plane I'm trying to focus but can't. I attempt to read over the information that Cade and his attorneys have been emailing back and forth but my focus is all over the place. There are so many questions in my brain that I'm afraid to ask — about Ansel's situation and my own.

Why didn't I tell them? Why didn't I just tell them?

I know why. I was embarrassed and had resigned myself to take heat leave. It was on my calendar to ask Cade for the time off tomorrow. Then also on my calendar to maybe talk to Deacon about it.

Coincidentally, we've been seated next to each other. I understand why Cade and Thalia would sit together, and it only makes sense that the two of us would be put together, but part of me wishes I could have traded with one of them. It's hard to avoid Deacon when he's sitting next to me.

My wolf focuses on him. *Heat with Deacon would be fun, we could be mates.*

We can't be mates with him. I argue with her. Illogically.

Just because you don't want to be doesn't mean we can't. She makes a valid point.

I look back at the email again, trying to focus on the words, and I make a note in my notepad. I don't know the extent of the arrest, but one thing that's always good is character witnesses. People Ansel's helped and rehabilitated need to be interviewed by the media and for depositions.

"What's wrong?" Deacon whispers, slouching in his seat to get closer to me, keeping the conversation relatively private given the airliner.

"Uhm." I close my eyes, and the angry tears well up again. Tensing my shoulders, I force myself to stop freaking out. "There was an issue with my heat meds . . ."

Stop covering for him! My wolf snarls inside me.

It's a slap to the face from within, and I speak out about Nathan, obeying her demand. "Nathan threw them out, and I only have my reserve supply left."

"Shhh," Deacon whispers. He puts a comforting hand on my leg, fingers gripping my thigh, squeezing gently. "How long is that?"

"Three pills after I take today's. I was going to talk to Cade about heat leave." I swallow hard, looking at him and meeting his eyes before gesturing back to the scary emails on my laptop. "What if it's not enough time?"

"We'll think of something," Deacon answers calmly. "Don't freak out. Start spacing your pills out. Instead of exactly twenty-four hours, move them to thirty-two hours. It gives us a little extra time."

"Is that safe?" I whisper.

"I know it is. They built fail-safes into the pills for the forgetful kind of wolves. It'll technically hold for thirty-six hours, but I don't want to risk it with Ansel's pack." Deacon slides his fingers against the fabric of my pants in small strokes, and the touch calms me.

Relaxing in my seat for a minute, I try to let his reassurances sink deep into my body, all the way to my bones.

Our mate will care for us. My wolf tries to steady me.

CHAPTER 53
DEACON

As IF I wasn't already terrified of losing Ansel, now Henri is going to go into heat. I can try and beg Lena to bend the rules to get Henri another set of pills. However, my adamant rule-follower little sister is bound and determined to make it so the lab stays firmly above reproach.

I would hope, with this not being an accident or misuse, that I can appeal to her softer side.

Maybe I should go through Finn? How else to get pills? There's a black market for everything, right? Heat pills are probably an exception to that though.

Lena doesn't take them, and Dinah's pills are way too strong for Henri. But if we cut the pills in half . . . No, that won't work. It's still going to be too strong. The size difference and the issue with Dinah being an Alpha Female means the calculation would be all wrong.

The seat belt light comes on, and as if the dinging bell rings a spot in my brain, an idea strikes.

Ansel's mate isn't an Alpha Female. She would have the

lower dosage, and if she's similar in build to Henri, the pills should be effective, at least enough.

As the plane descends, I start doing the math for the best-case scenario.

Assuming Ansel's mate was smart, she didn't start them immediately after her last heat. *Why would she?* She'd have five and a half months to make up her mind before needing to take them. It's practically a year of coverage at that point — five and a half months of her natural cycle plus the six months of pills.

For wolves farther away from our pack, Lena and the lab always send a week extra in case of a postage delay. It depends on the dosage. The numbers tabulate through my brain, the low and the high ends coming together.

It's shitty to steal Morrigan's pills, but Ansel can handle his pack with his mate. They've already gone through one heat together to prove it. But Henri, going into heat, would be a temptation to the nearly fractured wolves.

A temptation to us. My wolf wags his tail at first. *But we'd kill anyone near her.*

With Ansel missing, though, that sort of bloodshed wouldn't be good. We need to get Henri's pills sorted or get her out of there before her heat sets in.

Plan in place, I try to go back to worrying about Ansel. Worrying isn't going to do anyone any good, but it feels like the best waste of the extra energy I've got.

The plane touches down, and some idiot in the back claps.

I pull out my phone and text Lena to be sure we can't do something the right way first. Without looking where I'm going, I follow Henri by scent through the airport, texting Lena along the way.

Major issue with Henri's suppressants. Her asshole ex tossed her new script. Chances we can get another set expedited here?

LENA:

Fuck me.

Deacon, I can't get her new pills.

Policy since day one. Scripts can only be renewed when she'd naturally have gone into heat.

An exception for shit like this?

I didn't write the rules, Dea.

I don't know what to type back. I knew not to expect her to be able to get around the rules. It wasn't fair of me to ask her to do that. Looking at luggage claim, I watch a suitcase come down and slam into the rail before texting Lena my borderline-illegal-activity idea.

Hypothetically speaking . . . what would Morrigan's dosage do to Henri?

I was just typing that.

Morrigan's script is a super small dose. Like a fraction of a fraction. And I only sent her a 30-day supply so we could calibrate and see how she was feeling on them. Henri, hypothetically, would need to take one pill every 90 to 120 minutes. It would buy her a couple of days. Max.

Anything we can do to naturally slow it down?

No. She's been on suppressants a long time. Once they clear her system it'll be full force. Hopefully, this issue with Ansel is a misunderstanding, and we can get her home ASAP.

I'm going to be everyone's problem until you get some sort of exception written in for this sort of thing in the future.

I promise it'll be one of the first things I bring up when we get back.

Lena sends me a picture of a calendar reminder in her phone for two weeks from now.

I'll see you in Nameless.

We've got extra time. Lena's right. We'll probably be on our way home before we even need to worry about running out of time.

Famous last words. My wolf laughs. *It is irrefutable that Henri's ours. The Mother said so. You can't keep being miserable when we have our mate.*

I'm conflicted. It complicates life too much being mates. If Henri goes into heat, I'll stay under the influence enough to make sure we can't connect. No wolf, no mates. Surely Cade or Finn can get her home. There's not going to be any problems.

My wolf grumbles a mockery of my resolve that this won't happen.

But hope exists at Ansel's house, and that's where we're headed.

CHAPTER 54
HENRI

CADE HAD these new prefab cabins shipped in, and my team has been working nonstop from one of them. I'm almost completely out of pills, and we are nowhere near going home. The thoughts are keeping me up at night. Being here, with this pack, there's no privacy.

What am I going to do?

I get up in the early hours of the morning. The kind that Deacon and Lena claim should be illegal to operate during. Regardless of the time of day, I exit the little bedroom I've claimed as my own. There's a mountain of work to be done, so four hours of sleep is going to have to be enough.

On top of my laptop is an amber pill bottle. I squint at it from the kitchen, where I'm filling the drip coffee maker's filter.

Did I leave my pills out?

The bottle looks smaller than mine.

After I get the coffee started, I walk over to it, and my heart rate picks up. A note is underneath the bottle.

HENRI,

TAKE ONE EVERY 2 HOURS AFTER YOUR LAST PILL HITS THE 24-HOUR MARK AND YOU'D NORMALLY TAKE ANOTHER ONE. EXACTLY 2 HOURS. NO EXCEPTIONS. NOT EVEN SLEEP.

— DEACON

I don't even question whose they are. The instructions tell me they're not mine. It's not an emergency order that was rushed to get to me. There aren't a lot of options here as to who they were originally intended for.

Guilt sinks in, causing me to shiver.

No. Whoever they were for, Deacon wouldn't screw someone else over for me. He wouldn't hurt someone else for me.

But I know that's not true. Deacon has said he would hurt Nathan for me. But Lena, Dinah, Morrigan, Meaghan? He wouldn't hurt them to help me. So, it must be that someone doesn't need these.

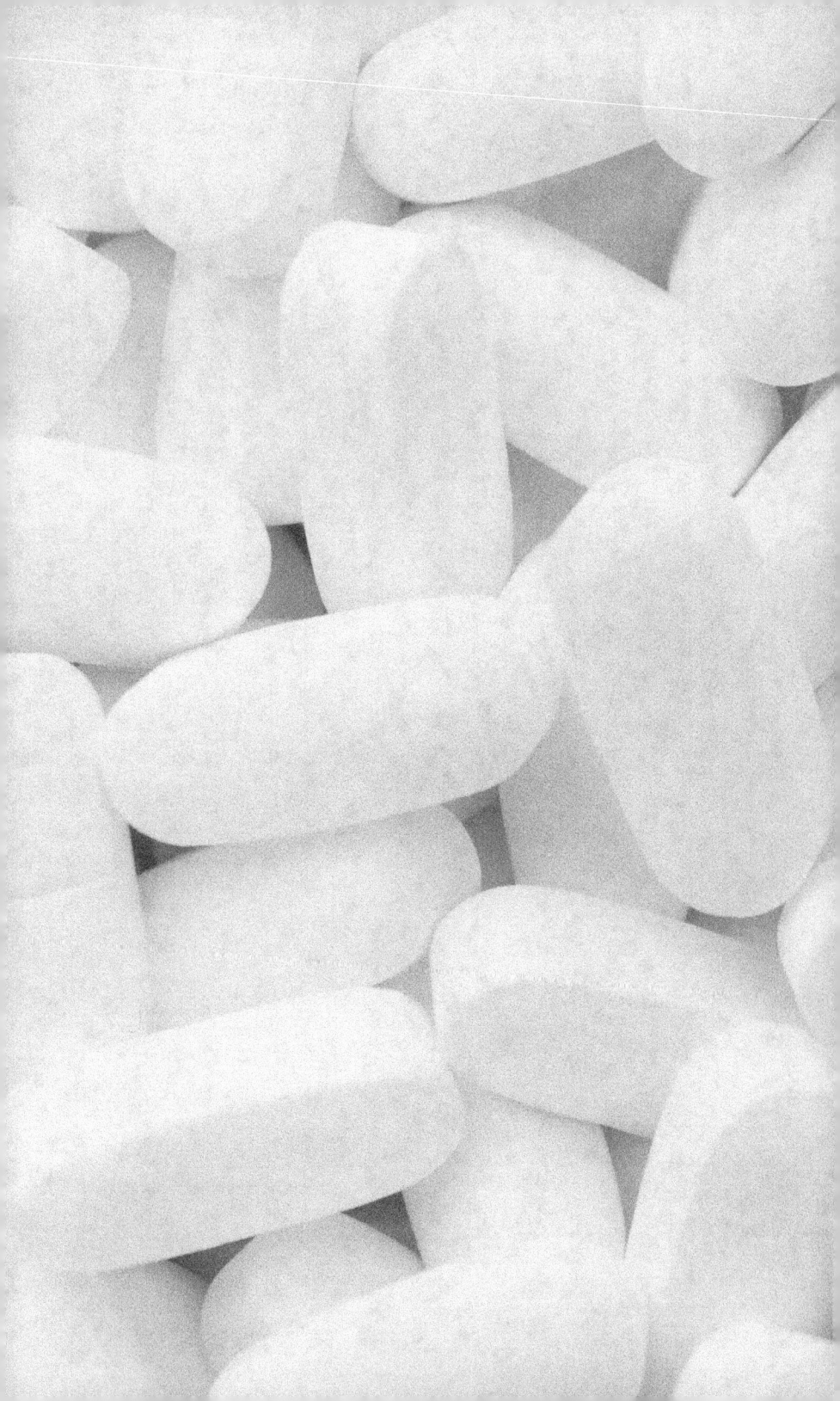

CHAPTER 55
DEACON

I KNOW I'm sobering up because that man's been dead for a very long time. "Hey, Walt."

"Deacon, what's the sermon?" He comes to sit down next to me in the dirt.

"You and Finn with that joke." I shake my head. "It's not looking great, Walt."

He huffs a single laugh. "That sick son of a bitch. When Ersilia said he was the one, I should have killed him and let Ansel kill me then."

"Pft. He's a wolf, as far as we'd all seen it. Would have been justified," I answer but hang my head because violence isn't supposed to be the answer. "You been haunting these guys all this time?"

"I mean, this is my home. Someone's gotta watch out for 'em?" Walt sighs, and his brown-black hair falls into his eyes. "You gotta go pull Ben out of the bottle. He's not gonna climb out himself."

"Is that you telling me he's about to drink himself to death or that he needs a friend?" My heart rate picks up.

I'm not about to let someone overdose or drown while I sit here. *Not when it's supposed to be me.*

Walt tosses his head toward Ben's cabin. "Last time I checked, he was on his side."

"Fuckin' hell." I get up out of the dirt and jog down the path past the trailers to Ben's cabin.

The back door is unlocked, and I walk into the kitchen, turning on lights as I go to the main bathroom. Ben's boots are still on. He's lying on the bathroom floor. Vomit all over the toilet and the floor.

"Ben!" I shout, kicking him in the shin.

He's breathing for now, but his mess and a bottle of cheap tequila are too close for comfort. If that idiot rolls over and dies in filth like this, I'm never gonna hear the end of it.

"Fuck off," he groans, rolling onto his back.

"Fat fuckin' chance." I step past his legs into the small space, grabbing hold of the front of his button-down canvas shirt. "Ansel wouldn't fucking forgive me if I let his second-best best friend drown in his own vomit."

"The fuck he wouldn't." Walt laughs, the dead man sitting on the vanity watching us. "But he's gonna be so happy to have a brother."

"You're not supposed to know that." I glare at Walt.

"Know what?" Ben growls. He manages to open his eyes, but they're bleary.

This is what I get for being mostly sober.

"Walt's haunting you. Don't worry about it." I pull him up to his feet. He's a fucking giant, but with a tiny bit of help from him, I get him up. "Hydrate."

Ben heads toward the kitchen.

"With water," I stress.

Apparently, my time to be the one falling apart is over. I'm cleaning up everyone's messes left, right, and center.

My wolf stretches out. *Let's check on Henri.*

I ignore him.

Checking on Ben in the kitchen, I find him doing exactly what I told him not to do.

I pull the beer out of his hand and drink it myself.

He growls at me.

I point to the water tap. "Hydrate. You don't wake up in a pool of your own vomit and get another beer. It's not classy."

NAPS IN THIRTY-MINUTE increments are not ideal, but it's all I've managed. The ancestors, Morrigan, Ansel's pack, checking on Henri, hunting down every person Ansel has ever helped, managing communications with Finn's brother Magnus, and making meals . . . it's all I can do.

I'm everywhere and nowhere. I sleep where and when I can.

In the dead of night, I'm taking a lap past the trailers and my sleeping family members when I hear just one tiny little sniffle.

Henri. My wolf pushes.

I slide open the glass door of her cabin and find her wrapped up in the fetal position on the end of the sofa, her laptop on the seat beside her.

Fear and sadness flood the room with their acidic scents.

I know why she's sad and scared. None of us want Ansel's imprisonment to be the reason we're here for this long. It's been a week of hell for all of us. But beyond that, Henri is running out of time before her heat comes, and it scares the shit out of me as much as it does her.

Tomorrow, we find out if Ansel lives, dies, or 'miraculously' escapes from federal custody. And regardless of that outcome, I have to do everything in my power to get Henri back to Minnesota for her own safety. *No pressure.*

I move her laptop before sitting next to her on the sofa. It's easy to pick up the little ball Henri has made herself into and shuffle her into my lap.

"Deacon," she groans and wiggles, trying to escape. She sniffles again. "We can't. There's work."

"Shut up. Be a wolf for two minutes and accept that you need physical touch," I murmur, nuzzling my head against hers.

Her objections stop, and she sits still. Her breathing and crying regulate, but the smell of fear still clings to her.

Another minute or two passes before she whispers, "It's not nice to tell people to shut up."

"I'm sorry. I should have told you to suck it up, buttercup. I'm holding on to you until you're done crying." I squeeze her a little tighter.

She snorts, and when she tries to stretch out of my arms, I let her. Henri maneuvers off my lap until just her calves are resting across my thighs.

"Talk to me, Henri." I run my hands up and down her shins, keeping the physical touch for both of our sanities.

Shaking her head, Henri wipes her eyes. "What if I fail?"

"Fail?" I cock my head. "What on earth could you fail at?"

"I needed to get all those letters and testimonies together. What if it wasn't enough? What if we didn't coach the people on how to write them good enough?" She draws a deep breath. "What if —"

I nod and try to reassure her, squeezing her legs. "You've been throwing yourself into your work here. But what you haven't seen, outside of these four walls, is those letters pouring in. The people of Nameless have all written letters, and they're signing their kids' names, hell even some dogs and cats and horses' names to them too. That all happened because of you. You and this campaign were not the only ball in the court. You're not the only player on the team."

Henri nods. "But —"

"No buts." I shake my head and reach over, wiping a tear off her cheek. "Cade has more legal staff, attorneys, lobbyists, senate pages, and other lawmakers working on this too. If tomorrow doesn't go exactly in our favor, it's not going to be because you failed to get people to write letters or because you didn't get Ansel's reputation and image to shine like a star. You did more than enough."

With a few deep breaths, Henri answers. "Okay."

I pat her legs and go to move them off me, but she grabs my sleeve.

"I'll be out of pills by morning," she admits. "Morrigan's pills."

"I know." I squeeze her calf. Though I'm not sure how she figured out they were Morrigan's. *I probably only have twenty-four hours to get her home.* "How are you feeling?"

"So far so good." Henri tries to make me believe there's nothing wrong when we both know she's lying, and I hate that she lies to me, but at least she has the decency to be bad at lying.

"You're already feeling warm and anxious and wanting to be someplace safe," I infer.

Biting her bottom lip together, she doesn't say anything.

Correction, I have less than twenty-four hours to get her some place safe. She's metabolizing the pills too fast.

"I'll see if I can book a flight out of Salt Lake City immediately after court. It's only a two-and-a-half-hour flight back home. Then the hour drive to the house." I look at the screen saver on her computer with the time. *Fuck, that's a minimum of thirty-two hours.* I try to infuse as much confidence into my voice as possible. "It'll cut it close, but we'll get you where you need to be."

"Okay." She gestures to the computer. "I've gotta . . ."

"Get back to work. I'm gonna go coordinate a flight. It's safer to put you on a flight with the Corinth agents." When I lift my hands off her legs, Henri kicks them down to the floor, and I'm free to move. "I'll sort it. You get everything you can done." With my finger under her chin, I make sure she's looking into my eyes. "But remember, this isn't all on you."

Henri looks away, back at her computer, and I go to tell Cade I'm taking his favorite staff member from him.

Cade's sitting at Ansel's kitchen table, glaring at his computer screen like it's going to give him different answers. It's where he is sixty percent of the time, so I'm not surprised to find him in the first place I look.

Listening, I hear Thalia's voice up in the loft above, which makes me think Dinah and Lena are up there with her. The door to Ansel's bedroom is closed, so it's hard to know for sure where Morrigan is. But this isn't private enough for me to talk to him about what I need to ask.

"Cade." I draw his attention from the computer.

He raises an eyebrow at me. "Can this wait?"

I shake my head. "Really can't."

He growls, The Leviathan trying to intimidate me into backing down.

I let my wolf rise to the surface, the bastard staring The Leviathan down and letting out an animalistic snarl.

That gets Cade's attention.

"Quick walk around the house." It comes out as an alpha command, and it won't do anything to him, but it furthers Cade's skepticism of me and the situation.

"What?" Cade growls.

414

"I swear, two minutes." I raise my hands, trying to surrender, falsely, to the aggression.

It's weird having a changing wolf within me. All this new pull. I don't love it, but it's got some perks.

The chair objects loudly, scraping on the floor as Cade pushes it back to stand.

I lead the way out through the sliding glass door, and it isn't until Cade has drawn a few deep breaths of fresh air and is reminded that he's a wolf, not a human pushing buttons on a keyboard all day, that I get a real answer from him. "Sorry, what's up, Dea?"

"Between the two of us, Henri is going into heat."

I let those words sink in, the gears turning in his brain practically visible through his eyes.

"Fuck," Cade groans. "How did this happen?"

I roll my eyes. "The deadweight wanted to service her through heat, and the reason she left was that he tossed her suppressants."

"Okay. Can you handle getting her on a flight? She needs to be at home where she's safe and can be taken care of." Cade runs his hand back through his hair.

"No work went into making someone that vile." Just thinking about Nathan has my wolf's hackles rising.

Cade locks eyes with me. "The calls and texts are still nonstop. Clearly the message wasn't received."

"I've been working on it. But it's complicated."

The sliding glass door opens behind us, and Thalia peeks her head out. "Your phone literally will not stop making noise, and it won't let me answer it."

"On it." Cade pats my shoulder. "Tell me what you need, and as soon as I have a second, I'll make it happen."

"I've got it for now," I assure him, but he's halfway up the deck stairs.

CHAPTER 56
HENRI

THE FIRST CRAMP HITS, and I dismiss myself out the back door of the courtroom. The guard gives me a pointed look, but I ignore him. Immediately two Corinth Security agents are following me down the hallway. I push my way into the bathroom, and one of the male agents follows me in.

"Women's room," I hiss at him, trying to shoo him out.

He barely acknowledges my remark, checking the stalls, which thankfully are all empty, before walking back out the door.

I turn the faucet on to cold water and stick my wrists under the flow. Resting my elbows on the countertop, I draw deep breaths, hoping the cool water and the stretch of my low back will ease the ache of the cramp.

It doesn't take long before I feel better. *Just a little one, then.*

Straightening, I look at myself in the mirror. My cheeks are flushed, but beyond that, I don't look any different.

We need Deacon, my wolf demands.

"Miss Greene." A male voice comes at the same time as a knock on the door. My security agent. "We're moving."

I grab my bag off the counter and leave the bathroom.

Ansel walks by with Morrigan in his arms, headed toward the exit. I fall into line toward the back of the Ardelean pack and get moving with the group through the police escort to where our vehicles are parked.

"Henri," Deacon shouts.

I spin around, looking for him, but I can't find him.

"Henri," he calls again, and this time I zone in on him standing by one of the smaller SUVs. Deacon beckons me, gesturing me toward him.

With brisk steps, I move around people piling into SUVs to get to him.

"You're going with these agents, you're on the first flight back to Minnesota." He nods.

"Deacon, hurry up!" someone shouts from across the group.

Deacon holds his hand up with his middle finger extended. "Just a minute."

"Oh, for fuck's sake." I pull his arm down, grabbing hold of the suit jacket. "We talked about this."

"You gotta go." Deacon opens the door for me and ushers me around it.

Not without him. My wolf protests.

"You're not coming with?" I shake my head, leaning around him to look at his family, nearly all in their vehicles. "No, that's ridiculous, you should celebrate with your family. I'll go."

Deacon locks eyes with me. "Ask me to come, Henri."

I look back at his family and then to Deacon. "I'm scared. Please?"

"Let's go." Deacon motions for me to get in the SUV, and when I do, he closes the door.

Instantly, I feel trapped and uncomfortable. My heart starts hammering in my chest. I reach for the handle, but he doesn't walk away to the other cars. He walks around the front of ours and climbs in the back seat next to me.

Deacon closing his car door only helps in the slightest to bring me back to center. I still don't like how confined I feel in this SUV.

"Seat belts," the security agent in the front instructs, looking in his rearview mirror.

My fingers fumble with it, and Deacon slides over, pulling it out of my grasp and buckling me in with ease.

He then handles his own.

CHAPTER 57

HENRI

"You're going into heat," the upperclassman whispers to me.

"I don't know what you're talking about." I try to back away from him, but my back meets the school's brick wall.

"What do you mean you don't know?" He shakes his head. "Who are your parents?"

I return the gesture, matching his shaking. "Paulina and Frank Greene."

"They're not pack." His brow furrows.

"I don't know what that means." I keep watching him watch me, growing increasingly uncomfortable.

My stomach hurts again. I should have known it would be too good to be true to never get periods.

His eyes change to the funny gold mine do before the world changes and I shift into my wolf.

"You." I point to his eyes. "How did you do that?"

"Who are you?" He shakes his head. "We don't have time. You're about to go into full-on heat in the middle of the fucking school day."

He pulls his phone out of his pocket. The late bell rings, and

Mr. Olson, the senior history teacher, sticks his head out into the hallway. "Excuse me. Miss Greene. Mr. Tucker. You're late."

"Just calling my dad, we've a small problem." The upperclassman, apparently Mr. Tucker, waves him off.

"Ah, I assumed it was me just . . . smelling things." Mr. Olson closes the door to his classroom.

"Come on, Miss Greene." Mr. Tucker leads me down the hallway and tucks his phone into his pocket.

"I have to get to class," I argue, trying to step around him.

Help, he can help. The little voice in my head tells me.

"You can't go to class. You've been having symptoms all week. I thought by now you'd have opted to stay home." He growls, actually growls. It's a low rumbling in his chest. "I don't understand how you thought it was okay to come to school when you're literally going into heat today. It's like you're trying to get attacked."

"I don't know what you're talking about. What is heat? Why would I be attacked?" I keep my words down, trying to talk fast. "I'm not feeling well. It's not the end of the world."

He looks at me and stops walking. "You know you're a wolf, right?"

My blood runs cold. *How could he know that?*

Because he's one of us, the voice in my head whispers.

CHAPTER 58
DEACON

WE PULL up into the departures lane of Salt Lake City Airport, and I hop out of the car, grabbing Henri's and my bags from the back before helping Henri out.

It was perhaps bold of me to assume she'd ask me to go with her. But I'm glad I bet on it enough to put my bags in this SUV.

Henri's wolf floods her eyes. She's jumpy and winces at the loud noises, cars, and bustling people walking around.

"Are you okay?" I try to judge her reaction.

"Yeah. Little overwhelmed." Her voice starts at a whine. "But I'll be okay."

Henri believes the words she says. But I'm not sure I believe them. I shuffle our bags into one hand and wrap my arm around her.

My wolf, not held quite far enough down, approves of me pulling her close and guiding her through the people. The minute the doors open to the check-in desks and the TSA lines, Henri loses it.

"No. I can't." She backs up, pushing against my arm, heading toward the door.

Her wolf is completely freaking out, pushed forward in her eyes.

"Okay." I move with her back out into the open air. "It's okay. Shhh."

Ushering her away from the crowds, I guide us down to a quieter section of the sidewalk. I pull out my phone and dial the Corinth Security emergency number.

"Deacon?" Cade questions, answering the phone.

"Can you turn my security detail around? We've an issue. I'm going to need to drive back to Minnesota. Not fly." I thread my fingers into Henri's, hoping the touch calms her wolf.

"On it. Want the help driving?" Cade offers, and I know I should take it.

Fuck, I should stick Henri in an SUV with a human driver and not risk the danger of the two of us alone together.

"No," Henri whines, and it's a breathy objection. "I can't handle other people. I'm messing everything up. I'm so sorry."

"No driver. It'll be safer with what's going on if I do it myself." I agree with Henri to him over the phone.

"Okay. I'll get them turned around," Cade says before hanging up the phone.

Henri jumps when a horn honks down the road.

"I'm sorry," she whispers. "I'm not normally like this. The people and it hurts and . . ."

"Shhh." I tuck my phone back into my pocket so I can run my fingers back through her hair. "It's okay. I can't imagine what you're going through right now. But I'm going to do everything I can to get you home where you'll feel safe for this."

Henri nuzzles against my hand, and I rub against her a little bit, the touch calming her down.

It takes ten more minutes and near-constant reassuring

touches, which I'm committing to memory to sustain me until I no longer have to suffer this earth, before the security vehicle comes rolling back toward us. The driver, without question, pulls a go bag out of the back and hands over the key fob for the push-start vehicle. I load our bags back in, and we're on our way out of the airport and cruising.

Traffic thins out as we leave Salt Lake City, and Henri relaxes. The drive starts to get more comfortable, and maybe, just maybe, with her relaxed, it'll slow her heat, and we'll make it to Minnesota in time.

It's almost nineteen hours without stops, and I know we'll have to take a night unless I can find some sort of uppers. But I'm guessing the amount of illegal drug sales in Wyoming is limited, and I don't have time to find a dealer.

I'll need at least four hours of sleep. That's twenty-three hours total.

We're racing against a clock. She's already having hot flashes and cramps. Those will only get worse, and the number of miles before we're both fighting for control is limited.

"We're going to have to stop for a night." I glance over at Henri, where she's sitting in the passenger seat, hopefully trying to think not-heat-inducing thoughts.

"Okay." Her voice holds a note of uncertainty.

"I'll need four hours of sleep. And I think it's probably best if we do that tonight rather than waiting for tomorrow night." I try to explain my logic.

"That makes the most sense," Henri says. She pulls both feet up, tucking them under herself on the seat. "I'm sorry about this. I bet you'd rather be back celebrating with your family. This was a big win and . . . I'm sorry."

The devastating regret in her voice pulls at every single one of my heartstrings.

Comforting her, I take my right hand off the steering wheel

and pick up one of hers, giving it a reassuring squeeze. "I'll see Ansel at Solstice. He's going to get some news that might be easier for him to process if I'm not there."

"Oh?" Henri squeezes my hand back. "You don't have to tell me. It's not my place."

"It's going to come out when we update the pack registry anyway." I clench my jaw before I let the words out. "Whoever . . ." That doesn't feel like the right way to say this; it's not fair to either of us. "Ansel and I are half siblings. I met our mother when I was in Romania. I'm not planning on telling him that tidbit because she's pretty much comatose. But it might be easier on Ansel if he can just have a minute to process before seeing me again."

Henri doesn't say anything.

A knot forms in my stomach. "Yeah. I'm sure that's gonna be a hard one for you and Kyle to spin. At least everyone loves Ansel after all the news coverage."

"No. It's not that. I was trying that thing Cade does when he waits you out until you spill all the secrets." She squeezes my hand harder. I can't tell if it's a cramp or just overcompensating for her words. "I was more wondering how you felt about it? I don't know Ansel at all, really, other than what I've learned in those letters and interviews, but it seems like you lived very different lifestyles."

"Yeah." I comfort myself by running my thumb back and forth across the back of her hand. "I've hidden it from Cade and Lena, but I've known I wasn't an Alden for a long time. There were a lot of inconsistencies in my life that didn't make sense. But I feel incredibly guilty for growing up in a mansion knowing he didn't."

"Do you think Ansel would want you to feel guilty?" Henri's voice softens, and her question causes a tightness in my chest. "Based on what I've learned, I don't think so."

She's right. I know she is.

I draw a breath, and the tightness dissipates. "He's complicated. Ansel will never hold it against me, and he'll take the information with a nod and a shrug and move on. Who you are, by blood or on paper, has never mattered to Ansel. Which makes the fact that he's weirded out by his mate being his best friend's kid kind of funny and a little contradictory . . . but then again, that's the sort of thing that I think we would all question."

"I . . . do you worry about what we are to each other?" Henri shakes her head.

I turn my head away from her, pretending to check the side mirror and blind spot. "No, Henri. I don't. The reality is, our lives are linked, and while I don't wish my burden on anyone else, it's not . . . If I can't get us home in time . . ."

"Do you want us?" Henri's voice is strange.

It isn't a tone I'm used to hearing, and I can't place it.

Apprehension? my wolf offers, but I don't voice it. *She's going to be ours. Quit drugging me and show her,* he demands. *Show her how much we want her.*

But I know the truth. I'm not going to be able to stay drunk enough to keep him under and drive. Our fate together, as mates, is going to get abundantly clear *very* soon.

"I've wanted you more than I've wanted anything."

"Okay." Henri draws a ragged breath. "We'll figure it out."

It pains me that she won't voice similar feelings, but I can't force or expect her to embrace complex emotions during her heat. The reality is her body is going through hell and demanding so much of her energy that nothing can be trusted as reality.

A little dark spot in my soul wrinkles. *She is feeling it, isn't she?*

CHAPTER 59
HENRI

MAKE HIM STOP HIDING. *I can almost feel him. I'm so sure,* my wolf begs, thinking about Deacon.

He drank this morning. And then I saw him pop a pill from a prescription bottle at the courthouse. He's not sober, and I know we both must be without substances in our system to recognize our mates.

His hand has been warming mine and quelling the raging storm that drives me to want to be connected. But surely, it's the heat talking. I'm sleep-deprived and homesick. I've worked nearly around the clock for the last week. The heat is playing on the fact that I'm touch starved and tired.

While at Ansel's, I avoided Deacon, focusing on work and making things better with Cade. I had intended to try to talk to Deacon, to get to this comfort level with him, especially with this . . . disaster. I just never did. The worst and best part of Deacon is, other than last night, he's completely respected me pushing him away and telling him to keep his distance.

He could have been with us this whole time. My wolf scolds me. *It would have been so good with him.*

The memory of us on the floor in the living room brings back all the emotions. *He's perfect.*

My body flushes again, and it stirs the fire within me. I've had a taste of sex with Deacon. That single taste explains the social media page dedicated to people who have hooked up with Deacon, well, and Ezra.

Or at least have claimed to. Some, I've been able to verify and others not so much. But my looking was purely business.

The Cousins Grimm's . . . proclivities . . . are well documented. There are some details that, unless you've spent time with Deacon, wouldn't have been detected, mostly because there aren't that many pictures of him online, and after extensive digging, I know there's only one where he's without a shirt.

We could take a bite out of that thigh. My wolf imagines his firm ass that we've seen just before he's shifted.

It's the heat talking, I remind myself.

There's no way I would be thinking about biting his thigh otherwise.

Trying to distract myself, I pull out my phone. "Should I try to find accommodations somewhere? I guess, do you need directions? Do we know where we're going?"

Too many questions at once. *Good job, Henri. Let's just freak out.*

Removing his only hand that was on the steering wheel, he increases the danger by pulling his phone from the pocket of his door. He angles it toward me so I can see his maps app is running. "I've got the navigation turned on, so she'll talk to us, but it's pretty much a straight shot along this highway to South Dakota and then straight on the ninety to home."

My face heats, and I'm wondering if it's from embarrassment or another hot flash.

"Why don't you scout another two hours ahead for food

and a hotel. We can start getting you fueled for your heat, and once we get to a hotel, I'll crash. We can get back on the road around after midnight," he suggests, and I start making myself busy.

A hundred and twenty emails alone are waiting in my inbox for attention, but I can't focus. There are also a ton of text messages. And before flipping into the map app, I open those.

CADE:

> Use the pack card for anything you need. I mean it, Henri. Next two weeks. Anything you need. It's literally the least I can do.

> I've had your assistant take over your calls and emails. Your team and the Corinth Security PR team will be able to handle anything in the aftermath.

> I'm not implying there are problems, but if there are any, they'll be covered, to ease your mind.

LENA:

> I know I'm sorry doesn't help. But I am. I've already started conversations with the board.

> I feel terrible for not having a contingency for something like this in place.

DINAH:

> You're going to be okay.

> I know it's scary especially if you haven't done this in a while. But trust your body and go with it.

> Trust Deacon.

Someday, I'll adjust to my boss's entire family knowing my life and problems, but that's some soul-searching for another day.

"Everything okay on that side of the car?" Deacon drums his fingers against the steering wheel.

"Yeah. It's fine," I answer.

A low groan comes from him. "Can I be honest with you for a second?"

"Uh. Sure?"

Deacon scrubs his hand down his face. "You're a really shitty fucking liar. I've told you, Henri. I've already judged you and decided that I love you. That's not going to change. So be honest about what's happening."

"It's just that everyone in your life is so loving and supportive. It probably sounds dumb, but I just don't know how to deal with everyone trying to take care of me. And I like it, but what if they stop? It will hurt too much to start caring about people and accept that they care about me when they quit." My voice falters when I say those words. "I am sorry."

"Henri." Deacon's voice is soft and sweet. "I can't think of a single act you could personally commit that they wouldn't forgive you for."

"Murder?" I'm quick to offer.

My wolf huffs in disagreement. *Deacon would love us more if you did that.*

"Oh, Henri. We'll help you dispose of the body." Deacon smiles and shakes his head. "But don't lie to me. Please, don't lie to me," he pleads.

"Okay," I agree. "I'll try to do better."

I go back to my emails. I know Cade told me to take the time off, but while I feel fine, I have to do something, and trying to play catch-up on the game of rescheduling Cade's events is something to focus on that isn't the elephant in the vehicle. But there's an unexpected email sitting on top of my inbox.

"Huh." I open it up, recognizing the email as one Nathan uses for his online gaming stuff.

"Huh, what?" Deacon spares me a sideways glance.

"Oh, it's not —" *Really, Henri? You just promised to try to stop lying to him.* I swallow and start again. "Nathan sent me an email with an account he doesn't ever really use, and I'm just wondering . . . why? Like he quit messaging me entirely. So, why a complete change of contact now?"

"About that." Deacon starts to pass a slow-moving minivan on the open road. "We, uh."

"You what?" I skim his message, cringing.

Deacon draws a deep breath, letting it out with a groan, "When we put you on time-out, the tech guys did something to clone your phone number, and there's now a set list of contacts who have instant access to you. The contacts we disallowed get filtered out like spam. Well, exactly like a spam filter. Unknown and blocked numbers can get through because of the usage of those for the high-profile people and their offices. We're working on a system for that, but we were kind of short on time."

"Deacon," I growl. "The whole point of not blocking him was so that he wouldn't try to contact me through di —" I cut myself off, shaking my head. *They were doing a nice thing. I needed the mental space to deal with Ansel's stuff.* "Well, one got through."

"I gathered." Deacon sighs. "I'm sorry, Hen. I should have told you, but I saw some of the messages. Cade made it a point to tell me how much they upset you, and Finn told me the volume. I just made a judgment call on it. I thought he'd have given up by now."

"Yeah. No. He didn't, and now it's . . . These messages are . . . distastefully explicit. It's like he knew how many pills I had left." I look at the message. Crude sex acts laid out in bad form. It seems so out of character for him. "How did this get past?"

"Well, it's not a content block, I didn't want your privacy invaded." Deacon maneuvers us back into the right-hand lane.

"Well, maybe we should." My cheeks heat, and this feels more like embarrassment than a hot flash. "He literally just wrote that he wants to stick his schlong into my lady garden and spray me down with his fire hose of cum."

"Oh, that's bad. I'm getting soft just hearing it." He shudders.

"That implies you're hard to start with." The observation comes out of my mouth before I realize what I'm saying.

Deacon doesn't contradict me.

I look over at him, and he shrugs, changing lanes and passing a semitruck.

"What? Do you want me to deny it?" Deacon merges back into our original lane after the pass. When I don't answer, he continues. "Henri, there's going to come a moment very soon when we're going to be forced to see a truth that we've both been avoiding. But beyond that, on a stupid base, biological level, a male wolf in an SUV with a woman they're attracted to, going into heat . . . is going to create a physiological response."

He knows. My wolf wags her tail. *He's right, we're mates. Let him claim us. He loves us.*

"I."

"You don't have to say anything, Hen. I know." Deacon looks ahead at the road. "Let's stop and stretch, get some snacks. Figure out where to grab a few hours of sleep. Oh, and forward that email to Adam at Corinth. Just put 'Deacon said *What the fuck? Show this to Millie*' in the body. She'll get a kick out of that."

He's been holding back. I think about the Wisconsin house and how things didn't progress after that because he was respecting my decision — or what he understood about it. Then, of course, well, Ansel's wasn't exactly the time or the place.

He wants me. And he means it.

AFTER OUR PIT STOP, Deacon continues driving. But I'm feeling more and more nervous with every passing mile marker. Memories of my first heat, feelings of being trapped, not safe, and alone, encroach on my well-being.

"How did it work being raised by humans?" Deacon asks.

I'm sure my nerves are practically a third occupant in the car, so he's just trying to distract me.

I shake my head and am forced to draw a deep breath, but it doesn't help my panting. "Um. I." Words don't come easily; focusing past the pain in my abdomen that never stops, only fluctuating in intensity, is getting impossible. "I was a late bloomer. I didn't shift at all as a child. From what I've learned, shifting is a modeled behavior."

"True." He squeezes my hand.

"But when we figured it out, I was a teenager. I was so scared. But I didn't tell anyone. I was afraid they'd tell me I was crazy or lock me away or —" Through the haze of it, the realization of what Deacon's lived through pulls a thought out of my brain. *He's been called those things.*

"Don't worry about it. Keep talking. I'm not offended." Deacon encourages me to tell more of my story.

Nathan never cared about that. My wolf is quick to point out the surmounting differences between them.

"But my adoptive parents saw me shift." I draw in a deep breath through my nose and try to steady my breathing. "And sure there was" — a slow ragged exhale, but when my lungs empty, I'm forced to take a gasping breath — "a small freak out." I pause and try to bring my breaths under control, but the pain is getting more intense again.

Fuck. Fuck. Fuck. Fuck.

My wolf whines, and it escapes from my mouth.

"But they just wanted me to find people like me." I try another deep inhale through my nose and a slow exhale through the mouth. "They were so supportive."

Am I rambling?

I try to wrap up what I'm saying. With a wince, I suck in a sharp breath to push the words out. "I didn't find anyone right away. I was looking, but I didn't even know what to look for." I have to stop talking again when I run out of air.

Why can't I just breathe?

Need Deacon, my wolf insists.

"Every time I thought I found shifters, it was humans being weird." I squeeze Deacon's hand extra hard as another wave crests.

Fuck him. Please let him fuck us, my wolf begs.

"It wasn't until I went into heat for the first time that I found someone." I shift in my seat, trying to relieve some of the pressure in my pelvis.

Deacon growls, maybe in anticipation of the worst-case scenarios. It's sweet how he cares so deeply for me, even with things he couldn't ever change.

"It wasn't like that." I reassure him. "It could have been. When he found me, fuck, it was like this but scarier. He brought the pack Alpha to me. I was safe. He gave me instructions, ways to get through it. Women from the pack brought me food and water. It was hell, but it could have been worse." The cramp finally subsides, and I yawn, trying to dispel the stress of the pain. "I know I got lucky. That it could have been bad. I appreciate it so much."

That seems to alleviate his frustration a bit.

"What about you? Do you do this often?" A new discomfort settles in my stomach. The kind that tells me I'm being judgmental, but I can't help it nor hold it back.

Deacon draws a deep breath. "I used to guard Lena through her heat. We had an incident with a lone wolf. Cade made it a point to be home after that."

"Okay." My breaths are ragged. "We're not going to make it home, are we?"

"I'm going to try. I'll push the engine as hard as I can, but it's not my bike. It'll only drive this fast for so long." His answer doesn't settle my worries.

I groan.

Deacon is silent for a few miles before backtracking the conversation. "To answer your question, yes. I've serviced someone through heat before."

"Deacon," I gasp as a sharp stab cramps my insides. "I fucking hate him for this," I growl, and another cramp hits. "Fuck!"

"I hate him too." Deacon's soft, calming tone soothes me a tiny bit. "But I'm not beneath spending almost a week making you forget his name." Deacon clenches his teeth, the muscle feathering along his jawline. "But you're lawful good. And if I bring you to chaotic evil . . . it'll ruin you to be with me."

"I want you too," I whine.

I'm reluctant to trust this, and maybe he's right that biology is playing a major part in my desires, but there's something about how Deacon cares.

"I know, Hen. I know." He focuses on the road.

My wolf whines louder, and the pain has me rocking in my seat, trying to relieve the growing need.

CHAPTER 60
DEACON

"ONE ROOM," Henri says to the woman at the front desk. "Two queens, please."

I open my mouth to object. I should, but instead I shut it. *This is how she thinks she'll be comfortable. It's not like we can't cuddle in a queen.*

My wolf is rising faster than I want. He's grumbling and pushing me toward her.

The last of the suppressants are entirely out of Henri's system. Within the next two hours, the 'it's undeniable she's your mate' moment is going to happen.

Who am I kidding? That moment happened the second Cade sent me the files of all the known players in Robert's support network. I was just too arrogant. I thought I was above it and would be able to resist.

Cade had asked me to do some digging into Robert's staff. Not trusting them, Cade didn't want to take any risks that there were ulterior motives going on within the ranks. We trimmed down Robert's lavish staff and only kept those who were most likely involved enough to know what was going on but not enough that they were pushing buttons and pulling strings.

The new intern, who was just getting her feet wet, wasn't the ideal candidate for the Alden pack publicist. But I wanted her from the first time I saw her picture. Conveniently, the PR staff all seemed to quit the night Cade killed Robert, except for the intern with zero experience, so he had no choice but to keep her.

In my defense, I was left unsupervised.

As soon as the receptionist slides the key card onto the counter, Henri grabs it and heads down the hallway to our room. She opens the door, and I follow her inside, putting our bags on the first bed.

"I'm sorry. If you want a separate room, we can get one, but I just . . . I just . . ." She trips over her words.

Standing behind her, I'm not able to see the emotions play on her face, but I can hear the muted tones of sadness.

"You're going into heat very quickly and don't want to be alone." I can't help myself, and if I could . . . I wouldn't, so I wrap my arms around her. Hugging her from behind, I nuzzle my nose into her hair and draw deep breaths.

She takes a few deep breaths. "Lena went through how many heats alone?"

"Uhhh, I guess I never counted." I don't bother trying to do the math now.

Lust and concern for her well-being are in the way of any deep thinking.

"I feel so weak. I'm falling apart. Lena did this all by herself for years, and I can't even stay in a hotel room alone. I'm not even all the way in heat." Henri berates herself.

It breaks my heart hearing her talk about herself, the woman I love, like she's not perfect.

"Hen, I'm going to need you to stop talking about my mate

like that." I let her go, but only so I can spin her to look at me. "You have gone through heat once. It was your first one. Anything any woman has ever said to me about it is that it's the worst thing in the entire world." Her bottom lip quivers, and I place my hand on the side of her face. "You're responding rationally to something scary."

Accepting my words, she nods but steps away from my touch. "How long before you're sober?"

"Two, two and a half hours, tops." I hang my head.

She takes a deep breath. "Then we'll know if my wolf and Revecca are right."

Her wolf is right. My wolf battles the last pill burning off.

Fuck off. I stuff him down. But I can't just push this off any further. "Henri, you know, at this point, it's a technicality that I'm still a little woobly, right?"

"Woobly?" Henri rolls her eyes.

"Really, that's . . ." I shake my head and say the words one of us needs to. "Henri, you're my mate. I am your mate. This isn't *just* the heat talking. This isn't wishful thinking or me doing or saying something to get a reaction."

Henri shakes her head. "Let's get some sleep. Early day tomorrow."

"No." I put my foot down. "Henri, we have to talk about where these big feels are coming from."

"You wouldn't understand, okay?" Tears are welling in her eyes.

"Try me anyway." I coax her.

Henri looks down at my shoes and twists her jaw back and forth. "It's like, without going into heat, I'm . . . close to being human."

"Back to when your life was easier. Things made sense," I offer, stopping myself from lifting her head up to look at me. "The first time you went into heat, your entire world changed."

She looks at me and nods. "I don't know how to be wolf. But I knew how to be human."

"I don't know what it's like to be human, but I think I've got a vague understanding of what you're going through. It's a struggle to be who you are and the person everyone believes you to be." There are so many things I've locked away in boxes around my brain that it looks like a disorganized warehouse of forgotten valuables.

I look at the beds, and the pillow is already calling my name.

"Why do you make everything sound so smart?" Henri wraps her arms around herself, the last hot flash having left her cold.

"I don't know." I shrug off the probably rhetorical question. *Finish the job, Deacon. Keep her safe and taken care of.* "Are you still hungry? We could have some snacks before bed."

Henri puts her hand on her stomach. "No, you made sure I was sufficiently fed even if I didn't want to eat my vegetables."

"What is it with the women in my life and vegetables? Only Thalia eats them without argument." I roll my eyes and pretend to be completely exasperated, and finally, the overdramatics get a small laugh out of her.

"Let's toss on a movie or some trashy TV and go to bed, then." I yawn, mostly out of stress, trying to release the tension. Busying my hands, I open my backpack. "Is it going to bother you if I sleep without a shirt on?"

"Oh." I watch Henri out of my peripheral. She opens her mouth and then pulls her bottom lip in before answering. "That's okay. I can deal with that."

The lack of real objection makes my heart flutter like I'm some teenager. *Get it together. We've already had sex.*

Obviously, our mate finds us attractive. My wolf gives me a ridiculous huff.

But not even the smug asshole can dampen the feeling of being wanted.

CHAPTER 61
HENRI

I THINK we slept for four hours when Deacon's alarm goes off. No, I think I slept for two hours because my body was one temperature change away from insanity. Deacon, however, is nearly bright-eyed and bushy-tailed after our four-hour nap as he comes back from the bathroom . . . But it's more than that.

Deacon's wolf rises to the surface, and mine rushes forward to meet his. I feel warmth and connectedness. It's all-consuming, and that obsessive part of me, who has always wanted to know where he was, clicks into place.

Our mate. You get it now, right? My wolf begs me to see and accept what she's saying.

"Fuck." Deacon laughs. He runs his hand across the back of his neck, and his face reddens a little bit. "You feel that too?"

I make him nervous?

I nod, biting my lips together, keeping in all the word vomit threatening to escape.

"I knew it would be intense, but no wonder no one can explain this feeling to you." He steps toward me, closing the gap between us, but hesitates when he gets to me, coming to a standstill.

I extend my hand, reaching for him. My body and wolf call for him despite my brain's hesitation.

Slowly, and like he's afraid I'll spook, Deacon takes my hand. His touch stokes the fire that's been growing under my skin. I'm salivating, and my heart rate picks up like I'm running with the pack, not just getting out of bed.

When Deacon wraps his arms around me, I could let the heat take me and melt me into a puddle on the floor. I would be content to be puddled for the rest of my life. *But is this just the heat talking?*

My cell phone rings.

With one last squeeze, Deacon lets me out of his arms so I can answer it. The contented warmth fizzles from my body with every vibration of the phone, flash of the screen, and by the time my hand wraps around the metal device, I'm nearly freezing cold.

In the last ring before voicemail, I slide my finger across the screen to accept the call. "Hello?"

"Where are you?" Nathan barks into the phone. "Why haven't you been answering me?"

"I don't know why that matters." I check, and the phone call came from an unidentified number. *One of the few things that Deacon couldn't figure out how to block.*

"Don't bother, Henri." He huffs and then grumbles, "I know you're with *him*. I thought we were getting back together."

My stomach sinks. "We are not getting back together. What are you talking about?"

"Henri, it's on social media. The two of you checking into a hotel together. The poster said you only got one room and went into it together."

I look at Deacon, and he's pulling his phone out of his pocket.

"Okay? What does that matter?" Tears prickle my eyes. *Why is this happening?*

Deacon steps up behind me, pushing his phone into my line of sight. It's right at the top of the Cousins Grimm social media page. Deacon and I at the front desk, and then him holding the door open behind me.

Things are slamming in the background on Nathan's side of the call. "I should have fucking known you'd cheat on me. Wolves aren't meant to be loyal to one person, it's why you all run in shitty packs. Hope his dick was good enough for you, Henri. You cheated on me, and now you're just some whore."

"Nathan, I'm not cheating on you." I'm firm with him. My mate has his arms wrapped around me, standing here listening, so why am I even talking to Nathan? "I don't owe you anything. We're not dating. Unless you've something extremely urgent to tell me about something from the time we were together, please don't contact me again." My voice shakes.

"You're a slut, Henri. Nothing more than all those fucked up things you wanted to do in the bedroom. I should have known better the first time you wanted to try something new. I wasn't ever good —"

Deacon pulls my phone out of my hand.

"Nathan. Hi. Deacon Alden. So, I'm a pretty tolerant individual, but you're quickly becoming the most notable coward I've ever met. Quite frankly, I've yet to find one good quality in your possession. And I say that because the best part of you was Henri, and she's mine now. Do not contact her again for any reason." Deacon waits.

Nathan is screaming loud enough that I can hear him, even

with my phone volume all the way down. "Fuckin' bastard. Dirtying her with your disgusting hands."

Deacon snorts and then answers with words thick with implications and veiled threats. "Nathan, don't bother trying to see or contact her again. If you do, there will be consequences that are directly proportionate to the amount of disdain I'm feeling for you at any given second. Please note, it's currently immeasurable." Deacon hands me back my phone. The call is disconnected, and his voice is back to his usual, friendly Deacon tone. "I'll get Adam to figure out a way to prevent that again."

"Did you just threaten Nathan?" My brain is fuzzy with the details of what just happened.

"Oh, well, if you're questioning it, then clearly, I haven't learned to do it well enough." With his hands on my shoulders, Deacon spins me to face him. He runs his finger up my cheek, and I feel the wetness of a tear that escaped. "Chin up, Hen. No boy like that is worth crying over. Remember?"

"Deacon, what should we do?" I want to shake my head away from his hand, but instead, I melt into him. "I mean, it's hardly abnormal that you and I have roomed together in the past as your media manager."

He wraps himself around me, holding me close. "You're going to go shower and get into comfy clothes. Then you're going to see how you're feeling and if you think you can handle going to breakfast. If not, we're going to do some gas-station and drive-through food before we get on the road. We're going to handle the media once we're done making sure you're through your heat safely."

My phone rings in my hand, and I look at it. Nathan calling again. His words hang heavy in my brain: *Slut. Whore. Cheater.*

Deacon pulls my phone out of my hand, rejects the call, and tosses it on the bed. With his forefinger, he tips my head back to face him and then kisses me. Soothing. He's not hurried but dedicated.

If the mating bond pull hadn't been there before, if I hadn't felt it so assuredly less than ten minutes ago, this would have been all the proof I needed. The way Deacon tastes my mouth, letting his tongue explore, is the hottest thing ever.

He breaks the kiss when my phone rings again. "I'm going make some calls and get Cade's people aware of his threatening behavior. You get ready to go."

My brain is foggy after the kiss, and I nod, agreeing with his request despite the many questions I should have. They're just impossible to pick out of the cloud he's pushed me into. So much is happening at once, and the emotions are amplified ten times over. But Deacon's directions on what to do feel right. I follow them, feeling comfort in the way he knows what to do.

CHAPTER 62
DEACON

Her arousal is suffocating me, and we've only been in the car for three hours. But I don't dare open the windows and try to push fresh air through the cab. It's April, and while we're out of the mountains, it's still cold.

Henri reaches for the air dials and turns them all the way to cold, blasting the AC. She fans herself and tries to make the hot flash more manageable.

Coming up behind a snowplow, I'm forced to slow down. I grip the steering wheel, ready to throttle it for being an inconvenient necessity on the road.

She gasps, and it startles me. I glance over to make sure she's not in any danger and put my eyes back on the road and the hazards.

"Sorry. Sorry. Sorry. Sorry." She whines between heavy pants. "Fuck. I forgot how bad these hurt. I think the worst thing is the cramps."

"It's okay. I've got you, Hen."

The idea to grab the entire box off Ansel's fridge was probably my best one. Knowing it's hard to believe just the pills would disappear, taking the entire box meant that they would wonder where it got moved to and eventually stop looking.

I take the next exit off the freeway. We don't need fuel, but the rule of a long-distance drive is if you stop, you fill it. I pull up to a pump at a gas station and set to fill the tank. While the nozzle pumps, I open the hatch and pull out the box, then carry it around to the passenger side and open Henri's door.

Her eyes had been glued shut, but they flutter open. She makes squinty eyes at the box and then back at me, making the devious dark part of my brain light up with delicious ideas. It sends shockwaves straight to my cock, and I'm glad for thick, well-constructed denim to contain me.

"Lena packed a box for Morrigan. And if you haven't figured it out yet, my little sister is a freak. Pick your poison."

The fuel pump clicks off, indicating it's full. But I can't pull myself away from her. Not. Just. Yet.

Henri's curiosity has been piqued. She takes the box from me and lifts the flaps. I wasn't sure which expression I was going to get.

At first, she freezes, then flicks her wide eyes to mine before stumbling through her words. "I don't know . . ."

"I know for a fact that Ansel and Morrigan didn't touch them." I try to assure her.

"It's not th —" A cramp hits her hard, and she pushes her head back against the headrest, covering her mouth with her hand to stop herself from making any noise.

Standing here, giving her space and time to decide, isn't the best way to care for her. But if I push her to relieve the cramps the only way I know how, here in this parking lot at a fuel pump, it . . .

I shake my head, clearing my thoughts. *She's probably not into that.*

Making sure she's safely tucked inside the car, I push her

door closed before replacing the gas nozzle. On my way back around to the driver's side, I close up the back of the SUV.

My heart is thundering in my chest. Breathing is hard. Forcing oxygen into my lungs, I try to calm my heart anyway. *Hold it together, Deacon. You can't fuck her right here. She might not even let you fuck her at all. The Wisconsin house wasn't exactly a relationship starter.*

My wolf growls. *She is ours. You're an idiot. Our mate needs us. Then she'll beg us to claim her. And you'll do it unless you're some sort of dumbass and fail to perform.*

Got it. Thanks. So supportive of the situation. I let the sarcasm hang heavy.

I jog up the side of the SUV and fling open the driver's door. Henri still has the box partly open on her lap, and she's staring at it, the lines on her forehead broadcasting the gears working in her brain.

After navigating us back onto the road, I explain, "Your heat is still early. We might be able to make it home if you stave off some of the . . . tension. I'm good to drive, and I'll drive through the night."

"Deacon," she snarls, her little wolf rising to the surface. "You want me to what, fuck myself with a dildo right here on the front seat of the SUV?"

"I mean, you can climb in the back if you'd feel more comfortable." It would probably make her more comfortable. I should have thought of it first. "But yes. I'm suggesting you fuck yourself in the car with a dildo to relieve the cramps. It will get you through, hopefully, to get us home."

Her heart rate picks up, but arousal, not fear, fills the cab. "What if someone sees?"

My cock throbs, and I drop one hand from white knuckling the steering wheel to try and adjust myself until it doesn't hurt. Try. Because it's not going to happen. *If an erection lasts longer than four hours, call your doctor.* The silly late-night commercial voice for a human erectile dysfunction medication plays in my head.

"Then someone gets the show of their fucking life."

Henri folds the flaps back all the way. The scent of her arousal spikes again, and I'm drowning in the sweet smell.

Don't look. Don't look. Don't look. I try to distract myself by changing the words to songs buzzing in my head and chanting to encourage my own good behavior.

One of the toys must be suitable because she leans forward and puts the box on the floor.

"You know how dangerous it is to put your feet up on the dash?" Henri's question draws my attention off the road to where she's adjusting herself in her seat.

The way she's sitting doesn't look comfortable. It looks clinical, like in pornos, where a doctor takes advantage of his patient.

"Put your seat back," I instruct carefully.

Henri drops her feet from the dash and does what I say.

"Shimmy out of your pants."

To keep myself in my seat, I start counting the lines on the road. *One, two, three, four, five, six, seven.* I look down and see we're going almost twenty over the speed limit. I take my foot off the gas and wait until we come down to a respectable five over, then set the cruise.

Henri's pants finally hit the floorboard.

"Now spread your legs, bend your knees, and rest your feet together on the seat in front of you. Think reclining horny butterfly pose."

"Oh," Henri whispers, "fuck."

"Fuck indeed."

The scent of her arousal through her pants was enough to drive me nuts, but now with her sex completely exposed, I take my hand from my dick to cover my mouth, the side of my index finger blocking my nose.

"Are you going to be okay?" Henri's voice wavers as she second-guesses herself.

"You got aroused at the idea of someone else maybe seeing you." I deflect, pulling my hand away from my face. I want to drop it back to my lap, but I force it to the steering wheel. "Ultimate exhibitionist experience, Henri. I can look all I fucking want, but I can't touch you."

"You could touch you." Henri's voice catches. It's thick with lust.

The throbbing in my cock radiates through my body, up my spine, and down to the soles of my feet. *It's the heat talking. It's the heat talking. This isn't her.*

It is her, my wolf argues. *It's the part of her she keeps away from us. From herself.*

"Touch yourself, Deacon. Please." She begs me so sweetly.

I slouch in my seat to better access my fly. Button, zipper, and boxers out of the way, the cock that's been plaguing my body finally has room to throb and breathe.

"Tell me what you're doing, Hen." I keep my eyes on the road, watching the white line rather than counting the passing lane stripes.

"I'm teasing the head against my clit. It feels so good." Henri immediately understands the assignment.

"I'm throbbing for you. My cock is so fucking hard right now," I tell her, encouraging her.

I wrap my hand around my shaft, squeezing in time to the pulses of my heartbeat.

Henri gasps, and I glance over just in time to catch the dildo sliding into her pussy. Oh, to be between her legs and watch it.

"Fuck. You're so smart," Henri whispers. "So, so, so, so smart."

"That feel good, Hen?" I smile, remembering what a blissed-out Henri looks like.

"Mm-hmm." She makes contented noises, and I can hear the dildo sliding in and out of her.

I match her pace, running my hand up and down my shaft. I roll my thumb over the tip, and beads of precum mix with my motions,

"What are you thinking?"

"About . . ." Henri hesitates. "Don't judge?"

My wolf growls, already angry.

"Too late. I've already judged you and decided I love you anyway." I say those words again.

I want her to fully understand what I mean and the radical honesty behind them. But fuck, perfect mate, wanting to be this free with it all. Should I spell it out for her?

"I'm imagining what it'd be like to have your full attention." She moans, and the pace of her fucking herself on the dildo picks up.

Don't crash the SUV, Deacon. My hand stops, and I swallow hard, focusing on driving for a few moments before I go back to stroking myself and trying to keep time with her.

My wolf gets a better idea. *Pull over instead. All the better to watch her.*

Henri sighs and finds cohesive words again. "This is so hot. Fuck."

"What do you like about this, Henri?" I ask, prompting her for more, but I don't need more. I'm already trying to hold myself back from coming. "Just knowing I'm watching?"

"Not just you," she moans, but it turns into a whine. "Nathan said it's shameful . . ." Her voice quivers, and I know she's going back to the horrible things he called her this morning. Despite that memory, she keeps talking to me. "But I . . . The idea of getting caught. That someone could see."

458

"Do you want me to push that, Henri?" I ask, eyeing the semi a half mile in front of us.

I turn my head, fully taking my eyes off the road to look at her. She's a vision. Fuck nude art and the classic works Thalia talks about. Henri beats them all.

I pull my eyes away from her and back to the road, watching as we pace the semi. "What do you say Henri? There's a semi up ahead. Want to risk being caught?"

She stops fucking herself, and it draws my eyes back to her.

She's biting her bottom lip.

I take it as a yes. My cock still craves attention desperately. But I tuck it back into my boxers and let my shirt drape over the top. Turning off cruise control, I change to the passing lane of the divided highway and gun it. The SUV climbs in speed with ease.

"You going to come for me, Henri? I'll pull up beside this truck, and you'll come as hard as you can."

"Hell" — she gasps for air — "yes."

I ride in the truck driver's mirror line of sight and see him check it, making note of my position. Creeping forward, I pull us up alongside the cab. I steal glances across the car as Henri pumps the dildo in and out of her pussy with fervor. She works her clit with her fingers, and I desperately want to help, but instead, I keep an eye on the semi cab, watching for his acknowledgment of us next to him.

"Fuck, Deacon. Deacon!" she screams as she comes.

It's loud, hard, and nearly eardrum shattering.

With the lane behind us completely void of any cars, I step on the brake and let the semi continue to barrel on, putting distance between us.

Memorizing the plate and the carrier, I keep it to myself to avoid pulling up next to them again at a stop. I don't know for sure what he did or didn't see, and it's best to avoid the possibility of another interaction.

Henri pants, coming down from her orgasm. She pulls the dildo from her pussy and lazily holds it in her hand.

"Here, I'll hold it. If the security guys haven't changed anything out, there are napkins in the glove box. I'll get you something nicer at our next stop. I didn't think about it. I'm sorry."

It was stupid of me not to think about it. No woman, especially not mine, should be cleaning herself with napkins after gifting me in such a magnificent way.

The pause and slight 'hmm' ultimately gives way to Henri giving me what I want. With the dildo in my hand and self-control out the window, I waste zero time or energy debating what I am dying to do. I run my tongue up the shaft, flattening it along the girth before turning the dildo and cleaning it again in the same long lap.

If Henri smelled good, she tastes that much better. It's like a kick of the good moonshine straight from Wyatt's extended family in the bayou. The strong kind that comes in a mason jar and you know came from a long line of bootleggers before you even get the lid off the jar.

I instantly want more. I want to feast straight from the source.

"Deacon!" Henri gasps.

I cast a sideways glance at her. "What? Did you want a taste? I'll share."

"No." Henri furrows her brow. "I didn't expect it."

"Figured this was a perfectly fine idea to clean it up. I'm helping." I can't help but smile as I turn the dildo again, taking a slower, longer lick.

My balls throb with the desire to fuck her, taste her, play with her. Anything.

She leans forward and opens the glove box. Finally comfortable enough with me to share perverse thoughts — maybe post-orgasm clarity or, at the very least, she's given up on trying to keep me at arm's reach — she tells me, "I didn't know I was attracted to that."

Thankfully there's a wad of napkins from a fast-food restaurant. She cleans herself, and I take the last lick up the final side of the dildo.

"You like a man who knows his way around a shaft?"

Henri stops breathing, and I know by the way she freezes entirely that she's gathering her thoughts, delaying her answer. "I . . . I've always wanted an experience with two men."

Her feeling free enough to confess that is like being given the most precious gift, and it unlocks a piece of my soul.

"And it feels wrong to expect guys to want to . . ." She clears her throat. "You look so . . . comfortable, licking that toy." Henri mumbles, "It's gotta be the heat talking, making me want this . . . Assuming you'd want that."

I smile, putting the dildo into the cupholder. "Confession: I'm monogamous, but unlike the cavemen, Cade and Finn, I am open to adding trusted others to playtime to fulfill certain fantasies."

Uncomfortable with the dildo so exposed, Henri awkwardly wraps it up in a few napkins and places it inside the center console. She then moves in her seat, pulling her pants back into place before returning the seat to the upright position. She fans herself and reaches for the knob to turn the SUV's heat down to cool off her body before the next wave of primal needs takes over.

"Confession: I've never had an orgasm that good." She leans her head back against the headrest. "I'm also more than slightly impressed with your ability to keep us safely on the road during all that."

That strokes the ego just right, and my smile grows. "I drive under the influence more than I drive sober. Hot woman in the passenger seat fucking her brains out is a distraction, but it's still significantly easier to keep track of the lines."

"Helps that the road is straight?" She makes note of the very flat, very boring, part of Wyoming.

"Does help that the road is straight." I agree.

Another mile rolls past, or rather, the electric number ticks up, before she speaks in a sheepish tone lightly laced with a tinge of fear. "So how much of a distraction would it be if I . . ."

Her words trailing off make me jump to conclusions. The optimistic brain kicks in. *Stroke me off? I'd kill for a Henri hand job.* I try to muffle the optimistic, dirty brain, but it gets louder. *Suck us off.* That sends a painful throb to my dick. *No. It's probably something mund—*

"Took care of you." Henri's words are tentative. She tucks her hair behind her ear and backpedals. "Unless, of course, you don't want me to. I wouldn't . . . Oh fuck, bad idea. Horny Henri talking."

"Henri," I groan. The metaphorical devil and angel battle on my shoulders, but as he always does, the devil wins out. "You can always touch me. I'm always available for your use." The angel forces me to add a clause. "But you don't owe me. This isn't one of those quid-pro-quo moments. I expect nothing from you."

"What if I really want to give it?" Henri's voice is barely above a whisper.

"I'm all yours, Hen." *I'll always be all yours.*

CHAPTER 63
HENRI

'I WOULD NEVER' is a phrase I haven't said a lot in my life, but I'm sure in college I said, 'I would never have car sex, especially not while it's moving.'

Well, I'm going to have to eat those words . . . Or rather, lick them off the side of Deacon's cock.

Unbuckling my seat belt, I try to figure out how to maneuver with the center console between us.

I pause, freezing when I get nearer.

"This isn't something you have to do." Deacon keeps his hands on the wheel.

The cruise control is set, so his legs are relaxed, but his cock is straining against his boxers and the fabric of his shirt.

"I want to. But you have to promise me something." I watch his face, looking for . . . deception? But I don't think Deacon would try to trick me.

"Anything." Deacon nods.

"Hands on the steering wheel at all times. Both hands," I reiterate.

The knife at the Wisconsin house was one thing, but the last thing we need is for me to freak out . . . I push the idea of a car crash out of my head.

He doesn't balk at the notion but gives a firm nod, looking over at me before returning his eyes to the road ahead, keeping us safe. "Understood."

"Can you, uh." *Get it together, Henri.* I draw a deep breath. "Get me better access?"

With a small shuffle, he slides his pants and boxers down and out of the way. He pulls his shirt up, and I get the first close-up look at his cock. It's . . . stunning. Hard, pink, and not super veiny, it's . . . pretty? It's not that I haven't seen it before, but not like this.

Deacon says nothing. He doesn't encourage me or dissuade me. His hands stay on the steering wheel, and everything stays constant.

It all waits for me.

I find the best way over the center console and lick the head of his cock. His stomach muscles clench, and it seems like a response to enjoying it.

When I lick him again, Deacon curses under his breath but, again, doesn't move. The respect he's giving me bolsters my confidence to take him into my mouth.

His breathing is ragged. But Deacon stays true to his word.

I explore his cock, sliding him into my mouth and swirling my tongue around the head as I pull back.

I wrap my hand around the base and stroke his shaft with the rise and fall of my head. Taking him deeper, I gag a little bit, and Deacon mutters. Over the sound of the car on the road, I can't make out what it was, but I know, from the throb of his cock, it's a good thing.

I press down again, thrusting deeper and gagging a little each time.

Deacon tenses under my touch. He pants, his core muscles clenching and spasming.

"Fuck."

This time when he curses, I hear him.

I'm in control, working his shaft, sucking him into my mouth, and hollowing my cheeks around him.

I move faster, encouraging Deacon to climax. He groans and his leg shakes.

I force him even deeper into my throat, ignoring my gag reflex, and Deacon curses again.

I love hearing those words come off his lips in that husky tone. Again and again, I repeat the movements that make him cuss.

"Henri," Deacon gasps. "Fuck, Henri, if you don't . . ."

I hum with approval, not needing him to spell out the end of that threat.

He lets out a guttural groan.

Body tense and on edge, Deacon comes.

I swallow it down the best I can, keeping my mouth wrapped around him until the throbbing stops.

When I run my tongue up his cock for the last time, Deacon is panting, his chest rattling in massive breaths.

With his eyes fixed down his nose at the road, he presses his head against the headrest. His hands, still firmly on the steering wheel, are red and pink from his white-knuckle grip.

It isn't until I'm back in my seat that he moves a hand from the steering wheel and scrubs it down his face.

"Fuck, Henri." He looks over at me. "You don't mess around. I've never." Deacon shakes his head, looking out at the road again. "I've never had anyone . . . that fucking good."

Deacon isn't a flatterer. He doesn't just say things to make me feel good. His praise brings a new heat to my face.

Pleased our mate well. He's going to take good care of us in heat. My wolf preens.

I buckle my seat belt and settle in.

A FEW MILES LATER, Deacon takes the next exit ramp, which boasts a single fast-food restaurant and a gas station.

Deacon pulls into a spot at the far end of a lot, and once he parks and cuts the engine, he squeezes my hand. "Stay right here."

He mostly shuffles his pants up before hopping out and doing the fly.

Sleepy, I nod at him and recline my seat so I can curl up better. I'm feeling cold and vulnerable again. Despite his praises, I'm worried I'm doing everything wrong.

When he closes his car door, I notice how alone I've become again.

Deacon uses the fob and locks me in. I try to relax, but every noise outside seems like a threat.

What if he doesn't come back? My wolf riots at him being gone.

I know that's not the case. Logic says Deacon wouldn't leave me like this. Staying as small as possible, I wait, listening to the minutes tick by.

"I'm saying that if they wanted to win the game, then they should have played better," one man says as he walks by the SUV.

Well, no shit, Sherlock.

I draw a deep breath and focus on the other sounds.

Birds in the distance squawking about who knows what.

A mother, scolding her child for running out from between cars in the parking lot.

They're normal sounds of a normal place. No one knows what's happening to me but me. I'm safe.

Are there wolf packs in Wyoming? My wolf tries to think through the map.

I reach for my phone and pull up the pack data that Cade has saved in the joint server.

I'm scrolling through the list, trying to get it to categorize on my phone when the doors unlock. I jump, yelping when the door behind me opens.

"Easy, Hen." Deacon's voice is soothing. The sweet undertone of reassurance is followed by the rustling of bags as he sets them on the floor. "You're okay. I didn't ask if you're okay, and I'll do better in the future. I was too eager to get you things that I didn't care for what you needed."

I uncurl from the ball I've been in and look over my shoulder at him.

Deacon leans against the doorframe and slowly runs his hand along my body, carefully working his way down my flesh. His smirk lights up his eyes. "There's my girl. How are you doing?"

"We're not going to make it to Minnesota, are we?" I whine, rolling over in the seat to face him.

Deacon hangs his head. "I don't think so. I'd much rather have you draped over my bed. But I don't think that's going to happen, and I don't think we should risk being stuck somewhere not safe."

He reaches down to the floor, and I see that the bags he bought are brimming with things.

"You shop fast." I observe blankly.

"Thank you." He starts pulling things out. The first thing is a fluffy sherpa and microfiber blanket. "I got you the white one with the little pattern because I know you like minimalism."

He crumples up that empty bag and throws it in the back

seat. The next bag has two bottles of water, one bottle of a sports drink, and one of my favorite sodas. Which he proceeds to fill every single cupholder with.

"You didn't have to do all this." I object.

He chuckles, shaking his head, and pulls out the most snacks I've ever seen come out of one bag. "Sweet, salty, sour, nutrient dense, not so nutrient dense, hot, and cold." He puts my favorite chocolate bar in my hand. Wrapping his fingers around mine, he locks eyes with me. "I know you think I don't have to do this, but it's my honor to be able to. And I'll be damned if it doesn't feel good to be able to do it."

A gust of wind kicks up, and he lets my hand go. Stepping out and closing the SUV door, he almost completely shields me from the gust. Once it passes, he opens it again before adjusting my seat up to sitting and tucking me in among the blankets.

"Thank you." I snuggle in, thrilled with how it feels on my skin.

"Anytime, Henri. Let's get back on the road. I've a couple calls to make. But I'll find some place to bunker you down."

I let him fuss over me, tucking me in and making sure everything is just so before he goes to close the door.

"Deacon?" I stop him.

"Yeah, Hen?" He waits.

I hold my arms out for a hug. The smile is back, and he wraps his arms around me the best he can with my position in the car.

"I judged you, and I love you too," I whisper in his ear.

Squeezing me tighter, he nuzzles his cold nose against my neck. After placing a kiss where he was nuzzled, he lets go of me. Deacon runs his hand along my jaw when stepping away with a huge smile on his face.

Back on his side of the car, he pulls out his phone and starts scrolling. A few minutes pass before he seems to have found what he was looking for, and the phone starts to ring. It rings through to voice mail.

"Hello, you've reached Emerson Witt of Rei Gato Properties. If this is an emergency, please hang up and call someone who cares. If this isn't an emergency, leave a number at the tone, and I'll call it to bitch you out for leaving me a message instead of texting like a normal person. Thank you and have a great day."

"I'm calling in a favor." Deacon hangs up without leaving his telephone number.

The voice on the recording was thick with a heavy Cajun accent that I recognize well enough. "Did you just casually call the Rei Gato, *THE* King of the Mountain Lions, and tell him he owes you one?"

"Oh, he owes me a hell of a lot more than one." Deacon laughs, shaking his head and pulling out of the parking lot. "So much more than one. Can you pull up directions to Sturgis, South Dakota?"

"Sturgis. Got it." I start typing it in. "Anywhere in particular in Sturgis?"

"Nope. He'll call back before I need turn by —" Deacon's phone starts to ring. "As I was saying." Deacon answers it. "It's about time you pick up the damn phone." His voice holds a note of humor, but it's accompanied by a scolding tone.

"Listen, next time you're balls deep, why don't you pick up your phone?"

The voice, which I recognize from a few conference calls with Cade, is in fact Emerson Witt. Though when talking to Deacon, he's a lot looser lipped but equally confident.

"Ouch. Apologize to Deanie for being a bad fuck, finishing that quick." Deacon tsks his tongue in disgust. "Your woman deserves way better than that since she puts up with your crazy ass all day." Deacon covers his mouth to keep the laugh in.

"Listen here, you little dog-breathed asshole," Emerson starts to threaten. "Ouch," he hisses. "Yikes. Woman. Alright. Alright. Deacon, what can I do for you?"

"I need a place to lay low for a week and not be bothered. Table for two and only two if you feel me." Deacon puts his hand on my lap.

"Ooh-ho-ho," Emerson chuckles. "How soon?"

Deacon gestures to me, so I turn my phone to face him. "Like ninety minutes."

"Deacon, you never make reservations in advance, do you?" Emerson sighs. "Lucky for you, I've got a place open. I'll go get it stocked for you. Anything in particular you need that I wouldn't think of?"

"Probably have Deanie help?" Deacon sighs. "Whole nine yards for a week, maybe ten days?"

"Aye, aye, Cap-i-tahn." Emerson puts on a very exaggerated accent. "Gotta go. I'll text you the address. Drive like you stole it."

"Only if you insist," Deacon groans and hangs up.

He looks down at the speedometer, and the vehicle slows down.

"So . . ." I look over at Deacon, trying to connect the dots between what I know of Emerson Witt and what just transpired. "He's significantly more fun when he talks to you than when he talks to Cade."

"Oh, it's because he fuckin' hates Cade and Cade hates him," Deacon admits. He runs his hand through his dark hair, ruffling it a little bit. "In Cade's defense . . . he did have to bail us both out one summer even though it was my fault, but you know Cade. In true loyal fashion, he blames Emerson."

"I'm sorry. What?" I shake my head. "You've been arrested?"

"More than once." Deacon nods. "The bad boy vibes aren't just vibes, Hen."

"Do I even want to know?" I scrub my hands down my face. "This is something I should have been told. Why did it not get mentioned to me? This could blow up on social media."

Deacon picks up a bottle of water from the cupholder and tries to hand it to me with strict instructions. "Drink the water. Take a deep breath and let it out."

"I don't want water. I want less chaos." I groan, pulling my hair.

"Don't we all." Deacon laughs, but he also insists with the water again, holding it out to me with a bit more force. "I'm sorry I upset you, but the reason you don't know about either of my arrests is that they've been taken off the books. They won't be on social media because, for one, I wasn't ever formally processed, just taken down to the station, and for two, Cade called in a favor. I own a nifty cool set of fingerprints though."

The reassurance makes me feel better, and I grab the offered water and take a sip. It does nothing for my hot flash, but I don't think that's Deacon's purpose in having me drink it.

"Sooo . . ." Deacon draws out. "I kind of just assumed you'd want me to spend your heat with you. I understand if not. And I've no problem telling Emerson to find me another accommodation. But I feel like a dick for making that assumption for you if it was wrong."

"I don't want to do this alone." I reach for his hand, and he gives it to me to hold. "I know I'm going into or am in heat and that things are going to look and feel different when I get to the other side, but I don't want to do this alone, and I can't think of another wolf I'd rather go through this with."

CHAPTER 64

HENRI

"GOOD MORNING."

The fear that had been filtering in through my sleep is banished with his voice and the feeling of his hand coming to rest on my hip. The touch melts the uncertainty of where I was sleeping and waking alone.

"We're here. I am pretty sure Deanie and Emerson are here too. We'll have to be social for a little bit, but if he's good at one thing, it's knowing when it's time to leave."

"Good afternoon." I yawn and stretch out. "It'll be nice to meet him."

Deacon helps me out of my blanket and then down to the ground, his hand cool against my warm skin. I just want to wrap myself around him to cool off.

"I'm going to apologize in advance for the 'hilariousness'" — Deacon's use of air quotes piques my curiosity — "that Emerson thinks he is. He's eccentric and will literally give you the shirt off his back, but sometimes he's a little loud and too friendly."

"Quit worrying." I can't resist and wrap myself around him in a tight hug.

After a second, he fully embraces me, holding me against him and drawing me close, then we both melt, relaxing into the affection. After several long, slow breaths, Deacon lets me go and leads the way along a crushed earth footpath up to the quirky little rental property.

A man with chestnut hair and tanned skin, wearing blue jeans and a dress shirt, stands on the deck enjoying the sun while he looks at his phone. His eyes pull up to us, and he tucks the device into his back pocket.

He claps his hands together and then shoots finger guns at Deacon. "Deacon! My man!"

In true Deacon form, he plays along with the antics, slamming one hand against his heart. "Ems, you've been up to no good?"

"Never. I thought I told you to drive it like you stole it. You know, all slow and inconspicuous like. You got here early." Emerson taps his watch in emphasis.

The screen door opens behind him, and a beautiful woman comes out of the house, green dress flowing around her ankles and her hair catching a coppery gold tone in the sun. Her hips sway back and forth in a very lanky and catlike walk. A walk that is heavily influenced by the fact that she is quite obviously pregnant.

"Well, as I live and breathe. It is Deacon, and he does, in fact, have a woman with him." Her voice is sweet and thick like honey, a different Southern drawl pulling at each syllable.

"Deanie, it is good to see you." Deacon offers his hand out to her, but she pushes it aside to pull him in for a hug.

My wolf doesn't like it. She eyes them suspiciously, and a protective need comes over me, creeping up my spine.

"I was just telling him how you don't come around

anywhere near enough now that you're all over television and the news. We used to see you at least once every other month. And now . . . I'm starting to think you are baby-phobic." She runs her hand across the top of her belly.

"Nah. It's that someone" — he gestures to me from head to toe — "seems to believe I'm charismatic and kind and that humans like me."

"They do." I defend with a huff. *Obviously. Because I can do my job.*

"Everyone loves Deacon." Emerson comes to my defense. "The trick is getting Deacon to love them."

"He says he loves me all the time," I muse, looking at the cute house.

Only heartbeats after it comes out do I realize what I just said.

Deacon saves me a half a breath later. "Well, anyway, we're thick in big cat country and shouldn't have any issues, right?"

"I put out a group text to the range. And for any strays . . . Well, Deanie and I did a little walkabout, so you should be well covered." Emerson nods, looking at me.

Deacon wraps an arm around me protectively, almost putting himself between us.

Deanie leans over and smacks Emerson on the stomach with the back of her hand. "Come on, you owe me ice cream."

"Oh. That's who you are. You're Henri Greene. The adorable woman who told Cade to quit being such a dick to me." Emerson lights up with a laugh. "Don't worry about me and old TL. He and I ain't never gonna see eye to eye. Gotta fight like cats and dogs, so to speak. But as long as his pack and my range stay friendly, it'll all be peachy keen."

Deanie rolls her eyes and shakes her head. "Come on, Emerson. Deacon, I love you, babe."

A whine escapes my lips.

My eyes widen, and I slap my hand over my mouth, murmuring behind it. "I'm so sorry. I'm sorry."

Taking a healthy step back, Deanie holds one hand up and keeps a large distance between us. "Text more. Oh, and to ease your mind, all that drama we had with the grizzlies a couple months back is over. Seems their funding ran out. Without all that big, city-slicker money, they had to pack up and go somewhere else."

"Strange how that works." Deacon gives her his 'guilty' and 'hiding something' shrug that I've seen him give Cade.

Emerson pulls him into a quick hug before wrapping an arm around Deanie, and the pair steps around us, farthest away from me and toward their SUV.

Emerson calls back from behind us. "Door code is on the counter. Text me if you need anything or when you leave, whichever happens first. Place isn't booked for another nineteen days, so you've got time."

"Come on, Hen, let's get you inside." Deacon coaxes me toward the door.

"Henri." Deacon runs his hand back through my hair.

I'm sitting on a soft dining room chair, and I don't remember getting here. A minute ago, we were coming in from outside.

"What are you feeling, Hen?"

"Hot," I whine, pulling at the collar of my shirt, trying to get it to be looser.

My wolf pants.

Deacon kneels before me and grabs the hem of my shirt. He pulls it over the top of my head, exposing me to the ambient temperature of the room.

"Too hot," I complain, fanning myself. I pull my hair up, holding it off the base of my neck.

Without wasting a second, Deacon stands and walks to the kitchen. I didn't notice how long his legs were until I see the amount of ground he covers in just a few steps. He's back in no time, holding a flexible ice pack.

I reach for it, wanting to press it against my body. "Can you live in Antarctica?"

"Roughly a thousand researchers live in Antarctica year-round," Deacon answers as he wraps the ice pack in my T-shirt. "In the summer, when it's milder, that number is about four thousand." Handing it to me, he warns, "Careful with it against your skin. We don't want to shock your system."

"Okay." I'll do anything he asks if I can just cool my body off.

I press it against my abdomen, and I shudder. It's blissful. My brain feels like it finally stops boiling.

I draw a breath, looking around the house again because the wave of heat that came over me blurred all my memories. "It's a cute cottage."

Deacon nods, and I know I must have said that once already. "It is. Deanie has amazing taste, and Emerson is a great carpenter. They own a ton of properties all over the West. But the Black Hills are their home base."

"That's cool." I shiver and my teeth chatter.

Tenderly, Deacon tries to pry the ice pack from my fingers.

I snarl, "Mine."

He holds his hands up in surrender. "The cabin is fully stocked for us, so I don't have to leave you unless there are specific things that'll make this easier for you."

"No leaving," I say before I can think. "Probably. Most likely. I don't know. I've only done this once. And I've already started repeating myself. You're going to get sick of it. I'm so sorry."

"Shh." Deacon crouches down on the balls of his feet, looking at me. "If you could see yourself through my eyes and hear yourself through my ears, then you'd stop apologizing for being who you are."

My face flushes, and it's not because of another hot flash. I hope he can't see it. Maybe I'm too pink still from the previous hot flash.

He rests his hand on my thigh. "You like hearing how special you are to me?"

I bite my lips together and look away from him, trying to control how obvious it is that I'm falling apart listening to him. It's not even dirty talk. It's not like he's telling me how he's going to pull me out of my pants and bend me over the table.

Fuck. That sounds good.

"I've never met anyone like you. I've never met anyone who's worth being sober for. Someone I want to be authentic with. You judge me a little bit, but the way you do it isn't malicious. You judge me because you want to find a way to fix what's bothering me. The way you stalk me is so pure. You never try to fix me, just fix my situation, and I think that's probably my favorite part about you."

If I didn't hear the tone of his voice, I'd worry these are backhanded compliments, but Deacon means every word.

He slides his hand up my thigh, and I gasp. I draw my eyes back to him, and instinct has me checking his pupils. They're blown wide, the darkness nearly overpowering the pupil. *So hot.* I don't dare move for fear he'll remove his hand, but the way my pussy is quickly becoming soaking wet is making wearing pants unbearable.

"The smell of how wet you are is escaping," he tells me

while rubbing his thumb up and down on the inner part of my thigh. "Do you want me to help you?"

Yes! My wolf screams. *Yes, we do! Say yes!* she demands.

I'm starting to feel the intense need. It's like the first time I went into heat but worse. It's so much worse.

My wolf is starting to drive.

Lust mixes with my fear, and the words don't come out, but my head bobbles with a nod.

Deacon drops to his knees, and I'm positive I've gone completely insane because skirting right past the fear are words I don't realize I'm thinking. "What does it say about me that I like seeing you on your knees?"

Once the words are out, I'm a little mortified. I'm not used to speaking so freely with someone. Everything for so long has been so censored. But that . . . *damn.*

"Fuck, Hen." Deacon adjusts himself in his pants. "Do you know you're pushing all the right buttons being so honest and open with me?"

I shake my head. "Word vomit. It's a symptom of stress. I can't help it, and it's just been so much with Ansel and now this. And it's not important because you're telling me it's hot. I probably shouldn't try to tell you otherwise." The word vomit continues, but it doesn't discourage Deacon.

No, it makes him smile wider at me.

"The fact that you like me on my knees says you take pride in knowing I'll worship you. That you want someone who's actively looking out for your pleasure. I'll humble myself to your every need, whim, and desire because you are my queen, and while I don't answer to The Leviathan, if you asked me to, I'd do anything." He slides his hands up my legs until his fingers are curled into my pants. "Lean back."

I draw a ragged breath, but I follow his instructions,

pushing back my shoulders until they come to rest on the chair back. Deacon pulls me forward by my waistband.

"Mmm." I hesitate, holding my breath.

With my shoulders pressing backward and my hips being pulled forward, the change in my center of gravity is uncomfortable. Plus, there's practically no support really on the edge of the seat.

Deacon pauses, watching me and studying. His head falls slightly to the side, and his wolf presses forward for a closer look. "You're in charge. Say stop and I will. No need for a fancy safe word or anything. Trust me?"

His patience must know no end because he waits stock-still for my answer.

I nod. "Yes."

He pulls my pants and underwear down, and I carefully lift my hips to help him slide them off.

Deacon runs his tongue down my leg following my pants. The warm, wet lap has me moaning. But the second my clothes slide past my feet, Deacon ascends back up my legs and tips the chair backward, bringing my legs over his shoulders. I'm steadying the chair on its two rear legs as Deacon steadies me.

I must squeak because Deacon laughs. "Trust me, Hen."

"Do this often?" I growl as my anticipation of what he's going to do to me shifts to fear . . . to what happens if he lets me go.

"Mmmm, not with a partner," he confesses.

He wraps his hands around my lower back, forcing me to arch farther. Deacon slides my ass closer to the edge of the chair, nose pushing apart my legs to get to my apex.

"For a while I was playing around with autoerotic asphyxiation."

His confession sparks fear for his safety, but it's followed by a warm exhale on my core.

Fear has left the building.

Deacon rolls the soft, warm underside of his tongue against my clit on a downward stroke, taking my breath away. He pulls one hand away from my ass, over the top of my thigh, and teases along my entrance with the pad of his fingers. He tests shallow plunges in and out of my pussy.

I know he knows I can physically take more, but my hesitation must be making him exercise some restraint.

The anticipation of what is coming grows. But my moans grow along with it.

My head falls, resting on the back of the chair, and I'm melting into his care. I trust that he won't let the chair — and me — topple over.

I'm trying to push my pussy into his face when his mouth breaks free from sucking on my clit.

"The blinds to the sliding door are wide open, Henri," he murmurs, his breath against my low stomach rather than my clit.

I know he's looking up at me, so I bring my eyes back to him.

I don't even bother hiding how hot that idea is. Not that I could because Deacon's fingers are now completely inside me, scissoring me open. "Hmmm."

The chair tips back farther, and Deacon encourages me. "Keep a look out the door. You can kind of see the neighbors from here."

That causes me to draw a deep breath, and I roll my head to look out the window. He's not wrong. Through the trees and brush, I get a little glimpse of their house.

"Cade will tell you that if you can see someone, they can also see you. Just depends on if they're looking." Deacon's fingers fuck me a little faster, his thumb working across my clit in a figure-eight pattern. "I wonder how nosy those neighbors are."

I can't do anything other than make a needy noise. But it's all the encouragement Deacon needs. He goes back to working me over with his mouth.

Fuck. It would be so hot if they could see. Speculation from them on how he's taking me. Maybe they'd assume we can't see them watching us.

Embarrassment heats my cheeks at the idea of them judging us. Why is this the only kind of judging I can stand?

"Fuck me, Hen," Deacon pants. "What the fuck did you just think about? Tell me, Henri, what dirty thought went through your brain because I swear you just got five times wetter."

He laps me up, waiting for a reply. His tongue was driving me closer to an orgasm with precise movements but is now a frenzy of feasting.

"How hot it is. How hot it would be to have them judge us for being so open with sex. If we . . ." I gasp as Deacon's fingers fuck me harder. He curls them up, pressing against a spot that intensifies what I'm feeling. "If we ran into them. They'd know what we did. How embarrassing that they'd judge us or say something but maybe not directly."

Deacon groans, but he's so dedicated to what he's doing he doesn't ask any more questions.

But something's . . . wrong? Right? My orgasm is building, but not in the usual way. Something inside me is creating an unusual pressure.

"You like the idea of them embarrassing you with a double entendre," he deduces.

"Yeah," I whine.

My body is growing tight, and I dig my heels into his back. *What is happening to me? Why?*

He keeps licking me until my legs are shaking, then Deacon moves his thumb back to my clit, but my building orgasm doesn't falter. The switch from his tongue to his finger is smooth and seamless. But it's that pressure inside that's got me on edge, worried about how I'm going to come. It's not the normal build.

"Oh, Henri," Deacon says, digging his fingers into my lower back. "You want to be humiliated. You want everyone to know just how naughty you can be."

He may like worshipping me, but I'm lost to being his and how it steadies the tumultuous seas of abandonment and disconnection. Even if this doesn't last, at least for now, someone understands me.

"Everyone will find out that you're my dirty little slut. They can judge you all they want, but you're perfect for me." Deacon speaks between long laps of his tongue against my warmth, flicking my clit on each pass.

Those words, claiming me as his and validating my feelings, send me over the edge. An uncontrollable feeling takes over, and the pressure inside erupts. Pushing out fluid.

Fuck.

I realize what's happening.

Deacon moans, the licking turning to sucking, and my pleasure intensifies. He pleasures me like he's ravenous for me and my body.

My scream echoes in the open floor plan of the house, and I come again.

I'm whining, unable to stop the violent tremors of my orgasm, and only when a cry comes out of me does Deacon slow and finally come to a rest.

The chair slowly sinks down, and he shrugs my legs off his shoulders.

Where I'm droopy eyed from the best orgasm of my entire

life, Deacon's smoldering, looking for a spark of something more.

He smiles, and it's sexy but devious. "You didn't tell me you were a squirter."

I let myself fall victim to his scolding, feeling the color run from my cheeks down my neck. "I've never."

"Fuck, Henri. Fuck." He shakes his head, rolling it back and forth between his shoulders as it falls forward. Deacon looks up at me, head tilted to see me. "Do I get to come now or later?"

The question is odd until I get puppy dog eyes. "You think I'd really deny you? After that?"

"You're in charge here, Hen." He squeezes my leg. "If you want me to keep my pants on and worship your pussy rather than fuck it the entire time you're in heat, I'll eat you out on every surface of this house ten times over."

That ignites a new feeling inside me. I experiment with how it feels. "Maybe later, if you behave."

He lets out a needy little whimper. It's so hot hearing him accept his fate even if it hurts him.

But without a comment or argument, he adjusts himself and then stands, drawing a ragged breath. "Let's get you cleaned up and fed before that next wave hits."

The wait for the next wave isn't long. I make it to the bathroom door when my body, against my will, doubles over.

Deacon's right there, scooping me into his arms and carrying me into the bathroom.

But as intense as that wave was, it disappears before he sets me on the countertop.

"Aftershock," he informs me.

We're nearly nose to nose.

Kiss him, my needy little wolf demands.

So I do.

He tenses and then relaxes into it, kissing me softly.

I fist his hair and control the kiss, and he takes it. His compliance isn't begrudging or miserable, and I *know* because he makes needy noises. He mimics my movements like he's learning how to kiss me despite already having proven that he can steal my breath away.

When I don't stop, Deacon does. "Really should clean you up. I don't want to but I should. At some point, I'll have to be the responsible adult."

"Fair." I release his hair.

Deacon turns on the sink to warm water. "Do you want me to help you, or would you be more comfortable doing this yourself?"

My brain stalls out, nervous in the after-orgasm clarity. I'm uncomfortable thinking about the touch. "I can do it."

He offers me a washcloth, and I take it, running the fabric through my fingers.

Deacon steps back. "Want some privacy?"

Do I?

I'm nodding before I can say anything.

He hasn't done anything to me. Not like Nathan. In fact, Deacon's done everything right. He's given me room to process and consent, and he's gone above and beyond to make sure I want this with him. He didn't just assume that because we've had sex, I'd want him to service me through my heat. But that doesn't erase the discomfort I still feel in my own skin once the fog of lust has faded.

Don't link how good Deacon is with how bad Nathan was. I'm not that person. I'm not going to compare him to an ex.

Fuck. Why is this happening?

Deacon pulls another washcloth from the cupboard and smiles. "I'm going to the kitchen. Find me there?"

More nods from me, and Deacon dismisses himself, closing the door behind him.

CHAPTER 65
DEACON

The water at the kitchen sink runs warm, and I clean myself off. The collar of my shirt is wet, so I pull it off over my head before remembering our bags are still in the car.

Henri's scent, still clinging to my shirt, is comforting when I pull it back on. I get to the front door when I pause.

She won't like it if she doesn't know where we went. My wolf concurs with my pause.

I stride to the bathroom, and with the back of my knuckles, I knock. "Hey, Hen, I'm gonna go get our bags, are you okay if I go outside, or do you want me to wait for you?"

"I'm okay." Henri doesn't sound sure of herself, but I take her words at face value.

Back across the cottage, I leave the front door open and sprint to the SUV. I swipe the bags and the box of fun from Lena's attempt to corrupt Ansel and Morrigan and sprint back, closing the door behind me. I'm gone less than a minute.

"I'm back," I tell her, walking close to the bathroom door.

"Thank you. Can . . ." Henri hesitates. "Can you grab me some pants?"

"Sure thing, Henri."

I put the bags on the bed and rifle through hers, finding a single pair of sweatpants. Hesitantly, I bring them to my nose and sniff. They haven't even been worn since they were washed after being purchased during the week in Utah. She doesn't have anything comfortable to put on, and digging through her bag, I find a separate pouch with only one clean pair of underwear. It's a thong and doesn't look super comfortable, but there's a washer and dryer off the kitchen I can use. There are no T-shirts or soft clothing in the bag.

But it's not like I could have packed her bag for her. We weren't supposed to be gone this long, let alone at all. Almost all the clothes I'm wearing are ones bought by Meaghan and her team while we were out at Ansel's. The shopping haul they came back with was divided out as best it could be, and laundry machines ran practically around the clock everywhere.

Henri didn't even change to sleep at Ansel's house. The stress she was under held her too captive.

Fuck. I'm a shit mate. I'll make up for it.

I run my hand back through my hair before I open the zipper on my bag. I've got two clean T-shirts left, so I add one to the stack of clothes for her.

I shoot off a text to Emerson, asking for comfortable clothing in Henri's size to be washed and left on the deck. I don't even set my phone down before there's an acknowledgment and a timeframe for the request from a concierge number associated with the property.

It's no wonder they're the top-rated rental properties anywhere they open them.

I take the few comfortable items I have for her to the bathroom. "I brought some clean clothes for you. I noticed you didn't have any soft, comfy shirts, so I brought you one of mine, if you want it."

My eyes squeeze shut involuntarily while I wait for her response, hoping she says yes. Henri owns me even if she hasn't fully come to realize it, but damn it if I don't want her in my things, my space, my arms. I want to possess her too.

Strangely, Henri opens the door only far enough to stick her hand out. I place the pile in her hand and let her recoil in and close the bathroom door behind her.

"I'm going to start a load of laundry and then dinner. Is there anything in your clothes you're afraid I might ruin?"

"There's one shirt that's dry clean only, it's the light blue one, and my blazer." She's talking about the clothes we wore to Ansel's house and then to the trial. "But you don't have to do my laundry. I can handle it."

"It's my privilege," I assure her, not positive she completely comprehends how I'm yearning for her. "Don't listen to Lena's groans, which I'm sure you've heard. Most of her stuff I ruined in the machine was me being a protective older brother."

Henri laughs from the other side of the door, breaking some of the tension. "Fair enough."

Fish, more fish, beef, chicken, more fish. I shake my head. *Cats and their damn fish.*

I still have my nose in the refrigerator, trying to make sense of the food Deanie and Emerson left us, when Henri emerges from the bathroom.

"Hey," Henri says softly.

My blood runs cold through me. That single 'hey' is not settling.

She walks around the peninsula to join me in the kitchen but pauses, further raising the 'oh shit' feeling in my stomach, and I turn to devote my full attention to her.

"So." Henri draws a deep breath. "I'm afraid."

We can fix fear. What is she afraid of? We can kill it. My wolf immediately assumes it's not us.

Henri covers her face with her hands, and I'm positive the answer is going to be me.

"You're going to be so mad when I say this, and just, please remember it's over, it's done. It's not going to happen again."

Not us. My wolf corrects me.

"I haven't . . ." Henri swallows hard. "I haven't." She draws a deep breath, then pulls her hands from her face and looks me square in the eye. "I haven't had sex that I really wanted or enjoyed in a really long time, with the exception of our time at the Wisconsin house, and I'm afraid because . . ."

"Because you don't know how you're going to react or handle it." I nod, filling in the gaps, but leave off the judgmental answer — *because he's been using sex as a weapon against you* — locked in my head.

She nods. "I just don't know."

I keep my distance from her, giving her my absolute best behavior despite wanting to wrap her in my arms. She doesn't need me to force love on her; she needs me to respect that she doesn't know what anything other than Nathan's abuse looks like.

"You're in charge here, Hen," I reiterate. "I'm here for you, and if you don't want me here, then I'll leave." *It'll kill me, but I'll leave.* "Nothing is going to happen between us that you don't fully consent to. If you want a safeword, name one. If you want me to ask before we do anything, I will. If you want me to stay and not touch you, I will."

Henri shakes her head adamantly at that last one.

"I meant it, Henri." I nod, reassuring her. "If you want me to leave my pants on through this, then this'll be the last time we talk about it. You will not hear a complaint from me. If you want a big knife out of the butcher block, you can have it. This isn't about me."

When Henri turns her head away from me, the light glints off the moisture in her eyes.

Anything you want, Henri. I don't keep pushing her for a decision aloud.

"What if I freak out?" Her question is a jump in logic.

Normally, I can follow her thought process, but I can't connect the dots this time.

"Give me a little more to work with?" I try to piece it together. "Freak out, how or about what?"

"What if I panic, or we're trying, and I can't?" With the pads of her fingers, she brushes away some but not all of her tears.

My fingers itch to finish the job.

"How would you like to handle that?" I wait before offering her suggestions.

I know how I would normally handle it, but this isn't about me stopping and giving her space, which would be the absolute first instinct.

"I don't know." She shakes her head and looks at me. "I don't want to disappoint you."

I'm going to kill Nathan for every fucked-up thing he's ever made her think or feel about herself. It might have to be years from now to avoid suspicion. But I'm going to disembowel him and make him watch me do it.

"You will never disappoint me." I reassure her. "I can't be disappointed because every second you let me stay in the same room, breathing the same air as you, is just another gift. Disappointment only happens when you have an expectation. My expectation was that you would send me packing the moment we got here."

Henri frowns. "I wouldn't do that. You've been so good to me."

"You owe me nothing, Henri." I don't know how to get that through to her.

She's our mate, my wolf presses.

"Mate or not, there's no score to keep. I am good to you because you deserve someone to be good to you. The fact that I could do the bare minimum and you would thank me for it hurts my heart." I swallow hard and look away from her. "I guess what I'm trying to say is: believe me. Believe what I say. Don't fight what you want because you think I'm going to do or be something different. I'm exactly what I say I am."

Henri is quiet. In my periphery, I can see her fighting with herself. She wrings the hem of her shirt, a full breath of air held in her lungs waiting to be released.

What I wouldn't give to ease that turmoil.

"You wouldn't touch me? If we . . ." She stalls. "If we had sex, you wouldn't touch me. I know we've had sex and the knife, and it helped. I'm just . . . What if I can't?"

My wolf cocks his head, equally confused with the logistics of that.

Then a lightbulb turns on. "Tie me to a chair, the bed, the couch, or bind me on my own. If all you want is my cock it's yours."

"Now that's an idea," she says under her breath.

"Okay, when you say it that way, it sounds like you want to cut it off, and there's already a box of disembodied ones so can I at least keep mine attached?" I wince, the words coming out before my brain can stifle them.

But unexpectedly, Henri laughs. Her socks and pants rustle on the floor as she slides closer to me across the hardwood. "I meant the chair, Deacon."

She rests her hand on my chest, and I bring my head back

494

to face her and shrug. "That's probably a safer and more convenient plan than removing it."

Henri snakes her arms around my waist and hugs me. Normally, I would hug her back, but something about my touch unsettled her, and I'm not pushing it.

With a huff, she presses her head harder against my chest. "Quit sucking at hugging."

At her encouragement, I wrap my arms around her. Gently holding her to my chest, I free the tension I'd been holding.

Do we have to wait years to kill Nathan? My wolf nuzzles forward, trying to get more of Henri's touch, pulling for her wolf.

I don't answer him. I don't need to. The murder plots are already growing.

THE GOOD NEWS is Henri likes fish. The bad news is that after dinner and we've settled in for a movie, we aren't through the opening credits when her heat takes a turn south and she grows warm.

She whines. The very wolf sound tugs at my heart and cock with equal force.

Calm down, I remind myself. *She's just starting to get being a wolf.*

"You were serious, right?" Henri kicks the blanket off her legs.

"I'm mostly always serious." I lie.

Henri laughs, but it turns into a frustrated sigh. "You were serious that I could . . ."

The embarrassment increases her heat. Her face flushes, and I rest my hand on it. She seems to be okay with general comforting touches, the kinds that wolves are supposed to want, to crave.

"Could . . . ?" I try to figure out which of the million suggestions I feel like I offered her that she could be referring to.

"Tie you down," she whispers.

My cock goes to half-mast just at the thought of letting Henri use me. "Yeah, Hen. Anything and everything if it'll make you feel comfortable."

"Okay. How?"

Henri's innocence causes my heart to flutter happily.

"I can think of a few options."

The box of fun my deviant sister sent Ansel for one.

I nod and let her lead the way back to the dining room. I open the box and set out a couple of options for her.

"Does Lena just assume everyone is kinky?" Henri picks up a pair of fluffy handcuffs.

I nod. "Yeah. Pretty much."

Henri nibbles her bottom lip, and it makes me jealous, wanting to do it too. "You should get naked now."

Not needing to be told twice, I pull my shirt off over the top of my head and set it on the table before reaching for the button on my jeans.

"Wait." Henri stops me.

Frozen stiff, I'm only breathing enough to sustain brain function.

She steps closer to me and moves my hands out of the way to do it herself.

I'm short-circuiting with desire. *Pull it together.*

I try, but it was different in the car. Henri sucked me off like it was her fucking job, and it was amazing. But that was before I knew she was afraid. It was before I knew I had to behave.

Everything I do going forward has to empower her to be the woman from the car.

She pops the button open and then slides the zipper down, relieving some of the uncomfortable pressure of my stiff cock confined by clothes.

Henri's breathing is ragged.

"You don't have to do this," I remind her.

She growls at me. It's fierce and intimidating.

I take that as my cue to shut my mouth.

You pissed off our mate, my wolf snaps, chastising me.

She slides her fingers into my waistband and pulls down both my jeans and boxers.

Teased by the thought of what might be to come has left me hard and protruding for her.

"Did I mention how nice this is?" She looks up at me.

Avoiding speaking, I shake my head. *Did she just . . . call my cock nice?*

"Well, I was acquainted with it earlier, and I have to admit I very much approve." She puts a hand on my sternum and then points to the chair.

My wolf practically rolls belly up inside me, giving her everything just for more of her approval. And if it weren't for being given an order by Henri, I probably would too.

I follow the silent order and seat myself.

There's a soft confidence in Henri, hiding behind fear, as she walks behind me and handcuffs my wrists behind me and the chair.

My cock is painfully throbbing as I watch her. It's the sweetest kind of torture.

Henri's wolf assesses me, and a fire crackles in her eyes. The gold irises drag my wolf forward to meet hers.

"Like what you see, Hen?" I wet my bottom lip. "I know I do."

497

She nods, and a hint of mischief has her biting her bottom lip. Then the little minx strips slowly. Henri drags my T-shirt up her frame like a fucking pro. It comes up, and the undersides of her breasts peek out.

I'm staring. I know I am, but this is what she wants: me a captivated captive.

Her arousal is spiking, the scent filling the space around us. Her skin is flushed, and sweat is starting to glisten across it. Needing to be free of the warmth of her clothing, she finally pulls the shirt over her head, exposing her tits.

I've seen them before. We're wolves. But like this, nothing compares to this. I let out a ragged breath, trying to will myself to calm down. It's not going awesome.

But now, with my eyes on her, Henri's found some new confidence, and she militarizes it against me. She breathes in deeply and pushes it out. "I didn't know this could be so hot."

"I've never been this aroused for a strip tease." I adjust in my seat, trying to ease some of the throbbing.

I know it's useless. The only thing that's going to fix this is emptying my balls.

Henri steps closer. The sweatpants she's wearing are tied loosely and sitting low, showing off the bottom of her stomach.

I'm salivating and I swallow, but I want another taste. I can't get enough of her.

Standing between my legs, Henri looks down at me. "Can I touch you?"

I hold back a laugh and nod. "You can do anything you want to me, Henri. Anything at all."

And I mean that because as much as I objected to the idea of cutting my cock off, I'd bleed out on the floor if it meant she was happy. I'd live and die at her hand a thousand times over for each second that she looks at me.

Henri runs the back of her knuckles across my face and

loops her fingers into my hair, pulling firmly. She comes nose to nose with me, and I stay perfectly still despite the devil inside me screaming to lean forward and kiss her.

That devil is left screaming because she doesn't kiss me. Henri pulls her face back but maintains contact, circling her hand around my dick. And I'm glad I looped my ankles behind the legs of the chair to keep me seated.

Fuck our mate, my wolf demands, not understanding, or caring, about the trust this is building with her.

She strokes me until I can't stay quiet, and I know she's waiting for me because the moment I open my mouth and utter 'fuck' Henri lets me go. Then she's back to teasing me in a whole different way. Henri tucks her thumbs into the waistband of her sweats and inches them down around her hips, leaving her underwear in place. I'm treated to the view of the front of her thighs being revealed in slow, calculated movements, and then when she bends at the waist, her tits hang, tempting me for a lick, a suck, a bite.

Her sweats hit the floor, and she steps out of them, kicking them to the side.

I've given up on anticipating anything she may or may not do. There is no rhyme or reason that I can deduce in this slow seduction.

Does she not know she already has me?

Henri turns away from me, and I cock my head to the side, already curling my fingers together, ready to push through the cuffs. I know Lena only gets escapable toys. These handcuffs are here for Henri's peace of mind. And I'm willing to blow my cover with them if she isn't okay.

But I've underestimated Henri because, with a glance over her shoulder, she gives a little smile before skimming her hands down her sides, sliding the panties off, and giving me a perfect view of her ass. She wiggles it, teasing me before stepping out of the panties.

"Fuck me." I look to the ceiling above her, trying not to explode.

"That's the idea." Henri steps closer to me and then pushes my chin down with her thumb until my eyes lock on hers. "Is this still okay?"

"Significantly more than okay." I nod.

Claim our mate. My wolf is starting to sound like a Neanderthal, begging me to drag her back to our den and keep her all to ourselves.

"How?" Henri looks down, and I follow her gaze.

I unhook my feet from the legs of the chair, and pins and needles flood the nerves, protesting the movement. But I make her a seat with my thighs, and Henri nods, understanding.

"You don't have to do this," I remind her. "I'm not expecting anything, especially this, from you."

"I know." She nods and moves to position herself. But she's unsteady and unbalanced, trying to work her way onto my lap.

"Hands on my shoulders." The metaphorical angel inside keeps me honest in the handcuffs. Shuffling out of them and helping her would be the easiest way to do this but the fastest way to break her trust.

Henri does as I instruct.

"Now, throw your leg over."

Henri's short, almost too short, to straddle me and the chair.

She positions herself with her weight resting on her butt on my lap. It feels like Henri's flesh is on fire.

She scrunches her face, trying to figure out the movement.

"When you're ready," I say, "you're going to lean against my chest and push yourself forward against me. Then, with one hand, guide my shaft to your center."

"Okay." Henri nods and immediately follows the instruction.

There is no slow settling in or further hesitation. Henri is a sex goddess hidden in a modest package. She slides herself all the way down my cock in a fluid motion until she's seated, entirely taking me.

My heartbeat is erratic. Her pussy pulses around my cock, and I'm so fucking close. This is what I get for taking almost a year sabbatical from sex. I'm fighting for my life against an orgasm just from her sitting on my lap.

"Fuck," Henri pants. "I can feel you twitching inside me. You can't possibly make sex better every time we fuck."

"And yet, I do." I can't keep my smart mouth contained *and* stop myself from coming.

"Don't judge me when I come in like four seconds because I'm so fucking hot right now." Henri says what I'm thinking.

She's focused, looking down at where we're joined. The rocking of her hips forward and backward fascinates her on some level.

I'm resisting kissing her. I could just place a little one on her temple. *But I promised to behave,* I remind myself and the little devil inside.

My toes curl, and Henri moans and gasps. Digging her fingers into my shoulder, she raises and lowers onto my cock, grinding forward, then up and backward and down.

It's pure torture.

The way she moans, the heady little breaths in between.

"Henri," I warn, fighting back my release to give her every second she needs to come. "So close."

"Mm-hmm" is all she gets out.

Her next moan is louder, and then she digs her sharp nails into my flesh, throwing her head back in the rapture of her orgasm.

501

Between the tension, the rise and fall of her hips against me, and her walls constricting around my cock, I follow her over the edge. Balls twitching, I come so hard I see stars behind my closed eyelids as I gasp her name.

She falls forward, and I kiss her neck, tasting her sweat. I lick her skin, savoring it. It's delicious.

Her pussy continues to pulse with such intensity I can feel her milking every drop from me.

I fight against my intense desire to embrace the deep relaxation and sink into sleep.

Henri murmurs sleepily against my neck, her head having come to rest with her hand on my shoulder.

I nuzzle against her. "Come on, Hen, we gotta get you cleaned up."

The saddest little groan comes from her. "Okay."

She struggles with her own body for lucidity. The movements she makes are an uncoordinated struggle to pull herself off me.

Frustrated, she huffs. "You're too fucking big."

Well, that's a compliment.

I jam open the handcuffs and let myself out on one side and then the other, catching it before it falls to the floor. I set it on the table with a soft thud and then carefully guide Henri up and off my cock to settle her on my lap.

She snuggles in, drawing slow breaths. The sweat on her skin is rapidly cooling her off now that the wave has passed.

"Wait a minute." Very groggy, Henri leans back, examining me and then my hands on her hips. "Weren't you . . . ?"

"Lena's big on safety. They're not super difficult to escape." I incline my head toward the handcuffs on the table but quickly deflect. "The important part was you felt safe enough to explore. You had trust in me not disrupting your pleasure because there was a barrier preventing it."

"And then you just let yourself out." Henri's face, despite being tired, holds annoyance.

No, not annoyance, something stronger that cuts me down.

"I wasn't sure it was safe for you to try to climb off my cock, so for your safety and mine, I took the appropriate measures to prevent an accident." I've never been on the defensive with her, and I don't like it.

She closes her eyes, seemingly letting it go. "How can you just come that hard and then still use big words?"

"No idea." I flex my fingers, getting ready to help her again.

Her face relaxes, and sleep looks like it's going to claim her, but before it gets that far, her eyes shoot open. "You did . . . didn't you?"

"Yeah, Henri." With a soft smile, I try to reassure her of the truth about to come out of my mouth. "Best orgasm of my life."

With a sigh and shake of her head, Henri tries to stand again. This time, she's more coordinated and less baby-fawn-like on her feet, but her voice is small. "Help me clean up?"

"My pleasure." I'm tired, but standing and following her to the bathroom to clean up is not an issue.

Henri lets me thoroughly clean her folds, inner thighs, and butt. I give myself a quick pass with the washcloth and then gently kiss the tip of her nose.

"I've gotta pee," Henri groans, and I take myself out of the bathroom.

While waiting, I pull on pajama pants, shake out her clothes from the floor, straighten the dining room, and, with the remaining time, panic that she's not okay in the bathroom.

She was really hurt that I could get out. I wring my hands. She's never given me that sort of a look.

The door finally opens, and Henri emerges, yawning. "Will you sleep with me?"

"Kinda just did." I tilt my chin toward the dining room table suggestively.

"Not what I meant, Deacon." She gives me a small growl, pulling the sweatpants and underwear back up over her legs.

To get the pants clear of her feet, she shuffles, and her perfect palm-sized tits bounce.

The traitorous cock, who just came, stirs at the sight.

Fuck, heat is a powerful aphrodisiac.

"If you'd like me to share a bed with you, it would be my pleasure." I prove that despite my smart mouth, I'm not completely lost.

"Can we go to bed now?" Henri pulls my shirt over her head and pulls her blonde hair out from under the collar.

"Lead the way." I offer my hand out in the direction of the bedroom.

Instead of walking away from me on the shortest path back to the bedroom, Henri walks directly up to me and wraps her arms around my waist.

"I'm sorry," Henri murmurs into my chest. "You didn't do anything wrong. I just . . . I'm trying."

"Don't apologize to me," I whisper.

"You smell nervous." Henri's words are news to me.

I deflect from my feelings, using humor instead as I give her the truth. "Of course I am, it's a wet dream to be holed up in a beautiful cottage in the middle of nowhere with the hottest woman in the entire world begging to fuck herself on my cock. What if I fuck it up?"

"You can't fuck it up." Henri fists my shirt but leans back to look up at me. "I'm trying not to let you get mad and, at the same time, balance how to get through this without freaking out."

"You're not responsible for my actions or my feelings." I bring my hands up her shoulders, hesitating, but I choose to trail my fingers up her throat and cup her face anyway. "I'm already plotting Nathan's murder, Henri. There's nothing I'm going to do about it until we get back home, and I won't negatively react about anything related to him."

"Deacon, no murder. We broke up and I blocked him. It's fine. It's over. You and I feel our wolves pulling to each other. We're mates." Henri's soft smile is groggy at best.

Let it go. She doesn't need to know that he's going to die regardless if she broke up with him.

I nod in theoretical agreement with her. "I understand. But it's not over for you. Whatever he's done to you is living in your brain, and you're working to get past it. Know that whatever you need, whatever you tell me, I'll follow as long as it keeps you safe."

She nuzzles against my hand like I've seen Lena do to Finn, and I've got to have Dinah listen to my heart because it's all sorts of erratic flailing and pushing around in my chest.

"Bedtime," she murmurs. "I hope you're a good big spoon."

"I'm a wolf, of course I'm a good big spoon," I assure her, following her dutifully to the bedroom.

In bed, I curl up behind Henri, making her the most perfect little spoon. I nuzzle my nose into her hair and kiss the back of her neck. Then I squeeze my arm around her waist.

"You take cuddling very seriously," she murmurs, half asleep. "Not that I'm super experienced, but I do believe you're a top-notch cuddler. This could be my favorite part."

Dark with thoughts of murder and heavy with the weight of sated lust, I relax into her praise and let sleep consume me.

CHAPTER 66

HENRI

I'VE NEVER BEEN this fucking horny and this fucking frustrated. Sure I've been frustrated with he who shall be forgotten because sex was always on his timetable. It was never to be initiated by me. I was expected to be ready for his whims, no matter how I felt or what I wanted or didn't want. That's a hard lesson to override.

I can't wake up Deacon. I don't. There's a chance he won't reject me. No, I know he won't reject me. My logical brain knows that the minute I wake him up, he'll give me everything. The horny part of my brain begs me to. But the irrational fear, the part that's so afraid of rejection, has me grabbing a pillow from the bed and a towel from the bathroom, taking it to the far side of the house.

The sitting room is fairly private, designed for TV viewing with smaller windows. Throwing the pillow down on the floor, I drape the towel over the top.

This has been the only way I've gotten off by myself in the last four years. Today has been a clear deviation of my norm.

Toys were shunned and it was dirty for me to touch myself. Especially after I told him about my first heat.

This was the only thing that I felt like I could do. Here I am, doing it again, to avoid waking Deacon up. Shame is funny that way.

The pillow is a little small and the towel is a little softer than the ones I used at home. There's not enough friction.

I groan and squeeze the pillow tighter with my knees. It hits better, and I grind, a little frustrated but finding some relief.

"Am I doing so poorly taking care of you that you'd rather ride a pillow than me?" Deacon mocks offense but embarrassment flames my cheeks.

He steps closer, pajama pants slung low around his waist.

"I just —" My pussy clenches, cutting off my words.

"Ask me to help, Henri."

His command isn't a command, not really. It's posed as a question, and his words drip with arousal and sex appeal.

"Deacon, help me."

He comes and kneels behind me, his knees spreading my calves and thighs. "Can I touch you?"

"Mm-hmm," I answer, willing my body to relax, but it doesn't.

I expected Deacon to go straight for my sex, but instead he massages small circles down my spine with his thumbs, and I almost buckle from how good the physical touch feels. It puts me physically at ease. But I'm still mentally unsure.

"Do you like getting off this way?"

His words aren't meant to shame me, but I immediately feel that way. "Mmm."

"You don't." Deacon seems to read my monosyllabic response. "Can I help, Hen?"

Deacon's always been about embracing what feels good:

the adrenaline of his bike, the emotional high of the nightclub, and of course the buzz that keeps him feeling normal.

Why shouldn't I let him help?

Let him help, my wolf urges.

I answer Deacon with a nod.

"Use those words, Henri," Deacon urges me, continuing to respectfully rub my back.

"Please." My wolf pushes forward, and my word hits a high-pitch, needy sound.

A pleased groan comes from Deacon, and he slides his hand around my waist.

Anticipating his needs, I raise my ass to him.

"Let's take this back for you. We'll remove the shame and replace all the bad memories with something better."

I expected him to touch me, ease the painful arousal that's been growing, and then fuck me hard until he comes. But Deacon doesn't. He stands up, leaving me on the floor. It feels like the rejection I was expecting.

But I said please.

Stepping around me, he pulls me up from the floor to my feet. "You're too perfect to be fucked into the floor."

Deacon picks up the pilfered pillow and towel and takes them over to the sofa. It's pressed back against the windows on the far wall. Deacon bypasses the couch cushions and places the pillow on the arm with the towel on top of it.

With ease, he pulls the side table out of the way, creating room. Standing behind me, Deacon points out the window toward the neighbor's house. It's quite a ways away, and it's dark inside.

"I can't tell if their blinds are open or not," he whispers in my ear like they'd be able to hear us watching them. "But if we turn the lamp on —"

"Yes." I cut him off knowing exactly what he's suggesting.

Despite not being able to anticipate his motivations and movements, I understand this. Deacon has fully embraced my kink to risk being seen.

"So. Fucking. Dirty. Henri." Spoken from anyone else, Deacon's words would feel condescending, but the praise, with a deep rumble in his voice, elevates my emotions from negative to positive.

He clicks on the lamp behind us. The light illuminates the room and makes seeing outside into the night difficult.

Done talking, Deacon helps me straddle the couch arm. The pillow is in the perfect position to support me, and with a little bit of maneuvering, Deacon's exposed me to him.

The way he drags his fingers along my sides, down around my thighs, then back up my ass is excruciatingly erotic.

His sleep pants land on the floor with a soft thud followed by a shuffle as he kicks out of them.

"Please, fuck me." The words come out of my mouth with a little growl before he can ask me what I want him to do to me.

"Impatient, hmm?" Deacon slides his fingers into the wetness I created by grinding on the pillow, and it electrifies my body with a hum of need. "Can I use my fingers to fuck you, Henri?"

"Deacon," I gasp, trying to stop myself from begging. "Please."

He slowly inserts two fingers into my warmth, fucking me with them.

I moan and arch into him. The furious need that was staved off when he found me and soothed me is fast returning with a vengeance.

"Do you want my cock, Henri?" He keeps moving his fingers, curling them and hitting the right spots over and over again.

I rock back, trying to get him closer. "Yes."

Deacon pulls me back on the arm to be closer to him and slides his cock along my entrance. "So wet. So fucking wet."

In one fluid movement he sinks his cock into me. I moan so loud it's pornographic. I should be embarrassed by the sounds coming out of my mouth, but I'm not. I'm not because Deacon responds with his own moans and slow thrusts, dragging more sounds out of me. My position, facing the couch, isn't quite allowing me to grind my clit against the sofa's arm, but the fullness eases the cramping and the stiff desire.

Deacon, however, must notice that something isn't perfect because he bends over the top of me. "Tell me what you need, Hen. This is all about you. You're taking the power back."

"Not enough friction," I whimper, trying to push back into him.

He hasn't stopped, but the slow, careful pace while he listens to me is agonizingly sweet.

"Deacon, I need . . ."

When Deacon pulls out, I protest with a snarl, and he laughs. "Easy, killer."

He slides his arm underneath my stomach, bringing it upward to my chest, and with it, he helps me adjust so I can better support my weight with my hands. I reach out before me but note the window and stop.

Deacon nibbles the back of my neck and whispers into my ear. "Don't worry about smudging the glass."

I put my hands out flat and brace myself as he implied, but I do feel a little bad about touching the window with my hot sweaty palms. Not bad enough because when Deacon slides his hand down my stomach and slips two fingers underneath me, the pressure on my clit makes the guilt disappear. It makes all the thoughts disappear.

He tilts my pelvis just a little more forward, and I gasp, the shooting pleasure unexpectedly delicious.

There must be just enough room for Deacon to slip inside me. The way he fills me is a new stretch, the sensation already driving pleasure.

Mate fucks us perfectly. My wolf speaks like I don't already know the physical pleasures.

"Deacon," I caution him. "So close."

He nips at my ear and his fingers stroke my clit. "Tell me to stop if it gets to be too much. Tell me to stop when you don't think you can take anymore but focus on how you feel. Focus on how good it is and chase that pleasure as far as it takes you."

I can't speak because I don't remember what words are. The lightheaded feeling has me weak already. Deacon supports my weight with his free arm, hand cupping my breast and gently squeezing. Between the pace of his thrusts and grinding against his fingers while he takes me, it's bliss.

My head drops forward involuntarily. I'm floating somewhere along the path to an orgasm, and I arrive faster than I planned. The pressure builds in a single hard thrust, and I press my fingers into the glass.

His name comes out at the top of my lungs. "Deacon!"

"Fuck," he hisses but keeps fucking me.

Is he holding back?

It's a fleeting thought because Deacon fucks me in tandem with working his fingers. He plays with a nipple and kisses my shoulder.

My orgasm fades, and I wait for the clarity; I wait to come down from the peak. But it doesn't come. Rather it builds again. This time faster and stronger.

Panting, my lungs can't keep up with the call for oxygen my brain is putting out.

I'm gasping, struggling for breath between moans, making my voice hoarse, and I come again. His name doesn't make it past my lips because in this orgasm, I lose all strength, but Deacon doesn't let me fall. In my bliss, I feel safe and protected.

"Come. Please," I gasp, wanting and needing to feel him come undone.

My beg is enough.

"Henri. Fuck." The way he curses my name when he does fills me with pride.

I've given him this just as much as he's sated me. Two orgasms sound excessive, but I'm driven to feel his touch. It's a primal instinct anchoring me to his desire.

Deacon withdraws from me, and I want to cry at the absence. I do let out a pathetic little mewl.

"Trust, Hen, I don't want to either. You're so warm and inviting. I want to live inside you just as much as you want me there, probably even more." Deacon kisses across my shoulders as he sits me up, starting from one side and not stopping until he reaches the other.

With delicate touches, Deacon pulls me off the sofa and turns me to face him, quickly pulling me into his arms. I wrap my arms around his neck, and he lifts me, cupping my ass. With my legs around his waist, he carries me through the house to the bedroom.

Deacon cleans me like he did before and climbs into bed alongside me. "Don't hesitate to wake me up, Hen. You're not alone in this. I'll never turn you away."

He kisses the back of my neck and down my shoulder before wrapping himself around me like he has each time we've come to bed.

Deacon is the perfect big spoon, and the feeling of being safe in his arms is one I'm never going to forget.

CHAPTER 67
DEACON

WE'RE TWO DAYS IN, and heat hits Henri hard. She's more primal and needy. Her consent is fervent. I've never had this much of a connection with someone. The responsibilities of my life have never let me give this much dedicated time to a partner. And not once have I ever felt something for them. Duty yes. Love and care, never.

"Earth to Deacon." Henri fakes white noise like she's on a walkie-talkie.

When she cracks a joke, she's lucid. This more playful and carefree Henri is so different yet familiar. She's relaxed and at ease. I love this goofy side of her. I want more of it.

My back is to her, but turning my head over my shoulder, I hold up my hand like it's a walkie-talkie and make the crackle sound back to her. "Deacon to Ground Control, go ahead, Ground Control."

"What's your current objective?" Henri fakes the crackle, and the temptress, wearing one of my T-shirts, leans against the counter.

"Operation: fuel the sex machine. Over." I crackle again.

Henri giggles, dropping the walkie-talkie act. "You make me sound like a cyborg."

"With how often you're riding my dick, I'm starting to think you are a cyborg or a competitive sex-lete." I shrug with a nonchalant smile.

She lets out a 'hmmm' tapping a finger on her chin before deciding on "More like a heat-lete?"

Despite it being late in the day, I've made us breakfast. I plate the food, one for her and then one for myself, before bringing them to the breakfast bar in the kitchen rather than eating at the dining room table and the chairs we've defiled.

"It smells delicious. When did you learn to cook?" Henri walks around the breakfast bar and sits down.

It's such an innocent question. I should lie, but I don't. I'm okay letting her learn all the truth about me. I offer up all my ugly parts because I've seen her darkest ones.

"About three days after Cade left for basic training. It was me and Lena on our own. Mom and Dad didn't teach either of us how to cook because 'we have staff for that.'" I snort at how ridiculous my life must sound to someone not raised wolf. "So, I pulled up videos on the internet and figured it out. There was a lot of takeout in the beginning, called in after the dinner hour because of whatever I did wrong to a dish made it inedible."

Henri doesn't seem upset by my revelation. "Well, how else were you supposed to learn? You're really good at doing what you need to in order to survive. It's kind of sexy."

I set my fork on my plate, the bite of pancake speared on the end still attached. "I can't even tell anymore if that's you or the heat talking."

She shrugs and sends me one of my smirks, but it fades into a soft smile that's all her own. "I love how Cade cooks for Thalia. Burnt grilled cheese and all. Nathan never cooks for me."

"Cooked," I correct, not letting thoughts of him remain in the present tense.

Henri agrees with one stern nod. "Cooked. He never cooked for me. There was always 'if you wanted some, you should have asked' and 'there's leftovers if you want.' But it wasn't *for* me."

"You were an afterthought in the relationship." Those words come out a little harsh because they're tied to my beating heart that is crushed for her. She deserved so much more.

Henri pays my tone no mind. "Yeah. Completely." She moves on, directing the conversation back to me. "But you take care of everyone. It's like you're constantly in servant-leadership mode."

"I don't think of myself as a leader, and servant takes it a little too far. But it's just become a distraction. If I'm taking care of someone else, at least there's a purpose. And I've trained myself to do just about anything basic while under the influence of just about everything I've tried," I answer before going back to eating.

"Do you have any nondestructive coping mechanisms?" She looks me up and down.

"Coping mechanisms? One is supposed to cope?" My food is flavorless with that thought. It's not her fault. This is just what happens when I talk about myself. The hollowness grows, and I'll eat past it in a minute. "Until very recently, it's been day in and day out. You know, the same shit, different day for me. It wasn't until you made me be public facing that I had to learn to do something new."

"Oh." Henri goes silent eating.

The guilt my words carried wasn't intended for her to bear.

"This?" I gesture to myself because, let's face it, there isn't a part of me that's not touched by darkness. "Isn't on you. I am the sum of all my parts, the good, the bad, and the indifferent.

It's just until you . . . I lived in the dark cave watching the shadows of light, wondering what monster would come for me."

"Plato was an asshole." Henri surprises me, knowing the reference while violently stabbing into her pancake. The fork clicks on the plate. "Who the fuck thinks of chaining prisoners in a cave as an experiment?"

"Amen to that." I laugh and shake my head.

The people who don't think about chaining abusive asshole ex-boyfriends up in secluded basements and slowly torturing them to death. Henri doesn't need to know that. I'll always be honest with her, but that's not the sort of information one should volunteer.

Murder, or the thought of it, brings back my sense of taste.

We'll avenge her. It will be delicious. My wolf thinks of an all new taste.

My hunger grows when Henri hops on her stool, getting closer to me until we're brushing elbows.

CHAPTER 68
DEACON

She's a goddess lying on the bed with pillows surrounding her. The waves of her golden hair pick up rays of sunshine in the late afternoon sun. I haven't been watching her long while I drink my fifth — sixth? — cup of coffee in the last twenty-four hours, but I'm dreading her temperature returning to normal.

Inside this house, with Henri, it's been a solace for my soul.

"Oh, she's a looker." A voice comes from behind me.

My hackles rise, and I turn to look. The joy of the Black Hills, I'm certain the man before me is an apparition. The man wearing a hat, high-waisted denim jeans, boots, and suspenders over a button-down shirt would have made too much noise coming in the door.

I ignore him, going back to looking at Henri.

His hand passes through my shoulder, causing me to shiver as he walks into the bedroom. He stands and looks at Henri, and I let out a low growl when he bends over the bed to watch her.

"I get it. I get it. You don't want no one lookin' at your girl." He moves on his way out of the house through the wall.

He's the first one I've seen since I've been sober.

Because you let me handle it, my wolf notes like I'm the one being ridiculous.

It should be a relief to hear that he's making a difference, that somehow, he's figuring out and working the gift.

But I don't feel control over it.

Another second passes, and another ancestor is in the house. My frustration grows seeing an older woman looking around in the kitchen.

I thought you were handling this.

My wolf is too focused on Henri to even notice or care. The woman looks around the kitchen, and I focus on her, pretending I've got a clue how to make this work. *Just go away.*

Like a mirage dissipating, she fizzles, and then she's gone.

Would you look at that? He can learn. My wolf gets snarky with me, but I'm too impressed with myself to care that he's got an attitude today.

That didn't feel like a fluke, and his confirmation of it lends to reassurance that not all is lost for this world.

I turn back to watching Henri, who is fast asleep, completely unaware of me and the ancestors watching. *She's absolutely perfect.*

Claim our mate, my wolf urges me. He's forward, pushing me toward her.

I set my empty coffee cup down before I oblige him, at least in part, by moving closer to her. The bed dips with my weight, and she stirs, her eyes opening and blinking against the low light.

"Mmmm. Good morning." Her voice is husky and thick with sleep, and I'm smiling.

I can feel how it pulls at my lips and pushes up my cheeks so genuinely.

"Good evening." I greet her.

Lowering myself down to the bed a little bit, I kiss the inside of her calf. Her flesh is still hot under my touch. It's been four days, and her heat isn't showing signs of letting up.

Henri pushes her legs apart, welcoming me with a gasp.

I kiss and lick up her leg, and when I get to her apex, Henri hooks her finger under my chin and indicates her need. Never one to deny her, I kiss the rest of my way up her flushed pink skin. Painstakingly, I avoid her breasts to kiss her sternum, collarbone, and neck before planting a kiss straight on her lips.

My little minx raises her hips and hooks her legs around behind me, pulling me down to her on the bed. She fists my hair and pulls me closer, deepening the kiss, and I lick her lips, opening her mouth.

She runs her nails down my back and hitches her fingers into my sleep pants. Fumbling with them, she tries to slide them down my hips and growls when she struggles.

"Tell me what you want, Hen," I murmur against her lips.

"Fuck me," she demands.

I kiss her nose and back away from her, climbing off the bed. "Come with me."

She snarls, "No."

Hand extended to her, I encourage, "Come on. I'll make it worth it."

Henri groans, "Fine."

In only my T-shirt, she lets me lead her out onto the deck and then up the stairs to the upper deck. Aside from the pillows and blankets she was sleeping with, I dragged every single one up here.

This cycle that's become our life together feels like it needs to come to this, and I'm nervous about whether she'll like it.

Up on the rooftop deck, there's an amazing view of the sun sinking down toward the skyline. I moved the little café table and chairs out of the way to make the blanket nest.

"Awww." Henri looks at it and scurries toward the pillow pile before looking back to me.

"I hope you don't mind, but I left the knife downstairs." I laugh, thinking about the first time I made her a blanket nest on the ground. How was that almost a month ago?

Henri looks out at the quiet neighborhood, our single neighbor whose house is empty, and the little wilderness area around us.

She bites her lip, looking back at me. "We can fuck up here?"

I shrug my shoulders. "I don't see why not."

Lazily I step toward her, and when I'm within arm's reach, Henri grabs the hem of my shirt and tugs on it until I'm as close to her as possible. She reaches up and kisses me. The way she claims my mouth only makes me push back harder against her. I entwine my fingers into her hair and pull gently, getting one of those sexy moans from her.

We break the kiss, and I follow Henri down to the mess of pillows on the deck, lying beside her. Henri adjusts next to me until we're kissing again, hands exploring the flesh we've already come to know.

"Too many clothes," she pants against my lips.

I remove my hand from where I was stroking along her hip to the cord holding up my sweatpants.

Without her on top of me, it's easier to slide them down, my cock springing free. Henri immediately wraps her hand around it.

"Henri," I gasp before chastising her. "Let me get my pants off first."

She snarls at me.

Does she see how much more wolf she already is? Though, maybe it's just the heat talking.

With a low growl, I press myself up and plant a kiss on her

lips. "I've let you lead, but don't think I'm afraid to get a little bit more hands on in all this."

"Mmmm." Henri contemplates but doesn't argue any further with me.

I kick the sweatpants off and pull her on top of me, pressing my fingers into her hips. I counter her statement from earlier. "Too many clothes."

Seductively, Henri teases me, raising the hem, slowly trailing it up toward her tits, exposing her perfect pink skin along the way. When she frees herself of the T-shirt, I get a full look at her in the early evening sun, the red and golden light casting her in a glow. It's a near-religious experience seeing her like this, a goddess among mortals.

Gold wolf eyes flicker in the light. And I let mine forward to meet with hers.

If she claims us, we claim her, he demands of me like I would even think of not.

But he knows I won't tie her to me first.

More practiced, Henri shuffles down my torso to tease my cock with her warmth. My head slides between her folds and presses at her clit until she shifts her hips back so it's at her entrance.

I groan, my eyes falling closed. "Henri."

"Yes, Deacon?" She taunts, keeping that slow, steady rocking movement.

"You're tormenting me." I shake my head, opening my eyes again.

The view isn't any less beautiful.

Henri smirks and leans forward, bracing her hands against my pecs, and then she rolls her hips back, impaling herself on me.

My groan echoes in the world around us, and tension flees

my body. Henri presses herself off my chest and begins to ride unassisted, playing with her breasts with one hand.

I test my luck and slide my hand down from her hip to work her clit with my thumb. She gasps and grinds down to increase the contact. Rising and falling on my cock and grinding her clit against my thumb, Henri pants as an orgasm rocks through her. She holds back her beautiful screams, but her sexy moans fill the silence and the space surrounding us.

Restraining myself is nearly impossible. Her pussy flutters around my cock, squeezing me and daring me to erupt. I force myself to stay down, my shoulders pressed against the decking, and I'm rigid beneath her.

Henri collapses down on top of me in one swift waterfall of movement. She has me pinned down, and I can tell she's not done. I can feel the tension in her body and how this new angle is going to change the stimulation she so desperately needs to come again.

Henri's eyes blaze the yellow gold I love when the animal inside her chooses to come forward. Her fangs elongate, and I tilt my head to the side, exposing my neck, shoulder, and chest as an offering for her to put a fresh mating mark on me.

From the corner of my eye, I watch her, all the while submitting to her.

My eyes fall closed, and I dig my fingers into her hips. My body arches. I'm about to come, but I won't rush her. I won't force her to do more or go faster. Henri grinds her clit against the base of my cock, and she screams out.

But it's muted by her mouth filled with my flesh as she bites into the base of my neck with all the force the tightening orgasm has built in her body.

The pressure is intense and chilling.

Her orgasm spurs me to the edge.

Claim. Her, my wolf reminds me.

So, I do, raising myself gently, not wanting to disrupt her as she uses me for her pleasure. No, if anything, Henri just fucks me harder.

I'm over the edge, lost to my release. It's not a lucid thought as my teeth sink squarely into her shoulder. My fangs cut through the muscle and nip at her clavicle.

She yelps in pain, but it gives way to a moan as I come hard, screaming into her shoulder. Bucking up to meet her thrusts, I drag another orgasm from her.

It's in that moment that I can feel fate breathing into me. And finally, it takes a full breath.

I never thought I would feel this. I imagined I would take my dying breath before I would ever have a chance to feel something like this, something so good, happen. And yet, this feels like a stuttered breath, a gasp you take while drowning, delaying the inevitable.

Death and rebirth.

This is the burning breath of life.

With my cock deep inside her, it's damn near euphoria.

Henri continues working her body over mine. She rides my cock like I'm going to disappear, and she only has a few seconds of bliss left.

"Fuck," she whispers. "Fuck. Deacon." She pants a few heaving breaths and then softly calls my name again. "Deacon."

I slide my hands from her thighs up to her hips. The world is new with whatever magic the mating bond brings. None of the euphoric highs I've tried have ever hit like this.

"You're feeling this?" she mutters. "It's like —"

Henri struggles to draw a breath, and when she finally does, the air seeps into her; it expands her chest, and her tits bounce.

"Yeah, Hen, I feel it. All of it." I've felt this pull with her for a year, only for it now to be tenfold.

Minutes, hours, maybe days for all I know, pass as we come down from this natural high. All I know is that by the time we move from our spot on the pillows, the sun is close to the horizon. The illustrious glow of the atmosphere's orange-red light can't compare to the bright light of the mating bond inside my brain.

She leans against me, forehead to forehead, and whispers, "It's so much better than I thought it would be."

"I don't understand how Lena and Finn could have let this fade away." I wiggle my nose against hers. "One thing's for sure. This is a high I'm never going to let go."

"You fucking better not." She gives me a fake little growl.

Henri's arms wobble with the exhaustion that follows sex. Rather than let her fall, I roll us to our sides, staying inside her the best I can, knowing it'll only be a moment or two before I'm not hard enough to.

I think she might be asleep, but Henri's voice, hoarse post the screaming we did together, permeates the silence. "Deacon?"

"Yeah, Hen?" I ask, rolling back and separating us in favor of seeing her face.

Henri's silence worries me, but there's no anxiety in our growing mating bond, only a peaceful calm. "I don't think I'm afraid of you."

"You're not supposed to be afraid of me, Henri." I drag her chin up to meet my gaze. "You deserve to be loved and coveted. I didn't think I knew how to give you those feelings, and I'm still not sure now, but I can tell you that you're never to be afraid of me. You have me wrapped so tightly around your finger that a twitch in the wrong direction could end me. Your disapproval would draw my last breath."

"You're not allowed to leave me," Henri says softly, her wolf rising to the surface, calmly presenting before me.

Ours. My wolf rises to meet hers.

"You couldn't get rid of me if you tried." I kiss her again softly and whisper against her lips, "I've just found you. I'll never let you go."

CHAPTER 69
HENRI

DEACON LOOKS like an angel when he's asleep. His soft brown hair, which is getting long, falls in his face.

"I can feel you staring at me," Deacon murmurs.

Busted. "Sorry."

He opens his eyes, and they're soft and full of sleep. He blinks a bit. "What time is it?"

"Early. Like six a.m.," I answer, earning a wrinkled nose from him and mock disgust.

"Ew. They make one of those in the morning still?" Deacon pulls me into his arms, dragging me across the small space of the bed to hold me against his chest. "You're feeling better?"

I nod against his collarbone. "I feel more like me."

"I'm glad." He draws long, deep breaths of my scent from the top of my head, and in the silence, I think he's gone back to sleep.

Moving very slowly and methodically, I try to slip out of his arms.

Deacon's grip firms up. "Where we going?"

"I was going to let you sleep a little bit," I whisper as

quietly as I can. "You go back to sleep. I'll go clean up from last night."

"Already did." Deacon yawns and rolls onto his back, dragging me with him. His chest rumbles as he speaks. "After you passed out, I carried you down here and tucked you into bed, then brought everything inside."

"All the more reason for you to sleep. You've been amazing. You deserve rest." *Let me care for you now.* I keep that to myself because something tells me he's going to argue that he's still taking care of me.

"Can't." Deacon's voice drops, that one word marked with defeat. "The longer I lie around and do nothing, the more stuff catches up with me."

I think through things, trying not to be dense, but come up empty. "Like what?"

He stills, even his breathing cuts off, and I look up at him. His eyes are vacant, staring at the ceiling. "Everything?"

You're being nosey, Henri, I remind myself.

It's not nosey if it's out of a place of love. My wolf pushes.

There's a tightness in the connection between us and what must be the mating bond.

I'm still trying to think of something to say when Deacon breaks through. "We almost lost Ansel."

Moisture is gathering in his eyes, and I push up onto my elbow to better talk with him and be equals.

"As long as I've fucking known him, he's been invincible." Deacon shakes his head. "Maybe it's silly to believe that of someone. But he's always been larger than life to me. After meeting our mother, I knew I would probably never tell him because he wouldn't know how to handle that or process that type of news. For someone who lives finding the best in people, it —" Deacon cuts himself off, laughing and shaking his head. "The reason I can't tell him lines up with what Revecca called me. The Ardelean wolves are reincarnated time and time again. They call my wolf the guardsman, and fuck if that doesn't feel like the most ridiculous and fitting title I could ever have. I'll protect the rest of the world so long as no one looks too closely at me and my post."

I don't know what to say. I know I should say something, and words are on the tip of my tongue, but nothing comes out.

"We almost lost Ansel," Deacon repeats. "You fell apart so badly that I had to be the responsible one to put you back together." He sighs. "Lena was her own science experiment, and it nearly became a study on Darwin." His chest rises and falls erratically. "Thalia was an amazing human." He forces air into his lungs. "At what point do I admit that I've failed because everyone I've ever loved has been hurt on so many levels."

"Stop." I cut him off, climbing on top of him and straddling his chest. "I'm going to need you to talk nicer about my best friend."

He looks up at me and shakes his head. "We've gotta get you some old ladies to crochet with. I'm a really dangerous friend. Didn't you hear about all the people I've ever loved?"

Shaking my head right back at him, I lean down until our noses press together. I plant a chaste kiss on his lips and then rest our foreheads together.

My wolf hums in pleased, connected delight. *Ours.*

"Ansel had you rallying for him and holding his pack together. Lena let Finn in because you were there to meddle and push them together. Thalia has never been happier. Cade has never been prouder of you." I add that last one in and feel him furrow his brow against mine. "You don't have to believe me for it to be true."

Deacon gives a small laugh and wraps his arms around me,

holding me to his chest as if gravity wouldn't do a good enough job.

"You don't have coping mechanisms that are healthy, so should we get you some old lady friends to crochet with?" I try to break some of his tension.

"The advice I've received recently is to embrace my wolf," Deacon grumbles.

"Okay." I push up off him, forcing him to let me go. "Let's do it."

"Do what?" He pushes up, trying to grab for me again, but I bound off the bed quicker than his long arms can reach.

"Be more wolf." I smile at him, hoping he's catching on.

Even the wolf inside me is surprised. *You? You want to shift?*

"Well, alright. Fuck it. Let's go." Deacon rolls out of bed and follows me through the cabin to the door leading to the deck.

I pause at the door. *You can do this, Henri.* I coach myself.

"You're still on the cusp of heat," Deacon whispers.

He snakes his arm around my waist and warps his hand around mine on the doorknob.

"I know there aren't other wolves here. But it would be understandable if you're uncomfortable and don't want to go. I'm okay. I promise."

He'll protect us, my wolf confirms, her tail wagging softly.

"We could get the range up here. But I'm going to warn you, cougars smell." Deacon laughs. "Okay, no, they don't smell that was mean. Don't tell Deanie."

"She's so nice. I can't believe I got jealous of her." I get up the courage and twist the doorknob, Deacon moving with me.

Out on the deck, the cool morning air immediately pebbles my nipples and cools the red embarrassment off my face.

"She's all good. Deanie didn't get to being Reinha Gata by being afraid of a little jealousy," Deacon says before letting out a loud shiver.

I turn around to offer going back inside, but he's already sliding his pants off.

"But don't worry about me and Deanie. Never went there. Ems is head over heels for her and called dibs within like two seconds of seeing her. Fuckin' cats. They have to actually draw blood from each other to figure out if they're mates. It's nuts. I'll take this weird 'know it when you see it, but it's not pornography' any day."

He looks at me, pants around his ankles, and gestures up and down his body and then mine. "Henri, are you overdressed for this party, or am I underdressed?"

I pull his T-shirt off, revealing that I didn't find panties or he didn't put me on them last night.

"Fuck. That is never not going to be the hottest fucking thing I've ever seen." His eyes are heavy with desire as he looks at me.

"Come on," I urge. "We're learning how to cope."

"Yes, ma'am." Deacon draws a deep breath and effortlessly falls into the large whiteish, cream-colored wolf.

Come on. I call to mine, and she responds quickly, dropping me to all four feet with ease.

We are one in an instant. I've never shifted so effortlessly. All four feet land on the ground, and I feel different physically and mentally. We, my wolf and I, move without a struggle between us. *Is this what it's supposed to be like?*

He cocks his head to the side, watching me, but when we brush along his side, he relaxes, nibbling at the fur next to our ear before stepping into us and directing us toward the stairs. A new obstacle we navigate much easier than expected, managing not to face-plant into the ground.

Deacon stays right by my side, just like during all the pack runs in the past. We're slower than if we were running with the group, trotting small laps around the house before expanding our walk to a small game trail.

The woods smell different here than back home. There are all sorts of strange scents we don't know how to identify. Walking ahead, nose to the ground, we feel like we've lost Deacon and turn around to find him lifting his leg on a tree. *Ewww.*

His tongue lolls out the side of his mouth as he finishes and gives a full body shake before bounding and leaping, kicking his feet out on his way toward us. He pushes, nipping at our heels, indicating we move faster rather than the casual trot we'd been doing. We run down the trail at almost top speed. At one point it feels like flying with the sandy soil under our feet and the morning sun, bright and shining among newly budding life.

We flush a bird from the bush, and it flies off. Deacon jumps and snaps at it, only missing by a few inches.

He falls to the ground and rolls in the dirt. Wagging his tail, he contorts his body and throws his feet into the air like the puppies in the videos on the internet.

Awkwardly we dance back and forth between our paws. In a tight circle, he brushes around me before leading us back around through the woods to the cabin.

Contentment blankets me, and my world is warm and happy.

We shift back, and Deacon is immediately more laid back, his shoulders dropped into a carefree slouch, and for now, at least, I feel like we can do this.

CHAPTER 70
HENRI

"PENNY FOR YOUR THOUGHTS?" Out on the front deck of the rental property, Deacon offers me a glass of water, and while handing it to me, he gives me a kiss on the top of my head.

Only six hours ago we were fucking and having so much fun, but the real world is catching up to me again. Without the lust-filled smog of heat, my new reality is sinking in, and it's not all happy mating marks and newfound family.

"If you give me a penny for my thoughts, and I give you my two cents . . . what do you do with the extra penny?" I draw a sip of water.

"It's for the wishing well, so I can wish for a way to fix this for you." The genuine smile brings me out of my funk. He sits down in one of the deck chairs next to me. "So?"

The wind shifts, and I brush my hair out of my eyes. "I'm wondering how my parents are doing. If they miss me, and if I screwed up the opportunity to ever have them in my life anymore, all over an abusive asshole."

Deacon's genuine smile turns into a scrunched-up expression of guilt. "We've already decided I'm an obsessive stalker with little to no remorse in the notion of hurting myself or others, right?"

"What did you do?" I groan. *He's so lucky he's pretty with all this law-breaking trouble.*

"Broke into your really old social media account and checked in on your parents." He comes clean without any prompting or hesitation.

"Deacon," I snap at him. "Do you know any boundaries?"

"Consent for sex?" His cheeky smile lets him off the hook, but it doesn't settle my nerves.

I process in silence. *Do I want to know? What would knowing do?*

Deacon hangs his head, leaning forward in his chair to rest his elbows on his knees. "Where did your brain go?"

"I can't decide if I want to know or not." My voice trembles.

"It's like Shrödinger's cat. If you don't ask the question or I don't give an answer, then whatever you want it to be is real," Deacon offers.

This instance is just one of many where it's like I'm not smart enough to understand Deacon. "Is that really how that works?"

Rather than make me feel bad about it, he explains. "Without opening the box, the cat is both alive and dead simultaneously. However, when you choose to open the box, the answer is there. The cat is either alive or dead. It can no longer be both. Ultimately, it was about quantum mechanics, but that part, to most people, isn't as interesting as the psychology of the subject and how it reflects our own personal fears, beliefs, and happiness."

"What you're saying is that sometimes it's better for our own health to never open the box and just pick the cat's fate?" I clarify.

He nods. "And it's a valid option."

"Would I be upset if I knew the answer?" Tears well in my eyes.

"You're going to be upset either way." Deacon places his hand on my thigh. It's warm, comforting. "You're already upset not knowing. Is processing an answer better than the uncertainty? If it were me? I'd want to know."

I'm bobbing my head before I can even get words out. But Deacon waits for me to say it first. "I want to know."

"Your parents send you messages three times a week, every week," he says with a soft smile.

A sob runs through my entire body. "No."

"They haven't missed your birthday, a holiday, or adoption day." Deacon moves out of his chair to sit on the ground in front of me, resting his hands on my thighs. "There's hope for a reconciliation and their love for you . . . I can't fathom."

I nearly drop the water glass. Deacon pulls it from my hand and sets it on the ground beside him.

"I can't." *Can't what?*

"You don't have to message them right now. There's no reason to talk or try to figure things out right this second. You've got a complicated relationship. It's going to feel big for a little while." Deacon rubs my thighs, comforting me. "But if you want the relationship, it's there for you to have."

I slide out of the chair and land in his lap, wrapping my legs around his waist. When my head comes to rest on his shoulder where I marked him as mine, Deacon nuzzles in.

He firmly wraps his arms around me and whispers, "It's going to be okay. This will work out however it's supposed to."

We stay like this, in each other's arms, or rather, Deacon held hostage by me and my emotional breakdown. Tears trail down my face, and I sniffle until my head hurts.

At last, I gather a modicum of composure. "I want to contact them."

"Okay." Deacon nods against me. "It's your social media account. You can do it at any time. Or, if you'd like, I can reach out to them on your behalf."

The offer is sweet. It feels foreign. "You'd do that for me?"

"Henri, this is small potatoes compared to the things I would do for you." He kisses my shoulder right where my mating mark is. "You're mine. I'm yours. We've a whole lifetime together and a world around us. We will always come up with a way to solve problems together."

I make a small decision, at least for now. "I'm going to think about it for a little bit."

"You've got time to make the decision. They're both healthy and doing well," Deacon assures me.

My soul feels easier with that information. "So, about us?"

"Well," Deacon hums out. "I was hoping you'd consider moving into the main house. But I wouldn't mind moving down to your cabin. It does occur to me, though, that just because we've claimed each other, you may not be ready to be mates."

"We're mates." I'm quick to cut him off. "We're mates, and I'm moving in. Just means I've got farther to walk every morning for tea with Ms. Gertie."

His chin moves against my head, and I know he's smiling without seeing it. "I'm so glad you like her."

"What's not to love?" I correct.

"Nothing, but she's important to me and to Cade and Thalia." He adds them on quickly. "But I can't explain it. She's just a maternal figure even though I've known her such a short time. Someone I didn't know I needed."

"That is the best way to explain it." I agree, leaning back a little bit to face him. "Can we go home tomorrow?"

Deacon nods. "If you're feeling good, we can go home tomorrow."

CHAPTER 71
DEACON

SHOULD we have stopped for the night on the nearly twelve-hour drive home? Absolutely. Did we? No, we did not. But Henri wanted to drive, and it gave me a couple hours to sleep off the road fatigue, so I accepted her help.

The house is quiet when we walk through the door into the mudroom. I let out a sigh of relief. *How was it nearly three weeks since we rushed out of here with under ten minutes' notice? How did my entire life get so much better since then?*

"Shit, Deacon." Henri turns around to face me, terror written across her face. "Your bike is at the airport."

I lean to the side and open the door to the garage. "Had a friend pick it up for me."

"You let someone else ride your bike?" She squints at the bike and then at me. "I don't know a lot about motorcycles, but from what I've heard, their riders are very particular about them."

I close the door and step into her, putting my arms around her waist. "You worry far too much. No, my friend Romeo owns a towing company. He went down and hauled it home for me."

"Oh." She lets out a sigh but then stiffens and scrubs a hand down her face. "Oh, gross, I left my lunch in my office."

"I'm sure Lauren and her staff found it." I reassure her while trying to read between the lines of her yo-yoing emotions. "Henri, take a beat." I brush a lock of hair out of her face and tilt her chin up to look at me. "Talk about it?"

"Everything's changed." She looks away from me to the door that leads to the main portion of the house.

"This is one of those times where 'nothing has changed' even though you feel differently about it." I try to explain my thoughts without invalidating her feelings. "Your job is still right here waiting for you. Your office has been cleaned. Your staff has been working. Life's been going on in the usual way, which it does."

Carefully I let her go and kick off my shoes, nudging them over by the cubby, the bags of dirty clothes still in the car.

Henri pulls off her heels and pushes her shoes over next to mine, but she's squirming. "I could just take them to where they belong."

"Leave them." I correct her. "This is where they belong now. We've got a garage stall just for your personal vehicle. This will be your entrance and exit."

"Oh. Why?" Henri looks over at me, and it takes a minute before it dawns on her. She covers her face with her hands. "Okay, I swear I'm not stupid. Don't regret claiming me."

"You're my mate." I step back over to her and wrap my arms tightly around her, pulling her as close to me as possible. "I'm never going to regret you. But fuck do I ever sound as sappy as Cade."

That gets a small laugh and then a swoony, "But they're so cute together."

"They're here!" Lena yells from the main portion of the house.

I stiffen. "Shit, she's on to us. It's not too late to go to your cabin."

Henri tenses too. Her heart is beating like a bass drum at a rock concert. "I thought you said it would —"

"I was joking. Hen. I'm sorry." I relax my hold on her. "There's nothing to worry about. Come on, let's go see what has Lena excited."

It takes a minute, but Henri draws a breath and gets the fear under control. Making sure she's with me, I lead the way into the foyer and then into the large great room with the kitchen.

Our family is here, but so are the regular ancestors, Marielle, Bud, and Zachariah, the boy with the jacks from the stairs, and a few others who come and go.

I try to close them out, focusing like I did back in South Dakota. They don't budge. My wolf focuses on the room around us, mostly Henri, and I try to draw his attention to the ancestors. *It's useless.*

Lena is pouring champagne into flutes on the counter.

"What are we celebrating?" Henri's question has Cade looking between the two of us.

He's questioning our relationship together, but I give nothing away.

I clear my throat to explain, but Thalia beats me. "Well, Ansel being released and the great job you did . . ."

When Thalia trails off Lena picks up her thread. "And the fact that you spent a week in bed with Deacon and didn't kill him."

Finn pinches the bridge of his nose. "Christ almighty, faolan."

I place my hand on her shoulder where the mating mark is.

She looks up at me. "You told them?"

"Haven't talked to any of them since we left Ansel's."

Instantly, I realize how bad that kind of is as far as security risk goes and check Cade out of my peripheral vision.

"But you live with me," Lena says. She approaches and hands us each a champagne flute. "Congratulations."

"Apple juice for preggo." Lena slides one to Thalia. "To all of us and the impossible."

I clink my flute with theirs and raise it to my lips.

My wolf snarls and snaps at me, angry that I'm even considering it.

I pull the flute away and look down at the effervescent liquid in the cup. *Not worth it.*

The family breaks out in chatter as Henri catches up with Cade and Thalia. We hear about Ansel and Morrigan's mating ceremony and how my cousin had his wolf reset.

It seems hypocritical that Revecca would do something like that for him but not help me. But she wanted my wolf to be mature and for me to try getting control. Revecca said it's going to take time for my wolf to settle, but what if he never does?

Marielle watches me closely, arms crossed in front of her chest, as I clean up after my family, loading the champagne flutes into the dishwasher.

She hums. "It's not like you to not partake. Finally decided to do something with your life?"

Ignore her, and she'll go away. It's an old technique that never worked.

"What, you're ignoring us now?" She huffs. "After all the years and shit we've done for you?"

"Go away, Marielle," I say softly, trying not to distract from the room. *Should have fucking had the drink.*

My wolf, completely ignoring my request for assistance,

pushes me to walk away from the ancestor and back toward where my family has congregated on the couch. Bud's looking out the window, but Zachariah is looking menacingly at Henri.

It was so much easier in South Dakota. Maybe it only works on the ones you don't personally know?

I don't debate it too much but rather pull a blanket off the blanket rack and bring it over to the couch. I pull Henri into my lap and drape it over the top of us, cutting off any view Zachariah may have.

Maybe it'll just take more time.

I cuddle in against Henri, disconnecting from the world to decompress.

It's not until Henri moves in my lap, turning to kiss me, that I realize I drifted off to sleep.

"Take me to bed?"

"Of course, Hen." I kiss her back, letting her go.

CHAPTER 72
DEACON

I'M CONSTANTLY BATTLING BEING selfish. We've been home for two days, and Henri is in the trenches of reacclimating with all the 'stuff' that went on while we were away. Her team did a great job, but some things and people just need the 'Henri touch.' All I want to do, however, is glue myself to Henri's side because around every turn, more and more ancestors are coming out of the woodwork.

South Dakota and the woman in the kitchen had to have been a fluke. Not once since then have I been able to make one of the ancestors go away. I've tried everything. Except the one thing that I know works.

The reality of our situation is that I'm committed to being sober. Micro-dosing being a thing of the past is leaving me up to the good old-fashioned 'try hard' method for success. *Would it have been easier not to come home to the usual ancestors? Maybe the trouble is these ones know me too well, and I can't just make them go away.*

Spending time in the living room and catching Henri on breaks feels less pathetic than lying on the floor outside her office. That precise distance is the closest I can be to her and talk to the ancestors when they won't go away.

But it's also the farthest I can get from her before the little dark thoughts start infiltrating my brain. It's the darkness in my brain that's the worst of it. The little slivers of truth weave themselves into insecurities that have me questioning if it would have been easier had we not claimed each other.

She's worth it, I remind myself as I watch Lauren leave for the day. She walks out the back doors onto the deck, straight through Bud. He dissipates, not reforming, at least for now.

Embrace the wolf, control the gift, how hard could it fucking be?

Go see our mate. My wolf pushes me to move up off the couch, and I'm about to start stalking her again when footsteps come down the hall.

I close my eyes to shut out one sense in hopes of focusing on the others.

Ghosts don't make footsteps, so I know the footfalls are real. Finn's heavier steps. Cade's long strides. Thalia giggles, but no Henri.

Lena comes bounding down the stairs from the other direction. "Hey, Dea."

"Vell hello, Lena." I give her the fake Minnesotan accent. *Don't look too crushed.* I focus on being neutral.

"Yous gotcha self some dinner plans?" She wraps her arms around me tightly.

Giving her a squeeze, I'm quick to let her go. I drop the fake accent. "No, but I'd be glad to join you, assuming Henri didn't make us plans."

Lena nods. "Yeah. It'll be fun. We're thinking about running tonight too."

"Super nice out. It'd be a good night for it." I agree halfheartedly.

My wolf stretches at the promise of time outside.

It's been a long day, and Henri worked through lunch; I know she's not avoiding me. But I'd hoped we'd be able to at least talk. Even if it's just a couple sentences. I miss spending time with her every day.

These stolen glances, stalking her again, aren't sustaining me anymore. Not after I had weeks by her side.

Cade, Thalia, and Finn take over the kitchen, talking about their days. I sit and listen, but none of it catches or keeps my attention.

I could just slip down the hall and steal her out of her office?

"Deacon?" Finn says my name like he repeated it.

I blink and pull my focus back to him, making sure to watch him as he speaks. *Focus.* "Yeah, Finn?"

"How many days has it been now?"

I know Finn means it innocently. He's trying to show interest, and he's trying to be supportive, but fuck.

It rubs me the wrong way, bristling me from the inside out. The wolf I've been trying to adjust to owning rises to the surface.

"Seriously?" I growl at him, straightening from where I've leaned against the counter. "We're going to do this?"

"Hey, Dea." Thalia tries to draw my attention and my anger off Finn.

Not today, little red. Not today.

"We're going to act like this is some sort of goal or ridiculous triumph we're calculating? It's been nine days since our last velociraptor attack." I try to calm down, drawing a deep breath and forcing myself to look away.

But the words came out. I snapped. There's no putting the cat back in the bag it didn't like being in to start with.

My wolf snarls, trying to force me to look back at him. Anger boils within me. *Bite him. Force submission. We are Ardelean.*

I choose to draw another breath instead and push my hair out of my eyes. Most of the gravel from my growl is out of my voice. "It's been nine fucking days. I've been home for two days, and I've talked to at least a dozen people." I push my finger against the counter, emphasizing those words. "People who weren't there. I thought I'd try to distract myself, so I took my bike and went to the coffee shop in town. I was so sure he was alive that I asked him if there was a war reenactment taking place. Thank fuck the barista at the damn coffee shop thought I was a tourist looking at the corkboard posters."

"Deacon." Cade gives me his caring voice, and I know he means well, but it feels like more condescension. "One —"

"Cade, you finish that fucking sentence with 'day at a time,' and I might actually rip someone's throat out." I look around the room at all of them. Even little red isn't spared from my anger, and that guts me on a new level. *None of them are willing to put any belief in me.* "It used to be that I was suicidal with a slight sociopathic tendency toward vengeance against people who hurt my family. But now I'm on the verge of a killing spree with a dash of good old-fashioned murder-suicide."

Shaking my head, I slide off the stool and go to leave. *Fuck dinner. Fuck them. I want my mate.*

I nearly run straight into Henri.

Everything about her is wrong. It's not quite right. She looks away from me, and it's just another stab to my heart.

I'm nine days sober. It's the second longest time in I don't know how many years and just as awful as the time before.

Seeing the way Henri looks at me, disappointment and regret in her frown and soft eyes, makes me question how badly I want to keep that promise to Lena.

How do I know if he's fully matured for Revecca to take him?

Up in my room, Bud, one of my usual haunts, is sitting in my chair, looking at whatever I left open on my desk.

Rather than uproot him from the chair, I slump down along the wall and look at him. "Do you ever just sit back and look at your life and think: yeah, that tracks?"

"All the time," Bud replies. "Your life is a fucking mess."

"Yeah. I meant in general but fair." I thud my head back against the wall.

"Least you could do is get a job." He huffs.

It's interesting that he thinks that's the base of my problems.

Rolling my eyes, I shake my head. "I don't know how many people are alive or not in a room. Can't exactly be helping people if I don't know if they have a date of death, and I wouldn't even know if my boss is alive or dead."

"You could just ask." He tries to solve my problem with so little effort.

"Ahh, yes. Mr. Bossman Sir, could you please tell me which side of the turf you woke up on today? Oh, you don't remember waking up today. Well, I'm not sure you're alive. So, carry on." I run through the fake scenario in my head.

"Don't have to be such a dick." Bud shakes his head. "This is why that girl wolf of yours took so long to be interested in you. You don't take anything seriously."

If this conversation had happened last month, I would have considered what he was saying as true.

"She and I are more complicated than that," I explain to him. Gesturing to him, I add, "By trying to avoid you fuckers I messed up my wolf, and now I'm stuck waiting for my wolf to catch up maturity-wise. I thought I had it figured out, but here we are. I'm still forced to look at your ugly mug."

Bud turns to look at me and laughs a solid 'ha' before shaking his head. "So, total sobriety then?"

"Yeah, go tell Zachariah. I'm sure he'll pretty much move in." I glower, not actually wanting him to cause more chaos.

"Well, if there's anyone who could do it, it'd be you." Bud nods, inspecting me. "I've never seen someone get so fixated on something until he found a way to fix it. Think about all the left-for-dead motors you've cranked new life into."

The notion seems ridiculous, but stubbornness is very much an Ardelean trait.

"So, how many days do you need to be sober to fix it, and how many days has it been? You were gone for a long time." Bud, ever so analytical, starts in on the mechanics of the situation.

"Nine days sober." I think back to the last drink I had, and then further back to the conversation with Revecca. "And we have no idea how long before my wolf rights himself and I become the Alpha wolf I was intended to be. Again, I thought I'd done it by now. Made a ghost go away when we were gone just fine, but you fuckers are more stubborn."

"Well, then the answer is that it's not nine." Bud gives me a smile. "Guess we'll have to see if it's ten."

"Thanks." I change the subject. "Any chance you looked at the Comet in the garage?"

"Yeah. Needs a new head gasket. You were off your game if you missed that," he informs me.

I knew the gasket needed to be replaced, but seeing how much haunting he's done while I'm not around is just one of my favorite pastimes.

Bud doesn't hover. "I'll leave you to it then."

"Thanks." Closing my eyes, I stay seated against the wall.

CHAPTER 73
HENRI

CADE KNOCKED on my office door on his way to the kitchen, where we were going to make dinner together as a family. Finishing up my last email for the day, I was so excited to see Deacon.

Through the bond, he's felt kind of tense and off since we've been home. I asked about it yesterday, and he said it was just an adjustment period, that he was seeing ancestors, and that he was sure it would get better.

But hearing the conversation in the kitchen and learning that he wasn't giving me the whole truth stung.

Things were tense when I walked into the kitchen on the heels of Deacon's outburst. While the hostility fled the room after him, it was clear there was fallout, and the awkward tension hung tight in the air.

"I'm so sorry," I start.

It's a knee-jerk reaction. Instantly on the defense of him and our relationship. That brings hot tears to my eyes.

"No." Cade cuts me off with a shake of his head. "Deacon

sure as fuck doesn't need you covering for him. Come sit. I'll go talk to him."

That strikes me the wrong way. "No, thank you."

Cade freezes, looking at me.

"With all due respect, I don't know that anything any of you can say is going to help him." I stand my ground firmly.

Finn looks so guilty, his eyes lowered to the floor, head bowed.

Lena breaks the silence first. "Why don't you go up and see him? I'll have the big asshole here make extra, and we'll send it up to you if you don't want to come back down for dinner."

"Thank you. I'll just take some leftovers up." I go to the fridge and grab a couple of the reusable bottles of water and two of the containers of leftovers. Moving to the microwave, I reheat them, willing it to work faster.

Two and a half minutes feels like forever, but finally they're done and hot enough. I stack everything up on one of the trays and head out without another word. I don't even know if I'm mad or disappointed. All I know is that I feel how sad he is through our bond, and I want to be there for him.

Deacon's suite door is unlocked and ajar when I get up there. The curtains to the setting sun are drawn, and most of the lights are off, with the exception of some of his display cabinets and the large balanced arm lamp over his desk.

Big blueprint papers are rolled out across his desktop.

"Hey," I say, trying to look cool like he does while leaning against the doorframe.

He turns to look at me and gives me a pained, soft smile. "Hey."

"I brought food?" I offer the tray toward him.

Deacon moves quickly, pushing the blueprints aside. They curl themselves up, and he elevates the side of his desk and then grabs the folding chair, putting it on the opposite side. He offers me his desk chair and waits for me to set the tray down before joining me.

"I'm sorry," Deacon says softly.

"No." I echo Cade. "You don't have to apologize to me for that."

He furrows his brow. "The look you gave me downstairs says otherwise."

"What you saw on my face was me coming into a conversation confused, wondering what is hurting you." I open the lid on a container, super hungry and ready to eat. "You're the one who'll have to sort out whatever that conversation was and why it upset you, but I think they mean well."

Deacon smiles at me. It's unexpected, and the mood in the bond changes. "I fucking love you, Hen."

"I love you too." I answer, nodding, but it turns into a headshake. "What's . . . What did I say that's got you smiling?"

He laughs. "You're perfect. I need to do better."

Heat creeps up my neck, and I feel my cheeks turn pink. I turn the subject back away from me. "You've been different since we've been home. Are you doing okay?"

Deacon sighs and starts picking at the food. "I thought I had control of my gift, and maybe at one point I did, but I don't now. Wishful thinking, maybe? But I'm trying to do the right thing and deal with my gift in the right way. It's hard. I don't want to distract you, but—"

"But you don't think of suicide when we're in the same room." I repeat what he's told me before, pulling at the memories and confessions we've made to each other.

Deacon swallows hard. "It's not just that. I spent so much time with you and getting to know you that I miss you. I'm trying to adjust to being apart, but I don't want to."

"Well, there's lots of room in my office, and as long as

you're quiet on calls and out of sight for video chats, I don't see any reason why we couldn't spend more time together." I shrug, picking up the other container and taking a bite. *I bet we could fit a bigger couch for him to lie on if he wants to.*

"Seems to me that my brother is eventually going to demand that I get back out and handle the world." Deacon is a bit more forceful in stabbing into his container of food.

"Oh." Dread sinks through me. There are a ton of events on the calendar that would be Deacon-responsibility level, and the majority are scattered across the country. *I don't want to be away from him.* "Don't stress about it. I've got some ideas."

"No, you don't, but you'll think of some." Deacon laughs, calling me out on my little white lie.

Deacon eats with me in comfortable silence, his tension relaxing and settling in.

When we're done, he puts the food tray and the reusable water bottles outside on the table near his suite door.

"I can just take that downstairs?" I offer, guilt settling in that we're making a mess for someone else.

"We have staff for that, Henri." Deacon reminds me, lacing his fingers in mine. "I need to cuddle you more than I need to make their life easier."

"We have staff." I repeat his words, and they startle me, causing me to stiffen. "Deacon, *we* have staff. You bit me, and I'm pack Alden, but now I'm like . . . pack Alden."

"Technically when we file the paperwork, you'll be Pack Ardelean." Deacon smiles like that's any better. "Cade held a vote with the family. Lena gave me the name change documents to file. I figured I'd get around to it after I talked to you about it. I didn't know if you wanted to keep your last name."

"Deacon." I let him lead me into the bedroom as he walks backward through the space he knows so well.

"Hen." He echoes my tone back to me. It's mystified and breathy.

"No, I don't have any intelligent thoughts." I give up.

He stops me by the closet, unbuttoning my blouse.

"That's okay. I was kind of expecting this to sink in eventually." He starts sliding the shirt off my shoulders, and I help him pull it off me. "Henri, regardless of what happens to me or what happens to us, you're extremely wealthy and don't have to work a day in your life for the rest of your life. My assets, which can be liquidated outside the Ardelean Fund, are enough to live on for decades. Managed correctly, could be enough for a lifetime. Inside the fund, my contribution is well, I don't know that it's larger than Cade's acquisition of Corinth Security, but I've only reported a loss once."

"Deacon," I squeak when he starts unbuttoning my pants. "Why are you telling me this?"

"Just so you remember that you may be Cade's pack publicist, but inside the family dynamic, you're an equal." He runs his hands down my legs with the fabric of the pants, and it should be sexual, but it isn't. The care is a dedication met with a melancholy feeling in the bond that I can't place. "You're filthy fucking rich."

He's on his knees before me, and I push my fingers into his hair, pulling on it. Disheveled like this, the family resemblance is more noticeable with Ansel than Cade.

"I don't need to be rich. I just need to have you." I reassure him but step out of my dress slacks. "Come on, let's have a cuddle puddle on the bed and veg out for the rest of the night."

"Absolutely." Deacon kisses my stomach before picking up my pants as he comes to stand.

He tosses them in the dirty laundry before I can object that they're not that dirty and grabs a T-shirt out of the closet for me to put on.

"Sweatpants?" I ask, and he goes back, pulling those out for me and a pair for himself too.

How did this get to be the most comfortable thing in the world?

My wolf practically rolls her eyes, and that's answer enough.

CHAPTER 74
DEACON

IT'S TAKEN seventy-two hours to get my head on straight enough to bother being on the main levels with my siblings and outside of Henri's office for more than ten minutes at a time. The ten-minute increments were to procure more leftovers and say hello to Ms. Gertie.

Spending time with Henri, though, seems to be the answer to my problem with my wolf and my gift. Ancestors disappear when I tell them to, the control back to being what I had at the cabin. Even Marielle and Zachariah are forced away with my command. It's a breath of air when I was drowning.

Waking up late, I make my way down to visit Henri, planning on going back to working on the surprise I've been preparing for her, but as I walk past her office, something's new.

I know her smell. I take comfort in it. The usual smell of the fur of a wolf and the sweet, tender smell of honeysuckle is off. Different but not wrong. Her scent in the bedroom was the same, but now, down here, as I walk past, something doesn't fit, not quite right.

She's on an important video call with the mayor of St. Paul, trying to come up with a plan for the Summer Solstice gathering he wants to host, and if I'm being honest, it's one event I'm excited to go to, so interrupting her is not in my best interest.

Reading but not answering text messages on my phone means I know what the rest of my family is up to and how apologetic they are, but there's only one person I'm ready to apologize to. I go back up to the second floor to the nursery, ready to check in on Thalia. Anxious, she's sent me nursery inspiration pictures and is still fussing over choosing a paint color.

I'm at the door to the children's playroom when it hits me.

The change in Henri's smell is less than it is in Thalia's, but it has the same undernote.

It can't be. No. I'm going to be wrong. I shake my head, trying to dismiss the idea, but I can't.

I wanted to spend some time with Thalia, but she's not my mate.

Probably pregnant, my wolf pushes. He wags his tail in excitement like this is the best fuckin' news in the entire world.

The worst thing is that I can't even ask 'How did this fucking happen?' I know exactly how it happened. Some idiot didn't even bother looking for condoms, and as Lena has drilled into my head a hundred times over, there was an eighty percent chance that she'd get pregnant. Being on suppressants for as long as she was should have given me a little bit of hope and decreased that percentage, her system maybe needing time to flush the drugs, but it's me.

If there's a bad luck lottery, I'll win it.

Why the fuck didn't I think about it?

Because we want a family and want this. My wolf cocks his head.

I'll have to apologize to little red later. But I can offer an olive branch to her dumbass mate right now. I pull my phone out of my pocket and text my older brother.

ME:

> Your mate is looking at paint colors again. Go and reassure her that you all picked the right ones the first time.

I'm already halfway down the hallway to the stairs when I get a reply.

CADE:

Thank you. On it.

Cade and I bump into each other when we're on the stairs, and he grabs hold of my forearm as I walk past him. "You okay? You look a little spooked?"

I shake my head and lie through my teeth. "Ancestors pissed me off. It'll pass. Gonna clear my head."

"Be safe," Cade says and hangs his head for a second. "I'm sorry."

I don't want to apologize to him yet, but being angry isn't the right solution. Not apologizing to him and accepting his apology isn't growth or the right thing.

"Me too." I finally press out with a nod and divert the subject away from me. "Remind Thalia that yellow is a bad color for a nursery, makes kids crabby."

"Will do." Cade lets go of my arm and continues up the stairs.

We could be using that knowledge too. My wolf thinks of the third floor where there's space for hypothetical children for me.

It wasn't — it's not supposed to be — in the cards for me. I swore off the chance of passing this awful sort of gift on to someone else. I had every intention of keeping it. But my siblings insisted that we carve out space just in case. Dinah assured me it wasn't because she saw something. . . but Henri might be pregnant. And Dinah's been known to sugarcoat things for me.

Might, I remind myself, continuing back downstairs toward the garage. I could still be wrong.

My heart is hammering in my chest. Not even the purr of my motorcycle calms my body.

Go to town, get the test, bring it back, and figure it out.

AN HOUR AND A HALF LATER, I went to town, stared at pregnancy tests for like twenty minutes, purchased two different kinds, and came immediately back home. The thundering drum in my chest hasn't stopped yet.

Henri's meetings are over, and halfway down the hall, her office door is open and waiting for me.

Get it together, Deacon. I try to draw deep and steady breaths, matching my steps down the hall. *If you're freaking out, she'll freak out. It's all my fault. I fucked up. Make it better.*

Fucked right, my wolf corrects as he plays a tiny horn of victory in the back of my mind. *She's pregnant with our pup. She's ours, and now we'll have a family.*

Whose side are you on? She might not even want a kid. I stuff him back down.

Mine. He laughs like it's obvious.

I lean against her doorframe, watching her work, which I know she hates, but she's just so damn sexy, her hair pushed back in her headband to keep it out of her eyes. It's one pair of glasses away from a sexy librarian wet dream.

That might be why she's pregnant. Sexy librarian dirty

thoughts. Heat aside, the things I want to do to her should get her pregnant alone.

"Can I help you?" Henri growls, but it's adorable.

The glare she gives me only makes me want to kiss her.

I know what I've done to piss her off, invading her space like this. She prefers I stalk her from a distance or just embrace being with her in the office. Obvious lurking makes her nervous.

Is there a right way to tell her this? I can't come up with one. "You're pregnant."

Her head rears back. "No. I'm not." She shakes her head, the glare falling away, eyes softening with fear. "No."

"Yeah, Hen." I focus on schooling my features to stay calm, at least on the outside. If she listens carefully, she'll hear my elevated heart rate, and I'm sure my own fear scent will mix with hers soon. "We risked it, and the odds weren't what we hoped."

"Deacon, I can't be. That's impossible." The fear in her eyes doesn't fade, but she looks back at the computer in front of her and ignores me.

I was going to sit in the chair on this side of the desk to talk to her and logic it out, but with a couple extra steps, I change trajectory. Squatting next to her in the desk chair, I put my hand on her thigh. "Henri, it is possible. And it's happened. I can smell it."

She turns to face me with a huge sigh. "No one gets pregnant on their first heat after suppressants. It's why they tell us to stop taking them a season before we want pups. Furthermore, scent changes are an old wives' tale."

I don't argue with the proof being Thalia upstairs and how we all knew. Instead, I pull one of the pregnancy tests out of my back pocket and place it in her lap. "Then take the test and prove me wrong."

"Deacon, I'm busy. Too busy for this." She tries to turn back from me to her desk, but I hold the chair still.

I lock my eyes on her, and mixed emotions hit me hard. I take a deep breath before urging her, "Hen. We'll figure it out. But you've got to take the test."

"If I take the test, will you fucking let it go?" she groans.

She hovers her hand over the box, afraid to touch it, like it might bite her. Maybe make her more pregnant.

"If you take the test and it's negative, I won't mention it ever again." I agree with a very firm nod. "I won't bring up pups until you do."

She's pregnant. My wolf laughs at my statement. *She's going to test positive, and you're an idiot for letting her think there's a chance she won't.*

I push him aside rather than pulling him forward and risking agitating her.

Standing up, I offer her my hand.

Henri stands without accepting my hand and clutches the box, the cardboard buckling a little with her grip.

Exiting her office, she goes toward the kitchen and the guest bathrooms that we have. I wrap my arm around her and guide her back toward the stairs that lead up to the second and third stories.

Whispering, I scold, "I'm not letting my mate take a pregnancy test in the pack's public bathrooms."

"It's not going to be positive. You're just wasting time." She argues with me but doesn't pull away from me.

Fuck, Hen. I want you to be right. I really do. Except there's this tiny little flicker in my chest that disagrees.

CHAPTER 75
HENRI

I LET Deacon lead me upstairs to his room. Begrudgingly, I follow him into his bathroom and then wait for him to leave.

"Okay, I've got it from here." I try to shoo him out the door with a few flicks of my hand.

Doing the opposite, Deacon closes the bathroom door and slumps against it until he's sitting on the floor.

"Great." Rolling my eyes, I head over to the toilet.

Luckily, Deacon caught me before my after-lunch bathroom break, and I have to go. In an attempt at modesty, I leave my dress mostly down while sitting on the toilet and get it out of the way before trying to do my business.

This is the most awkward thing in the entire world. *Human women go through this all the time? How does anyone make this work?* Through the grace of God or whatever deity there is, I manage to pee on the stick without getting urine everywhere.

I clear my throat, and Deacon trains his eyes on the floor while I clean up. The stick capped and set on the counter, I wash my hands, and the gravity of what we're doing sinks in.

Deny. Deny. Deny. It's not actually happening. The test isn't going to be positive. I'm not going to be pregnant. I watch the stick on the counter while drying my hands. Deacon's heart has been beating fast, and now mine matches the pace of his.

It hasn't changed yet.

"This is stupid." I groan, looking at Deacon.

In a fluid movement, giving away just how graceful he can be, Deacon comes to stand behind me, staring at the little test on the counter. He wraps his arms around me and rests his head on top of mine.

"It's not stupid," Deacon answers. "Even if it's negative, it's better to know for sure."

"It is going to be negative," I tell him. Again.

Our mate. My wolf presses hard inside me, and I can't help but let myself lean back into his embrace. *And a baby could be nice.*

Deacon tightens his arms around me.

"How long do we hav —" The test on the counter starts changing, and the rest of my words come out as a whisper. "To wait?"

"Gonna go with we've got an answer." Deacon holds me tighter.

Plain as day, the test reads in all spelled-out letters 'pregnant.'

My heart shatters into a million pieces. *No. No. No.* My heartbeat skyrockets further. I can feel my pulse in every part of my body, and I'm getting hot all over. My head throbs, and I forget how to breathe.

"Shhh." Deacon squeezes me. "We'll figure this out. It'll be okay."

I wobble, and it feels like the world is spinning, but Deacon's holding me. He pulls me up tight against his chest and carries me out of the bathroom.

Time is moving funny, and I'm gasping for air.

The bed squishes underneath me, and the world is blurry with my tears. I try to wipe them away, but I can't move fast enough.

Deacon lies on the bed next to me, and I try to move away from him. He pulls me back. Which is probably for the best because the room spins, and lying still stops the movement.

"I'm pregnant. That's going to change everything." I squeeze my eyes shut and try to picture this life with Deacon. I finally get the words out. "I can't do this. I never really wanted to be a mom. I don't know how to parent."

Our mate's pup, my wolf snarls at me. She pushes me closer to Deacon, and I turn, curling up against him.

I press my face against his chest, and despite everything, drawing in deep breaths of his scent calms me down. *I'm pregnant with Deacon's baby.*

He runs his hand listlessly up and down my arm. Silent and calming, Deacon doesn't interfere with my wallowing, but he comforts me so much.

Our mate will take care of us. Look at how he takes care of us. My wolf argues with me.

I'm quick to dismiss it. Moving on, the idea of being pregnant hits me again: swollen stomach and miserable. I'll be on my own doing it all. He's struggling with even taking care of himself. It's nice having him camping out in the office, but what if this is what it's like forever?

Our mate is doing a good job. He is great at caring for us, my wolf argues.

But beyond pregnancy, I don't know anything about raising a pup. Having been raised by humans has always made me feel on the outside. I can't raise a wolf because, despite the fluffy wolf inside, I'm not a true wolf.

Yes, you are. My wolf huffs. *I don't know how much more wolf you want to be.*

There's no way to make her understand. Deacon is good to me, but that doesn't mean this is the right thing.

"Hen." Deacon wipes the tears out of my eyes when I look at him. "I'm here, and I'm all in. You're not alone. We" — he reiterates by giving me a little squeeze — "can do this."

I want to agree with him. Fuck I want to let him take care of me, but what if he can't.

Shaking my head, I draw a deep breath. "We aren't supposed to be together."

"Says who?" Deacon laughs as he runs his fingers through my hair. He pulls me up to sit with him on the bed. Cross-legged, Deacon pulls me to sit in his lap, and I wrap my legs around either side of him. "I've got adorable little fang marks to prove it." He drops his voice to a whisper. "Yours are less little, but if I do say so myself, they're equally adorable. You are mine. I'm yours."

Mine. I feel that word as he says it.

I've envied Finn and Lena in how thoroughly they've claimed each other. Cade's entire world revolves around Thalia, and there's something so amazing in the possession on that level.

But Deacon can't give me that. He's inconsistent and a mess. Even if I wanted to be a parent, and I'm not sure I do, Deacon couldn't be there with me through everything.

Shaking my head, I can't give him words that won't hurt him. "You're holding it together the best you can. I know how hard you're trying. But now I have two people to think about." My voice catches. "I don't know that we can do this together."

The hurt is evident in every feature on Deacon's face. He bites his lips together and draws a deep breath. "I understand where you're coming from. You know I'm here with whatever need you have. Whatever you're willing and wanting to share with me, I'm here."

The pain in Deacon's face and the tension in his body echo the gutting pain of my wolf screaming inside me. She howls and rips at me from the inside out, threatening to shred me to pieces. The bond between us pulses with sadness like a boat being tossed about in a turbulent ocean.

The road to hell is paved with good intentions. No matter how much this hurts, I have to make the right choices and be the responsible one.

Ignoring her, I shake my head. I know it's a contradiction in our communication, but I can't force myself to nod in agreement. "Yeah. I'll let you know."

Deacon isn't hiding his pain, but he doesn't try to stop me. Instead he helps me to my feet. I'm halfway out of his suite when I stop walking. Something nagging me in the back of my brain forces me to look at him.

He pauses, focused completely on me. His eyes are glassy but not dazed out like when he's under the influence of something. They match the hurt on the rest of his face.

"Deacon?" His name is the dumbest question ever since I'm looking at him, but it doesn't stop me from asking it.

"Yeah, Hen?"

"You're sober, aren't you?"

He gives me a tiny smile and a nod. "Have been since we started your heat."

"The champagne when we came home?" I try.

"Slipped it to Lena. Don't tell Finn."

This is so fucking awkward. I don't know what to say. Walking away, I fight my wolf at every step. She tries to drag me back to Deacon and the reassurance that comes with staying in his arms. Hiding away in his suite from trouble and responsibilities would only compound the problem.

Instead, I go back to my office. Tonight, I need the space. I need my cabin by Ms. Gertie and to really think about what this is going to mean for us.

For all of us. My wolf projects the idea of a happy little three-person family. Me, Deacon, and a baby.

My little trip upstairs to Deacon's suite took almost a half hour. I sit down at my desk and open a private browser tab to type words I never thought I'd have to type into a search bar.

Wolf shifter pregnancy termination.

The search pulls up a number of websites, but I can't click on any of them.

Wait. I drum my fingers on the desktop and move my computer off my desk calendar, which hasn't been changed from last month.

Thirty-six hours . . . So it was this day. I hold my finger on that date and count down the rows and over to today. That was only two weeks ago.

He didn't drink his glass of champagne when we toasted Ansel's freedom once we got home.

Our mate, my wolf snarls, snapping at me, *is trying for us, and you're just pushing him away when he could be taking care of us.*

I close my eyes when the screen gets blurry from my tears. The memories of him trying to hold it together while I was managing him as the public-facing member of the Alden pack, the day drinking and pills, are all so recent in my brain. That's not a safe family environment.

But he's doing it. My wolf pushes the logic of it.

Okay, so even if Deacon is sober. Even if he gets his wolf under control, that doesn't make either of us a good candidate for parents.

But dammit, Deacon . . . I put my hand on my lower stomach, where apparently I'm growing a baby, a pup. I've seen him with children. *No. No. Being good with someone else's children doesn't make you a good parent.*

You're being stubborn. He'll be good. My wolf believes in Deacon. She's adamant.

I don't have to make any decisions today. Maybe . . . we'll see.

But I can't sit at my desk anymore. I pack up my shit and start out of my office, heading toward the back door and hopefully avoiding everyone on the way to my cabin. No reason I can't do the rest of my work today from there.

CHAPTER 76
DEACON

HENRI'S FUCKING PREGNANT. *What the fuck do we do?* I'm standing here, staring at the refrigerator, and I can't remember what I was trying to cook or that I was even hungry.

My wolf answers the rhetorical question. *I don't know. I thought you'd know. Raising pups isn't a wolf job.*

This is why I told you no. We didn't need to be looking for or finding our mate. I groan, gripping the refrigerator for support.

He's unsteady within me, wobbling with the same wooziness that tries to take me now. *Had I known you didn't know . . .* He stops, but it doesn't help my already deteriorating condition. *Had I known you didn't know . . . no. That's a lie.* The asshole pushes forward a picture of her smiling, and my body goes numb.

"Hey, Deacon." The refrigerator door leaves my hand, closing in front of me, and Finn's face moves into my line of sight. His hands are on my shoulders. "Are you okay?"

The way Finn cocks his head at me is funny.

My head is wobbly, and my heart is beating far too fast. "No."

"Let's sit you down." He guides me around the island to the couch and lets me fall back down into it.

He sits down on the couch across from me, leaning forward.

The room stops spinning.

"I haven't." I try to defend myself. *At least, I don't remember using.*

"Henri's pregnant?" Finn's voice is so much quieter. He looks past me toward the hall that leads to her office.

"Henri's pregnant." I nod, agreeing with him.

Finn's face lightens, and then he chuckles. "Could be worse."

"Could be worse?" I scrub my hand down my face, starting to feel my heart rate steady.

"Yeah." Finn nods. "Could be a velociraptor attack."

I laugh, and a weight lifts off my chest. Finn's joke isn't all that funny given how angry I was about that before, but it sure does put things into perspective.

"I'm sorry." I sigh after the laughter clears. "I know you're trying to be supportive. It comes from a good place but —"

"But we're all treating you like you're one second away from disappointing us, and it's pressure you don't need." Finn interrupts me.

"I was gonna say, but fuck off, I'm doing the best I can, but yeah, that probably surmises better." I shrug with the realization that he's labeled the feelings. "I'm sick of feeling like it's just expected that I'll fail. Would be really nice if someone just believed in me. Ms. Gertie doesn't count because I'm pretty sure she thinks I can do anything, but that's the good grandma energy."

Finn actively listens. He nods and lowers his eyes while processing my words, and it's the first time I think he might actually be seeing me. "I'll do better. I'm sorry for being an overbearing arsehole to you. You mean a lot to Lena, and there's something between the two of you she hasn't been ready to share with me. Whatever it is, it weighs heavily on her. It seems every day we get closer to her heat, she's more anxious about it and you." Finn shakes his head and shrugs. "Well, I know you can appreciate the lengths we'll go to for our mates." He reaches for a personal connection.

Do I tell him it's Lena's fault I'm still alive? The thought seems insensitive, so I share the information without placing blame directly on her. "I made Lena a promise that I wouldn't end my suffering until a certain date, and that day is approaching rapidly." It feels like a lifetime ago that I had to pick a new date. "If Lena's heat is on time, so to speak, I . . ." I shake my head, realizing how awful that must be for her. "I wouldn't be here when she gets back."

"Fuck," Finn whispers.

His whole body folds, shoulders slumped, waist bent, resting his weight on his elbows. Finn hangs his head, and it takes a minute before he pulls himself up. He studies me. Finn looks about as sick as I felt moments ago.

"Should I." Finn covers his mouth but stops the question and comes to a decision. "I'll talk to her about suppressants. That . . ."

That could be so dangerous after what she put her body through with her trial drug. It's not like we have a model for what she's been through, but suppressants have caused infertility in the past and with her compromised state . . . *Does Finn know that risk would be compounded?*

I see Finn doing the math, but he doesn't press.

Guilt seeps into my chest. *Am I that selfish?* I've waited this long. Henri changes everything. Henri pregnant with my pup changes everything indefinitely. It's a turning point, here in this moment. Suicidal ideation may never go away, but the intent is over. She might never choose me back, but I'll choose her and my pup.

"Thank you for telling me." Finn puts his hand on my shoulder as he steps toward the end of the house where their room is. "It helps me help her."

His hand falls away.

"Finn." I stop him, closing my eyes before forcing them open. I stand, legs not as wobbly and the world not as spiny as it was before. I lock eyes with him. "I'll talk to Lena. I can't promise we'll be velociraptor free forever, but I'll always be here. So, you should maybe pick up one of those baby name books for Lena. She's always wanted one but couldn't bring herself to buy one. No point if she wasn't ever going to have a mate, pups, and all that."

Those words lift every single weight from Finn's shoulders. They had worked themselves up around his ears, and now they drop to a normal position.

"Thank you." His eyes turn glossy. "I don't have words, Deacon. You mean so much to Kathleen, but don't discount what you mean to me."

I hang my head and come up with the only acceptable answer. "You make my sister very happy. Equally mad, but very happy. We may not always see eye to eye, but I can respect you for all the decisions you've made to protect her."

Finn nods, accepting what I'm saying, and this time when he turns to go, we part ways.

"Deacon! There you are." Zachariah comes charging in through the wall, and I pinch the bridge of my nose.

It would have been my luck to kill myself and get stuck haunting people in the same vicinity as him anyway.

"What do you want?" I snap at him, walking up the stairs to the second and third stories.

"I think you need to have a talk with that Marielle lady.

She's on a tirade and acting crazy." Zachariah swings right into the role of sexist old white dude without any hesitation. "I swear. Back in my day the women respected men. They didn't go on about this nonsense like women's rights to their bodies. They trusted men to make the right decision."

I stop mid-flight of stairs and look at him. "What was Marielle talking about?"

"Something about an unhappy mother to be." He takes the shocked look on my face as agreement with his cause. "Yes! You get it. So, you'll talk to her then? I knew you'd get her sorted. Aside from seeing ghosts, you've quite a level head on you."

I walk away from Zachariah back down the stairs and across the house the long way toward Henri's office. But she's not there. Her computer is gone, and the lights are off.

"Henri, where did you go?" I ask mostly to myself while I pull my phone out of my pocket and press the call button. *Pick up. Pick up. Pick up.*

"Hello?" Henri sounds aggravated, and I hear keys in a door lock.

Not here. My wolf deduces.

"Hey, where are you?" I skip right to my need-to-know information.

"I'm at my cabin." Henri sighs. "I need to be alone, Deacon."

How do I tell her my ghosts ratted her out about looking into her options? I don't blame her. If that's what she wants to do, I'll support her through it. I sit on the stairs and confess. "Part of living with the ability to see ghosts is that they're the worst fucking snoops in the entire world. They will literally get all up in your business because they fucking can. Like, why does a bear shit in the woods? Because it can. That level of invasion of privacy."

Get it together, my wolf snarls.

587

"What's your point, Dea?" Henri's cabin door creeks closed with a thud.

Is it better if I don't flat-out tell her I know what she was considering? There doesn't seem to be a good answer. "I won't talk you out of any option you want to explore. But please don't ice me out of supporting you."

Her silence speaks volumes. My phone makes a very distinctive beep when it disconnects, so I know she's still on the other end of the line.

"All those conflicted feelings you're having, I'm having too." I don't know what to say. I don't know how to fix this.

"Come to the cabin." This time the phone makes the beep noise as Henri disconnects the call.

CHAPTER 77
HENRI

DEACON RAN TO MY CABIN. The amount of time to get here and the way he pants when he makes it to the door are great indicators.

I open the door, and Deacon stops himself from touching me. He forces himself to take a step back and away from me.

"Come in." I step aside, letting him into the little cabin.

He steps through the doorway, and his eyes take in the place. I haven't really been calling it home. I haven't even come here since we arrived back from South Dakota. My stuff is still in boxes from the movers, and I haven't even bothered to check that everything is there because there's nothing of real importance.

"We're having a baby," I say firmly.

It draws his eyes off the moving boxes to me. He nods but says nothing.

"Yes. I looked it up, and then I looked at a calendar."

Deacon cocks his head to the side, trying to see what I'm saying from a new perspective. "Henri, you gotta break it down for me because I can't see the connection between those two things."

"You've been sober fourteen days," I inform him.

Deacon stands up straight and gives a full-body sigh. "Fucking Velociraptors."

"What?" I rub my temple, trying to understand him.

"Everyone is so obsessed with my sobriety. Yeah, I'm trying. But —" His frustration hangs in the silence between us, echoing in the small cabin until he runs his hand back through his hair, pulling at the roots. "Henri, I've done nothing but think about how badly I've fucked things up my entire life."

"Tell me what you really mean, Deacon." I cross my arms in front of my chest.

"Just stay with me, try to keep up, no matter what fucked up shit I'm about to say, and then when I get to the end, you can scold me." Deacon waits for me to agree.

"Okay."

"I understand why I'm not a prime candidate for the father of your child. I'm not disillusioned by the imperfections of my existence." Deacon draws a ragged breath, leaning against the cabin's door.

My body aches to go to him and tell him that's not it. *I agreed to be quiet. Don't interrupt.*

"I have thought of killing myself no less than a hundred times since we've been back. And I know because I finally started keeping a tally on my phone. I have a tally mark per ancestor I've seen minimum. Double for Zachariah and the way he looks at you. But today when Finn sat me down and talked to me about a problem with Lena, I reassured him that I would talk to her about her heat. I guaranteed him that I would renew a promise." Deacon's eyes are glassy, and he swallows. "I would change the ending of my life story, and short of an act of god, when she gets back from her next heat, I'd still be here for her."

Hair has fallen into his eyes, and my fingers twitch.

Stay. My wolf reminds me that I can't go to him, not just yet.

"I promised him that despite the stupid fucking tally marks in my phone, I'd always be here. In a single conversation, over the course of ten minutes, I had the realization that no matter how much my brain says 'die,' there are some things I can't not see." A tear escapes his beautiful brown eyes, and he brushes it away quickly.

What do you say to that? I feel like I should say something, but nothing seems like it would be good or right. I promised to stay quiet, but he needs me. My heart aches in my chest.

My wolf whines but stays seated inside me, trying to anchor me for that promise.

But he keeps talking. "I can't not see Cade and Thalia's baby. I can't not see Cade freak out about how he's not sure if he'll be a good dad. The poor idiot doesn't realize how good of a job he does all the time with everything, and it's funny as fuck. But, more than that, I can't —" Deacon draws another deep breath and shallowly exhales.

I give him a soft smile, and it seems to be all he needs to continue.

"I can't leave knowing that Lena is going to have this minute like we just did. Where she's going to realize she's pregnant. Everything she's been too afraid to wish for will come true, and how could I miss that?" He makes soft taps of his head against the door repeatedly. "I fucking can't." He shrugs. "Because regardless of the suicidal ideation, I'd choose you. I would keep choosing you. All of you."

He wants us. My wolf thinks of the three of us as a little family together.

"In Romania, I asked Revecca if she would take my wolf."

Deacon slides down the door until he's sitting on the floor, looking up at me.

"Deacon," I gasp, not trying to cut him off. I put my hands over my mouth. He's blurry, and I blink away my tears. And I feel weird standing above him, so despite the living room furnishings, I sit near him in the entry.

"I asked her, and she said only after I let him come into his power." Deacon sighs before continuing. "Ha. I thought I'd be able to give him up if it meant saving you. Part of me is still a selfish asshole, Hen. I can't give him up."

Deacon pulls his phone out of his pocket and shakes it as if to strangle it. "So, I'm going to see how many tallies the note app can handle before it crashes and refuses to open because I can't guarantee that the thoughts won't be there. But my ability to willfully act on those thoughts is gone." He tucks his phone away and hangs his head.

Sadness but not pity weighs heavy on my shoulders. *My mate.*

"I'm struggling with these choices and these decisions, especially because the wolf doesn't seem to be doing anything differently. I'm not feeling any different, but after spending time with you, I can sometimes get the ancestors to go away. Maybe like Lena, I had to have you to get further control."

Deacon is silent, and I think maybe it's my turn to talk. But the tension in the air has me second-guessing. *I don't know how to help him.*

"I don't know how long it's going to take or if it will get better, but I'm doing the best I can. Humans have meetings. They go and talk to others like themselves, where they all share about how they got started on drugs and how they're working this system to get sober. They have therapy and can talk about their issues. And you'll laugh . . . but I've been to meetings and seen doctors in the past, no that's not true, you won't laugh."

Deacon realizes he's lost track and stops himself. He tucks his legs up underneath himself. "You'd never laugh. You take me more seriously than anyone else ever has. But the meetings and their conviction only made me realize the self-control I had. I stopped microdosing in the past. I tried to get to the point where I could handle my gift. I wished, I tried to put faith in some higher entity that it'll be okay or they're helping me, forgiving me or whatever. But I guess . . . I'm on my own for this."

He sighs, pressing his palms against his eyes for a moment before pulling them down and looking at me. "I'm not promising I'll be perfect. I'm never going to promise that I'll be able to pull myself up out of the frustration that comes with my gift and how hard it is to just exist sometimes. I'm only promising that every day I'm going to wake up, try, and if I die, it won't be at my own hand, intentionally or otherwise."

Our mate is hurt. My wolf nudges me now, thinking it's time to go to him.

But I know Deacon isn't done. Even though I want to comfort him, I won't until he's ready for me to. He needs to hear, though, that I'm choosing him and this life with him. Only when he's ready.

"I will not tell you what you can and cannot do with your body." Deacon nods, "But I can tell you that I will be here for anything, everything, day or night, for the rest of your life. If you pick me or you don't, and even if my wolf and I never get it together, I'm not leaving you or abandoning you. Your problems are my problems, and after being a big problem for a very long time, I've become *really* good at fixing them."

"Deacon." I interrupt him because, at this point, I can't stop myself from climbing into his lap. He keeps saying all these heartbreakingly beautiful words and I need to be close.

He nods, understanding it's my turn to talk.

SARAH JAEGER

"Yes, I searched wolf shifter pregnancy termination." I straddle his lap it's awkward this close to the door but I make it work looking him eye to eye, "Panic and fear set in, but before I even got into that doom spiral of searching, I looked at the calendar instead. I realized how long you'd been fighting. Regardless of if you thought you could do it or not . . . you were. You have been all this time. We are going to have setbacks, and there are going to be times when we both struggle. I'm going to have my own stuff and insecurities to work through. But I don't want to do this" — I put my hand on my stomach — "without you."

Tears well in his eyes, and he tries to blink them away, but it does no good. He wipes his eyes with the back of his hand.

He wraps me up in his arms, and then, at the most vulnerable I've ever seen him, Deacon buries his head into my shoulder and sobs. His body shudders against mine with each heaving breath.

Nearly crushing me against his chest, he runs his fingers through my hair, curling them at the base of my neck as he kisses the top of my head again and again.

My goofy and emotionally aloof man breaking down gets me.

Tears pour from my eyes, and at this point, I'm sure they're soaking his shirt.

Deacon's sobs subside, and his breathing evens out. He wraps his arms around me tighter, as if that were possible.

"I respect if you want your space, but it would make me obscenely happy if you'd come back to the main house," He whispers. "I just —"

"Let's go home, then." I'm firm pushing up off Deacon's lap.

He stands and scoops me up in his arms, and I yelp. "Deacon!"

"What?" He laughs. His face is red, and tear tracks still glisten on his cheeks.

"Put me down." I roll my eyes before wiping the moisture off his cheeks.

Deacon shakes his head, "Nope. No. No way."

"Oh my god. You cannot carry me my entire pregnancy." I sigh and give him the scolding face.

"That's not it." He kisses my nose, already walking the few steps to the door. "I'm afraid to lose you. I'll even paint my sitting room by hand a bright, cheery color if it'll make you happy." He crouches to get the knob open. "You know, Cade and Finn make this look so easy."

I help open the door and let him carry me out onto the porch and then help him close the door behind us. He nuzzles against me on the walk up the hill to the house.

A wolf whistle comes from the main part of the house as I help Deacon with the front door.

"He did it!" Lena shouts.

"Knew he could," Finn answers at a more normal volume.

Deacon carries me past them and then down the hall toward the office and stairs. He stops at the elevator. "Stairs are faster, but I have zero faith in my ability to do this gracefully." His honesty is adorable. "Can't risk denting you."

With my help, we get the elevator moving up to the third floor. Then it's through the doors to his study and then into the bedroom. Deacon sets me down on the bed before pulling off my shoes for me. He kicks his own off and climbs into bed beside me. I'm the perfect little spoon again, held tightly in his arms.

"Is there anything I can do to make this easier?" Deacon whispers.

I know the answer to that question immediately. "Promise to keep trying no matter what."

"Done." Deacon's voice is firm with conviction. "What else?"

"That's it." I settle in against him more.

He shakes his head against the back of mine but doesn't try to push me for more.

Deacon draws slow, deep breaths behind me. "I'm going to need to run later. Do you want to come with?"

"Oh. Can I?" I tilt my head. "Am I allowed to shift when I'm pregnant?"

"Yeah, Hen. You can." Per usual, Deacon doesn't even falter at my question.

I know it's something I should know being a wolf but don't.

Deacon presses our bodies closer together, and I don't think we could get any closer without him being inside me. "There's no such thing as a stupid question. We all have our deficiencies somewhere in life. And as far as 'things to not know' goes . . . I'm pretty sure we're allowed to not know about pregnancy."

"Should we tell Ms. Gertie before the rest of the family finds her?" I yawn before turning myself onto my back to see him.

"Absolutely. I think she'd be extremely disappointed. Not a lot of things feel worse than disappointing the most motherly figure I've ever had in my life." Deacon raises up onto his elbow to kiss me.

"Are we napping?" I yawn, rolling farther to nuzzle against his chest.

"Heck yes." He kisses my neck down my shoulder. "You've had a big day. We'll get some rest and then some snacks and get to work making plans to renovate this space."

"Too much work for today." I snuggle and roll back to my other side, letting him be the big spoon again. "We've got a long time before we need to do that. I'm comfortable here as is."

"Keep wiggling that ass against me, Henri, and you won't be so comfortable," he warns.

Nap or sex, nap or sex. The decision weighs back and forth, but before I can make one, Deacon's heart rate drops. His body goes slack, and I know he's lost to sleep.

Heavy emotions will do that to a person, and I'm pretty sure Deacon's felt them all today.

"I love you." I say the words quietly, and they feel satisfying and different from the first time I said them. "I've judged you too, and I already figured out that I love you."

CHAPTER 78

DEACON

W<small>E DIDN'T MAKE</small> it out of bed last night for anything more than food. And now this morning, between meetings, Henri came upstairs to our home to look at the blueprints I have laid out on my desk, a piece of tracing paper over the top of my existing walls and bookcases.

"You're serious about doing a full reno of your suite just to get me some space?" Henri looks so guilty. She chews on her bottom lip and looks around the space.

I pop down in my desk chair and open and close my hands, grabbing for her.

Henri walks over with smile on her face, and my heart flutters.

With a sigh, she runs her hand through my hair.

"I'm absolutely positive. When I built my suite, it was custom made for just me and me alone. But it's not just me — not anymore."

"Correct. You are, as one would say, stuck with me." She winks and then turns to look over at the floor plan. "Okay, so you like having your desk by the sliding glass door and your shelves of oddities in their own room."

"I like having a window where I spend most of my time for some regulation of night and day. But it's not necessarily a need for it to be the doors." I shrug, moving over the floor plan of Cade's suite from the floor below us. "Oddities can go anywhere. I can downsize my collection."

"Well." Henri looks at the two plans. "I'm keeping my office downstairs. It's more accessible for everyone who needs to contact me, and I really don't want people traipsing into our special place." She pauses, looking at me. "I really liked when we were at the cabin in South Dakota. We got lost in our own little world. But you don't have to get rid of your things to make room for me."

I sit up straight and kiss her. "Best part about the third floor? Aside from cleaning and maintenance, we're all by ourselves, and aside from the elevator and stairs, we have the whole west wing to work with."

"Oooo. The west wing. How very royal." Henri rolls her eyes. "So the bedrooms on both sides of the hall?"

"The other two are currently set up as guest bedrooms, but we could overtake them as needed." I assure her.

She smirks and cocks a brow with a devious glint in her eyes. "So, if we have six kids, we could use them?"

That hits me with a jolt in the stomach. Fear and panic sink in a cool wave from head to toe. "Oh. Let's not commit to six. I'd say two, max, so we're not outnumbered."

"Perfect compromise." She smiles at me with a shit-eating grin.

"You just conned me into two, didn't you?" I pull her down into my lap as she giggles, letting me nuzzle against her. "Fuck, it's so easy with you around."

"Same." She rests her head against me. "Okay, so wish list:

602

oddities storage, library, workspace for you, bigger bedroom with sitting area to watch TV."

I pick up the pencil and get to work, moving around walls and spaces. Henri watches me, and I start by expanding our bedroom out, making room to sit and look out the large windows.

"Bathroom and closet are okay?" I ask.

"Yeah. You've got plenty of room for my stuff." She muses, looking at her stomach like she's expecting to see a bump, "When do we tell everyone?"

"Well, Finn knows, so Lena knows, which means Cade knows and Thalia knows." I feel my face heat. "Finn found me kinda freaking out."

"Awww." Henri ruffles my hair.

Her happiness and smiles are contagious. They permeate my bones, relieving an ache of loneliness. I'm about to say something, but her phone starts going off.

It had been quiet all morning.

Dread fills my stomach, and I don't know why.

She pulls it out, and with one glance, her jaw goes slack. Henri murmurs, "Oh no. No. No. No. No. No."

I look over her shoulder, pulling the phone so I can read it.

Headline after headline:

James Alden, Pregnant Girlfriend?
Who is James Alden Buying
Pregnancy Tests For?
Mystery Woman of James Alden?
A Cousin Grimm off the Market?

"Shhh." I try to comfort her by running my hand up and down her back. "It's me buying a pregnancy test. They can't prove shit. This doesn't have to come out right now."

She stands up and starts uncharacteristically pacing, running one hand back through her hair while the other holds her phone, thumb scrolling.

"Fuck," she groans.

"What?" I stand up and move toward her.

"Ever get a message from Cade and think 'I'm getting called to the principal's office'?" She scrunches up her nose.

"Oh, yeah." I sigh, not even bothering to look for my phone because whatever text she has, I'm sure I do too.

I follow Henri's lead down the stairs.

"Library," Cade sighs, opening the library door for us.

Henri eyes me and mouths, 'I thought he knew.'

With a shrug, I do what I normally do when Cade's pissed off. Pretend I care less than he does.

I pull a chair out from the table and kick my feet up onto it.

"Ew. No." Lena scolds as she comes into the library a few seconds later, Finn barely two steps behind.

Giving her a massive eye roll, I pull my feet off the table and scoot the rest of the way into the table.

"Grabbing my computer and tablet," Henri calls over her shoulder before heading to her office.

I move to stand, but Finn shakes his head and steps back out into the hall. *Well, there goes the hope that this is about anything other than me.*

My handler, Kyle, Cade's personal assistant, Meaghan, and two of Henri's assistants file in, and Henri brings up the rear.

Cade locks his gaze on me before he growls, "When the fuck were you going to tell me?"

"Depends on what we're talking about." I go on the passive defense.

"First of all, you have people openly threatening you online. Second, that you're buying pregnancy tests." He doesn't cast Henri a sideways glance, but his muscles twitch like he wants to.

"First, that's news to me." I pause because my throat is scratchy as I swallow a growl. "Second, when it became your business."

"Henri, how did we miss the death threats?" Cade's voice and gaze aren't any softer when he turns and speaks to her.

How dare he! My wolf rises at the way Cade is glaring at her.

I snarl at him, standing up from the table, my wolf ready to snap. "Don't you fucking take that tone with her."

The Leviathan rises in Cade's eyes, and the look stalls my wolf, but it doesn't curb my anger.

We could beat the piss out of him. My wolf doesn't deny the fact that we'd probably lose, but the point would be made.

Cade is calculating. He looks between me and Henri before he softens and gives a nod.

"Apologize," I growl at him.

"Fuck, if I knew you'd be this . . ." He laughs, fizzling off some of his tension.

It's not funny, but maybe I'm being too sensitive.

He looks past me. "Henri, I'm sorry. You weren't here when the death threats came in. You don't deserve that. I'll do better."

"Accepted." Henri's voice is small.

I take my seat next to her and place my hand on her thigh.

She scrutinizes her staff, looking for an answer. Specifically, Kyle, and he crumples under her gaze.

He stammers, "Well . . . I was . . . You see . . . When you were . . ."

Cade's gaze locks on him.

Poor bastard doesn't stand a chance.

With a hard swallow, Kyle pulls at the collar of his shirt and manages to get words out. "I assumed they would stop because

Deacon's been out of the media for a while. Given Ansel's issues, the threats against Deacon seemed like small potatoes."

"Finn." Cade doesn't bother looking at his Second. "Tell Magnus I appreciate his assistance."

"My pleasure." Finn nods.

Lena and Finn came back from Ireland after her wedding five months ago, both sporting new black leather jackets. So it's not a surprise that Cade and Magnus have struck some kind of deal that's about to cover my social media manager's issue.

The threat is going to end up terminated or, at a minimum, wishing they had been.

Since I've been kept out of the dark, I'm trying to piece together everything at once. Death threats against me. Magnus's involvement in resolving them. The pregnancy test pictures leaked on the internet.

"Going forward." Cade draws a deep breath and lets it out, calming himself down like he would instruct Thalia. "Let's assume there is no such thing as a small death threat. I want it all logged. If you do not know how to log one, please ask for assistance."

CHAPTER 79

HENRI

THE MEETING COMES TO AN END, and Deacon goes with Finn to learn more about the threats, but I'm pulled into Cade's office for a one-on-one.

"Henri, please," he urges me as he takes a seat in one of the soft chairs in front of the fireplace. "I'm just checking in with you. No one here is in trouble."

I sit down and try to relax, but I'm too on edge.

"Call Deacon?" Cade suggests. "We don't have to talk until he's here if you're stressed."

The door opens before I can press call. Deacon comes over and sits on the floor in front of my chair without a word, his shoulders pressing against my legs. A blanket of peace falls over me, reducing the panic from the roar of a crowd to a dull whisper of worries.

"I am sorry I reacted the way I did to the news that came out this morning." Cade apologizes.

I feel my jaw drop at his opening statement to the conversation. It's not that Cade doesn't apologize. He's a good leader, but I felt guilty for everything.

"It was a clusterfuck of information. I am sorry that I did not behave like a good team leader." Cade hangs his head for a moment but draws it back up to me. "I'm so excited for the two of you, and anything that takes away from that happiness feels like a personal attack against two of my favorite people."

"I got a promotion." Deacon laughs, breaking the tension.

"I accept your apology." Tears well up in my eyes, and I brush them away quickly. "It's a lot at once."

"The good news is that the death threats are localized to Deacon. No one is currently bringing your name into the threats, but I'm still increasing your security as well." Cade reassures us both.

"The headlines all just ask about Deacon buying the tests." I agree, nodding. "It doesn't seem like they've connected us at all."

"Oh, I'm firing Kyle," Cade adds, and it feels random. "He's creating a gap in your team, and I'm having Michael look into him. But The Leviathan has some opinions, and I'm trying to trust his instincts more."

"Can I be the one to fire him?" Deacon volunteers a little too excitedly.

I run my fingers through his hair, and he rumbles, relaxing against me.

"No." Cade shakes his head. "You can be there, but I can't let you fire him."

"I'm sorry everything is so messy. I'll get it resolved as soon as possible." I start back on the defensive. A to-do list is forming in my head and getting longer by the second.

Cade laughs. "No. You and Deacon take some downtime. Figure out a game plan for yourselves. I'll prioritize the workload and send you anything I can't have covered relating to PR. Meaghan already has a list of things she's taking care of." He sits straighter in his chair. "I should have done it a long time ago. This year we've been in survival mode, and it's time we changed that."

"Are we good?" Deacon eyes his older brother, and a silent moment passes between them.

They're communicating on that wolfish-brotherly level that I haven't come to understand yet.

"Yeah. Whatever you're doing, it's doing something." Cade nods and runs his hand back through his hair. "Maybe we should run though? Recalibrate? With three Alpha males in one house, we're bound to have hiccups."

"Let us talk to Ms. Gertie, and then we can head out?" Deacon looks up at me over his shoulder with a goofy grin.

"Let's see Ms. Gertie, but you two run without me. I've gotta get some work done. My boss might get mad." I joke, pushing just a little bit on whatever new relationship I'm forming with Cade.

"Fuck, Henri. Make me sound like an asshole or something." Cade winces.

"Or something." Deacon mimics getting to his feet. He offers his hand out to me.

Leaving Cade's office, I feel both one hundred pounds lighter and one hundred pounds heavier. I've swapped all my fears and stresses. But we come out to the kitchen where Ms. Gertie is making snickerdoodles.

"Good Lord, don't you two look like you've been through the wringer." Uncharacteristically, Ms. Gertie isn't smiling at us. She looks increasingly upset the longer she looks at us. "What's this nonsense about me moving up to the house?"

"Yeah. There've been some death threats against me. I'm not the fondest of my own life, but if someone hurt you or Henri, to get to me, I wouldn't forgive myself. I would like you to stay here in the guest suites, where we have the most security, until it's been handled. Two weeks tops." Deacon assures her, giving her a hug and a peck on her forehead.

"I'm not missin' church," she starts. The more she talks, the sterner her voice gets. "Or bridge."

"Why don't you invite the bridge ladies here? We'll host at the main house in the dining room. Lunch, desserts, snacks, the whole nine yards. We can show them just how highfalutin you are." Deacon charms her so easily. "And I'll get you to church on time with a handsome young wolf to escort you. Make it all fancy and formal."

"Mm-hmm." Ms. Gertie shakes her head, scowling, but the light in her eyes says it's all for show. "I don't like it, but I'll allow it."

"Thank you, Ms. Gertie." He smiles at her, and then she cracks, giving him a little grin.

"When were you two gonna tell me I'm expecting grandbabies?" She raises an eyebrow, scolding Deacon.

"Well, the plan was Friday at dinner, but it seems social media beat me to it." Deacon hangs his head. "You're gonna be a grandma."

She smiles from ear to ear and looks at me. "If that's okay with you, dear?"

"Of course it is. You're family." I return her smile.

It's surreal. There's still this little bit of dread inside me. I'm terrified, but it's not the same scared I had before. Excitement laces the negative feelings, and they don't seem as bad.

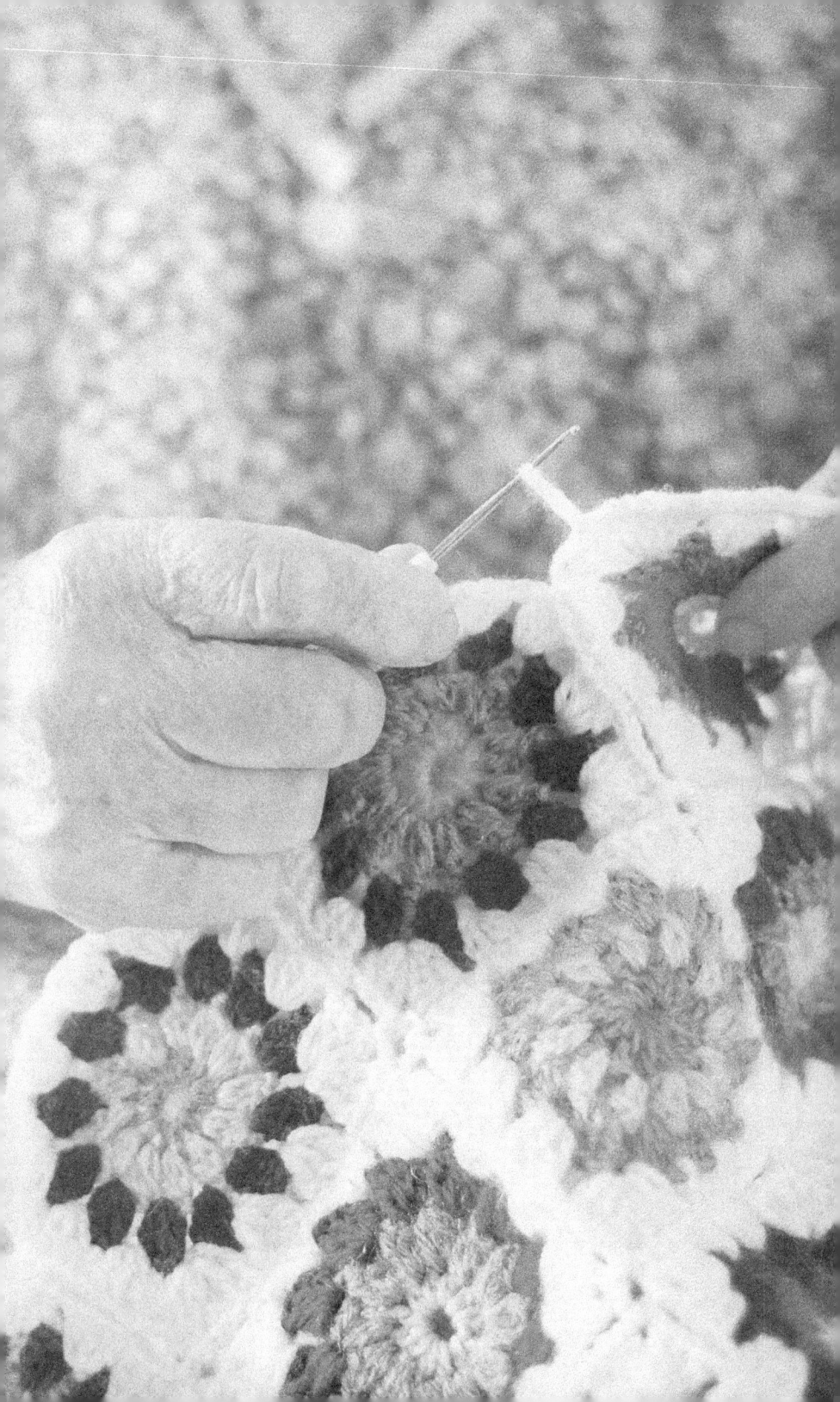

CHAPTER 80
HENRI

I'm getting a cup of tea and a sandwich from the fridge in the kitchen an hour later when snarls erupt outside. I freeze.

My wolf instantly comes forward, ready to protect me, her hackles raising.

Finn comes down the hall at a brisk clip and goes right out onto the deck. His quick movements send shivers up my spine.

Abandoning my lunch and with a more formidable wolf to lead the way, I follow Finn out onto the deck over to the rail.

The Leviathan squares off with the dusty white and cream wolf I know so well as Deacon. It looks brutal, and the noise coming from them only increases. I saw the fight between Finn and Deacon when Finn took Second. But The Leviathan is supposed to be unbeatable. Why would Deacon go up against him?

My words come out at a whisper. "What? No."

"Henri." Finn tries to pull my attention from the fight, but I can't look away.

My fingers squeeze the deck rail.

"They're playing. It's not even all that vicious. They're just being loud. See?" Finn points down to them. "Cade's not even biting him, just making contact, teeth to fur."

I watch more carefully, dismissing the sounds. There aren't any speckles of blood tarnishing Deacon's mostly white coat. The Leviathan stops, sneezing after getting a mouth full of fur, and Deacon stops circling to roll on the grass, seemingly scratching his back.

When Deacon gets up, Cade presses against him, and they head to the changing room.

"The boys needed this before it turned into a full-on brawl between them, with the two of them at odds and Deacon's wolf coming into himself. This letting off steam brings them to a better understanding of who they are now together." Finn pushes his shoulder against mine. "I know it seems like a lot all at once, and I don't have Dinah's gift to speak so definitely, but I've seen a lot of good men, like Deacon, either sort their shit or fail. And Deacon's not in the latter category."

"He's struggling." I worry my finger on the wood of the deck rail, looking at where the boys were play fighting a moment ago.

"Struggling is a part of the life experience. There's no way to truly stop it, despite how much we want to protect our loved ones from it. There's always something we need to fight through." Finn's words of wisdom match the worry I've been having. Life never gets easier.

The brothers climb the stairs to the deck, having dressed in the changing area down below, talking quietly between themselves.

As they crest the top step, Cade ruffles Deacon's hair and speaks intentionally at a volume to be heard. "Go hang out with your mate. I'm going to make Finn really pissed off about a whole bunch of things so that he and Lena can both be crabby today."

"Fan-fucking-tastic," Finn grumbles sarcastically.

Deacon offers his hand out to me. "Whatcha workin' on, and can I convince you to play hooky with me instead?"

"I'm setting up some new meeting schedules. There are conferences that, despite the changes with Ansel —" I cut myself off. "I can't play hooky, but I can take a lunch break, and then you can hang out in my office."

"Deal." He kisses the top of my head sweetly. "Let me go get cleaned up, and then we'll eat?"

Nightshade
Atropa belladonna.

MAY

CHAPTER 81

DEACON

IT TOOK PRACTICALLY every trick in the book to get myself out of the house without Henri. And it wasn't just Henri I had to lie to. The ends justify the means, so it'll probably be fine.

We're going home tonight. My wolf argues with me for the fifteenth time.

Yes. We're going home tonight. I reassure him, hoping I'm still not lying to him, but he's behaving, and I haven't seen too many people who haven't been real, according to Michael.

"This it?" Michael Tate, Cade's chief security officer for Corinth Security, asks, looking at the brick-front Cape Cod home we pulled up in front of.

"Numbers match." I shrug.

"What's the plan?" Michael asks as he chambers a round in his gun.

"Fuck. What do you think we're here for?" I hiss, pushing the gun down. "You're nowhere near on my first list of people to bring with me when going to kill someone."

Michael rolls his eyes. "I know you haven't forgotten about the death threats against you. That meeting was just the beginning. I'm going nowhere without being locked and loaded."

I sigh. "Yeah. Yeah. You're not even human, so let's not pretend we're going to need the bullets." I open the car door and get out.

When I turn back, Michael's staring at me with a mix of awe and horror.

I fucking knew it.

Michael is out of the car in a flash and following me up to the house.

He doesn't bother calling my name to get me to come back. We're in the middle of nowhere, Ohio, on a school night after supper. It's not the most dangerous place in the world. He'll chill out.

But my nerves are shot for another reason. I ran the conversation through my head a thousand times, so all that's left is to ring the damn doorbell and have it in person.

I don't focus on anything other than the blue door as I walk up to it, the tunnel vision of the task at hand setting in.

The doorbell casing is a little worn, but I push it instead of knocking, giving it a chance to do its job.

"I've got it," a woman calls from in the house.

Through the frosted glass window, I can see a shape moving through the space toward the door.

"Hello?" The woman looks just like her picture. Dark hair, glasses, more avian face than Henri's rounder one. No one would mistake them as biological family. "Can I help you?"

"Are you Paulina Greene?" I ask, trying to keep myself standing upright.

I'm not normally great with parents. I'm the guy you take home to scare Mom and Dad. No conversation I've had with parents in person has ever gone well. This would have been easier on the phone.

"I am." She eyes me and then leans to see Michael standing a few feet behind me before calling out, her voice pitching with fear. "Frank?"

"Coming," Frank, presumably, shouts back.

Rather than repeat myself, I wait for him to come to stand beside her.

"Oh, hello." He eyes me suspiciously. Which isn't even fair because I purposefully didn't wear all black because 'it would look like I was here for bad news.'

"My name is James Deacon Alden of The Ardelean Bloodline." I shuffle to the side. "This is Michael Tate of Corinth Security. We're here to talk with you about your adopted daughter, Henri."

"Daughter," Paulina says sharply. "We adopted her, yes, but she is our daughter."

I smile. I like her already.

"Is she okay?" Frank is quick to ask.

"She's doing quite well." This is as far as the conversation in my head really went in the form of details. I was hoping they'd ask some questions to guide it, but I'm still standing awkwardly on their front stoop. "She asked me to come speak with you."

CHAPTER 82
HENRI

I MISSED NOT DOING this regularly, coordinating meetings and talking events. Being at the heart of showing humans all the best parts of wolves and our impact on society became a mission I didn't even realize I'd had.

It's been good to get back out with the Ardeleans for positive public appearances, even with a reduced schedule over the past couple weeks.

I miss not being right at Deacon's side all the time, but as much as Kyle was a pain in my ass, he was a warm body, without which I wasn't able to attend the wolf's induction into the Rock N Roll Hall of fame with Deacon in Ohio because I had to handle events here.

He got in late last night, and we only had a few minutes to catch up before we collapsed into bed. My wolf is on edge without him, and she isn't settling with the promise that we're catching up with him after this discussion panel with Finn and Lena on the next steps with the lab.

Soon. We'll see him soon. I try to settle her.

My phone vibrates, and it instantly distracts me. One thing

that has massively changed is the difficulty to schedule a meeting with heads of state. *Please be the governor's office.*

I tap my security detail on the arm and indicate to my phone. He nods and steps out of the convention center into the hallway with me. We walk a ways down the corridor to a more private area.

I slide the green circle to answer. "Hello?"

"Hello, Henri," Nathan answers, but it's like I'm hearing him in surround sound, as though he's nearby.

A grunt sounds behind me, and as I turn, a scream lodges in my throat. My security detail is lying on the floor, one of Nathan's friends squatting over him.

Arms wrap around me from behind, and I don't need to look to know who they belong to. Nathan's familiar scent floods my nose.

No, my wolf snaps.

I fight hard, drawing on her strength to push against Nathan. But he only squeezes me tighter.

"If you don't want to get hurt, you need to stay quiet," he whispers in my ear.

Nathan's friend pulls my phone out of my hand and drops it next to the security agent.

"Scream and we'll kill you." Nathan's friend threatens me.

"They'll notice I'm missing," I warn them. *Fuck. Fuck. Fuck.*

I struggle harder against Nathan, but it doesn't do me any good. He's so much larger and stronger than me.

I try to shift to get away, but fear overwhelms any other thoughts or feelings. My wolf is there, but she won't crack the surface. I squeeze my eyes shut, focusing on her, but I can't take her form.

Nathan grips my arm and neck. He drags me down the hallway, walking backward, and then turns us, forcing me out into a corridor. He shoves me against the wall, and my head connects with it face first, rattling my brain with the force.

"You had to go and be a fuckin' slut." Nathan's voice cuts in through the ringing in my ears.

Disoriented, I struggle against him the best I can, but it's futile.

He drags me down the quiet hallway with me held to his side. Neck bent at an odd angle. Shoulder contorted in another. My feet stumble, trying to get purchase on the ground.

"Hel —"

Nathan removes his hand from my neck to put it over my mouth. "Don't. I'll kill you."

With his hand covering my mouth, it pushes up against my nostrils, cutting off my air entirely. I'm quickly losing energy from the lack of oxygen.

No. I can't die. I force my jaw down against his hand, sucking in a breath, prolonging what feels like the inevitable as blackness creeps in at the corners of my vision.

I'm thrown up against another wall — no, a door. The wood is different from the wallpaper. He pushes the central bar to open the latch, and I fall forward. Lightheaded, I get my hands out in front of me to catch myself.

As quickly as I can, I crawl to get away from him and attempt to push myself up to my feet.

Run. My wolf urges.

Nathan's hand wraps around my ankle, pulling me back to him. The low-pile carpet burns against my palms.

I yelp loudly.

Shift dammit! I scream in my head.

"You went and got yourself knocked up by some asshole. I wasn't good enough for you, Henri?" Nathan's foot connects with my stomach.

I curl in on myself with the impact.

Everything hurts. I can't breathe. I try to gasp for air, but my lungs refuse to cooperate. I can't hear anything over my pulse pounding in my ears and the panicked screams to *survive* in my brain.

When I gasp and finally fill my lungs, he lands another blow to my chest, but it's weaker, and I'm still able to draw ragged breaths.

"You're a fucking whore, Henri." Nathan laughs at me. He grabs my hair at the roots, pulling me up to almost sitting from where I'd been prone on the floor. "That's someone who gets paid to fuck. You've always said 'he's my employer.' Yeah, because he's your fuckin' pimp. Letting him fuck you while you get paid for it. That's disgusting."

I don't know what to do. Arguing with him has only escalated things in the past, and I'd hate to even imagine what an escalation from this would look like. Begging seems like what he wants.

My breaths are coming fast, and tremors are taking over my body as my fight-or-flight response doesn't know what to do.

Every conversation that Cade and Thalia have ever had in passing about hostage situations and negotiations goes out the window. Safety briefs with Finn are completely forgotten. My wolf isn't coming to save me.

Tears, however, pour from my eyes.

"You got off your heat pills for him. Bet you fuckin' couldn't wait to screw him," Nathan spits, dragging me by my hair along the ground.

I kick out at his leg, trying to trip him. When that doesn't work because I barely have any strength left, I dig my fingernails into his forearm.

"Fuck!" Nathan hisses, letting go of my hair.

My reprieve doesn't last long.

He grabs my arm, and his foot lands square in my ribs. I feel the crack after I hear it, but I can't get the scream out of my chest.

Through bleary eyes, I can just make out Nathan, but I don't miss the knife in his hand. Backpedaling on the floor, I try again to get away from him.

Pain shoots up my arm, through and across my chest, and I force myself to keep moving. But I'm no match for him.

"Should destroy you for cheating on me." Nathan pulls me back to him, my arms dragging on the floor.

I gasp and try to scream, but he's on top of me, and the pain is taking my breath away.

I've never felt something like this. But this must be where they get the term stabbing pain from.

Keep fighting, my wolf encourages.

Deacon's going to be crushed.

I keep trying to push him off me, but the thick, heavy scent of blood tells me it's hopeless. I'm going to die here like this.

Poor Deacon.

CHAPTER 83
DEACON

MORNINGS ARE ROUGH. It's like the ancestors know I'm still in that twilight between sleep and wakefulness, and it's those times when they sneak in. I feel like they're kicking my ass for being able to tune them out now with the help of my wolf.

Add in jet lag for the first time in my life, and it took me twice as long to remember what it's like to be alive.

Thirty minutes later than I wanted, I finally managed to wade through the sludge of waking up. After regaining my focus and getting more in tune with my wolf, I got on the road. Henri, Finn, and Lena are already in town doing Lena and Finn's first public appearance post Lena's heat and since having returned from Ansel's.

I didn't like letting Henri go without me, but the threats have lessened and localized strictly on me. No one even seems to care Henri exists outside of the fact that she's my mate. So, it's safe. Between Corinth Security and the hotel staff, she should be fine.

It doesn't feel fine, and I keep catching myself speeding. Our bond has been growing, but it's not so instantaneous like

Finn and Lena's or Cade and Thalia's, which is to be expected since my wolf is almost but not quite settled.

It's just that I feel fear.

This straight stretch of road is notorious for a police officer sitting in wait, and driving Lena's red SUV isn't worth the hassle of getting a speeding ticket.

It's nerves from dealing with Finn and Lena. She's fine.

I glance down at the dash to check my speed before setting the cruise control.

When I pull my eyes back to the road, someone is standing in the middle of the lane.

They weren't there a second ago, were they?

They're far too close.

I slam on the brake as hard as I can.

When I turn the wheel to divert, the SUV lurches.

Tires and brakes squeal loudly.

The vehicle fishtails, and I correct, but not fast enough.

Lena's going to kill me.

MY HEAD IS KILLING ME. Literally killing me. Swear to any fucking deity-like entity Ezra has studied and can talk to you about that this is the end of me.

There are voices and flashing lights beyond my eyelids. The stereo is still blaring in the car.

"Hey, can you hear me?" someone asks, and I open my eyes.

"Yeah, are you dead?" I squint at him. *Why is he upside . . . nope. I'm upside down.*

"No. You're not dead either." He assures me.

Fantastic.

"I'm going to lay this sheeting down, and we're going to get you out of here." They speak with that calm voice every emergency responder uses.

"No." I sigh. *Cade's never gonna fucking believe I was sober and did this.* "Don't waste the sheeting. I'm a wolf. Just fuckin' move."

"You could still be severely injured. A spinal cord injury could be aggravated. We'll help you." He tries to explain, his panic evident that I might hurt myself and he'll get in trouble.

"If you insist," I groan.

I pull my numb and tingly arm off the ground next to me and reach over, turning off the stereo. "Better."

It takes them twenty minutes to do what I'd have done on my own in two.

Out of the SUV and on the ground, I see Cade and Thalia. Their vastly different expressions further highlight the differences between them.

Thalia's eyes are wide, and her hands cover her mouth. Cade, however, wears his sweet disappointment in his pursed lips and furrowed brow. *Fan-fucking-tastic.*

I let the EMT check my pulse and blood pressure. But right about when he wants to cut my clothes off for further evaluation, I'm done playing patient. I sit up to a cacophony of objections from the three EMTs around me.

"Gentlemen, I appreciate it, but I'm still wolf, and I'm still good." I spring up to my feet and shake my T-shirt.

Shards of automotive glass plink off it and my pants when I dust them off.

"You're denying medical attention?" One of the EMTs finally officially clarifies.

"I am completely denying medical attention. Don't touch me." I nod with my words before adding, "Do not resuscitate."

The EMT in charge waves the cops over toward us.

A sinking feeling hits my stomach as the reason for the accident comes back.

He was real. I hit someone with the SUV.

I turn to look at the front end, but having ended up on its roof, the whole thing has become a bit too dented to tell. I don't smell blood though.

There'd be blood, right?

I look to Cade, who runs his hand back through his hair.

Am I really going to jail? I really killed someone. The irony doesn't escape me. *It was on accident. This time. Fuck.*

"Want to tell us what happened?" Cop number one gestures to the totaled vehicle.

Staying silent doesn't seem to be an option. "Saw something in the road. I tried to brake. Lost control."

"What did you see?" The cop pulls out a pad of paper and a pencil from one of his various pockets.

"I can't be sure." *Admit nothing.* I shake my head. "It all happened so fast."

"We'd like to run a breathalyzer," the cop informs me.

It's expected, so I follow him to have it administered.

My hip hurts, and there's a hitch in my step. I try to ignore the pain enough to not limp, but it doesn't go unnoticed.

One of the EMT guys interjects. "We should really have that looked at."

"It'll get looked at later, I promise." I lie, waving him off.

From my periphery, I can see a tow truck lumbering down the road, lights flashing.

Compliance is what has kept wolves alive since they were outed to the public. I give no one any reason to be suspicious of me. But it doesn't stop my hair from rising on the back of my neck. I'm 'legally' and 'technically' Cade's problem after the legislation he pushed through during Ansel's trial. But I could totally see him being mad enough to let them take me to county for the night to teach me a lesson.

The cops make me blow into three different breathalyzers. They all come up exactly the same: 0.00, and no one knows how to handle it.

"What did I hit?" I ask Cade under my breath when the cops walk away to have another meeting among themselves.

"Nothing." Cade shakes his head. "It literally just looks like you were driving too fast and lost control of the vehicle. Which, we thought for sure you'd be wasted."

"I made a promise. I'm keeping it. Just like I keep all the other ones," I tell him, looking down at my scuffed-up boots. I shuffle, giving my back to the cops to protect our privacy in the conversation. Raising my eyes back to meet him, I hold my older brother's gaze. "Cade, I saw someone in the road. Plain as day. Came out of nowhere. He seemed so real."

"No one has perfect control of their gift, Deacon. If you're saying you saw something, then that's what happened. There's no body, no witnesses, dashcam was clear," Cade whispers but then starts walking away. "Doesn't matter. We've gotta go."

"Ready to go?" a state trooper shouts.

"Well, okay then." Obediently I follow Cade. "Am I getting arrested anyway?"

"No," Cade snaps at me.

Granted, I just destroyed an SUV and caused quite a bit of a scene.

"If it matters, I'm sorry. It's not like I was trying for this." I keep following him.

Thalia climbs into the back seat of the SUV rather than the front. She doesn't even say she's glad I'm okay.

I stop walking, and panic sets in. "Cade, what aren't you saying?"

"Get in the SUV." Cade orders, the command of The Leviathan coming through.

I hold my ground for as long as I can, but even with my wolf coming to full power, it's not like I can overrule the law of wolves.

Getting into the SUV with my bum leg is difficult, and the pain shoots up through my back. Gonna need to try and get it back into alignment later. *If there is a later.*

The State Trooper lights and sirens start, and Cade presses a button and lights up the after-market lighting on the SUV. We're also flanked by cop cars in front of and behind us.

"What's going on?" I demand.

Cade is silent, so I look in the back at Thalia.

She caves. "Henri's been hurt."

My world breaks apart.

It feels like my chest hollows out with guilt for not toughing it out this morning. The fear and anger, everything shatters like a star crumpling under the gravity of the situation, a blackhole destroying it all.

"No." I pat my pockets. *It's not going to be true. It won't be. I'll just call her.* My phone isn't there. "Cade?"

"All I know is that they got her to the U of M. Doctor Thorpe and Doctor Bowes are there with her now." Cade keeps focused on the road. "We were chasing you down to try and get you to the clinic when we found you in that accident."

"I thought we sent her with security?" I snap at him, and the darkness starts driving my thoughts. *I am going to slaughter them all.*

Ever cool under pressure, Cade keeps his voice neutral. "They killed her security agent. Looks like they used a taser and then dragged him out into the alleyway and put a bullet through his head."

"So, it was Nathan?" I bang my hand against the passenger window.

"We don't have proof of that. Security tapes haven't come through," Cade answers.

Cars move into the ditch as we pass at top speeds with the State Troopers.

Thalia's phone rings in the back seat. She answers, her voice breaking with sadness and fear. "Hey, Finn."

She's finally turned her phone down to wolf volumes, so I can't hear Finn speaking.

"Okay, I'll let him know. Yeah. He's okay. Little fender bender." Thalia meets my eye and hangs up the phone. "Henri's in surgery. Vital signs are all strong."

It'll kill me if she dies. It'll kill me, and none of them can even say anything about it. *I don't survive not having Henri.*

CHAPTER 84

DEACON

LAST SEPTEMBER

LENA LOOKS so fucking small in that hospital bed. Dinah swears it's not Finn O'Leary's fault. But that doesn't mean I trust him, yet.

But at least, here at her bedside, the ancestors I'm familiar with leave me alone. They're respectful enough to let me focus on my little sister.

Lena stirs and rolls to face me. She's not all there. The painkillers they're giving her to keep her wolf under are leaving her in a hazy state. It's been two days, and while Dinah says not to worry too much, I'm not sold on giving up my fear for her life.

Dinah's been wrong. Ansel says things change.

She extends her hand out to me, flopping it over, and I place mine in hers. Lena tries to squeeze, but her fingers barely curl before she's out again.

Cade comes back from outside and sits in the other chair on the opposite side of the room. He scrubs his hand back through his hair and shakes his head. "Thoughts on Finn?"

Tell him the truth, my wolf demands.

I don't. I lie through my teeth. "I think he loves her, and that's all that matters."

My brother may own equal shares in a security company, and they may be excellent at what they do, mostly. But I'm doing digging of my own before I give any final judgments on Finn O'Leary O'Brien.

The underworld of society is a dark and scary place, but anyone who can learn to thrive in it has a past and a history. I need to know if the shadow is as untouchable as I think he is.

"Fair enough," Cade concedes. "If you want to go, I'll stay."

But Lena wanted to hold my hand, so I'll stay until it's unbearable. More than unbearable. As always, I'm staying for her.

I motion to where Lena and I are connected, hand in hand, and Cade understands. He goes back to looking at his phone.

He's working. He's always working. And I can't blame him for it. Shit's always been on his shoulders. He doesn't have to be in this alone. Finn is Lena's mate. He's an ex-Enforcer for the Irish mob. If Finn can't help keep Cade's life together, then I'll sober up. But the two of them have a lot in common, and you don't have to like your boss to do a good job.

Thirty minutes pass before Cade whispers, "Thoughts on Henri?"

Hearing her name brings a quickness to the beating of my heart. I force myself to keep my tone indifferent. "What about her?"

"She's a one-woman army, but I can't get a read on her. She's inconsistent. Hyper professional sometimes, and yet a little bit . . ." Cade searches for a word, pulling his eyes off his phone. "Softer others."

I think back to what she said at the wedding about her fear

of hiring staff. 'What if they find out I don't know as much as they do?' *Secrets are meant to be kept.*

"She's young, and let's be real, putting up with your ass every day and the mood swings? Hardly fair. We can't all be Thalia, whose biggest personality flaw is getting hangry."

Cade raises an eyebrow at me.

It wasn't the most polite observation.

"What I'm saying is, you ask a lot of her. She's bound to get overwhelmed." I draw a breath.

"I've off —" Cade tries to cut in.

"Offered to let her hire her staff." I keep talking over him. "I get it. But Henri is young. Has she ever had to hire someone before? You're doing that thing you do when you expect everyone to have the same life skills as you. I'm just saying. Maybe help her form a team rather than offer her the world."

Cade waits to be sure I'm done before he speaks. "You're right. I've got to find a way to make her life easier, not harder. And asking her to take a break from what she's doing to duplicate herself isn't realistic."

"See, and everyone thinks you're just a pretty face." I laugh thinking about the engagement announcement on social media, where the comments section was hundreds of women devastated by the fact that Cade Alden is off the market.

He runs his hand back through his hair. "Fuck, had that conversation with Thalia this morning. I thought when I got married, we'd see less crazed women trying to throw themselves at me."

"I know, you'd think her name written on your forearm would be enough for people to get it." I laugh almost too loudly.

Lena groans.

Cade covers his mouth and tries not to let a sound escape

as he laughs. When he has control of himself, he replies, "If only."

"But seriously, don't try to get Henri to take herself away from the shit she's already doing to try and figure out how to hire and form a team. Especially since her boss is literally a tactical team lead, who has built how many teams?" I growl, but Lena's groan reminds me that she's there, between us, and vulnerable.

"Too many to count." Cade nods. "You know, when I can pin you down, you're a great Second."

"Thanks," I answer, not knowing what else to say.

"Oh, look, one of you's lying around. Get up, lazy bones, we've got work to do," a man I don't recognize calls from the doorway.

He's dressed in a very stereotypical 1980s power suit. I look to Cade to see if he's reacted to the intrusion.

None the wiser, I try to ignore him and go back to looking at Lena's hand in mine.

She murmurs in her sleep and slowly wakes. "Hey."

I can tell she's not all there, the drugs holding on to her brain. She's in a fog, and she won't remember, but I take the opportunity to comfort her anyway. "Hey. You're doing great. How are you feeling?"

Lena blinks and then squints at me. "I'm fine."

She pulls her hand from me and shuffles in bed. She hisses in pain before drawing a few deep breaths.

"I love you," she whispers.

"I know Lena. It's okay. Get lots of rest, okay?" I curl my fingers, flexing them from their fatigued state.

"Okay," she grumbles.

It takes a few minutes, but then the deep breathing of sleep returns.

This is the longest Cade and I have spent in the same room in a long time. I haven't been keeping tabs on his office as well as I normally do, but I've been distracted. Henri, Thalia, Lena. It's one after another, and well, it's a job I don't mind, but it doesn't make it less time consuming.

CHAPTER 85
DEACON

I⊤'s ⊤oo much of the same. My life is one cycle after another. Sitting here in this same temporary hospital room, I'm facing the mortality of the people I love all over again. Cade, Ezra, Dinah, Thalia, Lena, Ansel, and now Henri. Too many people have almost been taken from me. My own mortality isn't an issue, but how could I picture a world separate from Henri?

Without any of my loved ones, the sun wouldn't dare shine, the wind wouldn't blow, and the rain wouldn't even bother trying to fall from the sky.

Underneath my fear for Henri's life, rage is brewing, but Doctor Thorpe said the surgery was completely necessary. Without medical intervention, Henri would have died.

We're wolves.

We're damn near indestructible.

But Nathan dented Henri.

No, not dented, he broke her.

"Deacon." Cade keeps his voice down.

I shake my head, unable to move from her side. It's not like with Lena. Nobody who could stay here with her loves her anywhere near as much as I do. "If I walk out of this room, she'll be alone."

My eyes are locked on Henri, and I flinch when a hand lands on my shoulder.

A quick glance tells me the small, delicate fingers belong to Lena. "Go with Cade. I'll be here, and that means Finn won't be far away either."

I shake my head, and the stupid room is foggy with my tears.

"I know." Lena comes to stand partly in front of me but doesn't block my view of Henri. "You can't leave her alone because no one loves her as much as you do."

"It's annoying how much you know about me." I glare at her.

"Yes, well, years of your bullshit, and I've gotten pretty good at figuring you out." She squats down, putting her hand on mine, and looks up at me with the softness in her eyes that melts me every fucking time. "You and Cade need to talk."

When she tugs on my hand, I stand up and plant a kiss as softly as I can on the small portion of Henri's forehead that isn't bruised.

Get information from Cade. Then we'll go and kill the asshole, my wolf demands, and it brings to life the darkness that lurks inside me wanting bloodshed. The brewing rage deep in my consciousness stirred.

Cade, waiting in the hallway, inclines his head toward the other end of the hall. We walk past Finn, who leans against a wall, watching the hospital room with laser focus.

Down two hallways, we're at some sort of lab, and Dinah is looking at one of the computers.

With a quick glance around the room, I find a clock on the wall. It's after suppertime, so I guess that's enough time for her to get here.

"Thanks for coming." I give her a nod but focus back on Cade. The sooner I get done dealing with him, the faster I'm back at Henri's bedside.

"Of course." Dinah gives me a soft smile. "I'm starting to think, though, that emergencies are the only way this family gets together anymore."

"Hey," Cade argues, "I just saw you for New Year's."

"Ugh. Fine." Dinah rolls her eyes.

"Really, assholes? Not the time," I snap. "What do you want?"

Dinah clears her throat. "It's really early to say for sure. But Deacon, I want you to be prepared for the very real possibility that Henri miscarries."

As if the pain I'd felt before was child's play, the dark and heavy emotions awaken from shallow graves in my heart.

I put my hand over my mouth to silence myself. A scream, a sob, a string of curses and threats —no, promises — of bloodshed are all there waiting to escape. Demanding to be heard.

Nearly dead, lying in a hospital bed, and fighting to heal, she needs me to hold it together. Only one of us can fall apart at a time.

To fall apart and put myself back together again in whatever time she's slumbering is going to be the hardest part. My whole body feels like it's being pulled into this vacuum, and the weight of it pulls me under.

I blink when the room becomes completely unrecognizable through my tears. Neither Cade nor Dinah moves to comfort me, and that's okay because if someone touches me right now, I'm going to break apart.

I can't fall apart now. The thought is on repeat. *How many times in the last ten seconds have I thought that?*

Don't fall apart. Not right here. Not right now. Don't fall apart.

The intensity of the black hole is too much, and my hand falls away from my mouth.

That's when Cade wraps me in a hug. Dinah follows. It's a group hug.

Dinah steps over next to me and strokes my hair, and I know she, of all people, understands my loss on a cosmic level.

My knees buckle, and Cade slowly drops with me to the floor.

"He'll pay for this, Deacon." Dinah assures me. I lean into her legs. "All the imaginable things we can do, we will do."

The darkness that's bloomed in her over the past few years plays well with mine. But she keeps it contained since she got her pounds of flesh.

"I'll tell her." My voice is locked in a snarl, cracking under the strain.

It's the first words I manage but the only important words needing to be said.

Cade's phone vibrates, but he doesn't look at it. It stops but picks up again and again. "Fucking what else could go wrong today?"

He pulls it out of his pocket and looks at the screen. "God, she's got the worst timing." Cade answers his phone, the irritation biting at his words. "Yes, Revecca." He hands it to me. "It's for you."

I take it, confused by her calling Cade for me, until I remember the accident and the fact I don't know where my phone is. "Hello?"

"I'm so sorry." Revecca sounds sad.

"How the fuck do you know al —" I stop myself. "Finn or your gift?"

"Both," Revecca admits. "Are you holding up?"

"Only one of us can fall apart at a time." I get that thought out into the world, hoping once it's spoken, it'll leave my head.

That I'll be able to just be strong by speaking it into existence. But that doesn't stop it from ruminating. "I'll have to be stable for her when she wakes up."

"I understand." Revecca pauses. "If it's too overwhelming. I'll come and borrow your gift back. Please, Deacon, seeing you and your wolf hurt more . . . don't be too proud to ask for assistance."

"I hear you," I answer. "I love you too. Want to talk to the idiot?"

Cade rolls his eyes.

"No, I only called him because your phone did not seem to be available." She sighs. "Give him my kindest regards."

"Will do, speak later." I hang up before this can turn into a Midwest goodbye. "Revecca says you don't suck as much as she originally thought you did."

Dinah chuckles. "The more I see of her, the less she sucks than I originally thought."

It's not until I'm standing that I realized I got up off the ground, time and autopilot seemingly kicking in. "I need a few minutes. I'll just be in the courtyard. Shout if she wakes up?"

"I'd like to keep her under until tomorrow morning at the earliest." Dinah nods. "If you want to go home, change, grab some—"

My vehement head shaking convinces her to stop offering.

I walk away knowing they're worried about me. It's well placed.

Outside in the courtyard, I walk in erratic lines because I can't settle into a rhythm to pace. I force deep breaths into my lungs, begging them to stay expanded while my heart cries for sweet and utter silence.

My wolf is howling. Grief and rage run in mismatched patterns in my mind. The sun is finally beginning its descent, and soon, welcomed darkness will cover the night sky.

With one step, I ache being away from her, but in the next step, guilt tells me I should stay away.

Stay entirely away. Without you here, she wouldn't be in that bed. She wouldn't be near grieving the loss of our child.

Lena pokes her head out the door. "Don't yell at me. Cade, Thalia, and Finn are with her."

She holds her phone out to me, the red case glinting. "Call him."

I don't have to ask who she wants me to call. It's who I've always called.

The minute her little phone is in my hand, I debate pocketing it and ignoring her instructions. But I thumb open the screen using the biometric scanner that, for whatever reason, she wanted me to be able to use. His number is already queued up on the screen, so I hit call.

"Deacon," Ezra answers.

"Funny since I called from Lena's phone." I laugh, but it's humorless.

"Deductive reasoning." Ezra sighs. The other side of the line picks up frogs, nighttime birds, and insects. "Primary thought?"

"If I wasn't here, this wouldn't have happened in the first place." I flop down in two general motions, uncaring that the earth is hard when it breaks my fall.

"Try again, kid," Ezra tells me like there are more than a handful of years between us.

"Why does this fucking hurt so much?" The hot, angry tears are back. "It's not like it was even really a thing. It was weeks. It wasn't a lot more than some divided cells."

"Stop," Ezra growls. He draws a deep breath, and I follow his example. His words come with a relaxed candor, each one chosen with care. "We both do this. We forget that we're not immune to grief and loss because we can think past and

650

beyond it. You have been denied the opportunity to ever know this child. It's not like you can hear them or speak with them when they're gone, and that must be an incredibly difficult concession for you to have to make. Because as much as it sucks that the ancestors literally give you no peace, you're used to knowing that it's not goodbye."

He's right. While I've been lucky enough not to be haunted by the people who raised us and Robert, it's always been a possibility. Much like Morrigan's dad, I could try and find them.

Silence sits between us, and I don't even know what to say anymore.

My wolf hasn't stopped thrashing in my mind. My body being prone on the ground isn't suitable enough for him and his rage. "Fuck, I'd kill for a drink."

"You won't do that." Ezra takes a minute. "Just to remind you . . . If you weren't there, she'd be dead."

"If I weren't here, she wouldn't have pissed him off this badly," I counter.

Not one to let me win, Ezra is firm but controlled. "If you weren't there, he would have found another reason."

"You don't know that," I argue.

"As much as I'd love to agree that I can't know that." Ezra blows out a long exhale. "You won't ever convince me that Henri's abuser wasn't the same as Dinah's. We've lived through this before and came out thriving on the other side."

"What do I do, Ez?" I close my eyes, listening for some sort of divine answer.

He snorts. "What we always do, Deacon. You do what we always do."

"I've squandered my most recent idea," I admit with a snarl. "Stupid fucking Finn. Too chaotic good. It took him way too long to make a move. I won't wait though."

"Hey, what was it you wanted to talk to me about? A car?" He starts a cryptic conversation. "You were saying there was someone else who was interested in it?"

"Well, that would require me getting in contact with the buyer, but I suppose it's worth it." My wolf settles with those words.

Grace's news article and the knowledge from the morgue told a tale of abuse, death, and the covering up of a crime. But it wasn't a crime I had considered.

"Double-check and be sure the mechanic does good work. Wouldn't want you to buy a lemon," Ezra encourages.

Justice for both Grace and Hen.

"Alright." Having a plan keeps the thoughts of not being here at bay.

The wolf settles, accepting my willingness to right the wrong of the universe. His commitment to behaving stops the urge to put him under by any means necessary. It's a gentleman's agreement. Silent but effective.

CHAPTER 86

DEACON

DINAH KNEW what was going to happen and didn't even question when I requested that there be no way for Henri to know I was missing. Before allowing Finn and Lena to give me a ride home, I give her hand a soft squeeze, reassuring her, even on a subconscious level, that I'll return.

Hours later, after the normal dinnertime, when people start thinking about what to watch on television for the night, the pain of loss begins to fade. And the phrase seeing red becomes meaningful.

Nathan is a dead man. Pacing my room, I'm stuck debating the best way to kill him. Poison isn't brutal enough. Straight up stabbing leaves too much evidence. Gunshot is too quick, too traceable . . . kinda. Ezra has a point about the car. It's easy enough. But it's not satisfying.

It's all my fault. The guilt hammers a spike into my heart. *If I had just pulled my ass out of bed.* No, before that, if I had a single thought about the risk of pregnancy rather than the amazing fucking sex, we wouldn't have been in this mess to begin with.

Or if I had stolen someone else's pills. I could have . . .

Could have what? Stolen Dinah's pills and put her in this mess? That was my only other option.

I should have done something for her. Instead, I was selfish. I wanted to play perfect mate and have just one heat with her. It was selfish of me to put her in danger, and she's the one who paid for it.

You let him hurt our mate because you didn't kill him early enough. My wolf snarls at me like I'm not already having those same fucking thoughts.

I don't want Nathan to go down easy. I want to watch. It's not like killing the punk Brayden who went quietly, heart attack, a potassium overdose that will never be caught. It's metabolized and long gone. But it would be the least traceable. It would be the safest bet for getting in and out without getting caught.

Cade would be pissed if I got caught. He literally just settled shit for Ansel.

Sure, he made it so that if a human has an issue with a wolf, it goes to our laws to be dealt with, or if I'm arrested by a human police system, it would go back to our people. If I killed Nathan and was caught, well, the new laws would at least allow Ansel to bail me out and put me down. Fuck could just end it all efficiently.

Death could be quick.

How many people is too many people close to us dying of a heart attack before it's suspicious? Potassium is easy to get. Untraceable. *No. Can't make this at all traceable.*

Killing Nathan isn't like the wolves I hunted down who escaped the heartlessness of Dinah's wolf. The ones who Cade, Ansel, and Judah let live.

It's not like Ersilia and Gerad. Ansel was brutal in ending them, tearing the bodies to pieces.

No, this is a different kind of personal. This isn't for

someone else. I've killed to protect my family, at all costs. But this is for me. It's for Henri. It's so we can stop the pain of injustice.

I don't believe in happy life after death. You don't walk around with other people's ghosts and believe that in death, you could be with your loved ones.

"Deacon! Just the man I was looking for." An ancestor walks through my bedroom wall and right into my space.

Zachariah was an awful human being in life, and in death, I think he's worse.

"Go the fuck away." My patience is wearing thin. I can't handle dealing with anyone else's bullshit today.

I'd hoped when we moved from the country house in Wisconsin to the house in Minnesota, he wouldn't have followed. But maybe it's the antique Harley sitting down in the garage, half taken apart, that he's somehow anchored to, despite the fact he's never been a biker. Fuck, maybe it's one of Cade's classic cars.

Focus Deacon. I shake my head, ignoring Zachariah as he goes on and on and on about something.

"I'm just saying if you're going to kill that fucker, I'd be glad to help." Zachariah's words stop me from pacing.

"How? You're dead remember?" I look at the bottle of pills on my desk and then to him.

I've been trying to stay sober, but this interruption is not helping me get my thinking done.

"Well, not to self-incriminate but I do know a thing or two about framing someone for embezzlement." Zachariah adds another layer to the fucked-up life he led.

It's not a bad idea, but embezzlement wouldn't exactly land him in jail for life. But Finn's got people in prisons. Finn has lots of people in prisons.

Fucking kill him. My wolf begs for bloodshed. *You let him hurt our mate. We will be the one to kill him.*

"Appreciate the offer now fuck off," I growl at Zachariah.

My wolf banishes him away from me. The control is nice to have.

Through my bedroom window, daylight is breaking.

I don't have a plan. But he's dying tonight, before Henri even has a chance to know I was gone.

I've waited too long as it is. He should have been cold and dead long before now.

I grab my boots without the tread on the bottom and the keys to the sport bike, and head down the stairs.

Finn is standing at the bottom of the steps, keys in hand, with a mischievous smirk. "Let's go."

"No." I try to argue with him, hitting right where it's going to hurt him most. "Lena needs you."

He snorts. "You're planning on getting caught?"

I don't answer.

Finn smirks. "Didn't think so. Let's go."

His shoes are already on, and he grabs a plain black jacket that covers his chest holster.

"I'm guessing you've a plan?" I climb into the black SUV, wishing I was taking the bike I have keys for, but this might be more necessary.

"The bunnies came up with an excellent idea back when we first talked," he informs me. "I've been hanging on to it for you. Repayment."

"I didn't kill him for you." I shake my head. "Neither of you owe me anything."

"We're family, Deacon," Finn reminds me. "I've killed for a lot less for my family."

I accept his help, and a feeling hits me. Something other than hollow anger. I don't know what it is, and it's unsettling.

"Want to walk me through it?" I try to distract myself from

it as Finn drives us down the driveway and we're flagged through the front gates.

"Breaking and entering." Finn gives me the first bit — the obvious way into the house. "It's suicide by remorse. You can have your pick on deaths."

"I was seen threatening him," I remind Finn. "What if they look into it too far?"

"They won't," Finn assures me. "County coroner is in his early sixties and has a gambling problem. He and I had a nice chat. His wife wants to retire, but they're never going to be able to at the rate he loses money to bookies. I've gotten his debt wiped with the bookies, blocked them all from ever letting him place another bet, blacklisted him at every casino in the state. His wife got a hefty raise at the little distribution company she works at. In three years when they retire, an estranged relative is going to die and leave them a hefty sum of money."

"If there is a change of heart and he doesn't rule it suicide? Or the family pushes for a second opinion?" I start looking for loopholes in his plan.

"If there's a change of heart, well, debt of that size can just as easily be doubled with interest." Finn pauses, and an uncharacteristic smile teases his lips. "It also seems that the little clinic Nathan's been seen at has located some of his backdated medical records, stating how deeply disturbed he was. He's had suicidal ideations for the last two years. Punctuated by his mistreatment of Henri."

"What if they find an inconsistency with the way he died? Bullet not lining up, stool not right, strangulation versus breaking the hyoid?" I look for other reasons.

"Deacon," Finn scolds. "Not my first time."

Finn's quiet resolve is comforting. It's no wonder Lena says he's such a pain in her ass. He's thought of everything.

"Neighbors? What if someone sees us?" I think of the next thing.

Finn shakes his head. "It seems they've all had to go in to work early today for various meetings. Paid, of course, at double time."

"You're so sure no one is going to rat us out," I growl.

"Money talks." Finn assures me, settling into the drive. "Seeing the pictures of what he did to Henri talked louder."

A pit sinks in my stomach. I want to be mad at him for showing anyone what happened to Henri. For violating what happened to her and letting her be vulnerable to someone else. But he's not wrong about what that sort of image does to people. Especially when it's someone as sweet as she is.

"How the fuck did you set this up so fast?" I'm mystified at the speed with which Finn works.

"It's been in motion since the visit you and Cade paid to him at the gym. All it took was a few phone calls to dispatch the orders." Finn's planning and forethought are unnerving.

"Cops?" I ask, knowing at this point Finn's going to have a solution.

He sighs. "Chief of police isn't exactly squeaky clean. But he's not on my payroll. We didn't approach him, but I've got enough to make it go away if we need to."

"Cell phone tower pings?" I'm grasping at straws, and I know it.

"We're stopping at a diner a few miles up ahead. The bunnies have contacts there. We'll have been there this morning having coffee and food," Finn answers.

"GPS on this beast?"

"Doesn't work." Finn sighs. "Deacon, I love you. I love Henri, and I love your sister more than I love life. There is nothing I would do to jeopardize losing that."

The ease with which he says those words is alarming. Finn

does love everyone deeply, the loyalty there knowing no bounds.

I nod and relax into the seat. I wanted something more violent and to rip him limb from limb. But this will have to do.

"There is a plan B," Finn admits. "If this doesn't meet your needs."

I don't answer him, letting us get a few more miles down the road. He pulls into the diner parking lot and backs into a parking spot.

Before he turns off the engine, I ask, "What is it?"

"We turn him," Finn answers. "You take his car and follow me and him home. Then I or Cade, who did volunteer, turn him into a wolf. He's in too deep and is then subject to our laws."

Finn holds his hand out. I pull my phone out of my pocket and hand it to him.

"I'll be right back." Finn nods and takes the phones into the back door of the restaurant.

He's back in less than two minutes.

Behind the steering wheel, Finn gets us back on the road.

"You've an hour to decide."

I shake my head; his plan is good, but mine . . . it comes from beyond the grave. "I've got a better idea."

"This'll be good." Finn looks over at me.

I spend the next hour laying out my plan, the one I'd brewed in pieces over the last few months. In the quiet hours of the morning, when Henri was asleep, and the loud moments in my brain when I couldn't be with her. Then I add Ezra's suggestion, which makes it a near-perfect murder.

"Deacon, I say this with the utmost respect, but you're a twisted fuck." Finn laughs as he parks a block from Nathan's house.

It's in front of a park to avoid any potential security

systems or suspicion from a neighbor, even if Finn covered those bases.

"Thanks." There is no humor in the smile I give him. "Shall we?"

I've stalked Nathan plenty of times, but this time, my excitement is growing harder to contain.

Finn is at my back, letting me take the lead. If it weren't for being a wolf, I probably wouldn't even hear his footsteps on the ground. For a behemoth, he really does move like a shadow.

Casually I stroll up the sidewalk and right to the door. I lift the mat corner and pull the key out from underneath it.

"Christ, humans will do just about anything except keep themselves safe," Finn mutters.

I slide the key into the doorknob and unlock it. Using my shirt, I wipe my prints from the key and drop it back under the mat.

Finn twists the handle, the sleeve of his hooded sweatshirt covering his hand, and lets us in. "The hares will come for cleanup just to be safe."

The house is dark. But the blue glow of a TV spills into the hallway from the bedroom.

"Alright. That's it for me tonight, bitches. Gonna see if I can't get a booty call now that I know for sure that piece of wolf ass is out of the way."

Nathan almost sounds like he knows I'm here and is trying to infuriate me. The way he thinks he can talk about her and what he's done like it's nothing.

An office chair creaks and wheels roll against the floor. "I'll catch you tomorrow. We gotta get some more PRs."

Something is set down — on a desk or table? —and again, the chair objects, but this time as he stands from it.

Finn casually leans against the wall by the door, and I stand more toward the middle of the living room, just waiting and not for long.

The glow from the TV is cut off, and Nathan is plunged into darkness. It would be an advantage if humans were invading his home. If I'd given up my wolf even. But he's not, and I didn't. My eyes adjusted long ago.

He walks through the dark, down the hallway toward us, his phone screen illuminating his face but not the floor in front of him. He's within arm's reach before he even looks up and realizes he's not alone.

Through the dark, I reach out and grab his phone, pulling it out of his hand.

Nathan skitters backward toward the hallway from where he came. A loud high-pitched scream belts out from his lungs, much like one would associate with the first person who dies in a horror film. Fitting.

Finn flicks on the light.

Nathan is ghost white.

I start laughing. It's cruel and wicked, and I kind of like being able to laugh right now. Anger is still there, bubbling under the surface, right along with the pain of grief, but much like every time I've gotten to kill, the enjoyment comes from that dark spot on my soul.

"What the fuck are you doing in my house?" Nathan shouts, replacing his scream of fear with rage.

Passing Nathan's phone to Finn, I answer his question. "We've just come to kill you is all. Shouldn't take too long and then we'll be going."

Nathan steps forward from the hall he'd been trying to take refuge in. "You think, what? You can just break in here and kill me? Like no one's going to know? You're wolves. That doesn't make you untouchable. There are still laws."

My wolf hums. *Less politics. More murder.*

"Aww." Finn makes the soft mocking noise he's learned from Lena. "He's so stupid. I just texted all your buddies that you're hooking up with a new chick you just met. I then just texted all your hookups answering them with someone else's name. No one's going to be looking for you. We'd probably be able to torture you all night, and not a single person would know."

Nathan squares up with me and clenches his hands into fists.

"You don't want to do that." I casually point to his hand. "Listen, if you make this easy on us, I'll kill you quickly. You know why I'm here —"

"You're here because you're pissed off that I'm better than you." Nathan cuts me off with the most ridiculous statement ever.

Finn lets out a huff. "Is that so?"

Nathan charges forward toward me. He telegraphs his punch, allowing me to easily move around it and shove my knee up into his chest. Having the wind knocked out of him drops him straight to the floor.

"He's a heavy fuck." Finn looks down at Nathan gasping for air. "Slow too."

"Slow, dumb, and heavy." I list the obvious traits that comprise the worthless piece of shit.

Nathan, not quite recovered, scrambles to his feet. He tries to grab me around the middle, but Finn wraps his long arm around Nathan's neck.

I take the short trip to the garage, remembering seeing sporting equipment there while stalking Nathan. As much as I'd love to trust all of Finn's fail-safes, for tonight, some things should look like they're part of the final accident in all of this.

I grab a baseball bat from where it leans against the wall.

Finn has Nathan lifted by his neck so high off the ground

his feet are dangling, and he's on the verge of passing out. *Show off.*

Nathan kicks out and tries to tear through Finn's thick forearm.

When I return, Finn drops him, and Nathan crumples to a heap on the floor.

I don't waste time.

Approaching, I line up a golf-like swing with the baseball bat, striking him from his left shoulder across his chest. The metal reverberates in my hand, and he lets out a gasping scream of pain.

I let him recover, my darkness reveling in the way he's suffering.

Crouching down in front of him, I pat the aluminum bat against the palm of my hand. "Broken collarbone. Hurts like a bitch, doesn't it? You'll lose some of the range of motion in your shoulder if I did it right."

"We should check." Finn steps behind Nathan and fluidly yanks him to his feet by the wrist, pulling Nathan's arm above his head.

Another glorious scream.

"Should have brought my shooting muffs." Finn winces. "I didn't take him for a screaming little bitch."

"Why?" Nathan cries.

"I think the words you used were 'cheating whore.'" I line up another swing, letting the blunt force trauma break his shin. Then I quickly follow it up with a knock into his ribs.

He's sniveling and blowing snot bubbles already.

Finn drops him to the floor.

"Help!" Nathan tries.

Finn bribing the neighbors, brilliant.

The darkness rises, and I quote it while it mocks him. "Help me! Oh, help me! I'm not as big and bad as I thought I was. Help! I can beat a woman but can't take the same torment."

Pathetic as he is, Nathan swipes out at me, still trying to throw a punch with his good arm.

"You know, I thought I'd enjoy torturing you more." I sigh watching him struggle. "I thought torturing you and making you suffer would make me feel better about everything you've taken from me. Everything you've taken from my mate and from Grace."

Nathan's eyes shoot up to me. "I didn't —"

"Don't deny it, Nathan. You're insufferable enough without being a delusional liar." Grabbing hold of Nathan's hand, I explain, "But I don't feel anything. Torturing you isn't bringing me joy."

I push his hand down against the floor. He tries to take it back, but I use the bat to hold it in place. Then I bear my weight down, shattering the bones of his hand.

He's crying and flailing, his face ashen white.

"It's not bringing me any sort of relief. The truth is, Nathan, you're no longer worth my time. You're not anything."

Nathan starts spitting up blood, and it splatters across the floor.

He vomits.

"If you want to go, I'll have the hares pick me up," Finn offers. "I've got some pent-up rage I could really stand to get out."

Mate, my wolf pushes. *End this and go to her.*

I nod, but the darkness doesn't recede. I can't not be the one to kill him. I put my hand out to Finn and he pulls his knife out of his jacket.

Nathan sputters as he foams at the mouth. The whites of his eyes are huge as I stand over the top of him. I put my foot on his stomach, practically standing all my weight on him, and he screams.

His eyes lock with mine, and my wolf pushes forward.

It's fitting that my wolf is the last thing he sees.

For our mate. And Grace.

The knife sinks easily between his ribs, puncturing a lung and then his heart. Of all my kills, this was the most important but the least fulfilling.

Later, I'll have to come to terms with not having done it soon enough.

CHAPTER 87
HENRI

IT'S DARK, and I'm cold until the sun starts shining. I've never been to this place before, but the lush ferns and the sunlight dancing through the trees are peaceful. A path emerges before me, and I follow it, letting the trail take me where it pleases.

Birds sing overhead in a steady tune, and the intermittent rustle of leaves comes and goes with a wind I cannot feel. I'm alone. Though, there are no woodland creatures that come to visit.

I'm lonely, and soon the peaceful forest feels too vast. Does the trail know to take me home? How did I get here without Deacon?

When I go to call out, nothing comes from my throat. No sounds breach the quiet landscape.

I run along the path, but it only keeps opening before me, and if I try to go in a different direction it moves with me.

Stopping myself, I close my eyes. Surely, I'll feel Deacon in our bond. He would be here within me.

Somehow, despite not feeling him, I know the forest is peaceful because of him. My panic fades. Maybe this place is Deacon, and when I wake up, he will be with me.

The question is, when did I go to sleep?

CHAPTER 88
DEACON

S HE STIRS JUST a little before dawn.

Just after midnight, shivers racked her body from the cold, so I draped my jacket over her.

She's so small wrapped up in the leather and Kevlar. It doesn't suit her. Black just isn't meant for someone with so much life in them. Even now, on the gradual incline away from being half dead, there's too much life in Henri for her to wear black.

"Deacon?" She calls for me before her eyes flutter open.

"I'm here, Hen," I answer, squeezing her hand. I haven't been able to force myself to let go.

Her eyes blink once, not truly seeing, and then promptly close again. She drifts off to sleep.

She whimpers again, pulling me away from my phone.

"It's okay. I'm here, Hen." The sound of my voice soothes her, and she goes back to her soft slumber. But barely thirty seconds later, she's restless again.

I open the reading app on my phone and flip through a few books. I look for an option that suits her, but I don't know if she likes to reread books she's already read, and that's all I've downloaded lately in trying to catch up to what sort of literature she likes . . . I'd hate to start reading her something she hasn't read and spoil it.

Laughing at myself, I open what I had been reading to talk with Ezra about at the next family gathering: Shakespearean sonnets, and at what point is it loving sonnets or your inability to love any one person?

"'What is your substance, whereof are you made, that millions of strange shadows on you tend?'"

Henri calms down again, and her peaceful breathing resumes.

I continue picking my way through the lines.

I finish the page and go to flip it to the next one when I hear her small voice. "It figures you're a Shakespeare fan."

CHAPTER 89
HENRI

EVERYTHING HURTS.

I try to sit up, but my muscles don't behave. I don't understand.

My wolf isn't there. I look for her, but even squeezing my eyes shut to try and find her hurts.

"Henri." Deacon's voice soothes me. "You're okay. The sedation has your wolf nice and cozy inside you. You'll probably feel a little hollow, but it's okay."

I open my eyes, and only a faint glow illuminates the room around me. The dark outline of someone sitting in a chair is to my left.

"Deacon?" My voice spikes with panic that I can't push away.

The figure in the dark comes closer. I smell him, that distinctive whiskey and cedar.

He puts his hand in mine and squeezes so softly, like he's afraid I'm going to break. With how much I hurt, I just might.

"What happened? There's so much darkness I don't

remember. I know I went in the hallway." I try to piece it together.

I'm panicking, and it hurts to breathe. *It hurts to fucking breathe.*

Deacon doesn't answer right away. He brushes his thumb against mine. "You stepped out in the hallway at the meeting to take a call. Nathan and one of his goons attacked you and your security detail."

He tries to answer flatly, but I know that gravel in his voice. It's the disdain that's always there when he talks about Nathan. It's sharper now, though, more of a cutting edge.

"They killed the guard and dragged you to a different event space. Nathan —" Deacon's voice cracks. "It's all my fault, Henri. I should have just stayed up when I got home, and this wouldn't have happened."

Slowly the memory of being on the ground and Nathan's shoe connecting with my stomach comes back. The way he spit cruel worlds, the violence of them and the attack.

Tears well in my eyes, the memory of the pain drawing more to the surface, making me aware of every inch of my body.

"No." I bite my lips together, stopping more of my assumptions from coming to the surface. I know what Deacon is going to say even if I don't want it to be true.

Deacon growls, "What he did —" He huffs out a breath. "Henri, he kicked you repeatedly and then nearly gutted you with his knife. You're lucky to be alive. A hotel employee was giving a tour and spooked him off."

He looks away from me, but in the low light of whatever room I'm in, moisture glints in his eyes.

"The . . ." I stop myself, not sure why I'm bothering to ask. *I need him to say it to be sure.*

"I'm sorry," Deacon whispers and wipes the tears from

under his eyes. "Dinah says that it's —" He cups my face. "It's possible that you'll miscarry."

I nuzzle into his touch. I'm sleepy, and I know what he's telling me is bad, but I'm so tired.

Deacon whispers, "I'm so sorry, Hen."

Just a little more sleep, I beg my body, but I'm afraid it won't come.

"Hold me?" I barely get the words out. It's more like breathing than speaking.

"Let me know if I hurt you when I move you. We'll go slow."

True to his word, Deacon takes care to move me slowly. Even with how gently he shifts me, some movements hurt, and I yelp in pain.

Deacon settles into the hospital bed next to me, and it eases my mind.

There are thoughts I need to have. I know there are because there are so many crowding at the edge of my brain. But sleep spreads like the warmth of Deacon's body next to me, pushing me off the precipice into the darkness. I'm only faintly aware of Deacon's erratic breathing and the wetness of his tears against my neck.

CHAPTER 90
DEACON

THE DARKNESS I feel from Henri is so uncharacteristic that I check the bond a hundred thousand times over to make sure it's not me. I never thought I'd be learning something about interpersonal relationships from Lena, but her lessons on feeling the bond have become the best ones I've had to work with. Cade's attempt was 'It's like a string-can telephone but better' and 'think of the old school walkie-talkies but with feelings.' He tried.

'We're wolf shifters. We're not indestructible. She's been through hell. It's going to take time, Deacon.' was an explanation I didn't like hearing, but everyone swears she's going to be fine in a week or so.

It's only been four days. I feel like she should have been monitored for longer.

I *hate* worrying about her. I *hate* that the bright point of my life is a shadow of hurt and suffering. The book on grief Ezra suggested was nearly seven hundred pages, but I dedicated nighttime hours, sitting next to Henri's bedside, to reading it. As much as I disdain self-help books, this felt easier than talking about it. Even with Dinah, the one who would understand the most.

My wolf is diligently watching her. Studying and noting all the changes in her movement, the feedback we're getting in the bond, and how it could mean different things. But the drugs she's on are potent. Even with my tolerance, I wouldn't be able to find my wolf, so any chance he has of interpreting hers is on hold.

I'm finally pulling the car into the driveway. Doctor Thorpe and Doctor Bowes were certain she'd be safe to travel and more comfortable at home, but that didn't stop me from cautiously navigating away from every single pothole I could. Since Henri still has some complaints about stomach pain, the suspension of our new, near-indestructible SUV was put to the test and passed.

Henri lets me open the SUV door for her, and I help her out.

"Do you want to go upstairs or stay down here for a bit?" I offer direct choices, trying to keep her brain from needing to think through her options.

"I need to eat." Henri uses the same casual tone she's adopted since having woken up.

The way she avoids looking at me feels personal, but I want to give her space to adjust before we talk about this and about us. It doesn't stop it from hurting.

Thalia pokes her head into the kitchen while I'm preparing a snack. Or, rather, the most wolf charcuterie board I've ever made.

With a little cant of my head, I welcome her in.

"I'm glad you're home." Thalia breaks the silence and starts to carry on with normal life. "We were talking about the Winter Solstice run and how weird it was without the two of you goofballs running at the back, messing around."

"I resent that." I shake my head. "I am not a goofball. I'm

clearly a silly goose and we're not messing around, we're lollygagging."

We could run. My wolf debates. *We should kill first.* He points to the darkness of my heart and soul. *His friend, the one who was with him.*

He makes valid points, but I'm going to enjoy that hunt. I'll spend the next six months making him aware that a predator is chasing him, but not blatantly enough that he can prove it.

Henri shakes her head. "We're not lollygagging. We're dillydallying."

I feel sweet relief when she joins the conversation. My heart soars, but I don't press her too much. "What's the difference between those two anyway?"

"Well, one thing's for certain. We can *all* agree that you're not monkeying around." Thalia laughs.

"Now I'll have to make that a new goal. Next pack run I will most certainly find a way to monkey around." I set the board in front of Henri. "Here you are, Hen."

Medium-rare roast beef wrapped with a sharp cheddar. Thick-cut bacon with brown-sugar melted butter and flakey crackers. Strips of moose jerky and dried cranberries. Spinach leaves wrapped around mozzarella balls with balsamic vinegar. And then little cheesy crackers in the shape of bunny rabbits that I've seen her eat on occasion.

I start making up another one for me and Thalia to share.

"I can't wait to get back to work." Henri gives a short laugh, and she brings her hand to her stomach. "Ugh. No laughing."

"I think you like working too much. You need a hobby." Thalia goes to the fridge and pulls out some juice and a pitcher of water. Then she starts digging in the fancy ice drawer she put in there a few weeks ago. She comes up with a mocktail, filling three glasses.

"I started crocheting. But there's just something about keeping my brain busy." She groans.

"Well, you're always more than welcome to keep me company in the archive." Thalia sighs. "I don't think I'm ever going to get" — she pauses and changes direction — "done with all those boxes. Whoever stored these documents, books, and art clearly never heard of organization."

"It's okay to talk about being pregnant." Henri takes a bite of food and chews.

Thalia and I hold our breath. *How did it not occur to me that Thalia is pregnant, and it could be a trigger?*

"Oh, for fuck's sake, would you two breathe?" Henri looks between the two of us. "I was barely pregnant. It's not like it was really anything."

She doesn't mean everything in that sentence, the feelings in our bond betraying her.

"I just want to try and go back to normal. It's not like I'm the only woman in this house who is struggling with this." Henri takes a sip of her drink.

"Okay." Thalia nods. "So, anyway . . . I could maybe convince you to come keep me company. Deacon's been awful at it. He met this girl and has been completely obsessed with her. Which, fair because she's pretty much perfect but rude because we're best friends."

Henri snorts. "In his defense, I'm a shitty stalker, so he needs to make it easy for me."

My wolf wags his tail thinking of all the times we've caught her watching us but ignored it. *She is really bad at it.*

So bad. I agree. I object and try to defend her from herself anyway. "You're not shitty at it. You just clearly need more practice and perhaps to wear fewer pairs of high heels." My defense isn't exactly doing a great job.

It gets us all smiling, but while munching on the food from

the board I made Thalia and myself, I watch Henri pick at hers. She at least eats a little of everything.

The drugs that she's on make your appetite smaller, I remind myself.

Quite a bit later, Cade finds Thalia and drags her away, and I finally get Henri on our way up to our room. When we get to the elevator, it's already on the ground floor. I let her lead the way in and she pushes the button.

"I'm so glad to be home." She sighs as I unlock the door to our suite.

The staff and construction company had been working overtime to get the front of my suite more habitable and the bedroom finished off while we were gone. It paid off because it feels more like home than a wreck.

Henri doesn't comment on the space, and I take it as a good sign as I follow her extra closely to the bedroom.

"Can I wear one of your shirts?" She grumbles as she tries to strip off the one I brought her to the hospital.

I rush past her, getting her fluffy sweatpants, a T-shirt, and underwear. The spotting from the miscarriage stopped late last night so I don't put one of the pads that Dinah sent home in the underwear for her.

When I return to the bedroom, Henri lets me dress her. Kissing up her legs, I slide the pants up at the same time as the underwear. She strokes my hair absentmindedly.

I tie the little strings snugly but not tight around her waist. Then I roll up the T-shirt and plop it over her head, getting a soft smile when her head is through the neck of the shirt.

Her eyelids are heavy, and I'm sure, between the drugs that are still in her system and the basic movements of changing clothes, she's already exhausted. Arms through the sleeves, she's ready for another nap.

"How's your pain?" It's such a valid concern, but it feels

shameful that I'm just hoping she takes the pain meds as an escape from her own mind.

"I'm sore," Henri admits. "I feel so weak having to take something. Like —"

I cut her off with a kiss. Then I correct her as empathetically as I possibly can. "You're not weak for admitting you hurt after nearly being killed. The doctors and Dinah wouldn't have sent you home with pain meds if you weren't supposed to take them."

Henri sighs and leans against me, not in a hug but just a lean.

I wrap my arms around her, letting the sorrow hit me again. If I could take it all from her, I would. My darkness, used to pain and suffering, could bear this for her. It wouldn't be a burden. Not if it meant saving her from it.

I'm built for the dark despair that comes with life. But no matter how hard I try to pull it out of the bond for her, there's just more, and it's heart wrenching. I remember the grief book and how sorrow at first is an inescapable pit.

Just so long as it isn't a permanent visit, my wolf warns.

The staff brought up the bags from the car, and I know it's behind-the-scenes meddling that either Lauren or my siblings were involved in. So when Henri seems content in our hug, I step back and go to the dresser. The pill bottle is right on top of it, and bottles of water are stocked in a mini fridge that I didn't have before.

Not looking a gift horse in the mouth, I bring them to her.

Henri swallows the pill and nearly drinks the entire bottle of water. I set it on the nightstand and tuck her into bed.

"Stay?" She hesitates to ask the question.

"I wouldn't dare leave." I give her a soft smile, glad that I took care of the problem so I could be here when she's awake.

CHAPTER 91
DEACON

HENRI IS LEANING against the wall, looking out the window, when I find her, and the whole room seems dark and dim with her somber expression.

"Hen?" I call to her as I lean against the doorframe.

She doesn't look at me, and alarm bells sound in my brain, tension creeping into my shoulders.

"Hen?" I say a bit louder, hoping she's just lost in thought.

This time she turns her head slightly.

"What's going on?" I'm struggling with how to comfort her again. Do I approach her? Don't?

Her arms are crossed, wrapped around herself. Is she guarding herself from the world or holding herself together?

"What . . ." She cuts herself off, and many long breaths live their life during the pause before she starts again. "What are suicidal thoughts like?"

My wolf pushes, trying to get me to go to her. But I'm the one with experience here, so I stay away from her, giving her that space.

"For me?" I offer, and she gives a brief nod. On a ragged

breath, I answer her with a sick feeling in my stomach, knowing she's not asking because she's curious. "For me, they're a dark feeling. Questions like how to end the suffering? How to not feel like this anymore? That I would do just about anything for a moment of happiness, but since that will never happen . . ." I swallow hard, putting to words, the best that I can, the torture that wanting to die feels like. "Since happiness wasn't supposed to be a possibility in my life, I should quit trying to find it. Chasing happiness seems so futile."

Henri nods, not saying anything. But I need to know if she's safe or if I need to put the family on alert. I'm not intentionally letting her out of my sight, but I can't shoulder this alone. They wouldn't want me to.

"It's different. I feel and know the difference between ideation and intent. Intent feels harmful, like I'm running out of oxygen on command, and if I don't take my own life in this next breath, something worse is going to happen." Henri shakes her head almost imperceptibly, and when I blink, she's blurry through tears. My beautiful mate is feeling my darkness on her own. I hope she identifies with this next bit because it would be easier for me if this was what she was struggling with. "Ideation is soft and sweet and lulls me into believing that there's hope of freedom from pain. It's right there, so close I could touch it."

I nearly miss her single head bob while wiping the tears from my eyes.

"I'm sorry, Henri." I try to keep myself from falling apart because it's only fair that I give her this. Henri needs to be the one grieving and sad.

"Me too." It takes maybe another dozen breaths before she turns away from the window.

It's an invitation to her side, and I accept it faster than ever.

Henri doesn't meet me halfway across the room, but when I

get to her, she wraps her arms around my torso faster than I can envelop her with my body.

"I just want the pain to stop," she admits, sobs shaking her whole body. "What makes the pain stop?"

"Time."

It's a pathetic answer, and I know it. But it's better than what I really feel, which is 'Only you.' How can you tell someone that they're the only thing keeping you alive? Especially when they're struggling to keep themselves on this earth too? It's not fair.

I'd kill him again if I could.

"Are you in physical pain?" I feel like I should know that.

Our mating bond is thrumming, but so much emotional pain can mask the physical beyond measure.

Henri pushes back from me. "Why does that matter?"

"Answer the question." I push back, sassing her a little bit.

We're both mourning in our own ways, but I can't let her live in her head like this.

I give her the smirk I know she loves.

"Joys of being a wolf. You can take a stabbing and be up and walking around in no time." She gives me an uncharacteristically snide remark.

"No, you know, you're right. When you're back at work, maybe we can start a campaign of reasons people should want to become a wolf. 'Take a stabbing, keep on walking' or something." I laugh, and she rolls her eyes at me.

"It would at least have to rhyme." Henri scoffs. "Besides I don't think we should be encouraging people to ask to be turned."

"Okay, but if we were going to, you agree that we could start by marketing it to potential mafia members? I bet that would help Finn quite a bit." I'm biting my lips together by the end, trying not to laugh.

Fake frustration is changing Henri's face from sad to a little livelier.

"Come with me?" I offer my hand out to her.

"Where?" Henri eyes my hand, not accepting it.

"You'll have to come with to find out." I look at what she's wearing, and it's not suitable for where I want to take her.

My taunt piques her curiosity enough that she places her hand in mine. I lead her into our closet, pulling clothes off hangers on the way.

"I don't want to go out," she objects.

"Mm-hmm." I ignore her objections, turning on the shower to warm it for her, and start stripping her clothes off.

When her sweatpants and panties are down around her ankles, Henri steps out of them. She covers the silver healing scars from her attack.

I don't fight her to move her hands because she's not ready to heal like that. Instead, I step back and open the shower door for her.

"What, you're not coming?" Henri looks me up and down.

I shrug and pull off my shirt. "Lead the way."

Henri is slow to get washed and then to dry off and get dressed. I wonder if she's doing it because she's tired or because she really doesn't want to go, and she thinks that if it gets to be late enough, I won't make her go anywhere.

When I pull a band T-shirt on, Henri looks at what we're wearing. "Okay, so where are we going?"

"Out." I step close to her and tip her head up toward me, planting a kiss on her nose. "We're going out."

When she gives me a ridiculously big sigh, I clarify. "We're going out of the house, and then down the driveway, and then out the gate, and then down the road. And then to a place with other people. And we're going to have a good time, and then we're going to come home. But to know if it's bingo with Ms.

Gertie or something more fun, you'll have to come with and find out."

"Deacon —" Henri starts to object.

"I mean you're already showered and dressed, would be a shame to waste that clean hair." I smirk, and she knows I've got her. "Besides, if we get there, you walk inside the building, and you decide you don't like it, then we'll turn around and come home, and I won't make you try to do anything new for at least two weeks. And I'll let you book me something ridiculously boring to go to, and I'll even pretend to care about it. Maybe some sort of charity for illiterate kittens or something?"

Come on, Hen. Come on. I'm pushing her. I know I am. But I can't let her sit up here and wilt away.

"Okay, but if it sucks, we're coming right home," she reiterates.

"If it sucks, we are coming right home." I nod, walking backward through our sitting room and out to the hallway.

I keep walking backward until I get to the elevator and push the button.

"We could take the stairs," Henri offers.

"Mmmmm, pass." I shake my head.

The doors open, and I lead her in, pressing the button for the main floor. And then I push Henri up against the wall and kiss her deeply.

She kisses me back, fisting my shirt. When the elevator comes to a stop on the bottom floor, Henri growls.

"Mmm." I smile against her lips. "Alright. I could be convinced to give up on our outing to take you to bed."

"Nope." Henri pops the *p*, walking out of the elevator. "You tricked me into cleaning my hair."

Henri and I get to the kitchen, where family dinner is wrapping up.

"Don't you two look lovely." Ms. Gertie smiles at us.

"It's not bingo." Henri looks over her shoulder at me.

"It's not bingo," I agree.

Confused expressions stare back at us around the room, and Henri engages our family. "Deacon is apparently taking me somewhere of such national security that he can't tell me where it is."

"Ahh." Cade nods, playing into her joke. "Well, as we know, Deacon does have a higher security clearance than I do, so it must be true."

"It's not an emergency. I even told her if I got her all the way to where we're going and she didn't like it, we could come back." I shoot them daggers with my eyes, and they all get the message.

"I'm sure it'll be fine. He's wearing a random band T-shirt. Anytime he's been arrested, it's been wearing something much more inconspicuous." Cade misses the mark, but he tried.

"Oooo, if it's early enough when you come home, could you bring back donuts?" Thalia bites her bottom lip. "Chocolate ones with the fun fillings?"

"You got it, little red." I put my hands on Henri's shoulders and guide her past my family through the kitchen to the mudroom.

"If I promise to go, no matter what, will you tell me where we're going?" Henri whispers.

She had put on a brave face for my family but now darkness and uncertainty clouds her expression again.

"I got info on a DJ coming here on a trial tour back in January, and I thought for sure he'd cancel this tour since he was picked up by a bigger label, but he's still doing these shows as a trial run." I cock my head to the side.

"No." Henri shakes her head, disbelief widening her eyes. "No fucking way." She covers her mouth with her hands. "I mean, I saw the message because it was my job. But I . . ."

"Come on, Hen." I smile at her and open the door to the garage.

She pulls her sneakers out of the bin and walks with stocking foot into the garage, nearly running for the SUV.

I follow Henri, glad to see her excitement. She's scrambled into the passenger seat with the door closed before I get there, and I barely get my ass in the seat before she's trying to push start the ignition.

"I take it you're excited?" I ask, easing the SUV out of the garage.

The question hits wrong because Henri pauses. Darkness flickers into her body as she deflates into her seat. "Is it wrong to be excited?"

I shake my head, and our security detail joins behind us down the driveway. "We are allowed to feel happy after loss. It doesn't make us less alive or empathetic. Life is meant to keep moving, even after someone we've loved has left us."

"It just . . ." Henri waits for us to go through the checkpoint and, when our windows are rolled back up, adds, "I sound like a terrible person."

Playing back the conversation, I try to guess which of the many emotions I have that she might feel too. "You feel like a terrible person because how could something, someone, so small, who we weren't even fully excited about when we first knew about, cause us so much grief?"

"And then I feel guilty for not being happy about it in the first place." Henri volunteers.

"Because," I attempt while setting the cruise control, "Finn and Lena are struggling with something we idiots couldn't remember to think about preventing?"

"We are terrible people aren't we?" Henri scrubs her hand down her face.

When I put my hand on her lap, some of her tension floods

away. "We're not terrible people. Our path and Finn and Lena's path are very different. I mean, you saw the hell Cade went through for Thalia."

"I've lots of thoughts and feels on that now that we're together, and I feel like I can ask a couple more questions." Henri redirects herself. "But now isn't the time. I just don't know how to be sad and move on and be okay with being sad and moving on."

"Well, if it's any help at all." I shrug, drumming my fingers on the bottom of the steering wheel for a beat. "I just keep reminding myself that the thoughts are gone when I'm in the same room with you, that the tally marks in the notepad on my phone are still there, and so are you. That I can take all the hurt and the suffering and live in it. Or I can live with you and work to make the world make sense."

"What if it doesn't ever make sense again?" Henri whispers.

"Well, I was kind of hoping you'd look past the part where it didn't really make sense in the first place." I tilt my head over, looking at her with a grin. "Come on, Alice, we're all a little mad here."

CHAPTER 92
HENRI

SINCE COMING HOME to the Alden pack property, I haven't left. It's been two weeks, and I haven't even gone so far as the back lawn. I shifted, because I had to, but even then, all the mental energy I could handle was just walking around the green space.

And I wasn't aware of how awkward, alone, and unguarded I've been until we pull up to a stop at a warehouse district venue. There aren't more people than I've ever seen in one place before because I've been to plenty of packed events. But it feels so big.

My head is swimming, and I wrap my fingers around the door handle to hold myself inside.

"What's the soup of the day?" Deacon scrubs his hand down his face.

"Oh, I don't know, about forty?" I answer instinctively.

"Sweet, that's about how many I'm seeing. The wolf is working." Deacon opens his car door just a crack. "I'm going to sound like Finn, and I don't know that I hate it, but wait for me?"

He indicates to the door that I'm clinging to for dear life with a soft nod.

Deacon climbs out and walks around in front of the SUV to come around to my side. It's painful to make myself let go of the door to let him pull it open.

"I hear your heart, Hen." Deacon puts his hand in mine in place of the door.

I squeeze, trying to meld us together into one person.

"I'm trying." The words come out halfhearted. *I should try harder.*

"Would it make it easier if I told you Ezra is already inside with a security agent and ours are already behind us? Oh, and that I made Cade send Michael Tate with us." Deacon lowers his voice and whispers, "And I think he's a dragon shifter, but don't tell anyone I said that. Revecca couldn't confirm or deny it, but I didn't get a 'would you quit being ridiculous,' sooo."

I blink through the information overload, looking at Deacon again. "I'm sorry. What?"

"Ezra's inside, our security is with us. Come on, Hen." Deacon extends his arm, pushing the door out of the way. "You've gotta go inside the venue, and if you still don't want to be here, we'll go home."

My wolf pushes me, so I unbuckle and then climb out of the vehicle, making me get closer to Deacon. Warm desire to nuzzle in against him runs through me, and when I do, I'm quickly comforted further by Deacon's hand running into my hair.

"Dragon shifter?" I whisper. "That can't be real."

"I don't think I'm wrong." Deacon laughs. "Come on, we can share theories later."

Grumbling, I let Deacon pull away. He steps back and shifts me out of the way of the door closing. Keeping an arm draped across me, he leads us, from behind, to the sidewalk and then to the building.

We're glued together, fused tighter than I've ever seen Cade and Thalia. It's everything I've ever wanted, but not how I thought I'd get it. Yet, when I look for sadness in the circumstance, it's not there.

We get wristbands, and Deacon is directed up the stairs to a VIP area for before the show.

I'm winded when we reach the top, angry that my body, while pain free, is not in any better physical shape. *It's only a matter of time. Deacon promised.*

Ezra is the only person up here, aside from a bartender, who's flushed and goes wide eyed seeing us.

"He worked fast tonight," Deacon mutters under his breath, confirming my suspicion that Ezra and the bartender were just a little busy together.

"Alright, Henri." Ezra smiles. "What'll it be? We go home or hang out up here all night?"

I look at the bartender and then the room around us.

"Atta girl." Ezra laughs. "Say the word, little Grimm. We'll carry you up and down the stairs to dance."

"Little Grimm?" Deacon cocks a brow at him and then me. "Sure, why not."

Lily of the Valley
Convallaria majalis

JUNE

CHAPTER 93
HENRI

"HEN?" Deacon calls my name from my office door.

"Yeah?" I ask checking my calendar out of habit, that I don't have something going on that I'm missing. I'm 'back' at work, but I feel scatterbrained at times, but I don't think I'm missing a meeting right this minute.

My calendar is completely cleared. *I hate when he does that.*

"I know." Deacon nods like he's reading my mind. "You hate when I clear your calendar and don't tell you. But . . ."

He has a guilty look on his face.

"What?" I get that uncomfortable feeling up my spine.

"I brought someone to see you. Two someones, specifically." Deacon steps back out of my office door.

Who the hell would Deacon bring to see me? Curiosity alone is enough to get me out of my office chair. Wolf healing, despite being faster than human healing, is still slow. Apparently, the worse the trauma, the harder to heal from it, and from my understanding, it's not about the physical aspect of it.

I'm not sure I entirely understand, but I just know each day, I feel a little less like I've been violated on every single level.

Deacon offers his hand out, and when I put mine in his, he gives it a soft squeeze.

My heart rate picks up the farther down the hall we get.

"Who's here?" I whisper as we get closer.

"Frank and Paulina Greene." Deacon's voice holds a breath of hesitation.

I come to a full stop in the hallway.

He doesn't let go of my hand. "You had said you wanted me to reach out, and I did. I'd told them a little bit about what happened and delayed their coming, but I couldn't keep you from them. If you don't want to see them, I won't make you. But —"

I cut Deacon off, pulling my hand out of his and darting to the living room.

Mom and Dad are looking out the window at the birds hopping around eating bird seed off the deck from the feeders. Finn and Deacon installed them because something about a squirrel.

"Mom?" I try to say it strongly but fail.

The word is not clean and crisp. It's broken and sad — how I feel inside.

My body is broken, and my brain is numb. The one thing I hadn't even considered wishing for — a hug from Mom — sounds like the best thing in the world.

When we meet in the middle of the living room, she wraps her arms around me, and tears fall until I can't breathe and have to find a tissue box.

Deacon is off to the side, holding one out for me. Because he's always there for me.

I've almost got the tears under control, and then I see Dad with tears in his eyes, and I lose it all over again. I'm hugged tightly against his body the thick smell of the pipe tobacco he smokes enveloping me.

SMOG

"Thank you," Mom whispers to Deacon.

He doesn't say anything, so I'm guessing there was an acknowledging nod.

"I'm so sorry." I get out between sobs, forcing myself out of Dad's arms and looking at the two of them. "I'm so sorry. You were right. And I'm sorry. I'm so sorry."

"Shhh." Mom pets my hair, and I draw deep breaths, trying to get the sobbing back under control. "There's nothing to apologize for."

Deacon's hand comes to rest on my back, and then he gestures to the couches. "Please, make yourself comfortable. I'll let the three of you catch up."

"No," I whine, and my wolf rises with the sound.

"I'll stay." Deacon nods. "Let me grab some refreshments. Ms. Gertie will shame me for letting someone make this journey and not offer them some sweet tea, snickerdoodles, and banana bread."

"Just water for me." Dad walks to take a seat on an oversized chair.

Mom sits on the end of a sofa nearest him. I take a seat, turned to look at the two of them, and can hear Deacon behind me in the kitchen.

"I'm so proud of you," Mom says. "You've done such a good job with your career. I'm so glad that you've been working with your people all this time."

She doesn't bring up Nathan. I know someday we'll have to talk about him.

"And Deacon is very nice. I was a little concerned with that grim reaper nickname nonsense." Dad misquotes the social media but not surprisingly nails Deacon's personality.

My own personal murderer.

Deacon comes over with a tray of treats and then back again with pitchers of sweet tea, water, and orange juice.

Vitamin C and iron from Dinah's suggestions, I'm sure. So, when Deacon pours me a glass of orange juice, I don't object to him handing it to me.

Silence descends among us, and Deacon breaks it. "Well, there's a lot to speak about, and there's really no good way or place to start." He turns to look at me, placing his hand on my thigh just above my knee. He looks back at my parents. "When we spoke, I made my intention for your daughter clear, but it feels necessary to restate the facts. I am your daughter's mate, and in the very near future, I'll be claiming her as such. I will never come between the three of you. And I'd like to extend a formal invitation for you to take up residency here on pack property. From my understanding, you're nearing retirement age, and I'd like to assist you as you transition into retirement if you'd so choose to do so."

"I think I like him." Dad nods firmly. "He doesn't beat around the bush, does he?"

A snort comes from the stairwell, and Lena rounds the stairs, the thermal cup Finn bought her in hand. "Not snooping just coming down for snacks and to hydrate. Your guests are early."

"Oh my goodness," Mom whispers. "Is that Lena?"

"Yeah, last time I checked," Deacon whispers back with a goofy grin.

The familiarity between them is starting to feel a little suspicious.

"I can hear you," Lena whisper yells from the kitchen.

Mom puts her hand over her mouth.

Dad, however, laughs and outs Mom. "She's been obsessed with shifters since you all came out to the public. I'm fairly certain she's read every article that has been published."

"I've just been trying to stay up to date on our baby's life." Mom defends herself.

Deacon is looking past me at Lena, his facial expressions broadcasting a whole silent conversation between them.

"Shhh," Thalia whispers, and I can tell she and Cade are trying to sneak down the back access to the hallway toward the second-story stairs.

"Yeah. Little red, we can hear you too," Deacon says with a sigh. He looks at me. "I should have set us up in the library. I knew I couldn't trust the three of them not to be here."

"Four." Finn's voice is behind me and Mom. It startles her, and she jumps. "You really shouldn't have expected us to stay away. Our sister-in-law's parents come by, and we're not going to sniff around?"

Deacon scrubs his hand down his face.

Mom's eyes go wide, taking in the Ardeleans.

"Well, this trip is gonna completely blow away our trip to New England this year." Dad sighs, almost sounding disappointed. "I'd just gotten her excited for maybe seeing the mountains."

"Oh." I turn and look at Dad. "Give me your itinerary, and I'll make sure Judah Alloway is available to give you a tour of Mount Katahdin." My brain is apparently accepting everything as normal.

"That's it. She's going on a leave of absence. Effective immediately." Cade, arm wrapped around Thalia, comes into the living space. "You literally just see your parents for the first time in" — he holds his hand up in question before gesturing to Deacon — "I'm sure Deacon knows how long, and you're already organizing itineraries. Break, rest, relaxation, and something fun."

I bite my lips together, feeling embarrassed.

Rhododendron
Literally all of them

EPILOGUES

HENRI

Together with their beloved family and friends,
The Ardeleans
formally invite you to
Pack Alden
in celebration of the mating between
James Deacon Ardelean
&
Henrietta Elaine Greene

IT's PROBABLY the weirdest sentence I've ever written with my name in it. But it feels so right.

Sitting out on the deck, enjoying the summer air, waiting for full moon festivities to begin, I'm feeling itchy all over

We'll go running now, my wolf pushes, looking for the excitement of the coming run.

I tuck my tablet back into my bag and go to hunt down Deacon.

It doesn't take me long to find him. He's sitting in the stairwell, seemingly by himself.

"Alright, kiddo. I've gotta get going. Good to see you." He waves at the landing, and I can't help but smile. The differences with Deacon are night and day.

Am I that different now too?

Pushing himself up off the floor, Deacon takes two strides and wraps his arms around me. "Hey, Hen."

"Hey." I kiss him, wrapping my arms around his neck and pulling him close. "I was thinking maybe we could run now and later, both? I'm just feeling antsy."

"Anything you want." Deacon kisses me on the nose, then backs me up against the wall.

Yeah, let's run later. My wolf changes her mind, pushing forward. *We want him now.*

Deacon's wolf is staring back at me when he breaks the kiss. The dark eyes are beautiful. "Let's run first. Then we can play. We'll see how adventurous you want to be."

I back away from him, then turn and start back down the stairs. At the bottom, I take off in a sprint, hearing him race behind me. Shifting more and after healing, I've found myself stronger and faster, but I'm still no match for Deacon's long legs. He bear-hugs me from behind before I make it to the doors leading outside.

"I love you so much," he whispers in my ear. "So fucking much."

DEACON

APRIL

Sitting outside in the cold night air, I watch as a satellite blinks across the sky.

The door to the deck opens, and Finn steps out into the dark. "Thought I'd find you out here."

"Yeah. Little overwhelming. I'll be back in in a minute."

"Well, glad I caught you. Actually." Finn takes a seat next to me and offers out his hand to give me something.

I hold open my palm, trusting whatever he's going to give me is something I want and not disturbing.

Heavy metal drops in my hand, and I pull it back to inspect it.

"I know we joked about it, and maybe it's in bad taste, but I didn't want you to think none of us noticed." Finn lets me look at the metal.

The thick metal coin features a velociraptor on one side and a number — 366 — on the back.

I look at him, raising my eyebrow. "Uh, thanks?"

Finn explains, "Velociraptor attack free for a full leap year. I know you've done it without any of the human meetings or really recognized support. So, you miss out on people seeing the milestones."

I roll the coin in my fingers, looking at it, blinking away the moisture in my eyes. "Thank you."

ALSO BY SARAH JAEGER

The Ardelean Bloodline:

Smoke

Haze

Blaze

Scorch

Stay up to date on all things Sarah Jaeger.

Follow me on social media:

ABOUT THE AUTHOR

Sarah Jaeger is a human being from the Upper Midwest, even though she is certain she was born to be a shifter. A dreamer since birth, the idea for the Ardelean Bloodlines popped into Sarah's teenage brain and refused to leave. Finally, that idea is taking shape in the form of a fully-fledged paranormal romance series. When she's not writing, Sarah likes to recharge with solid TV show binges, playing cards and games with her family, and caring for her fur babies. Stay in touch with Sarah at www.authorsarahjaeger.com.